ALSO BY BERYL KINGSTON

HISTORICAL FICTION

Hearts and Farthings

Kisses and Ha'pennies

A Time to Love

London Pride

War Baby

Two Silver Crosses

A Stitch in Time

Avalanche of Daisies

Suki

Gates of Paradise

Hearts of Oak

Off the Rails

THE EASTER EMPIRE TRILOGY

Tuppenny Times

Fourpenny Flyer

Sixpenny Stalls

THE OCTAVIA TRILOGY

Octavia

Octavia's War

The Internet Revolutionary

THE JACKSON FAMILY SAGA

Everybody's Somebody
Citizen Armies

FICTION

Maggie's Boy
Laura's Way
Gemma's Journey
Neptune's Daughter
Francesca and the Mermaid

NON-FICTION

Lifting the Curse
A Family at War

OCTAVIA

BERYL KINGSTON

AGORA BOOKS

ABOUT THE AUTHOR

Beryl Kingston is the author of 30 novels with over a million copies sold. She has been a writer since she was 7 when she started producing poetry. She was evacuated to Felpham at the start of WWII, igniting an interest in one-time resident poet William Blake which later inspired her novel *The Gates of Paradise*. She was an English teacher from 1952 until 1985 when she became a full-time writer after her debut novel, *Hearts and Farthings*, became a bestseller. Kingston continued writing best-sellers for the next 14 years with titles ranging from family sagas to modern stories and historical novels. She currently lives in West Sussex and has three children, five grandchildren, and ten great-grandchild.

 twitter.com/berylkingston

OCTAVIA

BERYL KINGSTON

This is a work of fiction. All characters and events in this work, other than those clearly in the public domain, are entirely fictitious. Any resemblance to any persons, living or dead, is entirely coincidental.

Copyright © Beryl Kingston, 2007

All rights reserved

Cover Design By: Dissect Designs

Cover Images © Adobe Stock

This edition published in 2021 by Agora Books

First published in Great Britain 2007 by Allison & Busby

Agora Books is a division of Peters Fraser + Dunlop Ltd

55 New Oxford Street, London WC1A 1BS

You may not copy, distribute, transmit, reproduce or otherwise make available this publication (or any part of it) in any form, or by any means (including without limitation electronic, digital, optical, mechanical, photocopying, printing, recording or otherwise), without the prior written permission of the publisher. Any person who does any unauthorised act in relation to this publication may be liable to criminal prosecution and civil claims for damages.

CHAPTER 1

'We shall call her Octavia,' the professor said, gazing down at the crumpled face of his newborn daughter.

It was stuffy in the bedroom and the air was spiked with unfamiliar scents and smells — an astringent trace of the lime tea the midwife would insist on having made, a heaviness of blood and sweat, a breath of warm linen, the brusque smell of carbolic soap — but Dr Smith was much too discreet to notice them. They were part of the great mystery of birth and that was something from which he had been rightly and gratefully debarred. Left on his own as the mystery proceeded, he'd spent the night fidgeting from study to parlour, aware that what he was suffering was nothing compared to the torments of his poor dear Amy. From time to time he'd found himself trembling with cold and anxiety and was relieved that there were no servants about to see the state he was in. But now the long hours were over and they were rewarded by this delicious child. He was breathless with pride and happiness, as he'd been from the moment the midwife first eased the baby into his arms, amazed that something so small could rouse him to such heights of protective rapture. Being a man with a logical intelligence, it occurred to him that the reason for his reaction was probably because she *was* so small — small, soft, sweet-smelling, wool-wrapped, trusting. Ah the trust of that tiny hand actually holding his finger! But for the moment logic was roared aside by the power of his feelings. 'Octavia Smith,' he said. 'It is the only possible name. Octavia Smith, born on the eighth day of the eighth month of the year 1888. Think of it, my love. She is a numerical delight.'

The numerical delight caught her breath and gave a short sharp sneeze, like a cat. 'Exquisite!' her father said.

Watching them from the needed support of her mound of lace-edged pillows, Amy Smith was warm with emotion too, flooded with the most passionate love for this new daughter of hers but caught up in the old half-amused, half-delighted affection for her dear JJ, standing there with his hair on end, his whiskers bristling and his brown eyes dark with adoration. How magnificently absurd he was and how loving. 'Perhaps, my dear,' she said, her voice gentle with exhaustion and affection, 'we should consider that Octavia is usually reserved for the eighth child. Might she not be teased for it?'

'Not a bit of it,' JJ said. 'She will have the strength of character not to be teased. No, no, it is a capital name for a capital baby. Besides, old conventions exist to be broken, need to be broken, one might almost say, or they stand in danger of growing stale.'

The midwife looked at him sharply. That sounded just a little bit too much like the beginning of an argument and the one thing she was not going to allow was an argument with a newly-delivered mother. It had been a strenuous birth and her patient needed rest and recuperation. She padded across the room, quiet in her house shoes, and took command.

'Time for our sleep, Professor Smith,' she said, removing the baby from his arms. 'It's been a long night.'

'It has, Nurse,' the professor agreed. 'A very long night, but it ends in triumph.' He realised that he was still in his evening clothes and now it was half past five in the morning and the sky beyond the window was pearl white with the promise of a hot summer's day. Not that he was allowed to catch more than a glimpse of it, for the midwife had tucked the baby into her crib and was already pulling down the blinds to darken the room. He tiptoed to the bedside and sat down gently, taking Amy's limp hand and kissing her fingers. 'My clever darling,' he said.

Amy's limbs were heavy with the need to sleep and it was all she could do to keep her eyes open but she asked her question nevertheless, even though she knew what his answer would be.

'Are you happy?'

'Beyond words.'

'After all these years,' she said. 'Eleven years. I'm so sorry I took so long.'

He gentled a forefinger across her lips, forbidding any more apology. 'It is behind us now,' he told her. 'Octavia is here and that is all that matters. Now I must go downstairs and leave you or Nurse will be after me for being a heartless husband.'

Amy smiled drowsily as she closed her eyes. 'You are never that,' she said. 'You are always the most loving...'

Downstairs in the book-lined masculinity of his study, the professor brisked into the day, folding back the shutters and lifting the window to let in some fresh air and reveal his first welcome sight of the square. There was something extremely satisfactory about the deliberate proportions of a Georgian square, even a small and rather humble one like this. He had felt it from that first afternoon, when he and Amy had moved in, newly wed and unsure of one another, she clinging to his arm for comfort, he soothed by the beautiful balance around him. Achieved according to mathematical principles of course. When Octavia grew older, he would explain it to her. Meantime he would enjoy it for a few seconds while he got his breath back.

The church in the centre of the square was sharp-edged with

sunlight, its doors open for matins, and the streets around it were already peopled and busy. A barefoot boy with a bucket and spade was hard at work on the south side, scooping up a pile of horse manure, and the housemaid at number 12 was on her hands and knees scrubbing the doorstep. He could hear the swish of her brush from where he stood. He noticed that the dairyman had arrived and was serving a group of aproned women, carefully measuring the milk from his churn into their jugs, as they stood in a semi-circle round his cart, enjoying the sun and gossiping, and the baker was on his rounds too, bent sideways by the weight of his wicker basket, his pony waiting quietly between the shafts of his dusty bread van.

How patient labouring creatures are, the professor thought, and how easily taken for granted. There is much in our lives that needs change. And now change had come to his own life, sneezing like a cat, and all thought and action had been turned in a new direction.

His journal lay open on the desk waiting to receive the first and best of the day, he took up his pen and started to write in his admirable copperplate, taking pains with every word as he always did.

'*Mirabile dictu,*' he began. Only the grace and elegance of Latin was good enough for such an occasion. '*Octavia Smith born 4.45 this morning. Amy came through the ordeal well, but somewhat exhausted. Baby strong. Weight 6lbs 2ounces. Eyes large, blue. Hair fair as far as I can ascertain. Temperament equable. We shall expect great things of her.*'

CHAPTER 2

'There's that dratted child up to no good again,' the housemaid said, glancing up at the kitchen ceiling. It was only four o'clock in the afternoon but her face was already pinched with fatigue. 'She's running about in the hall. That's what she's doing, naughty little thing. Hark at her, crashing all about. She's worse than a wagonload of monkeys.' She picked up the nursery tea tray with both hands, partly to show how cross she was and partly to hold it steady. 'She needs taking in hand, that's my opinion. They should give her a good hiding instead of letting her run wild all over the place. Well she'd better not get under my feet, that's all. I got enough to do without a spoilt brat under my feet all the time.'

Mrs Wilkins was lacing a leg of mutton with sprigs of rosemary. As cook-housekeeper to the family, she had more important things to attend to than the antics of a naughty six-year-old. That was Nurse's business and let her get on with it. There was going to be a very special dinner party that evening and Professor Smith wanted everything just so. It made a lot of extra work, even though she'd managed to spread it over two days, and even though she'd got two parlour maids in from the agency to help lay the table and serve and clear. Still, all things considered, she was doing pretty well. The chocolate Bavarois were set and ready, all lined up on the dresser in their pretty cups, the soup was in the stockpot and only needed heating up and a curl of cream, Molly was peeling the potatoes, Mary'd made the nursery tea, so that was taken care of, but there was still the fish course to prepare, to say nothing of all the other vegetables, and time was getting on. 'She's just a pickle,' she said mildly. 'Little girls are like that the world over. Make sure you put enough salt in them potatoes, Molly.'

Molly sprinkled salt obediently but Mary was disgruntled. 'Never mind pickle,' she complained. 'You don't see the half of it down here all the time. Not like we do, eh Molly? She's a fiend. Charging about all over the place! An' it's ten times worse when them cousins come. They're like a bunch a' lunatics.'

'Mind how you go then,' Mrs Wilkins advised, as the maid headed for the door. 'Oh an' tell Boots to light the gas when he's done the fires or you won't be able to see what you're about.' Afternoon light in late September was always difficult to judge and she'd been so preoccupied with the joint she hadn't noticed how dark it was getting.

Mary toiled up the stairs through the sooty shadows, muttering to herself. 'And where's Boots when you want him? Tell me that. Stupid boy. Never mind tell him to light the gas. If I wants it done I shall have to do it mesself.'

To her relief, the hall was clear. No sign of the child or the cousins, although she could hear them whispering somewhere nearby. Thank the Lord for small mercies, she thought, and she carried the tray to the hallstand, balancing it carefully. It'ud be safe there while she lit the gas.

But she never got the chance to set it down. The door to the master's study was flung open so suddenly and violently that it thudded against the jamb, and the three children erupted into the hall, squealing and shrieking. They were running so fast they'd banged into her legs before she could get out of the way. She jumped and screamed, as the tray tilted sideways, teacups rattling, then the biscuits slid off the doyley, milk leapt from the jug in a curved slopping dollop and the teapot threw its lid into the air and sprayed hot tea all over the hallstand, across the runner and up the wall.

'Oh you nasty, horrible, beastly girl!' Mary yelled, putting the wrecked tray on the stand. 'Now look what you've gone and made me do. Why can't you stay in the nursery where you belong?'

Octavia put her hand to her mouth in alarm. 'I never meant...' she began.

But the hall was too rushed with action for her voice to be heard, the cousins retreating backwards towards the stairs, owl-eyed, Boots and the agency maids pushing one another out of the dining room, delighted by the sound of disaster, Mrs Smith calling from the landing, 'Is everything all right?' And before anyone could call back to reassure her, there was the sound of a key in the lock and the professor stood before them, booming like a cannon and making them all jump, because they weren't expecting him home so soon. 'What's this? What's this?'

'They come out the study sir, 'fore I could stop 'em,' Mary said, getting her explanation in before her character could be blackened. 'They was like bats out a' hell, sir, begging your pardon. It's a wonder I never dropped the lot. I couldn't help it. Miss Octavia run right into me legs.'

'Is this true, Tavy?' JJ boomed at his daughter.

Octavia had to swallow before she answered him. He looked so fierce and tall with the columns of those long black legs rising before her and that brown beard bristling like a lion's mane and his brown eyes so stern, and she did so hate it when he was cross. Besides, it had all happened so quickly she couldn't remember running into anybody's legs. But somebody had or the tea wouldn't be spilt. Somebody had and it could have been her. So she spoke up honestly and admitted her fault, because that was what you had to do. Tell the truth and shame the devil. 'Yes, Papa.'

'You ran into her legs?'

Oh dear, Octavia thought. He is cross. He won't let me stay up and see the people now. And she did so want to see the people. They were the most important people in London. She knew because he'd told her. But she'd accepted the blame and now she had to stick to it. 'Yes, Papa,' she said, miserably. 'I didn't mean to.'

'Your intentions are immaterial,' her father told her sternly. 'It is the consequence of our actions that we have to consider. You were the cause of this mess. Very well then. You must clear it up. Go down to the kitchen with Mary and get a bucket and a dust-shovel and brush and whatever else you need.'

The listening servants drew in their assembled breath in surprise, That's a skivvy's work. He ain't never going to make a child do it. Surely to goodness. That ain't right.

His judgement had baffled Octavia too. She looked from his steady face to the dark patches spreading across the Turkey carpet and wondered what she would have to do to clean them. Until that moment cleaning was something that was done by the servants, something that happened out of sight that she didn't have to bother about. There was a swish of skirts on the stairs, and she glanced up to see that her mother was halfway down, and looking protective. Perhaps she would be able to make him change his mind. She could sometimes. 'Mama,' she said. 'I'm dreadfully sorry. I didn't mean to.'

Her appeal was answered at once. 'JJ, my dear,' Amy said, in her soft way, descending the last three stairs, one elegantly lace-edged hand on the banister. 'She is very young. Perhaps we should consider.'

'I have considered,' JJ said, handing his hat and gloves to Mary in the manner of a man to whom reconsideration is impossible. 'She has been foolish and admitted it and now she must make amends. I don't expect to come home to a hall swimming in tea.' Then he frowned at Boots and the agency maids. 'Have you no work to do that you stand here gawping? Why are the lights not lit?'

The maids slithered back into the dining room, avoiding his eye, while Boots took a matchbox from his apron pocket and rushed forwards to make his own amends. 'I was just a-going to do it, sir.'

'Then be about it,' his master said. 'Don't just stand there. This is an important evening. I want everything just so. Set a fresh tray Mary, and bring it up to us directly. Octavia, I depend upon you to do your best. Come and tell me when everything is clean and proper.' And he took his wife's hand and walked them both upstairs, with the cousins trailing behind him, looking sheepish.

'She is very young,' Amy tried again. Her voice was more determined now that they'd reached the landing and the servants were out of earshot but her forehead was wrinkled with doubt and anxiety. 'Only six. Could we not find some other way?'

'She is being raised according to the best libertarian principles,' JJ said, speaking firmly because he was beginning to have doubts himself, 'to take responsibility for her actions. Actions have consequences, no matter what age you may be. It is never too young to learn that. She has given us test of our intentions rather earlier than I expected, that is true, but all the more reason to stand firm upon what we believe.'

Left behind in the hall, Octavia stood firm beside the jardinière, twisting the hem of her pinafore between her finger and thumb, and looking at the mess. The hall grew larger by the second, the gaslight more revealing, the stains deeper. There was tea everywhere. How would she manage to clean it all up? She knew it would have to be done but where would she begin?

Mary watched her as she set the tray to rights. Now that the child was actually being punished she felt quite sorry for her. It was no joke to be asked to clean up a carpet runner and wash down a hallstand and get spots off a wallpaper, as she knew only too well. She looked at the thin wrists above those twisting fingers, the pale troubled face beneath that fuzz of fair hair, those skinny black-stockinged legs, the awkward stance of those black boots, and the sight wrung her heart. 'Never mind, eh?' she said. 'I'll help yer.'

The words stiffened Octavia's spine. She couldn't bear to be pitied and especially by a servant. 'No thank you,' she said. She was instantly determined, chin up, mouth set, blue eyes hardening, 'I'll manage.'

She's just like her father, Mary thought. Pig-headed the pair of 'em. 'Wait there then,' she said, 'an' I'll get the things. Shan't be a tick.'

She was as good as her word, returning in three minutes with a pail full of water, a dust-shovel and brush, two mops, polish, clean cloths and a thick slice of stale bread. 'That's fer the wallpaper,' she explained. 'I'd better do that, 'cause it's a tricky business, wallpaper, an' I'm certain sure he never meant you to do everything. You can start on the carpet, can't yer. That's took the worst of it. Take one a' them little cloths and press it right down on the stain, hard as you can. That's right. That's took up a lot of it. See? Now rinse it in the pail and wring it out tight as you can. Then you got it about right fer the next bit. Be quick though. Tea can stain sommink chronic.'

They worked in silence for a few minutes except for the splash of water, the occasional plop of the gaslight and the soft frotting of bread on wallpaper. Octavia found that it was easier to press the cloth into the carpet if she stood on it and, as there was no one around to tell her she shouldn't, that was what she did. She was impressed by the way the maid was easing the tea stains from the wallpaper with her slice of bread, brushing down and down, always in the same direction. And Mary was touched by the child's determination, wringing out the cloth with those skinny little hands and going at it like a good 'un. She might be a bit of a pickle, she thought, but she's got spunk. There's no denying *that*. An' she could've ratted on her cousins. They was every bit as bad as her. But she never.

After a while, Molly appeared with the second tea tray and carried it carefully upstairs, cups rattling. They could hear the clatter from the kitchen, the clink of cutlery in the dining room, the regular tick of the hall clock. And at last the carpet was clean again, the floorboards swept and polished, the hallstand buffed to a sheen, and there was only the tiniest spatter of brown teardrops among the vine leaves of the wallpaper.

Their labours had brought them together, like conspirators outwitting the rest of the house, smiling at one another. Mary had quite forgotten how cross she'd been; Octavia was relieved to see what a good job they'd done — except for the marks on the wallpaper.

'He won't be cross about the little stains, will he?' she asked her ally.

'No, course not,' Mary said, as she gathered up her mops and brushes. 'He won't even see 'em. He'll be proud of yer. See if he ain't. Pop upstairs an' tell him you've finished.'

So Octavia said, 'Thank you for helping me,' because you have to remember your manners, and ran up the stairs to collect her father. And he *did* seem pleased with her, for he stood in the hall, fairly beaming. So perhaps she was forgiven.

'Good,' he said. 'Now you must come up to the nursery and have a bite to eat with your cousins. I've made them wait for you so I expect they're hungry too.'

'Am I still allowed to stay up and see the people?' Octavia asked as she followed him back upstairs.

He was looking at her hands and noticing how red and sore they were. Poor little thing, he thought. I've been very hard on her and she's no age. Amy was right. I should have found another way. 'Why should you not be?' he said gruffly.

'Because I was naughty.'

'You have made amends,' he said, taking her roughened hand and patting it, 'and now the matter is closed. Over and done with. Of course you shall see our guests. They are great men and women. The best of our society. You can't miss a chance like this. I've given Nurse instructions to tell you who they all are, one by one as they come in. You won't miss any of it. You're to sit just inside my study. You can see everything from there.'

Octavia smiled at him, her solemn face lifted and rounded, her blue eyes shining in the gaslight. Then she put up her arms to hug him, and he stooped towards her so that she could fling them round his neck and kiss him. 'Oh thank you, Papa. Thank you, thank you, thank you.'

He was warmed by her affection, as he always was. But this time he was shamed by it too. She might be naughty — that was only to be expected — but she was so loving and such a nice child. She never bore grudges, she hadn't told tales on her cousins — and they were every bit as much to blame as she was — and she'd taken her punishment like a trooper. 'I gave you my word,' he said, 'and I always keep my word.'

So that evening, when the cousins had gone home and she'd had her supper and changed into her nightgown ready for bed and said goodnight to Mama, who'd rubbed some of her special cream on her sore hands, he led her downstairs and installed her in his great leather armchair in the study, with a shawl over her shoulders and a rug round her legs to keep her warm, and Nurse sitting on the Windsor chair behind her with a list of all the guests so that she could be kept informed, and left her to watch the arrival of the great and the good.

They were certainly very grand in their evening dress. Some of the gentlemen had capes over their shoulders and the ladies were in elaborate gowns made of satin and velvet with tiny waists and huge puffed sleeves, and some of them wore beautiful necklaces that glittered in the gaslight. Mr Wilkins was sporting his butler's suit with a very stiff collar and making a great fuss of greeting them and taking their capes and hats and gloves. It was quite a while before he escorted them upstairs to the drawing room, where Mama and Papa were waiting for them, so she had a really good view.

The third pair to arrive were an odd looking couple, she very tall and grand in a beautiful blue dress with huge leg a' mutton sleeves, he small and dark with glasses and an odd-looking black beard.

'Mr and Mrs Webb,' Nurse whispered. 'They're the leaders of the Fabian Society.'

'What's that?'

'I'm not exactly sure of the ins and outs of it,' Nurse whispered. 'I think it's politics. You'd better ask your father. See the man who's just come in? Now that's Mr Bernard Shaw. I've seen his picture in the papers.'

He was very tall and straight and had lots of ginger hair and a big ginger beard and a jolly way of moving, as if he was going to break out into a dance. And he wasn't wearing evening dress, just a brown suit, which was rather odd.

Octavia watched him closely, intrigued by his appearance. 'Is he a foreign gentleman?' she whispered.

'He's Irish, I believe,' Nurse said. 'I suppose that's foreign. He makes speeches.'

'What about?'

'I couldn't say. But I know he does because I read it in the papers.'

Octavia looked at him again. He was standing aside to make room for two more arrivals, a large fat man and a lady with a lot of frizzy hair drawn up into a bun on the top of her head. He obviously knew them because they were greeting one another like old friends.

'Now that's Mr William Morris,' Nurse said, with great satisfaction. 'I'd know him anywhere. He's been here before. Your Papa thinks the world of him.'

Mr William Morris was coughing, his big fat shoulders shaking with effort and his face quite puce. And his wife was watching him, looking anxious.

'He's got an awful cough,' Octavia said, feeling sorry for him.

'Something the matter with his lungs so they say,' Nurse told her. 'Poor man. He made the wallpaper in the hall.'

Octavia wasn't sure she wanted to know that. What if he saw the stains? But he didn't. He and the ginger man were following Mr Wilkins up the stairs, talking to one another in very loud voices and Boots was opening the door to the next arrivals.

Another couple, a pompous looking man with white hair plastered to his skull with Macassar oil and a gold-rimmed monocle jammed into his left eye, and close behind him, a very beautiful lady with thick dark curly hair and huge dark eyes. She was wearing an extraordinary green dress, quite unlike anything Octavia had ever seen before, long and flowing and patterned at the neck and wrists with blue and green embroidery and little glass beads. She looked like someone from a fairy story, as if she could cast spells, or grant wishes, or fly in the air, or read your thoughts. It was necessary to whisper very very quietly while she was in the hall. 'Who is the lady, Nurse?'

'Her married name is Mrs Bland,' Nurse said, 'so the gentleman must be Mr Bland, but it says here she writes under the name of E. Nesbit.'

'What does she write?'

'I couldn't say. You'll have to ask your father.'

The hall was emptying. Boots had gone back to the kitchen and the three guests were following Mr Wilkins upstairs.

'That's the lot,' Nurse said, speaking in her normal voice and becoming her usual brisk self again. 'You've seen them all now. Time you were in bed. Chop chop!'

It was hard to be in bed with all those important voices talking and laughing in the dining room below her. Papa said they were the best and the wisest of their generation and they were going to change the world, so perhaps that's what they were doing. They were certainly making enough noise.

I wonder what the world will be like when they've changed it, she thought. I hope they won't change the square. Or this house. I like this house, even when I have to clean the carpet. It's a jolly sort of house. She wished she could sneak downstairs and sit in a corner of the dining room and watch these important people and hear what they were saying. She couldn't, of course, because little girls weren't allowed at dinner. And anyway she probably wouldn't understand them. Grown-ups talked in such riddles.

But in fact it would have been instructive for her, for they were discussing education in general and her own education in particular.

'I can see no harm in children being educated at home,' Mrs Bland was saying, 'providing their parents can provide them with the necessary books and have the time and patience to use them.'

'And the wit,' her husband put in, wiping his lips on his napkin.

'I'm afraid I can't agree with you,' Mr Morris told them, happily mischievous. 'Parents are the worst possible people to educate their young.'

'You're surely not suggesting that we should send our children to school?' JJ teased. 'What was it you said in your article?'

'That board schools are instruments of repression,' William Morris agreed. 'Yes, so I did, and it's entirely true. They exist to provide subservient hands for factories in peacetime and cannon fodder for armies when we are at war. That is their function, which is why they are such unpleasant places. Don't you agree, Bernard?'

'I can't think of a single school I would be prepared to send my children to,' Mr Shaw said, 'ever supposing I have any. But as to what is to be done with them if we don't send them to school, I couldn't say. Perhaps we should take the advice of the good Dean Swift and make roast joints and meat pies of them.'

The agency maids were so shocked that they forgot they weren't supposed to gasp, but fortunately the guests were laughing so loudly that nobody noticed.

'On the whole,' JJ said when the noise had subsided a little, 'I think I would prefer not to eat my Octavia. At least not yet. So what is to be done with her?'

'If you must send her to school,' Mrs Bland advised, 'make sure it is one that will encourage her to think and allow her space and time to develop.'

'That is my opinion entirely,' Amy said, 'but where are we to find such a place?'

'I'm told there is a very good girls' school in Hampstead,' Mrs Bland said. 'The North London Collegiate School. It's a little out of the way but you might consider it.'

'We might indeed,' Amy agreed, smiling at her husband and thinking, we could move house and then we would be nearer. This house is far too small for all the people he invites into it. The nursery is positively cramped and you can barely turn round in his study and Mrs Wilkins really ought to have a bigger kitchen for all these dinner parties. It's high time we had something better. She would have to be tactful about suggesting it, for she knew, who better, how stubborn he could be and how resistant he was to change, despite the versatility of his mind. But then, glancing at him again, she noticed that he was beginning to get upset so the subject had to be dropped. Dear JJ, she thought. He simply can't bear the thought of handing his darling over to someone else. He'll be stubborn about that too. But it will have to be done sooner or later. Education is too important to be left to one person, however loving.

CHAPTER 3

Octavia was looking forward to her first great adventure. Mama said she was a very privileged little girl to be given such an opportunity, and although she wasn't quite sure what being privileged meant nor what an opportunity was, she knew it was something good because of the sound of Mama's voice when she told her.

'You've learnt to read and write quite splendidly,' Mama said one afternoon when they were snuggled up together on the big settee in the drawing room, 'and you can do all your sums, thanks to Papa, and now you're eight years old and I've got something quite wonderful to tell you. In September, when you are nine, your Papa and I are going to let you go to school. Think of that. You'll be able to learn all sorts of things at school — History and Geography and French and Botany and Science. The headmistress is the first lady ever to become a Doctor of Science. The very first. Won't it be grand?'

Octavia agreed that it would be. Very grand. But, as she found out in the next few days, it was also going to be complicated, for besides being sent to school it seemed they were all going to move house and live in another part of London.

'It's a fine big house,' her father told her, 'which will be better for all of us, but it will be an upheaval for your Mama so I must be quite sure it is a wise move. You *do* want to go to school, don't you?'

She assured him that she did, very much, but instead of smiling as she expected, he looked away from her and sighed, which was very odd.

'You must be very good on moving day,' he warned. 'You must do as you're told in every particular. Do you promise me?'

Of course she did, most earnestly.

'If everything goes as it should,' he said, 'I will take you up to London to see the Jubilee. How would you like that?'

Oh she would, very very much. The Jubilee was going to be the finest show that London had ever seen. It said so in the papers. There was going to be a grand parade with thousands of soldiers and hundreds of horses and people were coming to take part in it from all over the empire because the Queen had been reigning for sixty years.

'Very well then,' Papa said. 'It's settled. Just be sure not to worry your mother.'

But as the days went by Mama didn't seem to be worrying about anything. She was just cheerfully busy. First, she ordered a removal van and escorted two strange men in overalls all over the house, explaining things to them while they made notes in a dog-eared pocketbook, then she spent days and days packing all Papa's books into enormous tea chests, and checking while Molly and Mary emptied the linen cupboard and folded up their clothes and stacked piles and piles of things into the travelling trunk, and while Mrs Wilkins took everything out of the cupboards in the kitchen and wrapped all the china in news-paper until there was nothing left on the dresser, and when that was done she went from room to room tying labels on all the furniture, as happily and easily as if she'd been doing it all her life. Now and then she even broke into a song. And now here they were in a cab smelling of leather and horses, clopping through the streets to a place called Hampstead, because that was where they were going to live. It was right near the school and next to a fine common called Hampstead Heath where there were ponds and trees and they could go for some splendid walks, and a town where there were lots of shops that sold everything you could possibly think of. Mama was so excited the tip of her nose was pink.

'Here we are,' she said, leaning forward to look out of the window. 'This is the street.'

It was a very long street, built on the side of a hill and the houses were all very grand, three stories high with great sloping roofs covered in grey tiles and huge windows — not straight flat ones like they'd had in their old house, but curved into bays with three window frames in every one — and a white porch over the front door with two white pillars to hold it up.

'Isn't it splendid?' Mama said, admiring it. 'What do you think of it?'

Octavia looked at it too. 'It's not like our old house.'

'No,' Mama agreed as the driver reined in his horse. 'It isn't. This is a new house with a bathroom and a garden and everything just as it ought to be. We're only the second family to live in it. Think of that. It will be much much nicer than our old house.'

It was certainly much much bigger. And very grand. There was a path of black and white tiles leading to the front door, like a long chequer board, and the door itself was like a stained glass window in a church, all reds and blues and golds in oblongs and diamonds and shapes like flattened flowers. But there wasn't time to admire it because the removal van was drawn up beside the gate and one of the removal men was carrying Papa's great leather chair into the house, holding it in front of him and staggering under the weight of it. She and Mama stood together on the little front lawn while he struggled it into the hall and after a while Octavia saw a shape approaching from the darkness at the end of the hall and there was Aunt Maud. She was wearing a thick Holland apron and her hair had fallen out of its bun and was curling in damp strands onto her cheeks.

'Such a to-do,' she said, as they stepped into the hall. 'I don't know where they think they've put the tea chests. They're all over the shop. I can't find a thing.'

'Well I'm here now,' Mama said. 'It'll be better with the two of us. Where are the children?'

'I put them in the garden,' Aunt Maud said. 'We don't want them under our feet all the time.'

'Very sensible,' Mama agreed. 'Octavia can go and join them, can't you, Tavy. Is Baby there too?'

'All the lot of them,' Aunt Maud said. 'One thing I will say, Mrs Wilkins has done marvels in the kitchen. Come and see. That's the back door, Tavy. Just go through.'

It led into a garden like a little park. Octavia could hardly believe her luck. There was the dearest little cherry tree on one side and quite a big apple tree on the other and two flower beds edged with terracotta tiles and simply full of flowers and a lawn like a meadow, all tall grass and buttercups. But best of all was the view beyond the wall, for the garden sloped down to the edge of the heath and there was an enormous blue lake just outside the gate simply asking to be explored or paddled in — or even swum in. What fun!

Her cousins were sitting on a wooden seat under the cherry tree with the baby's pram parked in the tall grasses alongside them. Cyril was scowling and the baby was fully absorbed in hitting the side of the pram with his rattle but Emmeline looked up and called to her. "'Lo Tavy.'

'Are we to go in now?' Cyril asked.

'I don't think so,' Octavia told him. 'They said I was to stay out here with you.'

'I don't see why we have to stay here the whole time,' Cyril said, kicking a flowerpot. 'It's not fair.'

'Because we do,' his sister told him firmly. She was very nearly eleven and a quarter now and two superior years older than Cyril so she knew how a little brother should be treated. 'They're carrying the furniture in and they don't want us under their feet. It's no good getting ratty, Squirrel. You've just got to put up with it. They'll let us in presently. Ma promised. Make room for Tavy. I tell you what, let's play cat's cradle.'

Cyril stood up and kicked the flowerpot into the middle of the lawn. 'Pooh to cat's cradle,' he said. 'That's a baby game. I don't want to sit on a rotten old seat all day, playing cat's cradle. I want to see inside the house. What's the good of bringing us here if they're not going to let us in? I don't see why I should spend my half term sitting in a rotten garden. I'm going to climb that tree.'

'It's not a rotten garden,' Emmeline said, pulling the string into its first pattern ready to start the game. 'It's lovely. And mind you don't fall. Your turn, Tavy.'

Octavia was just as eager to see the house as he was but she had greater patience and besides she knew she had to be good or Papa wouldn't take her to see the Jubilee. So she settled herself onto the seat next to her cousin and lifted the string into its next pattern. 'Fish in a dish!' she said.

'You've cut out two goes,' Emmeline said much impressed. 'How did you do that?' Then the baby dropped his rattle over the edge of the pram and began to cry for it so she had to stop to attend to him. 'There it is, Podge! Don't cry. There it is.' But he went on crying even when the rattle was put in his hand and in the end she had to undo his reins and lift him out to comfort him. 'Isn't he a little duck,' she said, bouncing him on her knee.

'Quack, quack!' Cyril mocked from the apple tree.

'Don't take any notice of your brother,' Emmeline advised.

'He's just being ratty. I think you're a darling and so does Tavy. When I grow up I'm going to have lots and lots of babies.'

'When I grow up,' Cyril said, in his most superior way, 'I'm going to be a famous explorer and travel all over the world discovering things. I'll bet they won't say I can't come into the house *then*.'

'They won't let you be an explorer if you don't do as you're told,' his sister said scathingly.

'That's all you know!' Cyril said, climbing higher. 'You don't have to do as you're told if you're an explorer. You just have to explore and find new countries and do daring deeds. You two can stay at home and have babies but I'm going to be important. So there.'

'I'm going to be important too,' Octavia said, stung by his scathing tone.

'No you're not.'

'I am too. I'm going to change the world.'

He looked down on her from the twin heights of male superiority and the apple tree. 'Girls can't change the world,' he said.

'Why not?'

'Because they're girls. Boys change the world.'

'What about the Queen then?'

'You can't count her. Anyway she hasn't done anything. She's not like an explorer or a general. She doesn't *do* things. She's just the Queen.'

'I think you're horrid, Cyril.'

'I hope you're not quarrelling,' Mama's voice said behind them. 'I thought we'd have our picnic out here. Come down out of that tree, Cyril, and help me set it out.'

So the quarrel was deferred in favour of ham sandwiches and potted shrimps and glasses of Mrs Wilkin's lemonade. And after that they all went into the house and helped Mama to unpack Papa's books and set his study to rights so that when he came home that evening he would find everything exactly as he'd left it in the old house that morning, except that in this house the study was on the top floor with a huge window over-looking the heath and in the old house it had been right by the front door and very dark. But they arranged the furniture in exactly the same positions so that he would know where every-thing was and even opened his journal at the right page and put fresh ink in the inkwell for him. And he *was* pleased. He said he would never have believed it and told Mama she was the best wife a man could possibly have, which pleased her and made her nose pink for the second time that day.

Aunty Maud and the cousins stayed to dinner that evening and Uncle Ralph arrived at six o'clock to join them and although the meal was rather late because Mrs Wilkins couldn't get the hang of the stove it was very jolly. When it was over Papa said the house was warmed now and no mistake and thanked Aunt Maud for all she'd done to help them. And Aunt Maud said it was nothing and blushed and looked quite pretty. So what with eating and talking, there wasn't time for Octavia to think about whether girls could change the world until Mama was tucking her up in her old bed in her new bedroom late that night.

'What a day we've had, my Tavy,' Papa said, as he stopped to kiss her. 'So many changes.'

And that reminded her. 'Papa,' she said. 'May I ask you something?'

'Of course.'

'Can girls change the world?'

He smiled at Mama. 'They do it every day of their lives,' he said.

'No,' she persisted. 'I mean like Mr Morris. Really change the world.'

'What makes you ask?' Mama said.

'It was something C...' But then she stopped herself. Naming him might get him into trouble and she didn't want that. '... someone said.'

Cyril, JJ thought, admiring her discretion. Now he realised that this was a serious question so he answered it seriously. 'I see no reason why not,' he said. 'If Dr Pankhurst has his way women will soon be given the vote and then we shall see all manner of changes. The possibilities will be endless.'

Octavia didn't really understand what he was talking about but she recognised a positive answer when she heard one. 'Good,' she said. And closed her eyes. 'We *are* going to the Jubilee aren't we, Papa?'

'Of course,' he said, smoothing her hair.

'I thought you didn't approve of royalty,' Amy teased.

'I don't,' he told her, 'but the child has earned a reward and it will be an education for her to see it. I shall buy the tickets tomorrow.'

JUBILEE DAY WAS a long time coming. Waiting for it got more difficult as the weeks went by even though there was plenty to keep them occupied in their new house. Something different happened nearly every day. A gardener was hired to tidy the flower beds and mow the lawn — and spent a lot of time grumbling because the last tenants had let it 'run to rack and ruin'; there were three new servants to help Mr and Mrs Wilkins; decorators arrived to hang fresh wallpaper in all the downstairs rooms, which was nice because it turned out to be exactly the same paper as they'd had at the old house; and on Saturdays Emmeline and Squirrel came to visit and they all went out on the Heath and spent the day exploring. It was gloriously hot so they had to be careful that Podge didn't throw off his sunhat and get sunstroke but he was pretty good and kept it on, more or less. Cyril fell out of a tree and wouldn't let them see his bruises. And Emmeline arrived one Saturday to say that Uncle Ralph was going to let her go to the North London Collegiate School too and wouldn't that be nice. But no matter how much they did and how far they walked, the Jubilee was still ages away. The papers were full of it, with pictures of the Queen and her family and details of all the festivities that were planned for the great day. Papa said they were putting up a new grandstand near St Paul's and that he'd bought three excellent seats for them. 'You will have a bird's eye view, I promise you.' And Mama said if that was the case perhaps they ought to have new outfits for the occasion. What did Papa think?

So the outfits were ordered from the dressmaker in Flask Walk and very pretty they were. Amy's was a suit in lime green silk with ruched frills in the prettiest lilac set diagonally across the skirt and a lilac blouse that was all neat tucks with a white collar that covered her neck right up to her chin and rose in two curved wings on either side of her face and Octavia had her first proper grown-up costume, in rose pink, finished with grass green bows at shoulder and wrist, which she wore with white silk stockings and white silk gloves and the dearest little straw hat trimmed with pink roses. And then, just when everything was ready, the weather changed and they had a violent thunderstorm. Octavia stood by the drawing room window, watching as the rain whipped the fruit trees and violet clouds massed and brooded over the rooftops.

'What will happen if it rains on the day?' she asked Mrs Wilkins. 'Everyone will get wet.'

'It won't rain,' Mrs Wilkins reassured her. 'Don't you worry your pretty head. We shall have royal weather. It's always royal weather for the Queen. God bless her. Now come away from the window, there's a pet. We don't want you struck with lightning.'

But the morning of the Jubilee was muggy and not at all promising.

'You two must take your parasols and I will carry an umbrella,' JJ decided practically. 'Then we shall be prepared for every eventuality.'

So with every eventuality catered for, they set off for the City, travelling by horse bus because Papa said that was the best way. But when they got to King's Cross the driver couldn't take them any further because so many roads had been closed for the procession, so they had to get off and find some other way to proceed. Professor Smith took his family by the new underground, which Octavia found very exciting. She'd never travelled under the ground before and what with the smell of sulphur and hot oil and dust, the pressure of the crowds and the terrifying clicking of the train as it rushed in and out of the tunnels, she was quite breathless by the time they emerged into the air again.

They were in a wide street with very tall buildings on either side, all of them flying the Union Jack and hung about with so many garlands of green leaves that the air prickled with the scent of them and Octavia felt as though she was walking through a forest. The pavements swarmed with people, all very excited and all walking in the same direction. And the sun was shining.

'Hold my arms,' JJ said to his womenfolk. 'I don't want you getting lost.' And off they went along the pavement with all the other people, men in boaters and blazers, smoking cheroots, men in bowlers and brown suits and stiff white collars, smoking cigarettes, women carrying baskets and umbrellas and folding chairs, as if they were off to a picnic, women in summer dresses and bonnets high with flowers and feathers and bright wax fruits, and hordes and hordes of children clutching tiny flags, all of them crushed in close together and all talking at once. 'D'you ever see such a crowd!' 'Soon be there!' 'She's got the weather for it, bless her.' 'Watch what you're doing with that flag, Mildred. You go on like that, you'll put the lady's eye out.' And after several jostling minutes, pushed up against other people's bony arms and into the hot cloth on their backs, they emerged into a wide square in front of the biggest church that Octavia had ever seen and Papa said they'd arrived.

'St Paul's Cathedral,' he told her. 'One of the best examples of mathematical architecture in the world. Observe the grace of the columns, Octavia, and the balance of that architrave.' But his daughter was gazing up at the great grey-blue dome shining in the sunshine above her and was lost in amazement at the scale and beauty of it.

'You will see even better from our vantage point,' her father said, leading her through the crowds again. 'We go up these steps. Take care. They're rather rickety. That's the style. Second tier. Here we are. Now this is better.'

He was right. The view from their high grandstand was breathtaking, for now they could see the entire square in all its multicoloured detail, from the blur of the crowds on the pavements — all hats and faces and restless movement — to the stolid red backs of the guardsmen who lined the kerb, stiff as toy soldiers, their faces half hidden by great black bearskins. There was a statue on a plinth in the centre of the square, surrounded by iron railings, and the road that curved around it was empty, except for two cavalry officers on patient horseback. It looked very pretty because it had been sprinkled with pink sand. 'To save the horses' feet,' Mama explained. But the most impressive sight was the great mass of people who were standing on the cathedral steps in such a blaze of scarlet and gold and white that they looked as though they had burst into flame. There were two huge choirs, one in long red robes and the other in white, dozens of clergy, draped and dramatic, all gold and white and embroidered, generals and admirals in full fig, medals, swords and all, their shoulders hung about with gold braid and their hats plumed with ostrich feathers, several politicians strutting and looking important while their wives preened beside them, and on the bottommost step, a line of Yeomen Warders from the Tower, quaint in their odd red and gold jackets. It looked like a huge stage set, painted and peopled and ready for performance.

'Take a close look,' JJ advised his daughter. 'These are the people who run the country.'

'They're very grand,' Octavia said. 'Are they the great and the good?'

'Not what you and I understand by the term,' her father told her. 'Although to be fair I suppose some of them might qualify. We must allow for idealism.'

There was a flurry of activity in the sanded roadway. Two more cavalry officers had arrived and were trotting up to their companions. There was a short conversation and then all four took up positions on either side of the steps, the crowd began to buzz and from somewhere in the western distance they could hear cheers rolling and rising. The parade had begun.

Octavia was enraptured. So many horses, all stepping in line, snorting and tossing their heads, and all the same colour, so many riders in magnificent uniforms, first a troop of guardsmen riding chestnuts, then another in splendid helmets and breast-plates that flashed in the sun riding horses as black as silk. 'Horse Guards,' Mama explained. But Octavia didn't care what they were; the sight of them was enough. She leant over the edge of the stand, agog for the next troop, as they rounded the street into the square, one after the other, Dragoon Guards, Hussars, Scots Greys, Cape Mounted Rifles, Trinidad Light Horse, Jamaica Artillery, Lancers of the Indian Empire, magnificent in striped turbans and formidable beards. Even their names were magical. And what colours they wore! Sky blue and gold, scarlet and gold, purple and gold, emerald green and gold. She had never seen anything so gorgeous. The sixteen carriages that brought up the rear of the procession were quite dull by comparison although the ladies in them were beautifully gowned and held their elaborate parasols above their elabo-rately hatted heads as delicately as if they were holding flowers.

'Are there any more soldiers?' she asked her mother, leaning forward over the edge of the stand and straining to see. The crowd in Fleet Street were cheering like mad and there was a snowstorm of paper flags and white handkerchiefs so something special must be coming.

It was a black coach with crimson wheels pulled by eight cream coloured horses, all caparisoned in crimson and gold, with postilions in crimson and gold walking importantly beside them, and sitting all on her own on the back seat, facing two rather grand ladies in lilac gowns, was a little fat lady in black, with a small black cap on her white hair, a white parasol above her head and a huge smile on her round face. The Queen.

'Sixty years,' Amy said. 'Think of that, Octavia.'

'The richest woman in the world,' JJ parried. 'Think of that, Octavia.'

But Octavia was beyond thought, and cheering with the crowd. The noise they were making was so loud it was making her ears ring. 'Isn't it wonderful!' she said.

The coach had come to a stop right in front of the steps and the archbishop was walking down towards it. 'How will she get into the cathedral past all those people?' Octavia wondered.

But apparently she wasn't even going to get out of the coach. The ceremony was going to be conducted there on the steps and they were going to see it all. The two choirs were already clearing their throats and settling themselves to be ready. What fun!

It was a very short ceremony, just the Te Deum, the Old Hundredth, a blessing, the National Anthem and three cheers, but Octavia relished every minute of it. I've seen the Queen, she thought, on her Diamond Jubilee. And cheered again as the lovely cream horses pulled the coach away, slowly and gently, round the statue and out of her sight.

'What did you think of that?' her mother asked.

'I should like to see it all over again,' Octavia said. 'I feel quite sad now it's over.' And it *was* sad to see the way everything was breaking up after the event, the crowds shifting and beginning to walk away, the serried ranks of choirs and dignitaries turning and moving, breaking their wonderful patterns, the pink sand littered with discarded paper flags and smeared with trodden manure. 'But it was wonderful, wasn't it, Mama. When I grow up I'm going to be rich and famous and ride in a carriage too.'

They were negotiating the steps from the grandstand. 'Well if that's the case, miss,' her mother teased, 'you will have to find yourself a rich husband.'

Octavia grimaced with distaste at such a suggestion. 'Oh no, Mama,' she said seriously. 'That would be cheating. I mean to be famous in my own right because of something I've done.'

Amy smiled. 'And what will that be, pray?'

'I don't know yet,' Octavia admitted. 'Something good and helpful.'

'You still intend to change the world then,' her father said, handing her down the last rickety step and onto the pavement again.

'Yes, Papa,' she said. 'Of course.'

But her father was looking at Mama and offering his hand to help her down the step and the topic seemed to be over.

'We could take a little stroll and see the decorations, could we not, JJ?' Amy said, looking about the square.

Octavia was all for it. 'Could we, Papa? Oh do let's.'

'If that is what you would like,' he said and watched as she skipped towards the steps of St Paul's, bright and happy in her summer pink. 'There goes our world shaker,' he said to Amy half amused and half proud. 'Just look at her, my dear. I wouldn't put anything past her.'

Amy smiled. 'She's a good little girl,' she agreed, and added, because it was too apt an opportunity to miss. 'Once she's at school, we shall see great things of her.'

'You are still determined upon it,' he said, and his tone was almost reproachful, for they'd discussed the matter so often and at such length and he knew it was settled, but he wasn't convinced.

'Of course,' Amy said, in her mild way. 'You know I am, oh ye of little faith. You mustn't worry so, my dear. Nothing but good will come of it, I promise you.'

'I am sorry to have so little faith,' he said wryly, 'but schools can be cruel places. I would not wish her to suffer there. Or anywhere for that matter.'

'If it is wrong for her, JJ,' Amy reassured, 'we will remove her and find a better place. That is agreed.'

But he was frowning and pulling his beard.

'On the other hand, it could be just the right place at just the right time,' Amy said. She was so sure of it, yet nothing she said convinced him. She looked up at the great dome of St Paul's, strong and secure above her head, and knew in her bones that this precious daughter of theirs would move from success to acclaim, through school to university, to an eminent academic career, just like her father, and that school would be the making of her. Why was he so foolish as to doubt it?

Octavia had reached the top of the cathedral steps and turned to urge them to follow. 'Come *on*,' she called. 'You can see for miles up here.'

'If that is the case,' JJ called back, smiling again. 'We must join you, for what can be better than a clear view.' But as he strode towards her, he put one hand behind his back and crossed his fingers.

CHAPTER 4

Although her father worried about her all summer and grew more and more concerned as September approached, Octavia slipped into scholarship as easily as a swan into water. Learning was natural to her, for she was an inquisitive child and accustomed to having her questions answered; a classroom held no terrors, because her cousins had taught her how to wait her turn and stand her ground; but above all, she was happy in her skin so naturally she expected to find friends and helpers in this new adventure of hers and naturally she wasn't disappointed.

By the end of her first week she had made more than a dozen friends and by the end of the second had established one of them, a small pale rather nervous little girl with owl-like glasses, as 'my best friend, Betty Transom'. By the end of her first term she had decided that Mrs Bryant, their headmistress was the most wonderful woman she had ever met, not counting Mama, of course. 'She says we are all capable of great things,' she reported to her parents when she came home after the final assembly on the last day of term. 'All of us, every single one. She says times are changing and by the time we are in our twenties there will be all manner of opportunities for us and we are to seize them with both hands. Isn't that splendid?' It was so exactly what she wanted to hear that her face was glowing with the delight of it. 'I think being at school is the best thing ever.'

Her cousin Emmeline found the experience far more difficult and in that first term she spent many of her playtimes weeping on Octavia's shoulder, complaining that the other girls were beastly and she wished she hadn't come. 'It's all very well for you, Tavy,' she wept. 'You're clever. You know the answers.'

'Not all of them,' Octavia admitted honestly. 'Just say you don't know, Em. They won't kill you.'

But Emmeline took a lot of persuading. She'd been the big sister for so long it was hard to be an unimportant newcomer in a class full of larger and more determined girls who all knew their way around. 'I shall never fit in,' she mourned.

Cyril was delighted to see her at a disadvantage for once and said she was being a silly. He'd found himself a new friend that term and was full of reflected importance, quoting him on every occasion. 'Meriton Major says school stinks.' 'When he grows up, Meriton Major's going to be a Member of Parliament.' Now he offered his friend's philosophy to quell his sister's fears. 'I told Meriton Major about you, and he says it's sissy to be afraid of school.'

'I'm sick of Meriton Major,' Emmeline said. 'He should try being at our school.'

'It'll get better, Em. Truly,' Octavia soothed. 'It's just you're not quite used to it yet. Some of it's good, you've got to admit.'

But Emmeline couldn't see good in any of it. 'I think it's all horrid,' she said. 'You can't speak unless you're spoken to and you mustn't call out and you mustn't run and you have to say "please" all the time and they keep making you sign the Appearing Book — I've signed it four times already and I was only talking to Sissie — I don't see why you can't talk to your *best friend* — and Pa says I've got to stay there until I'm sixteen.

Sixteen! That's five whole years, Tavy, and I never wanted to go there in the first place. Oh I know I said I did but that was just to please people. What I really want is just to grow up and get married and have lots of babies.'

'Fathers are awfully funny,' Octavia observed. 'Here's yours really keen for you to be a scholar and I don't think mine wanted me to go to school at all.'

That surprised her cousin. 'How do you know that?' she asked. 'Did he say?'

'No,' Octavia admitted. 'He never actually says. That's how you know it's important. He goes round and round things, sort of talking at the edges. He was fussing about it all summer and asking me if I was really sure and saying I didn't have to go there if I didn't want to. And I love it.'

And loved it more with every new day. Even when the weather grew cold and the sports field was sharp with hoar frost, she couldn't wait to get out to play, and in the relative warmth of the classroom every lesson brought a new challenge. There were so many books to read and so much to find out. By the end of her second term she had established herself as one of the most intelligent girls in her class. By the time she was eleven and had been elevated to the main school she was being spoken of as 'university material' and her father had quite forgotten his anxieties and was happily admitting that he and Amy had made a wise choice in this school.

'She has a natural aptitude for French,' he quoted from her latest school report. 'Her grasp of mathematical principles is commendable. This is all very gratifying, Amy.'

'She is a natural scholar,' Amy agreed and smiled at him. 'Like her father.'

'She shall go to the pantomime,' he decided, 'as a reward for good work. And to the Egyptian Hall to see Mr Maskelyne and his magic.'

Octavia enjoyed the pantomime and was intrigued by the

famous magician but she would have worked well without any recompense, for learning was now its own reward. The months passed happily, punctuated by feasts and festivals and successes. Now there was a new century coming and the newspapers said it would be the start of a brave new world and would bring much change and progress, which didn't surprise Octavia at all for wasn't that exactly what the redoubtable Mrs Bryant had predicted. They all sat up to welcome it in and Octavia and her two older cousins were allowed to drink watered wine to toast its arrival, which was a first for all of them and made them all giggly.

But once the Christmas holiday was over, life at home continued in its old comfortable way and as far as Octavia could see the new century was just like the old one only with a different name. There were wars going on in various parts of the world — but weren't there always? — the Italian king was shot by anarchists, and in Great Britain a new political party was inaugurated. It called itself the Labour Party and was led by a man called Keir Hardie. Her father grew very animated at the news and said that Mr Hardie was first rate and that this was the start of a bloodless revolution and the masters would have to look to their laurels, but Octavia wasn't interested. She was more concerned with her Latin declensions.

Her life was changing but the change was so gradual and easy that she barely noticed it. She had grown taller — that was obvious because Mama had let down all her skirts and dresses and last years' gym slip didn't fit at all — but the face that looked back at her from her early morning mirror was unaltered, long and serious, the hair still sandy in colour and very frizzy, the eyes still blue under sandy eyebrows, nose long and straight, mouth wide and pale, teeth white and crooked, hands long-fingered and skinny. Out in the garden the cherry tree had doubled in size, but like her, it had grown gradually and in season and nobody remarked on it. Em and Squirrel had grown taller too, and, at fourteen, Em was beginning to round out into a pretty femininity, but they still wore the same childish faces and fought and argued in the same childish way. Only Podge revealed the passage of time. In the three years since she and Em had started school, he'd grown from a plump baby in a pram, to a roly-poly toddler, staggering about in his baby skirts, and eventually to a little boy in his first sailor suit with all his pretty curls cut off and his hair trimmed to a big boy's cut, four and a half years old and full of himself. Emmeline cried to see the sudden change in him and said she'd lost her darling baby but Cyril said it was high time he stopped being a duffer and learnt to stand up for himself. 'You want to be a big boy, don't you, Podge. Not a soppy baby.'

And Podge, who was standing on Octavia's knee so that he could admire his new image in the looking glass, said, yes, he did, and sounded defiantly confident even though the expression on his face was anxious and doubtful.

IN THE SUMMER of the first year of the new century the North London Collegiate School reached the fiftieth anniversary of its foundation and the entire school went to a special service in St Paul's Cathedral — no less — to celebrate. It was an impressive occasion and Octavia was duly impressed, thrilled to think that they were in the self-same cathedral that had welcomed the Queen, overawed by the imposing clergy, stirred by the wonderful sound the choir made as their voices echoed up and up into the high spaces of the great dome, uplifted by the rousing speeches in praise of the great work already done by the school, encouraged to think that even greater things lay in the future and that she would be part of them.

In the autumn the Conservative party won the General Election with four hundred and one seats to everybody else's two hundred and sixty-eight, and Keir Hardie was elected as Labour

MP for Merthyr Tydfil, to whoops of delight from Professor Smith. Then on the second of January in the second year of the new century, the papers were printed with black margins to announce the death of 'good Queen Victoria'. '*It is the end of an era,*' *The Times* said, '*and we shall never see her like again.*' Special prayers were offered up for her at school and in church, most social functions were cancelled as a mark of respect, and her death and its repercussions were the main topic of conversation wherever the Smith family went. This time Octavia wasn't impressed at all. It had been exciting to watch the living queen in her carriage by the steps of St Paul's but it seemed silly to make a fuss about her because she was dead. There was no need to go cancelling parties and staying at home all the time.

'If it had been someone we knew,' she said to her cousins when they were all sitting round the drawing room fire on Sunday afternoon, 'it would have been different. I can't see the point of making a fuss over someone we don't know. I don't see why they've got to cancel Betty Transom's party.'

'Nor do I,' Emmeline said. 'It's not her fault the queen's gone and died. What do you think, Squirrel?'

'Meriton Major's got one of those new bicycles,' Cyril said. 'I'm going to ask Pa if I can have one too. It's ripping fun.'

'It's always Meriton Major with you,' Emmeline said scornfully. 'I'm tired of hearing about him. Aren't you, Tavy? It's so boring, worse than the queen.'

'That's all you know,' her brother said, tossing his dark hair and picking up the poker to give the coals a good whacking. 'Actually he's a dashed good egg. If it hadn't been for them cancelling Betty's party you'd have seen him there and then you'd have known.'

But as it was they were denied sight of his hero and on the day of the party they had to content themselves with playing Pit and roasting chestnuts by the fire.

. . .

THE NEW CENTURY ROLLED ON. A wireless message was sent right across the Atlantic Ocean, which was quite amazing, the coronation was postponed because the new king had appendicitis and had to have an operation, which was very serious, the bell tower in Venice collapsed into a heap of rubble — there were pictures in the paper to prove it — and Emmeline finished her unwanted years at school, failed her final examinations and was allowed to leave. She was pretty with relief. Within a week she had put her hair up and left her childhood behind her. She and her mother visited the dressmaker in Flask Walk, on Amy's recommendation, studied the catalogues and went for several shopping expeditions to the West End. Soon she was fully kitted out as an adult, with all the clothes necessary to her new status, walking costume, day dresses, gloves, hat, silk stockings, button boots and all. She was totally and glowingly transformed.

'Pa's going to take me to a play on Friday,' she confided to Octavia, 'and a concert on Saturday. I intend to meet lots and lots of people. That's the best way if you mean to be married and I mean to be married just as soon as ever I can. Oh you don't know how lovely it is not to be at school! It's going to be such fun. You can't imagine all the things Ma's got planned for me. It's going to be a splendid summer.'

'Aren't you coming down to Eastbourne with us?' Octavia said. The two families always took their summer holidays together, always for four weeks and always in Eastbourne.

But apparently not. She and Aunt Maud were going to stay in Highgate all summer, Cyril was going to France with Meriton Major's family and only Podge would be playing on the Eastbourne sands that year. It was very disappointing.

'I shall miss you,' Octavia said. And did, for the holiday wasn't anywhere near so much fun on her own. Despite having a brand new swimming costume — and a very pretty one in sky blue cotton with two thick white frills at knee and elbow and another all round her cap — and despite excellent weather and having Podge to look after and with plenty to do and see, she was often lonely. The donkeys stood in patient lines on the beach, or plodded their well-worn hundred yards of sand, the band played its usual medley of cheerful tunes in the bandstand, the Pierrot company entertained as brashly as ever on the pier, the Punch and Judy man set up his customary stall at the top of the beach, but these things only increased her loneliness. What was the good of them, if there wasn't anyone to discuss them with? True, she had long talks with her mother and father when they all went for their daily promenade, but adult conversation is not at all the same thing as a gossip with your oldest friend, and a postcard isn't the same thing either, although she wrote one religiously every day. Emmeline did write back, but only now and then, and with diminishing interest, and by the time the four weeks were over, Octavia had begun to accept that her life had changed whether she would or no.

'It'll be nice to see Emmeline again,' her mother said, as they packed their clothes in the trunk on that last busy day.

Octavia agreed that it would, although privately she wasn't quite so sure and the expression on her face revealed her feelings to the perceptive eyes of her mother.

'And Cyril too,' Amy pressed on. 'I wonder how he got on in France. Don't stand on the towels, Podge, there's a good boy. You'll be glad to see your Mama again, won't you? And your brother and sister.'

'Not much,' Podge said. 'There's no fun in *them*. Squirrel's off with Meriton Major all the time on his rotten bicycle and Em's got new clothes. It's all she ever talks about. She says I'm a pest. I'd rather stay here with Tavy and ride the donkeys.'

Quite right, Octavia thought. He's got a lot of sense for a little'un. But the holiday was over and they would all be having tea together on Sunday, the way they usually did, so perhaps...

It was the oddest tea party. Emmeline was now a most superior young lady, wearing a pink tea gown and a knowing expression. She'd joined her father's tennis club in Brookfield, had been to so many plays and concerts she couldn't remember them all, had acquired an artless laugh and a new trick of patting her mounded hair, and was going to have what she called 'a proper party' at Christmas for all her new friends. 'You must come too, Tavy. You'll *adore* them.' And Cyril had come back from his holiday with hair as long as Oscar Wilde and the dark shadow of an incipient moustache on his upper lip, boasting that he'd been speaking French like billy-oh and dropping French phrases into the conversation all the time to prove it. Octavia wanted to laugh at him but she knew it would upset everybody if she did, for his parents were gazing at him in admiration and even Emmeline seemed wary of him.

'I suppose you'll soon be going back to school,' Aunt Maud said as they kissed goodbye. 'I wish you luck.'

'Thank you,' Octavia said. 'I'm looking forward to it.' Which was true. At school she knew where she was and what was expected of her. At school there were friends to confide in.

'I just don't understand my cousin,' she said to Betty Transom on their first day back. 'All she ever talks about is what she's going to wear. And what a lot of young men she's meeting. It's really boring.'

'Carlotta was just the same,' Betty said, polishing her glasses. 'Do you remember her? Long fair hair. Good at games. Sang in the choir. And then the minute she left it was all hats and gloves and "you'll never believe who I saw at the tennis club!" And putting on airs as if she'd never learnt anything in her life.'

'I hope I never get like that,' Octavia said. 'I think it's horrid.'

'You'll have to if you want to get married,' Betty said sagely. 'That's how they all go on then.'

'If that's the case, it's just as well I don't want to get married,' Octavia said.

'Don't you?'

'No,' Octavia said firmly. 'I don't. Not for ages and ages anyway.'

'What do you want to do then?'

Octavia had no doubt about that. 'I want to go to college,' she said, 'and get a degree and be a graduate like Mrs Bryant. And after that I want to find a cause, so that I can do something worthwhile. Something that will make a difference.'

'What sort of something?'

'I don't know yet,' Octavia admitted. 'I shall find out though. When I've got my degree probably.'

'You'll have to work ever so hard if you want to go to college,' Betty warned, putting on her glasses. 'You have to matriculate in Cambridge Junior for a start and then you have to stay on in the sixth form and do the senior exam and get a scholarship. It takes ages and ages. Pa told me.'

The earnestness on her friend's face revealed a fellow ambition. 'Is that what you want to do too?'

'I'd like to,' Betty admitted. 'The trouble is I don't think I'd be clever enough.'

'Of course you would,' Octavia said. 'Passing exams is just a matter of how hard you work. That's all. I'm going to pass mine with credits and distinctions. And so will you. I tell you what, we'll study together and compare notes. Two heads are better than one.'

'Will they let us?' Betty wondered. 'I mean, are we supposed to?'

'I ask my father when I'm not sure about things,' Octavia told her, 'so I can't see why you shouldn't ask me. Let's try it and see what happens. It's two years before the exams. We could learn an awful lot between us in two years.'

Betty was touched by the offer. 'You're my very best friend,' she said, her brown eyes moist with tears. 'My very very best.' She was trying to think of something she could offer in return, something equally worthwhile and important, but her mind was stuck in gratitude. 'If I can ever help *you* with anything,' she urged, 'you must tell me straight away. You promise.'

The promise was given with an easy kiss and their co-operation started that very evening with a difficult mathematical problem. It seemed intractable until Professor Smith enlightened them both in the quiet of his study and then it was perfectly simple.

'Fancy that!' Betty said, much impressed.

'What did I tell you?' Octavia said. 'It's just a matter of seeing straight. That's all.'

AFTER SUCH A REWARDING START, their lives rapidly acquired a pattern and the pattern didn't vary for the next three years. They did their homework together in Betty's house in Highgate every Tuesday evening and in Octavia's every Thursday and Friday and consulted Professor Smith whenever they had need of his mathematical clarity, and the longer they studied together the stronger their confidence became. Octavia still saw her cousins every week when the two families took tea but she and Emmeline had grown so far apart that they no longer had anything in common and Cyril got sillier and sillier with every passing week, showing off about his marvellous bicycle and his marvellous examination results and his marvellous friend Meriton Major. It was a relief to get back to school and talk to Betty Transom. By the time their mock examinations began, in the Spring term of their fifth year, they had grown into the sort of bosom friends who could tell one another almost anything and they were both so well prepared, especially in Mathematics, that Betty declared she was hardly nervous at all.

Which was obvious from their results, for both did well enough to stay on in the sixth form and to start studying for the Cambridge Senior Examination. The first year of their new studies passed easily enough and it seemed no time at all before they were sitting their second set of mock examinations.

'I feel as if I've been studying for ever and ever,' Betty sighed, late one January evening before their first English paper. Outside her bedroom it was dark and cold and she was feeling the strain of so much application.

'Once this is over and we've got our results, we'll go out and celebrate,' Octavia promised. 'I'll get Papa to look and see if there's anything nice on at the theatre or the music hall.'

But in the event it wasn't a theatre they went to visit. It was a hall in Central London.

On the morning after their mock results had been handed out — and most of them as good as they'd hoped — Betty came running into the form room waving a printed handbill. She was flushed with excitement. 'Look at this, Tavy!' she said, holding out the little paper. 'I've found our cause.'

Octavia caught her excitement. 'What is it?'

'Votes for Women,' Betty told her. 'It's what Mrs Bryant was telling us about at prayers last week. You remember. Women's suffrage. She called it the greatest cause of our time and I think it is. You just read it. Gwen got it last night when she was coming out of the telephone exchange. There was a lady there with a pile of them.' She spread the leaflet out on Octavia's desk. 'Read it. It's all about a meeting they're going to have right here in London and how they're going to make the government change the law so that women can vote the same as men and what a scandal it is that women are ignored. All sorts of things. Gwen says she's a good mind to go and I've a good mind too. What d'you think? Shall we?'

Octavia was reading the leaflet, scanning the close-printed lines, her heart throbbing with excitement. 'Yes,' she said, looking up. 'Let's. It sounds wonderful. We can't miss it.' Then a thought struck her. 'I'll have to ask Papa of course.'

'Ask him tonight,' Betty urged. 'He'll let you, won't he? He's into all sorts of things like that, isn't he? I mean, the Fabians and everything.'

So Octavia asked him.

'Well, well, well,' he said, beaming at her, 'so my little bird is going to stretch her political wings.'

'Yes, Papa. If that's all right.'

'It will be an education,' he said and beamed at her. 'Wear warm clothes and try not to get arrested, that's all.'

Mama was looking worried, biting her lower lip, her forehead wrinkled. 'Don't say such things, JJ,' she reproved him. 'Even in jest. There's many a true word spoken in jest.'

Why is she scolding him? Octavia wondered. Meetings aren't dangerous, are they? It was only a joke. He's always making jokes. They don't arrest you for going to meetings.

'You've worried her, my love,' JJ said, patting his wife's hand. 'No, no. You go, Tavy. Go, look, mark, learn and inwardly digest. And then come home and tell us all about it. I think you will enjoy it.'

'We're barely into March,' Mama objected. 'Wouldn't it be better to wait for warmer weather? March and April can be such difficult months. Think how they were last year. I wouldn't want you taking cold.'

'I'll wrap up really warm,' Octavia promised. 'Muff and everything.'

Her father spoke up for her in the same breath, 'She'll be fine, my love.'

'It's all very worrying,' Mama said, biting her lip again. 'She's too young for this sort of thing.'

'I shall be with Gwendoline, Mama,' Octavia pointed out. 'She's nineteen. She's been out at work for nearly three years.'

'That's as may be,' her mother said. 'But you are only sixteen.'

Octavia bristled. 'I shall be seventeen in August.'

'That is still too young,' Amy said, firmly, and she turned to scold her husband again. 'It's all very well for you to be light-hearted, JJ, but there are women in this movement who go out on the streets to demonstrate. I was reading about it only the other day. Do we really want her mixing with that sort?'

'From what I've read of the Pankhurst ladies,' JJ said, 'they are altogether reasonable and proper. Bernard Shaw speaks highly of them. However, since you are concerned, — and yes, yes I can see how concerned you are, my love — I will don my chaperone's hat for the evening and pack my duelling pistols or wear my broadsword, whichever you wish, and we will wrap our young firebrand in cotton wool and I will accompany all three of them to and from their appointment. Would that reassure you?'

'It would,' Amy said, smiling at the thought of her gentle JJ carrying any sort of weapon, let alone a broadsword, and thinking what a dear, sensitive, ridiculous man he was. 'If you are with them, my love, I shan't worry at all.'

So that Saturday, the three girls put on their best hats and their buttoned boots, hung their muffs about their necks, and with Professor Smith to squire them, took a tram to Westminster to attend their first political meeting.

CHAPTER 5

The hall was full of flamboyant hats, bold, curvaceous, positive hats, nodding in the gallery, busy above the wooden seats in the body of the hall, embellished by swoops and swirls of extravagant trimming. There were sunflower hats, tilting their petalled faces to the light from the high windows, birds' nest hats, shimmering with feathers, fur hats, crouched over their owners' foreheads as though they were about to spring upon the nearest prey. Whatever else the politicians and leader writers might say about them, and they usually had plenty to say and most of it detrimental, the ladies of the Women's Social and Political Union dressed in formidable style.

There were very few men in the audience but that didn't worry Professor Smith, for this was just the sort of revolutionary assembly in which he felt most at home. He tucked Octavia's gloved hand into the crook of his left elbow and escorted his three charges to the nearest row of empty seats, smiling to right and left as he progressed.

Octavia was too overawed to smile. She settled beside him quietly, looking at the grand clothes of the platform party and the huge banner that hung above their heads declaring 'DEEDS

NOT WORDS' in bold green letters. It made her remember how she'd felt years and years ago, when she was six, half-hidden in the shadows of her father's study, watching the great and the good as they arrived for dinner, knowing how small and young she was and yet feeling hopeful and uplifted and breathlessly excited to be so near to the people who were going to change the world. And now, here she was, half-hidden among all these strong, determined women, in this grand high-ceilinged hall, feeling almost exactly the same — only not quite so small. And as she looked around her, she suddenly remembered what hard work it had been to clean the tea stains from the carpet and recalled, in sharp still-shaming detail, the little pale brown splashes on Mr Morris' famous wallpaper. How odd, she thought. Memory is very peculiar.

The platform party were discussing something, looking round the half-empty hall and conversing urgently, their fine hats dipping towards one another, like great birds in flight.

'Time to start, I think,' Professor Smith observed.

'There aren't many people here,' Betty whispered.

'It's not the quantity that counts on occasions like this,' he told her, 'it's the quality.'

Which was more or less what the Chairman said when she made her opening remarks, thanking her audience for attending and expressing the hope that the speech they were about to hear would make them feel that their journeys had been worthwhile. 'We have a great task in hand,' she said, 'and every person who supports our noble cause is valued and valuable. I welcome you most warmly, one and all.' Then she introduced the speaker, 'somebody who is so well known to us that she hardly needs any introduction at all. Mrs Christabel Pankhurst.'

The applause and the expectation were intense, for this was the lady who had founded the WSPU and was the driving force behind all its activities. She stood, elegant in her grey suit with the thick white frill of her blouse framing her chin, smiled, waited until her audience had settled and began, speaking in a voice so soft and gentle that they had to strain forward to hear her.

Octavia listened with all her attention, determined not to miss a word, for what was being said was right and true and needed saying. The world was neither just nor fair — she had always known that — and something had to be done about it — she knew that too — and now here was a lady who knew exactly what it had to be. Before long she was nodding in agreement as each new point was made. If a woman does the same work as a man she should receive the same rate of pay. Of course. If she has studied law at University and earned a degree she should be allowed to practice alongside her gentlemen colleagues. Quite right. If her husband deserts her she should be allowed to petition for divorce, in exactly the same way as he could were the position reversed, despite the recent ruling in the High Court. Of course, of course. It was all so reasonable, so correct, so utterly sensible. She felt as if she was flying, up and up, lifted on stronger and stronger wings with every stated truth. Yes, yes, of course.

'However,' Mrs Pankhurst went on seriously, 'it must be said, here and now, and over and over again, that legal, economic and educational inequalities will not be redressed until women have the right to make their will known through the ballot box. Without the vote women will continue to be second-class citizens, without the vote we are without a voice, without the vote we have no rights and no power. It must also be said that, in this country, the right to vote has never been given willingly and never without a struggle. During the last century, men were gradually granted the suffrage for which they fought but only by grudging degrees. The Chartists began their campaign in the 1830s, as you will remember, but it wasn't until the third Reform Act in 1884 that they were finally taken seriously and even now, although five million men are enfranchised, this is by no means the universal suffrage the original Chartists sought. All these new voters together only make up two thirds of the adult male population. We have a long and difficult struggle ahead of us, but it is a noble struggle. Our cause is just, ladies and gentlemen and in the end we will prevail.'

The applause was immediate and prolonged although a little muffled because so many hands were politely gloved. Octavia took her gloves off for better effect and clapped until her palms were sore and by then the audience was on its feet and cheering and Mrs Pankhurst was acknowledging a standing ovation. 'Hurray!' Octavia called. 'Hurray! Hurray!' Dust motes swirled in the air before her, like specks of gold in the gaslight, the applause rose and fell in reverberating waves of sound, the banner throbbed in the current of their approbation as if it covered a beating heart. 'Oh hurray!'

'I must join,' she said to her father, as the cheering subsided.

He was putting on his own gloves. 'I thought you might.'

'Now,' she said passionately. 'This minute. I want to shake her hand and tell how wonderful she is.'

'So do I,' Betty and Gwen said together and amended it, half-laughing, to, 'So do we.'

'Then you will all need a shilling,' he said, smiling at them.

'Shall we?' Octavia said.

'Indeed yes,' her father said, as he took the coins from his pocket. 'That is the price of commitment.'

Oh what bliss it was to stand in such a splendid line with so many strong-minded determined women and to know that she and her friends would soon be part of this extraordinary Union. What a thrill to touch the gloved fingers of her new heroine and to hear herself welcomed — by name what's more. 'You have joined a great crusade, Miss Smith.'

She was still glowing with the wonder of it all as she climbed aboard the tram for her journey home. 'Didn't I always say I'd find a cause?' she asked her friends, rhetorically. 'And now I have, we all have, and it couldn't be a better one. We shall make history. Think of that. Once we've got the vote, the world will never be the same again.' It was a perfect, blissful moment, the cause so right and just, her friends thrilled and happy, beaming at her, her father so obviously proud of her. 'Oh I can't wait to tell Mama.' She was taut with excitement, twisting in her seat to talk to her friends behind her, turning back to look at her father, her hair tousled and her cheeks flushed.

'Perhaps you had better leave me to break this to your mama,' JJ said as he eased into the slatted seat beside her. 'We don't want to make her anxious.'

'Why should she be anxious?' Octavia said, amazed that he would even entertain such an idea. 'She'll be proud. As I am. How could she be anything else? Oh Pa, my dear, dear Pa, this is the most wonderful moment of my life.'

Her father gazed at her rapturous face with affection and concern. 'You must be prepared for heavy opposition, my dear,' he said. 'It is not an easy road you have chosen.'

But Octavia was beyond warning. The future was full of hope; difficulties would be faced and overcome no matter how hard they might be; this great change was possible, necessary, inevitable. She was still talking as they delivered Betty and Gwen to their gate and still tremulous with excitement when they reached South Park Hill. It was a dark evening and the gaslights were globes of such very bright yellow that the windows below them gleamed with their reflected gold. To her dazzled eyes it all seemed just as it should be, richly coloured, bright and welcoming. How could it be anything else on such an evening? Then she reached the front path to her own house and saw that there were people in the parlour. She could see some-one's silhouette against the blinds.

'We've got company,' she said to her father. 'I wonder who it is.' And she led the way into the house, ready for warmth and welcome, eager to tell Mamma her good news and to share it with their visitors.

The parlour was hot after the chill of the night air outside and prickling with excitement, as if they knew her news already. Mrs Wilkins who was bending over the hearth to feed fresh coals to the fire, had cheeks as red as the coals, and their visitors were so excited she could hardly recognise them. Aunt Maud was sitting beside Mama, with her hair tumbling out of her bun like straw from a stack and giggling like a schoolgirl, and Emmeline was sitting in Pa's armchair, which was unusual to say the least. There was something different about her, an air that Octavia couldn't quite place, as though she were a queen receiving company — no that wasn't it — or the Cheshire cat in Alice in Wonderland — no that wasn't it either. You couldn't compare Em to a cat. Never mind, she thought, pushing the puzzle aside. Wait till she hears what I've done. She'll be just thrilled.

'Mama,' she said, striding into the room. 'It was the most amazing...'

But she didn't get any further for Aunt Maud was interrupting her. Actually interrupting her. Whatever next? You *never* interrupted people. It was one of the ground rules of politeness. Pa said so. But it was being done, ground rules or no.

'My dears,' Aunt Maud said, beaming at them all. 'Such wonderful news. Emmeline is engaged to be married.'

'And I've just...' Octavia struggled on. 'We've just...' But she was wasting her breath for Emmeline was on her feet and tripping towards her. Her news would have to be deferred. 'How lovely,' she said to her cousin. 'When did this happen?'

'This afternoon,' Emmeline said happily. 'He asked Papa before dinner. I wanted you to be the first to know. We're going up to the West End on Saturday to choose the ring. He says it's to be a ruby and diamond and I'm to choose the one I want. Oh

I'm so happy, Tavy, you wouldn't believe.' And she flung her arms round Octavia's neck and hugged her tight.

'Oh I would,' Octavia said, kissing her cousin's hot cheek. 'Dear Em, it's what you've always wanted. I'm so glad.' For a second it was on the tip of her tongue to ask which of Em's many suitors she'd chosen, but she checked herself in time. Just as long as it wasn't the bank manager one, Ernest Whoever-he-was. She stood back to look at her cousin's rapturous face. 'And guess what,' she said. 'You'll never believe this. I've got what I wanted tonight too.'

Emmeline blinked with surprise. 'Have you?'

Now her news could be told. 'I've joined the WSPU,' she said proudly. 'I'm going to be a suffragette.' And she smiled into her cousin's face, expecting pleasure and approval. But Emmeline was pulling away, her expression changing. 'Oh Tavy!' she said. 'You can't have.'

'I have though,' Octavia said, misunderstanding the changed expression and still beaming. 'Isn't it wonderful? You and me both. On the same day.'

'But you can't have,' Emmeline insisted. 'I mean, they're dreadful people. They're leading the country to rack and ruin.'

Her disapproval was like a slap in the face and so unexpected it stopped Octavia's breath. 'Oh Em!' she said. 'How can you say such a silly thing? They're not dreadful, they're wonderful. I've just spent the evening with them, and I've never heard such sensible women in my life. You should have been there.'

Emmeline's face was beginning to flush with distress but she stood her ground. 'They're dreadful,' she said, doggedly. 'Ernest says so. They're telling people to break the law.'

It would be Ernest, Octavia thought. I knew he was a fool. 'If a law's wrong it deserves to be broken,' she said. 'Everyone knows that. And this law's as wrong as it can be. Why should a man have the vote and a woman be denied it, just because she's a woman? You tell me that.'

'I don't know anything about that,' Emmeline told her. 'But the law's the law and if it's the law you have to keep it.'

'No you don't,' Octavia said, passionately. 'That's the whole point. If it's a bad law, you have to change it.'

Aunt Maud was on her feet, smoothing her hair, hanging her handbag over her arm. 'Time we were off, Emmeline,' she said, too brightly, and looked at her sister, her expression part appeal, part annoyance. 'We only came over for a minute just to tell you.'

'Of course,' Amy soothed, touching her arm in a placatory way. 'You can tell us everything else on Sunday when you come to tea. There's so much I want to hear, Emmeline my dear. And by then you will have your ring, won't you.'

Emmeline agreed that she would and tried to smile although her face was crinkling towards tears and she couldn't look at Octavia. It was horrid of her to quarrel, she thought, and especially tonight. She took her mother's proffered arm and made as good an exit as she could, her head held high and her spine stiff with distress and anger. Amy escorted them to the front door, gentling all the way, and JJ followed tugging at his beard with embarrassment. It was a very difficult departure and left on her own in the overheated room Octavia felt guilty for it, as though she were an infant caught out in some childish transgression. But really she could hardly have stood silent and allowed her foolish cousin to say such abominable things. Not that it *was* Emmeline of course. It was that pompous fiancé of hers. But whoever it was she had to speak up. She couldn't allow such prejudice to go uncorrected. That would have been cowardice and this wasn't a time for cowardice. It was a time for women to speak up. She could hear the voice of her heroine, '*You have joined a great crusade, Miss Smith.*' What would she have thought if I'd stayed silent at my very first test? No, she thought. I did the right thing. The only thing. It might have upset Emmeline for the moment but she'll thank me for it when she understands.

There was a cross swish of skirts and her mother was back in the room. 'That was no way to treat your cousin, Octavia,' she said. 'She was most upset.' She spoke gently but her annoyance was plain from the set of her mouth.

'Then she shouldn't have said such stupid things,' Octavia said, fighting back. 'I couldn't believe my ears. *"Leading the country to rack and ruin."* The very idea. That was just prejudice, and if there's one thing this campaign *must* do it's to speak out against prejudice.'

'At a political meeting maybe,' her mother told her, taking her seat by the fire, 'but not in your own home and not to one of your guests. That is discourteous and unkind and I cannot allow it. You will write to Emmeline and your aunt this evening before you go to bed and apologise.'

'No, Mama,' Octavia said, flushing at the distress of disobeying her mother but determined to follow this through. 'I know this will grieve you but I cannot possibly do such a thing. It would be tantamount to admitting I was in the wrong.'

'You *are* in the wrong,' her mother told her implacably. 'You were discourteous to your guests and now you must apologise.'

JJ was standing beside the dresser pouring himself a whisky, trying to look unconcerned and failing. 'Pa,' Octavia said, turning to him for support, 'you know what this means to me. Tell Mama it isn't possible.'

His answer was a profound disappointment. 'Your mother is the arbiter of proper behaviour in this house, my dear,' he said, 'and, as such, I stand by her decision. My advice to you would be to apologise with a good grace and put this whole rather silly business to rest. Any other course of behaviour would prolong the unpleasantness.'

'Any other course of behaviour would be preferable to cowardice,' Octavia said hotly. 'Can't you see what you are asking me to do?' The longer they talked about it the more deeply entrenched in her opinion she was becoming. 'It isn't possible. It would be treachery.' And then tears began to swell in her throat and she had to leave the room, before she lost control of her feelings. She managed to pause at the door to wish them goodnight but then she had to move away as quickly as she could. Oh how can they be so unkind? she thought, as she ran up the stairs to her bedroom. I'm not a child. Why can't they trust me to do the right thing? And she flung herself face down on her counterpane and wept with abandon.

It was a long sleepless night. She relived the quarrel, endlessly and word for word, sure she'd been entirely in the right, but getting more and more upset to have quarrelled with her dear Em and wondering how on earth it could have happened. Her thoughts rolled over and over, as the hall clock turned the hours like pages and the darkness pressed in upon her like guilt, and when morning finally lightened the sky, she was no further to knowing what she ought to do. I'll talk to Betty Transom, she thought, and see what she has to say.

BETTY TRANSOM WAS INDIGNANT. 'For your own cousin to say such things!' she said. 'How could she be so insensitive? It beggars belief. Well don't take any notice of her, that's my advice. She's just being silly. Apologise if you must. You don't have to mean it. I've apologised hundreds of times in my life, over and over for all sorts of silly things and I've rarely meant it.'

'That wouldn't work for me,' Octavia told her, sadly. 'If I say a thing, I have to mean it. It wouldn't be honest otherwise.'

The bell was sounding for the end of break. 'Well,' Betty said, 'it's too great a cause for any of us to go back on it now. My lot weren't happy about it either. My Ma thinks I shall be sent to prison. But I'm not going to take any notice of any of them. Cheer up. I'm with you. And so is Mrs Pankhurst. It'll all come out in the wash.'

Unfortunately it was a tea party that Octavia had to face, not a washday, and the tea party was even worse than she feared.

FOR A START her mother was distinctly chilly with her, which was more upsetting than she cared to admit, and to make matters worse, she was uncomfortably aware that her father was ill at ease. He was frowning and stroking his beard and watching the conversation as if he was guarding it. Emmeline wouldn't so much as look in her direction, but that was understandable because she'd been placed at the end of the lengthened table, well out of the way, wedged between Podge, who was a big boy for a twelve-year-old and took up an inordinate amount of room, and Cyril, who talked about Oxford pretty well non-stop and stole the marzipan from her plate when she wasn't looking. Emmeline and her fiancé were in the seats of honour at the centre of the table, she quietly contented, displaying her new ring, eating very little and gazing at her lover with admiration, he holding forth — about the dependability of modern banking and what a first rate career it was 'for the up and coming young man', about stocks and shares and how happy he would be to advise his host on such matters, even about education, which he claimed provided the backbone of the nation, 'always provided it was administered with sufficient rigour and discipline'. The longer he talked, the more Octavia disliked him. She'd come to the table prepared to give him the benefit of the doubt because, to be fair to the man, she'd only met him on two or three occasions, and then only briefly, when he was arriving to take Emmeline out for the evening, and she really didn't know very much about him except that she didn't like him. But one meal was more than enough to give her his measure.

.   .   .

'HE'S pompous and boring and self-opinionated,' she told Betty Transom the next morning. 'I can't think what she sees in him. He isn't the least bit handsome. His face is too fat and he's got tiny little eyes and messy looking teeth and he oils his hair so much it sticks to his skull like a nasty bit of black leather and he talks about money all the time.'

'Ugh!' Betty grimaced. 'If that's what husbands are like it's just as well we're not going to get married.'

'Amen to that,' Octavia said. And that made them both laugh and cheered her a little.

BUT THE REAL cheer came the following morning when she brisked in to breakfast to find a letter waiting for her beside her plate. It was from the WSPU, signed by somebody called Dorothea Worth, welcoming her to the Union and asking if she would care to assist them in their shop on Hampstead High Street.

There is always work to be done, she said. *We meet on Tuesdays and Thursday and you would be most welcome, should these days be agreeable to you.*

They were more than agreeable. They were essential. She and Betty, having decided that they would start work at once, walked to the shop as soon as they'd had their tea that very afternoon.

It was an interesting place and not a bit like a shop, although there were the usual plate glass windows outside and the usual bottle green paint everywhere and pamphlets for sale on a counter just inside the door. But the real work was being done in the room behind the shop, where three young women were hard at it typing letters and addressing envelopes.

Dorothea turned out to be a plump middle-aged woman

with hair almost as untidy as Aunt Maud's and the same preoccupied habit of patting it and tucking at it while she was speaking. 'We're sending out information about the Manchester demonstration,' she told her new recruits. 'We want it to be the biggest and best there's ever been, so we can use all the help we can get. You'll be joining us of course.'

Oh of course. It almost went without saying. Although as they walked rather wearily home after an evening of letter folding and stamp licking, they both confessed they were none too sure about what their parents would have to say about it.

'Your Pa won't mind,' Betty said cheerfully, but added with a little more doubt. 'Will he?'

Octavia had to admit that she really didn't know. It would depend what her mother had to say, and with that horrible apology still not given and Emmeline unapproachable and the deplorable Ernest everlastingly around to prejudice her, it was hard to predict what anyone would say. Luckily it was only her father who was at home to greet her that evening. Amy was still at her sister's 'discussing menus or some such'. And her father approved.

'Capital,' he said. 'I can just see you carrying the banner, you and young Betty. Will Gwen be going too?'

'I don't know yet,' Octavia had to admit. 'She's on late shift this week so she wasn't there and we've only just sent out the letters. I expect so, though.'

'Well you're sensible girls,' JJ said. 'You won't do anything foolish.'

And that, rather surprisingly, was her mother's opinion too, although she added a proviso. 'If anything untoward were to happen you must promise me you would get out of the way of it at once.'

It was a promise easily given. For after all what could possibly go wrong when there were going to be so many of them and they would all be together to support one another?

. . .

THE MORNING of the demonstration was cold and overcast, threatening rain, and as she dressed for this first public test of her affiliation, Octavia was tremulous with nerves. Ever since she'd joined the WSPU and had that silly quarrel with Em — oh how she regretted that quarrel! — she'd made a point of reading every newspaper article about the suffragettes that she could find and she'd been appalled at the level of prejudice she'd discovered, especially in the cartoons that all depicted campaigning women as ugly and deformed. So she'd given a lot of thought to what she would wear, knowing how important appearances could be.

She'd chosen her dove grey costume and the prettiest blouse she possessed and had topped them off with a brand new, far too expensive hat, dove grey to match the costume and loaded with artificial fruit and flowers. Even though it was probably immodest to say so, she was pleased with the image she presented, and glad that Betty and Gwen were equally prettily dressed. The three of them strolled into Euston like visiting royalty, using their umbrellas as walking sticks and gathering admiring glances.

But the journey increased her nervousness with every mile. Her two friends gossiped and giggled and didn't seem at all perturbed by what was ahead of them, but Octavia rehearsed every possibility in her mind and the possibilities grew more alarming the nearer they got to their destination. What if they were arrested? Would she know how to behave if they were? What if there were fisticuffs? Or if she were hit by a truncheon? How would she cope with that? And the wheels sang a mocking accompaniment as they rattled along the rails. '*What if you were? What if you were?*' It was quite a relief to hear the brakes take hold and to know that they'd arrived.

CHAPTER 6

Manchester was an extremely dirty place and a very noisy one. Octavia was horrified by how black and tall the buildings were, and how roughly people were pushing past each other on the pavements. She felt she was walking in a chasm in a foreign land. After a while she noticed that she and her friends were not the only well-dressed women in the street and realised that all of them were all walking in the same direction and then she knew that this was going to be a very big demonstration and began to feel glad that she was part of it. Then they turned a corner and there were the placards saying, 'Votes for Women' in large bold letters and the familiar banner with its familiar legend 'Deeds not Words' swelling in the breeze and making a noise like the crack of a whip and she felt she was in familiar territory. Standing directly and loudly in front of the banner, there was a brass band tuning up and behind it there were rows and rows of women waiting in line, filling the square, turning their heads to smile at them as they approached.

They joined the tail of the procession and introduced themselves to the women on either side of them and then they waited, while the column got longer and longer. Police constables walked up and down beside it, looking important, and consulted with their sergeants, looking solemn, and patrolled again. And eventually the brass band gave a sort of garrumph and began to play a rousing march — something by Souza wasn't it? — and they were off.

It felt most peculiar to be marching down the middle if the road instead of walking on the pavement. And alarmingly exposed. But after a hundred yards Octavia got used to it and began to swing along as though she'd been marching all her life. Until she noticed the crowds.

At first they all looked the same, staring and blank and oddly unreal, standing in little groups at the edge of the pavement, the men grimy in their working clothes, their faces shadowed by cloth caps, or superior in dark suits and white wing collars and bowler hats, the women clogged and shawled and carrying heavy baskets, or wearing smart coats and gloves and grand hats. But then she realised that, despite their class differences, they were all disapproving and many were shouting insults. 'Go hoame to tha maister!' 'Shame on you!' 'Hussies!' 'You're a disgrace to womanhood!' Her spine stiffened with such anger at their stupidity that for a few seconds she couldn't walk normally and that annoyed her too.

'How can they be such fools?' she said to Betty. 'I can understand men shouting at us. They won't have the upper hand once we get the vote and they won't like that a bit. You can tell that already from this lot. "*Go hoame to tha maister*" indeed! Why should men be our masters? It's downright archaic. But the women are another matter. I don't understand them at all. When we get the vote, they'll get it too.'

'They're just showing their ignorance,' one of her new friends said. 'Don't take any notice of them. They're not worth it.'

But Octavia couldn't ignore them. They were too loud and too full of stabbing hatred. She was hot with annoyance all the way to St Peter's Field. But once there her mood changed, for there was Mrs Pankhurst standing on the hustings waiting to speak and the sight of her heroine lifted her spirits at once and made her feel proud of what she was doing. Let them shout, she thought. We have right on our side.

The speeches, when they began were a terrible disappointment. After the clear cool voices she'd heard and admired in Caxton Hall, these women sounded muffled and indistinct, their words blurred by the megaphones they were using and blown away by the wind. She struggled to disentangle what they were saying for several frustrating minutes and in the end she gave up the effort and decided that if she were to hear anything at all she would have to get nearer to the platform.

'Come on,' she said to Gwen and Betty. 'I'm going to the front.' And she began to ease and squeeze her way through the crowd, with her two friends following behind. Several other women had the same idea so it wasn't easy but Octavia was even more determined than they were and after ten striving minutes she arrived at the foot of the platform. The speaker was a young woman in rather a plain coat but her face was fiery and so was her message.

'The time is approaching,' she was saying, 'when we must decide upon militant action. We have tried marching and writing letters and petitioning the government and all the politicians do is to make soothing noises. They will never take us seriously from our strength of numbers alone, no matter how many of us there might be. They will never take us seriously while we write them polite letters. They will throw them in the bin. No, I tell you, they will only take us seriously when we disrupt their lives, when we make life uncomfortable for them. If it means breaking the law to draw attention to our cause, we must break the law. The longer we go on being quiet and respectable, the longer we shall wait for justice. This is a fight and we must fight with every means at our disposal.'

At that, the women who were near enough to hear her broke into a cheer. Yes, Octavia thought, cheering with the rest, she is absolutely right. We must take action. Even if it means being arrested and going to prison. At that moment, embedded among all those cheering women there was no doubt in her mind at all.

SHE WAS STILL BURNING with enthusiasm for her cause when she finally got back to Hampstead late that night.

Her parents had sat up for her and were eager to hear how she'd got on. Her father pressed her for every detail, beaming his pleasure at her boldness but her mother grew steadily more and more alarmed. Wasn't this just precisely what she'd feared? These campaigns were all the same. They began with marching and ended up breaking the law.

'I hope you won't do anything foolish,' she warned. 'I wouldn't want you getting hurt.'

'You mustn't worry so, Mama,' Octavia said. 'I shall be perfectly sensible whatever I do.' And she patted her mother's lace edged hand to comfort her.

Amy wasn't comforted. 'It will come to grief,' she predicted as she and her husband were preparing for bed. 'She's too head-strong, JJ. She'll go her own way no matter what we say. She won't listen.'

'She's a sensible young woman,' her father said, brushing his hair thoughtfully before the mirror. 'Let's trust her, shall we?'

'We can't even trust her to apologise for bad behaviour,' Amy pointed out. 'This silly quarrel's been dragging on for weeks and weeks and she won't write — I've asked and asked — and how it will all end I dread to think.'

But on this score at least she needn't have worried. Two evenings later Maud came to pay her a visit and Maud had arrived to be a peacemaker. She was even more dishevelled than usual, with her hair tumbled out of its pins and her cheeks flushed with apprehension, but she plunged into her mission as soon as she'd stepped foot inside the hall.

'Amy my dear,' she said. 'It's about the bridesmaids. My Em is worrying herself silly. She thinks Tavy won't want to do it. She's been in tears over it and that won't do. We can't have her making herself sick. So in the end I said to her, I'm sure she will, but there's no point sitting around worrying and crying. I'll go and find out for you. So here I am.'

'We'll ask her,' Amy said. 'She's in her bedroom writing an essay. Go through and I'll get her.' And she went off upstairs at once.

Octavia came down with her mother feeling rather apprehensive because the quarrel had been going on for such a long time and it really ought to have been settled ages ago and she still didn't know how to do it without losing face, but when she heard that her cousin was worrying and weeping, all her old affection reasserted itself and the whole thing was simple.

'Oh, Aunt Maud,' she said. 'Of course I'll do it. I always said I would now, didn't I? We promised one another. I wouldn't miss Em's wedding for the world.' She was warm with relief. Em might have said silly things about the suffragettes but that was only because Ernest had talked her into it. She wasn't like those poor silly women lining the pavement, shouting their stupid insults. There was no malice in her. Dear Em. Memories came cramming into her mind, disparate and jumbled, nudging and shifting, and all of them loving — the games they'd played in the house in Clerkenwell when they were little, the secrets they'd shared at school and on holiday in Eastbourne, the childish dreams they'd 'interpreted', the adolescent confidences they'd dared to reveal, she and this dear girl who'd so nearly been her sister.

Maud was smiling so much it looked as though her face was splitting in two. 'Can you come round tomorrow?' she asked.

'And I'll show the patterns. Some of them are *so* pretty. Oh my dear, she'll be so pleased.'

'AND AFTER ALL THAT NONSENSE, she said *"yes"* as meek as a lamb,' Amy reported to JJ later that evening. 'There are times when I just don't understand her.'

'She is a loving girl,' her father said. 'Love was sure to triumph in the end, even over a cause.'

Which in the following weeks, it most certainly did. To everybody's relief.

EMMELINE'S WEDDING day opened like a rose, luscious with sunshine and summer foliage under a dappled sky. 'Happy the bride the sun shines on,' her guests approved, smiling as she gleamed past them up the aisle, dreaming and beautiful in her white wedding gown. When they emerged into daylight again after the service, their mood changed, for a sudden breeze had sprung up and was soon scattering mischief and confusion in every direction, ruffling the lilac ostrich plumes in Aunt Maud's hat, flinging Emmeline's veil into the air, rippling the obedient silk of her wedding dress, tumbling the petals from the red roses in her bouquet. Within seconds her guests were laughing and holding on to their hats as the photographer fussed to arrange the family portraits to his satisfaction. 'In a little more on the left-hand side, *if* you please. Yes, yes, *my* left. That's the ticket. Now if you can just settle a little.'

Octavia stood beside the bride, feeling proud of her. Dear Emmeline, she thought, I *do* love you and I do so hope you'll be happy. You deserve to be happy — whatever you might think of the suffragettes. The breeze flapped the skirt of her blue gown like a flag and she turned to smile at her cousin, although turning made her aware of how cruelly her new corset was pinching. She knew she looked very grand in her long gown, with its delicate underskirt and all that expensive braid edging her bodice and cinching her waist like an embroidered belt, but being held in so tightly was a nipping price to pay for it. Still, she consoled herself, you have to look your best at a wedding. It's expected. All the other guests had put on the style quite splendidly, the ladies in fashionable dresses, lilac and rose pink, soft yellow, powder blue and wearing absolutely wonderful hats trimmed with ostrich feathers dyed to match, the gentlemen very fine in their morning suits with their lovely dove-grey toppers and their cream kid gloves and spats. There was one in particular who was especially handsome, tall and straight with thick fair hair and dark eyes and a lovely easy way of walking and standing, like a leading man at the theatre. She'd noticed him as soon as they walked out of the church. In fact, now she came to think about it, being at a wedding was very much like being at the theatre, all dressed up and being looked at. From the corner of her eye, she sensed that someone was trying to catch her attention, and turned her head to see who it was — and caught sight of the handsome young man again. He was standing on the edge of the group. I wonder who he is, she thought, and turned her head again in case someone noticed that she was staring.

'Nice smile!' the photographer called from beneath his black hood. The flashlight exploded with a flump of white light and when her eyes had adjusted to the sunlight again, the handsome young man had disappeared.

Then it was time for the bride and groom to climb into the two-horse carriage that was waiting for them and be driven away to their reception under a shower of rose petals and good wishes. Octavia went to look for her mother and father so that they could walk downhill to the hotel together with all the other guests. Everybody was talking at once as they progressed, laughing and chattering and saying what a pretty wedding it was and how well it had all gone. But there was no sign of the handsome young man, which was rather a disappointment.

At the hotel foyer, the guests had to wait because the groom's formidable mother was arranging the line, although strictly speaking it was nothing to do with her and should have been done by Aunt Maud.

'Come along, gels,' she said to the four bridesmaids. 'You are to stand behind the bride. Mr and Mrs Withington here, beside your daughter. That's right.'

It was a very long line, what with bride and groom and both sets of parents to be greeted, and the guests took a very long time to file past. Octavia was soon tired of hearing the same endless good wishes — 'Many congratulations, Ernest.' 'Such a delightful service.' 'We do wish you joy, Emmeline, my dear.' — and was beginning to feel cross at the way the bridegroom was smugly accepting everything that was being said as if it was his personal homage. He might be a distant relation of the great Coutts family, she thought, but there's really no need for him to lord it quite so much. I wish they'd hurry up and have done with all this. But the line stretched on and on beyond the hall.

'I don't know about you,' a voice said beside her, 'but I think they should speed things up a bit. I'm absolutely ravenous.' It was the handsome young man.

'I'm afraid we're in for a long wait,' she told him.

'So I see,' he grimaced. 'It's a jolly poor show! I'm so hungry I could eat a horse.'

'I don't think they're serving horse today,' she said. 'It's potted shrimps and ham on the bone and cold roast turkey.'

'How do you know?'

'I've seen the menu.'

'Well at least it won't go cold,' he said, sighing. 'My name's Thomas, by the way.'

She held out a gloved hand for him to shake. 'I'm Emmeline's cousin, Octavia.'

He took the hand, raised it to his lips and kissed it. Good heavens! 'Pleased to make your acquaintance,' he said.

He was standing so close to her and looked so very handsome she was suddenly breathless. He's like a Greek god, she thought, as if he's risen from the sea all dewy-fresh and sweet-smelling, and she looked at his soft skin and the golden hair falling over his forehead and those dark grey eyes and that wonderful straight nose and was weak with admiration. And what eyelashes he had! Thick and tender like a girl's. She was so overwhelmed by him she couldn't think what to say.

But he didn't seem to notice. 'They're calling me,' he said, gave her a graceful bow and went gliding off into the dining room.

The line seemed longer and the guests more ridiculously gushing than ever. If they don't hurry up, she thought, it won't be a wedding breakfast at all, it'll be a wedding supper.

But they didn't hurry up and it was more than an hour before the last of them had smiled past and the wedding party were free to make their ceremonial entry into the dining room and take their places at the high table. The bridesmaids were placed two by two at each end with the four parents sitting bulkily between them and the bride, which didn't please Octavia, because she couldn't even see her cousin, let alone smile at her. But then just as they were all settling into their seats, the handsome young man bounded up to the end of the table, pulled up a chair and sat down beside her, smiling broadly. 'Tucker,' he said. 'At last!' And turning to a hovering waiter. 'Set a place for me, there's a good chap. I've given up my seat to a lady.'

To Octavia's surprise a place was set, so whoever he was he obviously had the right to a seat at the high table, and he was the jolliest company, so easy to talk to that the meal suddenly took on quite a different aspect. Soon they were gossiping like old friends. He told her he was going up to Oxford in the autumn and, not to be outdone, she told him she was off to University College in Bloomsbury 'if my Higher Schools results are good enough.'

'Well bully for you,' he said. 'I never knew girls went to university.'

'They do now,' she told him, proudly. 'We're not in the nineteenth century any more, I'm glad to say.'

'Well bully for you,' he said again. 'What will you be reading?'

'English Honours. And you?'

'Oh Classics,' he said, as though the subject bored him. 'Like the Pater. I say this ham's not half bad. I hope they're going to give us more than one measly glass of wine.' He flashed a questioning eye-signal to his now attendant waiter and when the man paused for instructions, said, 'Fill this up for me, there's a good chap. Must have enough for the toasts.' And was instantly given a full glass. 'More for the lady too,' he said. 'You'd like another wouldn't you, Octavia.'

Octavia had never been given more than one glass of wine in her life but he was so confidently pressing and she was so thirsty, she agreed at once. So the meal and the conversation continued very pleasantly and she grew steadily warmer and more relaxed. They discussed the theatre and agreed that Bernard Shaw was a great playwright and that 'The Doctor's Dilemma' was a splendid drama. He told her she must see Pinero's latest. 'It's top hole. It'll make you laugh like billy-oh.' They shared opinions of the works of art they'd seen and the books they'd been reading. She admitted to a passion for Jane Austen and he confided that he'd always found that lady rather dull and much preferred Sir Walter Scott. By the time the master of ceremonies stood up to announce the first of the speeches, she felt as if she'd known him all her life.

Speeches — however many more are there going to be? — toasts — which required even more wine — the cutting of the cake, and finally bride and groom moved off to the ballroom and the master of ceremonies announced that the dancing would begin in twenty minutes. And just as Octavia was thinking what fun it would be to dance with this attentive young man, Squirrel appeared beside them and thumped her new friend between the shoulders.

'There you are, Tommy!' he said. 'I've been looking for you all over. Trust you to worm your way onto the top table. I see you've met our Tavy.'

She was puzzled and looked it. 'I thought you were part of the groom's family,' she said.

'Good heavens no!' Cyril said. 'You are a goose, Tavy. Whatever made you think that? This is my best friend. My very best friend. We're going up to Oxford together. This is Meriton Major.'

It was so exquisitely funny she was convulsed in giggles. 'Oh!' she laughed. 'Oh dear! Oh dear!' Meriton Major of all people! The dreadful Meriton Major. The one they'd suffered from all these years. The one she and Emmeline simply couldn't stand. 'Oh dear, oh dear!'

'It's the wine,' the dreadful Meriton Major said. 'You'll have to take a turn round the floor and dance it off. Bags I the first waltz.'

'Watch out for your feet then, Tavy,' Cyril warned, grinning at his friend. 'He dances like an elephant.' And got a table napkin flicked at his head for his impertinence.

The warning was unnecessary. The dreadful Meriton Major was as light-footed as a dream and the first waltz spun them both away into a wine-dizzied delight. 'Top hole!' he said when it was over, and he was escorting her back to her parents. 'Bags I the next one.'

But then Cyril came rollicking up to them with a face full of mischief to spoil the moment with one of his silly remarks. 'Has she signed you up yet, Tommy old thing?' he asked. His pale eyes were decidedly swimmy and his expression looked lopsided, as if it was slipping off his face. What's the matter with him? Octavia thought, peering at him. Is he drunk?

'She can sign me up any time she likes,' Tommy said bowing to her gallantly, but then he spoilt the impression he was making by adding, 'What to?'

'The Suffragettes,' Cyril said, grinning at his cousin. 'If you don't watch out, she'll have you carrying the banner.'

Tommy turned a quizzical expression in Octavia's direction. 'Is that true?' he asked. 'Or is it just Squirrel being squiffy?'

She admitted the truth of it at once, partly because she was proud of what she was doing and partly because she was curious to see what his reaction would be.

It was admirable. 'Well bully for you,' he said. 'I like a girl with spirit don'tcher know. Joan of Arc sort of thing. Capital.'

'All very well for you,' Cyril complained. 'You're not related to her. You wouldn't say she was Joan of Arc if you were, I can tell you. It can be dashed awkward for a chap.'

'Take no notice of him,' Tommy advised, turning to Octavia. 'He's squiffy. *I* think it's capital. I bet you look a corker in purple and green. I can just see you leading the drum band, waving your banner and everything. Top hole!'

Cyril was beginning to understand that his attempt to put his cousin down was failing and the knowledge made him truculent. 'You never take anything seriously,' he complained.

'I am maligned,' Tommy said cheerfully. 'I take my food most seriously. I defy you to prove otherwise. I follow the horses assiduously. I treat all trivial matters with the utmost gravity. What more can you want? And,' turning to Octavia again, 'I bags the next waltz. What could be more serious than that?'

From that moment, the wedding became a party. Octavia danced and giggled, drank more champagne and giggled even more, and by the end of the evening, when the guests were gathered outside the hall to wave goodbye to the newly married pair, confessed to her new friend Tommy that she'd never enjoyed herself so much in all her life.

'Tell you what,' he said. 'What say you and me and Cyril go up West and take in a show? Fitting end to the day, what? There are some corkers on at the moment.'

She was dizzied by the way he jumped from one pleasure to the next. 'Do you mean now?' she asked. 'Tonight?'

'Why not?' he said. 'You can't say you're not suitably dressed. You look a treat. Take the flowers out of your hair, find a coat or a wrap or something and Bob's your uncle.'

So she went to the theatre and sat between her cousin and his amazing friend and laughed until her ribs ached. And when the show was over, they all went on to supper at the Café de Paris — at Tommy's insistence of course — where they ate an enormous meal and drank an inordinate amount of champagne. By the time her two gallant escorts delivered her giggling to her door, it was past two in the morning and Octavia was light-headed. She had never been so carelessly happy.

'What say we have a picnic on the river?' Tommy said, as she put her key in the lock. 'Our cook does a capital hamper. We could take a punt. How about tomorrow?'

How could she resist? 'You mean today,' she giggled. 'It's tomorrow already. Or do you mean tomorrow, tomorrow?'

'Never mind all that,' he laughed back, daring her with those dark eyes. 'Shall you come?'

'Yes,' she said. 'I would love to.'

So they went punting on the Thames and Cyril dropped his boater into the river and was helpless with giggles when Tommy put the pole right through it as he was trying to fish it out. And they had a sumptuous picnic on the bank, cucumber sandwiches, pork pies, ginger beer and everything, even an iced cake that was melting in the heat and had to be eaten with a spoon. The next day they went to the races and Tommy lost rather a lot of money and didn't seem worried in the least, which Octavia thought was admirable. And that evening they went to another play that made them all laugh until Octavia had the hiccups. By the end of the week, they were inseparable friends.

From then on, the summer was bewitched, the long days soft and insubstantial as gossamer, the warm nights hazy with pleasure. It never seemed to rain, the skies were always cloudless and blue, the birds always singing, the gardens scented with flowers. Each new day brought a new delight, cycle rides out into the country, trips along the river to Hampton Court, or Greenwich, or the Tower of London, countless visits to the theatre and the music hall, frequent and delectable suppers. Now and then, when Betty nudged her memory, Octavia spent a virtuous evening at the shop in the High Street addressing envelopes for the cause, or running off pamphlets or copies of the newsletter, listening to the ardent talk around her — and agreeing with it — but for most of the time she simply forgot about it. For as Tommy said, 'We've finished at school and we don't go up until October so there's nothing else to do except have fun, and when you come to think about it, three months is no time at all for having fun. You can carry the banner and all that sort of thing when October comes, now it's *"Gather ye rosebuds"*. What say we go down to Kew for the day?'

Before Emmeline's wedding day Octavia would have argued with him, and in the more reasonable part of her mind she knew it. She would have pointed out how important the cause was, bombarded him with facts and figures and tried to show him the error of his opinion. Now she simply agreed with him and although she was faintly ashamed to be so easily diverted, she couldn't help herself. It was as if she'd become a different person.

And of course the time *was* short. October arrived much too quickly and soon — oh much much too soon — it was their last weekend, their last visit to the theatre, their last supper.

'I'll send you a postcard, old thing,' Tommy promised as he walked her to her door.

'So will I,' Cyril said. And when Octavia looked surprised. 'Honest!'

'No you won't,' Tommy said, joshing him. 'When have you ever sent a postcard? But I will. Never fear, Miss Smith! My word is my bond. Honour of a gentleman and all that.'

'I shall miss you,' she said.

'No you won't,' he told her. 'You'll be too busy at that college of yours. And anyway we shall be back at Christmas.'

But Christmas was ages away and she missed him more than she cared to admit, even though her new life at University College was absorbing, just as he'd predicted, and he *did* send her postcards — at disappointingly irregular intervals. She knew perfectly well that thinking about him so much was foolish. After all, she hadn't really seen him very often — perhaps three or four dozen times since they first met and always in company — so she ought to have forgotten him, more or less. But she hadn't. She couldn't. She knew him by heart as if his face was imprinted in her brain. Oh dear, she thought, what a way to go on. He'd never given her the slightest reason to feel anything about him. He'd been kind to her, but as her cousin's friend, no more, an entertaining young man who liked her but treated her as a brother. While she... Since that first extraordinary visit to the theatre she'd dreamt of him every night no matter how hard she tried not to. And she did try not to. Oh very very hard. By day she was happily involved in her college life, in lectures and tutorials, reading in the college library, out in the air with her new friends on the Surrey playing fields, attending rehearsals of the Dramatic Society for an ambitious play, which was fun but more difficult than she'd imagined it would be, but at night she fell into another world. Then his handsome face looked at her oh so lovingly, that full mouth kissed her, his arms held her oh so tenderly, and she woke trembling and confused, wondering if she was falling in love with him. No, she thought, lying in her quiet bed in the early morning light, trying to be sensible. I can't be. Not really. It isn't possible. But what a torture it would be to fall in love and be forced to stay silent. Why do women have to stay silent? That's unfair. If the position were reversed and he were falling in love with me... What an amazing thing that would be! Not possible, of course, but how wonderful it would be! And if he were, he could tell me and test my reaction and no one would think it wrong or improper. Oh, there is so much to be changed in this world.

CHAPTER 7

The Christmas holiday brought a terrible disappointment to Octavia Smith although it began well and in its usual loving way. Christmas Day was exactly what she expected. There was the usual luxurious dinner, with port wine and chestnuts by the fire afterwards, the usual dangling abundance of paper chains and lanterns to please her mother, one of the tallest Christmas trees her father had ever bought — 'to celebrate your success, Tavy my dear' — and so many presents she would have been unnatural not to be pleased and grateful. But there was no Christmas card from Tommy, which disappointed her, because she'd been hoping and hoping for one, and dreaming about what he would say, but she tried to be sensible about it. He'd probably thought it would compromise her or provoke awkward questions. It wouldn't have of course. She could have explained it to her parents easily but he wasn't to know that. Anyway, there would be a postcard in a day or two. She was sure of it. She only had to wait a little longer. Meantime there was another Christmas party to enjoy.

On Boxing Day they put on their Christmas finery and walked across the Heath to take high tea with Aunt Maud and

Uncle Ralph. There was no sign of Cyril but Emmeline was there, looking extremely pregnant and obviously happy about it. The only trouble was that now they had to endure Ernest's company too and he was pompous in the extreme, talking about his investments and the modern nursery he was planning for the baby and how he intended it to be brought up.

'I'm a firm believer in discipline and unvarying routine,' he said. 'That's the secret if you wish to produce a good child. Discipline and unvarying routine.'

It sounded rather oppressive to Octavia, but she couldn't say so being a guest, so she tried to change the subject. 'Where's Cyril?' she asked her cousin. 'Is he joining us later?'

'He's off with the dreadful Meriton Major,' Em said and laughed. 'He might be up at Oxford but nothing's changed. It's still Meriton Major this and Meriton Major that, except that he calls him Tommy now they're at Oxford.'

'We met young Meriton at your wedding,' JJ told her. 'We thought he was a charming young man, didn't we, Amy? He was keeping everyone entertained.'

'Oh he's charming enough,' Emmeline agreed. 'It's just that when he's around, we never see our Squirrel.'

'Which is rather a shame,' Amy said. 'I must agree with you there. I would have liked to have seen him.' But then sensing that she might have said something a little too critical, she turned to her sister to make amends. 'How is he getting on at Oxford?' she asked. And was told how wonderfully well he was doing, by both his proud parents, while his sister made faces at Octavia and fingered the salt cellar, to show that it should all be taken with a very large pinch.

Octavia grinned at her cousin but said little. She was thinking of Tommy and wondering when she would see him again. Sooner or later she would have to tell Emmeline what had happened over the summer and probably confess how much she liked him, which would surprise her after all the things they'd said about him, but that could wait until the post-card had arrived and they'd picked up where they left off. Oh what a lot there would be to tell her then!

But Tommy Meriton didn't send her a postcard, which was a daily disappointment, and he and Cyril didn't visit her either until three days before the start of term, when she'd almost given up hope of seeing them at all. Then they suddenly arrived in a great rush to tell her they'd got tickets for a capital show.

'Look sharp,' Cyril said. 'Put your coat on. Curtain up's in three quarters of an hour. We'll bring her back after supper, Uncle J.'

He talked all the way to the theatre and hardly let her say a word to Tommy, who sat behind them on the tram and smiled and said little. But she didn't mind. Soon she would be in the stalls, sitting beside him, and they could talk and laugh all they liked. But she was wrong. When they arrived at the theatre, she found she was one of a very large and noisy crowd, most of whom she didn't know and many of whom seemed rather the worse for drink. She had to sit between a stranger with a straggly moustache, who breathed cigar smoke all over her, and Meriton Minor, who was sixteen and spotty and extremely tire-some. She didn't get to exchange more than a sentence with Tommy during the entire evening and for most of the time he was so busy talking and laughing with his new friends he didn't even look at her. And then, when they'd all rushed off to a noisy supper and talked about Oxford in a new slang she didn't understand, he left Cyril to escort her home and said goodnight to her as she left as if they were mere acquaintances. She was crushed to be treated in such a casual hurtful way. It was too unkind to be borne.

That night she cried herself to sleep and slept badly. She woke at two o'clock and wept all over again, feeling angry that Tommy had treated her so cruelly and furious with herself for allowing him to get away with it. What was the matter with him? she thought. Did he mean to be cruel? Was it deliberate? Or was he drunk? He sounded drunk, now I come to think about it. He was talking very loudly. I should have taken him to task and asked him why he was being so horrid. That was the least I could have done. It was cowardly not to. Well all right then, I'll go to his house tomorrow morning, first thing, and have it out with him. He owes me an apology. But then she realised that she didn't know where he lived and she could hardly ask Cyril for his address. That would look awful. She'd have to find some other way. But what? Her mind spun round and round — a postcard? a letter? — but she couldn't think of anything that didn't involve asking Cyril and finally she fell asleep and dreamt that she was all on her own in a theatre and that everybody in the audience was laughing at her and she was struggling to get out of the place or to wake up.

When she did wake, it was three o'clock and she was utterly miserable, feeling cast down because she'd been rejected and inadequate because she was no beauty and couldn't — shouldn't — expect to be treated as though she were. Oh how could he be so cruel? she grieved. He must have known it would hurt me, ignoring me like that. And what am I supposed to do now? I've been publicly humiliated. He ignored me in a public place in full view of his friends. Not that they knew what he was doing. She had to admit that. They didn't know me from Adam, she thought. I was introduced as Cyril's cousin. But even if they didn't know, I do, and I can't just go on as if nothing's happened. Does he realise what he's done to me? Does he care? I thought he liked me. We had such fun in the summer. And the thought of all the fun they'd had made her weep all over again. It was all absolutely horrible. By half past four she gave up trying to sleep and got up and bathed her eyes. It was dark and cold but there was no point in grieving forever. She would have to take herself in hand. That was all there was for it. I shall think about it as if I'm someone else, she decided, and give myself a good talking-to.

Once she'd decided to play devil's advocate for her own case, several things became focused. It was galling to admit it but the first thing she had to do was to face the fact that she'd brought this whole miserable situation on herself. She'd read more into their friendship than he'd ever intended. That was obvious now. It had all been a daydream, a fantasy without any foundation, and now she was paying the price for being so silly. Well, she thought, I'm not one of those girls who only want to get married and have babies. There's a lot more in *my* life, college and a career — even if I haven't planned it yet — and the cause, of course. I must just stop being a fool and get on with the important things. But oh it did hurt to be rejected and he should have been kinder, he really should. He could at least have talked to her. The next time we meet I shall be cool to him, she decided. I shan't cut him because that would be impolite, but I shall be cool. See how he likes that. In the meantime there were things to be done and the sooner she got on with them the better.

She put her plan into operation on her first day back at college, seeking Betty Transom out at lunchtime and steering the conversation away from their Christmas holidays by talking about the cause.

'I'm beginning to feel rather ashamed of myself,' she confessed. 'I've given them so little time since I started here and there's so much work to be done.' And then she really *did* feel ashamed of herself because she wasn't telling her friend the exact truth and it was against her nature to be devious.

Fortunately, Betty Transom took her seriously. 'It's been worrying me a bit too,' she said. 'I know we've been busy with lectures and tutorials and the play and everything but even so... Maybe we should call in at the shop sometime.'

They went that very week before they could get overloaded

with essays. And were delighted to find that their fellow campaigners were really pleased to see them.

'You've come in the nick of time,' Mrs Emsworth said, trying to push the pins back into the tangle of her hair. 'There's so much work to do you wouldn't believe it. What with this meeting coming and the newspaper to get out and everything, it's all hands on deck.'

Betty and Octavia exchanged glances but they didn't ask questions. Whatever the meeting was they would find out soon enough. It would look bad to reveal that they didn't know.

It was to be held at Caxton Hall on the evening of February 13th, so as to coincide with the reopening of Parliament. Members of the WSPU were asked to attend in force as this was to be 'a meeting of the women's parliament' and they intended to make history. Christabel Pankhurst would be putting a resolution before them, to ask that the franchise be extended to include women, and when it was passed — as she was quite sure it would be — it would be escorted in procession to Parliament Square and taken into the House of Commons for their notice and approval. As Dorothea Emsworth had said, Betty and Octavia had rejoined the movement in the nick of time.

'You will come with us, won't you?' she asked them as they addressed envelopes and licked stamps. 'We need the biggest audience we can muster.'

They answered her with one voice. 'Of course.'

THE EVENING of February 13th was dank and cold but Caxton Hall was packed to the walls and warm with enthusiasm and the crush of a great crowd.

'We've come a long way since that first meeting,' Octavia said, looking round her at all the eager faces turned expectantly towards the well-known women on the platform and that bold familiar banner behind them. 'There were only a few of us then but look how many we are now. Oh Betty, this could be the turning point. They can't ignore us when we're here in such numbers. Surely to goodness.'

The excitement in the hall grew more and more palpable as the speeches were made, every hat a-tremble with the passion of it all, and when the resolution had been proposed and passed to unanimous acclaim, the cheers were so loud that they made Octavia's ears ring. 'And now we march,' she said to Betty.

'Yes,' Betty said cheerfully. 'Now we march. And let's see how easy we are to ignore tonight.'

It was chill out in the street and the air was congealing into a smoky darkness. There was much settling of hats and rearranging of fur stoles to keep out the cold. Woollen scarves were wound more tightly around their owners' necks, gloves and coats more firmly buttoned. Then the great banner was lifted aloft to lead the way and off they marched. This is better, Octavia thought, linking arms with Betty Transom. Not moping about after some stupid young man feeling sorry for myself, but taking action, doing something important.

She was so happily immersed in her thoughts that she didn't notice the horses until she heard cries coming from somewhere near the head of the column. Women to right and left of her stopped what they were saying and tried to peer over the heads of the procession, saying 'What is it? Is someone hurt?' and Betty and Octavia strode out into the middle the road where they would have a clearer view.

There was a troop of mounted police, galloping towards them. As they got nearer, Octavia could see that the horses were steaming with the effort they were making, and behind them she caught a glimpse of other horses being urged into the column, women scattering before them, screaming as they ran, women staggering as though they'd been hurt or wounded, and dark shapes lying on the ground. It was like a battlefield.

'They're attacking us,' she called to the others. 'With horses.

Look out!' And at that other voices took up the warning, yelling, 'Run!' and 'Get out of the way!' But the troop was upon them before she could move more than a yard and, in a confusion of arms and hooves and booted legs, she was pushed aside by the rump of a huge black stallion and the pressure of it was more than she could withstand and she felt herself falling forward, arms outstretched to break her fall.

For a few stunned seconds she lay where she'd landed, panting with the shock of the attack, and oddly unable to move. Then someone lifted her to her feet and a voice asked if she was all right and she took a deep breath and tried to get her bearings. There were people running all around her and from the corner of her eye she saw that the horses were regrouping, snorting and stamping and being hauled into line by their riders. Oh God, she thought, surely they're not going to charge us again. There was a strong smell of horseflesh and human sweat. And her gloves were streaked with blood. I've grazed my hands, she thought, watching the red stains as they seeped into the white kidskin and she tried to pull off the left glove to see what damage had been done and found she couldn't focus her eyes. But in the mist beyond her inadequate focus, she sensed that there were people who were hurt and in trouble and she knew she had to do something about them and stopped looking at her palms, took a deep breath and started to walk towards them.

Movement restored her balance. Now she could see that Betty Transom was staggering to her feet a few yards away from her, white faced and wild eyed and with no hat on her head and she quickened her pace so that she could offer her an arm to lean on. 'Are you all right?'

'Just stunned I think,' Betty said. 'They knocked me off my feet. Can you see my hat?'

It was yards away and trodden flat, lying on the pavement next to a woman who was sitting propped up against the railings holding a bloodstained handkerchief to her temples. 'I've got a bit of a cut,' she said, when Octavia asked her how she was and lifted the handkerchief to reveal it.

It was a deep cut and would obviously need stitches. 'Is there anyone with you?' Octavia asked. 'You ought to get home and call the doctor.'

'I came with Clara,' the woman said, 'but I don't know where she is.' And she began to cry.

'Don't worry,' Octavia said. 'We'll find her for you, won't we, Betty.'

Which rather amazingly, they did, by dint of calling her name extremely loudly and over and over again until she appeared. She was profoundly shocked to see the state her friend was in and kept saying she didn't know what the world was coming to and what were they to do but by this time Octavia had already decided what they were to do and was calling for a cab. She found one standing by the kerb a few yards back along the road. The driver was surly and said he didn't want 'no bleedin' women' in his nice clean vehicle, but he relented when Octavia told him she would pay him double, and Clara and her injured friend climbed unsteadily aboard.

By that time the horses had gone clopping off towards Parliament Square and Octavia had gathered a group of women around her and taken command. 'None of us are hurt,' she said, 'or not hurt much and the horses have gone, which is a blessing. I think we ought to go on with the march and try and get into the House, the way we planned.'

Some were unsure of the wisdom of such a plan — 'What if they charge at us again?' — but most agreed with her. So they set off for the second time that evening, without their banner and their leaders and walking on the pavement this time because they thought the road was too dangerous. At least the gas lamps had been lit and there was no sign of the police.

But in Parliament Square their way was barred by a line of

horses and there was no way they could push past such a determined barrier. 'We'll wait until we hear some news,' Octavia said. 'There's no sign of Christabel or any of the others, so they've either got in or been arrested. Someone will come out again sooner or later and we'll ask them.'

The person who came out nearly an hour later was a reporter with a notebook in his hand. He'd got his story and didn't mind telling them what he knew, even though the nearest policeman was glowering at him. 'Yes,' he said, 'they got to the Strangers' Gallery.'

'How many?'

'About fifteen as far as I could see. Anyway they were all arrested. Appearing at Bow Street tomorrow morning.'

The thought of being arrested made several women shiver.

'What shall we do now?'

'We will go home,' Octavia said, 'and patch ourselves up and be at Bow Street in the morning.' She was putting on a brave face but she suddenly felt cold and tired. It had been a dreadful evening. 'I'll see you to your door,' she said to Betty, 'because your house is nearest.'

'Will you be all right going back on your own,' Betty worried.

'I shall be fine,' Octavia said. But it was a lie.

By the time she reached her doorstep she was shaking with fatigue and delayed shock. It was all she could do to put her key in the lock and when she'd staggered into the sitting room she simply sank into the nearest chair and covered her face with her hands.

Amy was aghast. 'My dear child!' she said, rushing to her daughter's side. 'What have they done to you? Ring for Mrs Wilkins, JJ. She's been hurt.'

Octavia wanted to reassure her but for the moment she was too exhausted to speak and simply sat where she was while her mother swept into action, dispatching Mrs Wilkins to the kitchen for hot water, cotton wool and lint and Mr Wilkins to the chemist for witch hazel. She held out her hands and lifted her arms obediently so that her mother could ease her out of her gloves and remove her muddy coat and skirt, she allowed herself to be wrapped in a blanket and sat by the fire, she watched as her grazes were bathed and bandaged but for the moment conversation was impossible.

After the cold and terror of Victoria Street, the sitting room was as warm as a womb, enclosed, containing and protective, the red velvet curtains drawn against the night, their three easy chairs set around the hearth in a semi-circle, dappled by fire-light. Shadows flickered across Mr Morris's elaborate wallpaper, the gaslights popped and fluttered, and everything in the room was gilded by firelight. The brass fire irons gleamed as the flames leapt in the grate and above them on the mantelpiece the looking glass reflected light like water, the clock face was a golden disc, the lustres flashed blue and green fire like elongated diamonds. Octavia relaxed into the familiar ease of it. She was here in this still, peaceful room, being loved and cared for and that was enough. She would tell them what had happened in the morning.

'IT BEGGARS BELIEF,' Amy said, when she'd heard the story. 'Whatever were they thinking of to treat you so?'

'We were the enemy,' Octavia told her sadly, 'and they were the cavalry. They were attacking us. Obeying orders. It's a war, Mama.'

'It's monstrous,' her mother said, pouring the tea. 'Grown men on horseback riding into defenceless women. I don't know what the world's coming to, I really don't. Now then, my dear, eat up your breakfast while it's hot and then you must get back to bed. You're in no condition to go to college.'

'I'm sorry, Mama,' Octavia said. 'I can't do that. I've got to go to court. I want to be there at the trial.'

Amy turned to her husband for support. 'JJ,' she said, 'you must speak to her. She's in no fit state to go out.'

JJ had been stroking his beard for comfort while he listened to his daughter's story. Now he gave it one last tug and smiled at them both, looking from one to the other, at Tavy, pale and determined, with her mouth set and her face bruised and that frizz of pale ginger hair spreading like a halo, and at Amy who looked even more determined and was sending him eye messages begging his support. She looks so frail, he thought. Her hands were too thin and her hair too pale, with that odd salt and pepper greyness that redheads so often produce as they age. And she was ageing. He had to admit it. At fifty-two she was no longer the elegant woman he'd loved for so long. Since that last bout of bronchitis last spring, she'd taken to wearing a shawl round her shoulders and seemed to stoop even when she was sitting down. It made him love her more protectively than ever. But he couldn't take her part, even so.

'I think, my dear,' he said, 'we must allow our Tavy to make her own decisions.'

'And what if she gets hurt?'

'She has been hurt already, my love,' he said mildly, 'and acquitted herself quite splendidly in very difficult circumstances. I do not think we need to worry on her account this morning. There is unlikely to be a cavalry charge in a court of law. The judge would forbid it.'

'Yes, but what if she were?' Amy insisted. 'How would we know? We could be sitting here worrying for hours, not knowing. Oh if only we had a telephone, JJ. Then she could phone us and let us know.' She'd been hinting that they needed a telephone for weeks and weeks, ever since Maud and Ralph had had one installed.

JJ recognised that she was offering him a bargain. 'Very well,' he said. 'If we agree that it is right and proper that Tavy should go to Bow Street, as I truly believe it is, then I will buy a telephone.'

So Octavia dressed in a quiet costume, chose a sober hat and went to support her heroines.

THE COURTROOM WAS full by the time she and Betty Transom arrived so they had to wait outside on the pavement. But the police were no trouble that morning. They merely stood and watched, occasionally walking up and down like guardsmen, occasionally making a pretence of keeping the pavement cleared for passers-by, and after a long chilly wait the court began to empty and a crowd of women emerged, among them Mrs Emsworth who walked across to tell them that all the defendants had been sent to prison 'mostly six weeks but Christabel got three months' and that the Black Marias would be coming through at any minute. There was nothing more to be done except cheer the vans as they passed and hope that their imprisoned passengers could hear what was being shouted. 'God bless you!' they called. 'Votes for women!' 'The fight goes on!'

'They needn't think being sent to prison will stop us,' Mrs Emsworth said trenchantly as the vans were driven away. 'It will only make us more determined.'

Betty and Octavia agreed with her wholeheartedly. Oh it was a joy to be among such passion and purpose.

THE TELEPHONE WAS INSTALLED two weeks later and one of the first things JJ did was to use it to arrange a dinner party for his Fabian friends.

'And this time you must join us, my dear,' he said to Octavia. 'Edith Nesbit will be here and she particularly asked how you were.'

'Covered in bruises,' Octavia said, grimacing, 'that's how I am. Not a pretty sight for anyone to see.'

'But an honourable one,' her father told her. 'Wounded for the Cause.'

So she wore her bruises with pride and joined the party. And was praised for her courage by everyone around the table, and commended for her cool headedness, which her father had described to them in restrained and admiring detail.

'Mrs Pankhurst has written to us from prison,' Edith Nesbit told them. 'We shall be printing the letter in full in our next issue. Although I should warn you, it makes grim reading. Conditions there are truly dreadful.'

OCTAVIA READ the letter with mixed feelings, enormous pride that her heroines were willingly suffering such hardships, and admiration for their endurance and courage. But sneaking in among these noble feelings, there was a shrinking sense that sooner or later she too would have to break the law. Her conscience was too finely tuned to allow her to stand by and do nothing forever. And when she did, she too would be sent to prison, she too would have to face all the things Mrs Pankhurst had described, the inedible food and rough uniform, the all-pervasive smell, the lack of fresh air.

Her mother read the letter too and was appalled by it for she had no doubt that Tavy would break the law. It was in her nature to take the lead and sooner or later she would do it. In fact, there *were* days when she was beginning to wish she raised a daughter who simply wanted to marry and settle down and raise a family, like Emmeline.

CHAPTER 8

Emmeline's first baby was born in March, exactly nine months after her wedding. The news was relayed to Amy and JJ within an hour by means of their new magical telephone, to Amy's delight.

'You see what a blessing it is, JJ,' she said as she put the receiver back onto its hook. 'To know so soon. Don't you think that's wonderful? Maud says we can go and see her this afternoon. I wonder what she's like.'

She was a plump little thing, weighing nearly nine pounds, and really quite pretty, with fat cheeks, a fuzz of fair hair and big dark eyes. Emmeline was entranced by her.

'She's lovely,' Octavia agreed when she paid her own first visit on her way home from college later in the day. 'What are you going to call her?'

'Dora,' Emmeline said, firmly. She'd just finished feeding her infant and now she was sitting up in bed, relaxing against her mound of pillows with the child lying contentedly across her knees. 'Ernest wanted her to be Agnes, after his sister, but I couldn't have that. I mean to say, have you *seen* her?' She turned her head to talk to the baby, smiling and nodding. 'You don't look at bit like an Agnes, do you my precious?' she said. 'No, you don't. Anyway we settled for his second choice, so she's Dora. That's what you are, aren't you my duck, you're my dear little Dora.'

So she stands up to him, Octavia thought, and was glad of it. It wasn't good for a man like Ernest to have his own way all the time. 'I'm so happy for you, Em,' she said. 'You've got what you always wanted.'

'Yes,' Emmeline agreed, stroking the baby's cheek. 'I have — but so have you, haven't you, off to college and with the Cause and everything.' She gave her cousin a shy smile to show that there was peace between them, even over the Suffragettes.

'Yes,' Octavia said. 'I suppose I have.' Once she would have agreed wholeheartedly, and it *was* true, she *had* found her cause, and she *was* at university. The trouble was she knew the difference between dreams and reality now. And the cost of commitment. But there was some good news.

'Have you heard about the general election in Finland?' she asked. 'They've actually elected seven women as MPs. It was in the paper yesterday.'

Emmeline wasn't interested. Politics was boring. 'Um,' she said, gazing at her baby.

Octavia tried another tack. 'How do Podge and Cyril like being uncles?' she asked.

'Podge came over with Ma yesterday,' Emmeline said. 'He thought she was lovely. And so you are, aren't you, my duck. But it's no good talking to me about Cyril. We never see him these days. Ma phoned him. She told me. But I don't suppose he said much. There's no knowing what he thinks.'

'Oh!' Octavia said, rather surprised that he'd taken so little interest. 'He'll visit you at Easter though, won't he?'

'I doubt it. He's off to Paris at Easter.'

'With Meriton Major?' Octavia said. It was hardly a question she was so sure of the answer.

'Who else would it be? Paris at Easter and a summer touring Europe. They never do anything but gad about.'

Octavia had a sudden sharp-edged memory of Tommy Meriton, all long legs and thick fair hair and dark eyes. Oh how horrid he was. And what a good job she'd got over him. Let him gad about wherever he likes, she thought. I'm well rid of him.

Emmeline was looking at her again, wondering why she didn't speak. Probably because they'd been talking about Squirrel, she thought. He's such a bore. 'And how is this college of yours?' she asked, smiling encouragement. 'You must tell me all about it.'

'Well...' Octavia said and cast about in her mind for things that would be interesting. The play had been a great success, she said, and she and Betty and their new friends were all going to see 'Arms and the Man' on Saturday. 'Although whether I shall be able to see much of it from the gods, I can't say,' she confessed. Sitting in the front stalls with Tommy and Squirrel in that long ago summer — oh what a long time ago that summer was — she'd seen everything clearly, except the true nature of Tommy Meriton, of course, but now that she was demoted to the top of the theatre all the little distant faces had furry edges. 'I'm beginning to wonder whether I need spectacles.'

'It's all that reading you have to do,' Emmeline said sagely. 'Reading weakens the eyes. Does it give you headaches? Ernest has terrible headaches sometimes. He says he can't see the figures properly.'

Octavia could sympathise. She rarely studied figures these days but print had developed a worrying tendency to blur. Sometimes she had to blink until it returned to normal.

The baby gave a little burp and began to suck her fist. 'Oh what tales you tell!' her mother said, beaming at her. 'You couldn't possibly be hungry again. I don't believe a word of it. Not after all you've just eaten.' And she turned to beam at Octavia too. 'You never saw such an appetite. She'd suck all day if I'd let her. Tell you what, Tavy. When I've finished my lying-in, we'll go down to the opticians together and get your eyes tested. And afterwards we can have tea and cake at Fullers. How would that be?'

It was a happy outing, with the baby in her new pram, with a nursemaid to look after her, and Emmeline in her new clothes and the sun shining on them all. And the spectacles were really quite grand, steel-rimmed and as round as an owl's eyes. Her father said they made her look quite the scholar but she was more impressed by how much more easily they enabled her to see. 'I hadn't realised how poor my eyesight was,' she said to him. 'It's lovely to have everything in focus. I can see every word on the blackboard.'

'Then we shall expect even higher grades,' he said, teasing her.

'I will do my best,' she promised.

The good grades followed to nobody's surprise, for she was working easily now that she could see clearly again. What was a surprise — but only to Octavia herself and certainly not to be revealed to anyone else — was that being suddenly sharp-sighted taught her a new and extremely useful trick. She discovered that if she watched people's faces as they were speaking and was quick enough to catch the expressions that shadowed across them, she could tell what they were thinking. Even better, she was intrigued to notice that sometimes what they were thinking was at variance with what they were saying. It was like opening a window into their minds and made conversations extremely interesting. As the months passed she used her new skill more and more often, endlessly fascinated by the insights it revealed. It was like a private party trick. But it wasn't until the end of her second year at college, when Emmeline was expected her second baby, that she realised how useful it could be.

The year examinations were completed, term was over, she'd

just phoned Emmeline to see how she was and been told she was 'getting a bit weary', and at that moment, she was sitting in the garden in the sunshine in one of her mother's new cane chairs composing a letter. Earlier in the term and urged on by Betty Transom and Dorothea Emsworth, she'd stood for election to the local committee of the WSPU and now she was the branch secretary and responsible for all the official business of the group. The letter she was drafting was about the summer demonstration the movement were planning. It was to be in Hyde Park on June 21st which was just ten days before Em's baby was due, and the organisers intended it to be the biggest yet. Women were coming from all over England, there were going to be at least a dozen platforms for the speakers, and provision had already been made for a crowd of over a hundred and fifty thousand. 'Your support,' she was writing, 'will make...'

But at that moment, Minnie the parlour maid appeared in the garden to announce that Mr Cyril had arrived to see her, 'with his friend, Miss' and where should she show them.

'Tell them to come through into the garden,' Tavy said and prepared herself to do battle. Whatever happened next, it would be interesting.

They breezed out of the back door as though they'd been visiting her regularly for months. Cyril pulled up a chair and sat opposite her on the other side of the cane table. 'Grab a pew, old thing,' he said to Tommy.

Tavy watched them through her spectacles and was annoyed to see that Tommy was as sure of himself as ever, sprawling in the remaining chair with his long legs stretched before him and smiling at her as if they were old friends. Which they most certainly were not.

'We're off to have tea at the Ritz,' Cyril said, looking pleased with himself. 'Like to come? We've got seats for an absolute corker of a show. We thought tea first and then the show, didn't we, Tommy? We shall probably go on for supper somewhere afterwards. Make a night of it. Get your skates on.'

You really are insufferable, Octavia thought. You roll in here as if there's nothing the matter and expect me to drop everything and go rushing off with you, just because you've asked me. 'It might have escaped your notice, Cyril,' she said, coldly, 'but some of us have work to do.'

Cyril wasn't as abashed as she'd hoped he would be. In fact he wasn't abashed at all. 'You can work some other time,' he said. 'It's a ripping show. Absolutely top hole.'

'Yes,' Tommy said, smiling at her. 'Do come. You'll love it.'

And you're insufferable too, Octavia thought. She picked up her notebook so that he couldn't help noticing it. 'Since I last saw you, I've been elected to the committee of the Hampstead WSPU,' she said. 'In fact, I'm the secretary of the committee. The work I'm doing is for them and the Cause and just a trifle more important than a show — however ripping. Wouldn't you say so?' And she looked at him through her spectacles, observing.

He was put out although he hid it quickly, rearranging his expression and smiling again. 'Oh well,' he said, lightly, 'we mustn't get in the way of the Cause, must we, Squirrel. Another time maybe.'

'Maybe,' she said, still observing him, and even to her ears the word sounded cold. 'I hope you're going to visit your sister,' she said to Cyril. 'She's only got a few more weeks before this baby is born and she'd like to see you.'

'I might later,' Cyril said. 'I mean there's no rush is there.'

You won't go at all, Octavia thought, glaring at him. You're too busy gadding about and it's jolly selfish of you. It wouldn't hurt you to put yourself out a bit. It's no joke being pregnant especially when it's hot.

Her scrutiny was making her cousin uncomfortable. 'Better be off I suppose,' he said. 'Things to do don't you know.' And he got up and straightened his jacket ready to leave. 'Time for tea and all that. Come on, Tommy.'

Octavia watched as they disappeared into the house, Cyril waving and Tommy giving her a little bow, in that old-fashioned courteous way he'd done at the wedding when he'd kissed her hand. Was he upset? she wondered. It was hard to judge, his expression was so careful. But whether he was or not, she felt pleased with herself. I did that well, she thought. I was cold and I kept him at a distance. I'll bet no one's done that to him before. It'll do him good.

But as she picked up her pencil and returned to her notebook, she suddenly felt bleak. It would have been nice to have gone to the theatre with them, to sit in the stalls and laugh and joke, the way they'd done that summer. Oh if only he hadn't been so horrid!

CYRIL AND TOMMY went straight to the Ritz, where they made a very good tea. It wasn't until they were on their third plate of fancy cakes that they said anything about Octavia's refusal.

'Was she cross about something?' Tommy wondered, pondering the cakes.

'I shouldn't think so,' Cyril said, biting into a meringue. 'After all, I mean to say, what's she got to be cross about? Best seat in the house. Tea at the Ritz.'

'I got the feeling she was cross,' Tommy said, choosing an éclair. 'That's all. I mean she's never turned us down before.'

'Always a first,' Cyril said easily. 'No, no, she wasn't cross. She was just being Tavy. She can be dashed odd sometimes. You should have seen her when we were little. She was putting me down because I wouldn't go and visit Em the minute she told me to. Hey look who's coming in. It's old Tubby Ponsonby. There's a bit of luck. Come and sit here, Tubby, old thing. We're going on to a show. You wouldn't care to join us, would you?'

. . .

PREPARATIONS for the demonstration in Hyde Park took up all Octavia's attention for the best part of the next four weeks and by the time the Hampstead party were climbing aboard their chartered charabanc for the journey into the city she was feeling decidedly jaded. It was going to be a very big demonstration, they were all sure of that, but somehow she couldn't be hopeful of a happy outcome.

'We shall pass our resolution,' she said to Betty as the charabanc trundled through the Sunday streets, 'and everybody will say how wonderful it is, and of course it will be wonderful, we all know that, but the politicians will ignore us.'

Betty feared she was right. 'But what else can we do?' she asked. 'We've just got to keep on and on, haven't we?'

'Or break the law,' Octavia said.

'I'm not sure I could do that, 'Betty admitted. 'I don't think I could stand being sent to prison. I mean, not knowing what we know about it.' Mrs Pankhurst's revelations about prison life had left her deeply troubled. 'I mean to say, could *you*?'

Octavia looked out at the quiet rows of shops, all so respectable and shuttered and well-kept, and wondered whether she could. If this demonstration fails, she thought, I shall have to decide. The thought made her sigh. 'Ah well,' she said. 'We shall see, shan't we?'

It was an absolutely enormous demonstration. The crowds filled Hyde Park from one side to the other and stood packed together in front of all twenty platforms. The speakers wore elegant hats and sashes striped in the suffragette colours, purple, green and white. Annie Kenny brought a trainload of mill-girls with her from Lancashire and told her listeners that they had the support of men as well as women, Christabel Pankhurst asked the politicians to understand that the campaign had moved on from the days when it could be derided and belittled.

It had now won popular support and they would ignore it at their peril. 'You only have to look at the size of the crowd gathered here to understand what is happening,' she said. 'This is a great popular movement.'

But although the great popular movement passed yet another resolution at the conclusion of its mass meeting, petitioning parliament, yet again, to bring in legislation for an official women's suffrage bill, it was completely ignored. And at the end of the month, two suffragettes walked into Downing Street and made their own personal protest by smashing the windows. Militancy had begun.

The case for militant action was debated furiously at suffragette meetings and in committee rooms up and down the country. Octavia argued her own case passionately.

'I don't think breaking windows will do us any good at all,' she said. 'It will only irritate people and lose us support. And anyway they'll send for the glaziers and have them repaired in no time and it'll all be forgotten. We should be looking for something to show we're against bad laws but don't wish to harm anybody by opposing them. We need something symbolic. Something that will break a small unimportant law and catch attention without hurting anyone.' But for the moment she couldn't suggest anything suitable. And in any case she couldn't really think straight with Em's baby due at any moment.

He was born on June 30th and was called Edward, and was a lot smaller than his sister had been. Octavia thought he looked rather frail, but she didn't say so naturally. She stood by the bedside with the child in her arms and told her cousin he was a little dear.

'You've got a pigeon pair,' Amy said, enjoying the sight of her daughter with a baby in her arms. 'You clever girl.'

'She looked jolly tired,' Octavia said as she and her mother were walking home across the Heath.

'Giving birth is a tiring business,' Amy told her. 'But he's here now and she'll soon pick up again. Your Aunt Maud will make sure she has plenty of nourishing food. And she's got the rest of the summer to be out and about. That will make her stronger too. I wonder whether Ernest will employ another nursemaid.'

THE SUMMER WAS GIVEN over to Emmeline and her two babies. Octavia spent nearly every afternoon walking on the Heath arm in arm with her cousin while the nursemaids pushed the prams and Eddie slept and Dora sat up and babbled at the view.

The debate in the suffrage movement went on and various suggested tactics were attempted and failed. A group of women tried to rush the Houses of Parliament and were all arrested, another tried to smuggle their way in inside a furniture van, but were discovered and arrested too. Finally at the end of October a new and novel idea was mooted and Octavia she knew at once that this was the demonstration she'd been waiting for, the one she had to join. She knew she would be arrested and would suffer for it, but it was the right thing to do and she would do it.

'We are going to Parliament Square,' she told her parents, 'and we're going to chain ourselves to the railings. It will be perfectly peaceable, Mama. We're not going to break anything or shout or try to rush the building or anything like that. We're just going to march up to the railings and padlock ourselves in. We shall be arrested and I expect we shall be sent to prison but nobody's going to get hurt and with a bit of luck it will get into the newspapers and make people think.'

Her mother was upset and tried to persuade her against it. 'You are very young, my darling,' she said. 'I know you say it's going to be peaceable but can't be sure of it, can you. These things get out of hand and I wouldn't want you to get hurt. Wouldn't it be better to wait until you've graduated and then do things.'

Octavia put her arms round her mother's poor tense neck

and gave her a kiss. 'I'm nineteen,' she said. 'If I hadn't stayed on at school and gone to college I could have been out at work for five years. Think of that.'

'But what if you get hurt?' her mother worried.

'I shan't,' Octavia said, with more assurance than she actually felt. 'I promise you.'

'JJ,' Amy appealed. 'You speak to her.'

But he gave her a wry smile and said he was sure Octavia knew what she was doing. 'Just so long as you write and tell us what happens,' he said. 'Or telephone us perhaps?'

'Oh dear,' Amy sighed. 'It's such a worry. Well then, go if you must but don't wear your spectacles. If they throw you about and the glass gets broken it could blind you.'

So Octavia joined her first militant demonstration with her heart in her throat and her sight in her handbag.

IT WAS an afternoon of penetrating dampness and Parliament Square was uniformly grey, the air smoke-shrouded and smelling of sulphur, the sky leeched of all colour and coldly empty. The trunks of the nearly denuded trees were dark as coal, the grass in the central garden no longer green but a dull sludge grey that reminded Octavia of dirty linen, and the Houses of Parliament looked smudged and brooding, as though the great building was weeping sooty tears for all the iniquities of its long history.

The pavements were crowded with waiting women, dark in their winter coats and hats, parading slowly, two by two, or loitering as if they'd stopped to gossip, and there were one or two watchful policemen too, standing guard outside the Houses of Parliament, dour in their black uniforms. The banners were still folded up and hidden away in bags and holdalls, ready to be unfurled at the signal but for now everything was quiet and grey and watchful.

Octavia's heart was beating so powerfully it was making her throat pulse. She was glad she'd had the sense to wear a scarf and that the telltale signs were hidden. It wouldn't have done to let the others know what sort of state she was in especially as she wasn't entirely sure what sort of state it was herself. Fear? she thought. No don't let it be fear. That would be shameful. Excitement then? But it was too raw for excitement. Too raw and too immediate. It was very nearly time. There was no going back.

A whistle shrilled so suddenly it made her heart leap. She was propelled into action. Run! Now! No time to think. She rushed to the railings blindly, pulling out her chain and padlock as she ran. The grey scene broke into a jostling kaleidoscope, a gloved hand waved, a skirt swished, black boots skimmed the pavement, a hat fell from a tangle of hair, she had a glimpse of railings sharp as spears. Then the banners were out, unfurling in splashes of purple, green and white, bold as flowers in the darkness of the Square. People were shouting. 'Votes for women! Votes for women!' She arrived at the railings, and clung to them, panting. Now! She urged herself. Quickly. Before they can stop you. The padlock engaged with a crunch. The gesture was made. It was done.

After the rush, there were minutes of extraordinary stillness as the demonstration swirled around her and more and more women attached themselves to the railings beside her. Her heart steadied. Then she heard someone running, big boots heavy on the pavement, and a policeman's face loomed in upon her, round and hot and cross under his black helmet.

'Nah then,' he said, 'just undo that there padlock, *if* you please, miss. Let's not be havin' any trouble. You won't gain nothing with this sort a' carry-on.'

'It can't be done,' she told him, pleased by how calm she was. 'I've left the key at home.'

He breathed deeply, glaring at her. 'You're refusing my order,' he said. 'Is that what it is?'

'Yes,' she agreed. 'I'm refusing. Like the government. This is a protest against the refusal of the government to grant the vote to women. They refuse. I refuse.'

'Then I shall have to arrest you.'

'Yes,' she said. 'That is understood.'

He left her attached to the railings and clomped off to speak to his sergeant who was standing in the road, chewing the end of his waxed moustache. Another constable joined them and there were several minutes of earnest conversation. Then the sergeant walked away.

There was another woman in chains a few feet further along the road. 'Name of Polly,' she said, introducing herself. 'We've set them a problem.'

But not for long. They were soon back with another constable who was carrying a hacksaw. He moved along the line, cutting through the chains and grumbling. 'You'd better keep still if you don't want to get hurt,' he warned Octavia. 'I got no time fer silly women.'

A small crowd had gathered and there was a photographer on the other side of the street setting up his camera. Octavia watched him, hoping he worked for one of the newspapers. But then the Black Maria arrived and they were rounded up and led towards it, shouting 'Votes for women!' all the way.

I'm a criminal now, Octavia thought as she was pushed into one of the L-shaped cells inside the van. It was airless and dark in there, for there was only one small, blacked-out window, and unpleasantly claustrophobic, being designed to force a prisoner to sit bolt upright with his legs in the space under the unseen seat in front of him. Octavia's face was just a few inches from the wall in front of her, her back was jammed against the wall behind her and her legs were so tightly wedged under the seat that she couldn't turn her feet to left or right. She could hear other prisoners being pushed in behind her and recognised Polly's voice still shouting 'Votes for women!' and that encouraged her. We shall be sent to prison now, she thought, and even though she felt proud of what she was doing, she shuddered despite herself.

It was late the following evening before she got a chance to write the promised letter to her father and she was too weary to say much but she wrote what she could.

Holloway Gaol

Dear Pa,

I have been sentenced to six weeks and I am here in Holloway Gaol. It is not a pleasant place, I must confess to you, but then I did not imagine it would be. Prisons are designed to be unpleasant. However I think that being here will prove to be an educational experience, if nothing else. I am a category A prisoner, which means I shall be allowed books and writing paper and I intend to keep a diary so I shall do what I can to make the six weeks pass quickly.

We were booked in by a very unpleasant woman. She gave us our prison uniforms, which are rough and ugly, and took away our own clothes and all our personal belongings with the exception of my spectacles which she allowed me to keep, and said, "Don't go giving yourself airs. You're here to be punished and punished you will be." Strange to think that when we win the vote we shall be winning it for her too.

Tell Mama that I am looking after myself. I may be a convicted criminal but I am still your most loving daughter Tavy.

Her father wrote back by return of post to applaud her courage and ask if there was anything she needed that he could supply.

I hope you will tell me everything you can about life 'inside', he said. Your mother and I need to feel we are still close to you and letters must stand in lieu of conversation now.

I will do my best, Octavia replied, *although I fear that much of what I write will be censored, for opinion here is not free. Everything about this place is a punishment from the air we breathe, which smells of stale cabbage, dirty clothes, unwashed bodies sweat and used chamber pots, if you can imagine such a thing, to the discomfort of the cell. When I was first left alone here I felt like a caged animal and had to pace about. I simply couldn't sit down or keep still. However I am accustomed to it now. It is a matter of adjusting the way in which you think. There are still times when the walls seem to be looming in on me but I tell myself that this is because the cell is so small and the brickwork has been painted such a claustrophobic green; the barred window is so high I can't see out of it but I tell myself that at least it lets in light; the plank bed is hard and uncomfortable but no worse than a lot of women endure every night of their lives; the uniform is a shapeless dress made of rough cotton with large black arrows stamped all over it, a rough Holland apron and a mop cap like the ones skivvies wear. I think it is to show us how low we have sunk, but we wear it like a badge of pride. However there are some things that cannot be improved by thinking. The food is badly cooked and often inedible, cockroaches scuttle about the cell all night, and the warders still enjoy their power and bully whenever they can.*

The conversation continued. She wrote about the other prisoners she met in the yard, the petty thieves, 'who have no other way of earning a living', and were rough and tough and swore like troopers, the pickpockets, 'who take what they can, where they can', the prostitutes, 'who are weary and slipshod and old before their time', and one in particular who had become a friend.

She is an intelligent girl, sharp-witted and funny and quick to understand what is said to her. She has had very little education for there were six younger brothers and sisters for her to look after and schooling was a luxury. Her father has been in and out of prison all his life, so she says, and I can well believe her, and her mother has been so worn down by children and poverty that Lizzie has had to do most of the work for her. Now it is her earnings that keep the family going. It is little short of a scandal and a dreadful waste of her undoubted talent.

The long weeks passed slowly. But eventually she was serving her last few days and the punishment was nearly over.

I believe in the rightness of our cause, she wrote in her bold firm hand, *more passionately now than I did on the day I was arrested and nothing that is done or said to me in this place will change my mind in the slightest degree. Enduring things makes me aware that I am living to some purpose and that is a splendid thing because it is what I have always wanted to do. The more of us who are sent to prison the stronger we shall be. Now it is truly a fight and a fight for what is just and right. Eventually, no matter what is happening to us now, the government will have to give in and accede to our demands, just as earlier governments gave in to the Chartists. The longer I sit here on my own and think about it, the more obvious it seems to me. I wonder they can't see it too. Their opposition to us is cruel but it is also foolish. They are a House full of King Canutes trying to bully the incoming tide.*

I am well, or as well as I can be, and I think of you and Mama fondly and often. Your letters are a great strength to me. I wait for them impatiently. It will not be much longer now. In four more days I can walk across the Heath and breathe clean air again. Please reassure Mama and tell her that I am not changed by being labelled criminal and that I love her more than ever.

Your ever loving daughter,
   Tavy.

SHE WAS RELEASED ten days before Christmas and her father was waiting for her at the prison gate with a cab ready to take her home. He was horrified to see how pale and thin she was.

'We must build you up again, little one,' he said, holding her hand as they sat side by side in the cab. 'You must be fit and well for Christmas.' He was distressed to see that tears were falling down her cheeks.

It was the most special Christmas he could devise with the richest food, the best wines and the biggest family party they'd ever held. But it was the Christmas cards that pleased Octavia most. Details of her imprisonment had been published in the Suffragette newspaper, along with all the others, and she had cards from all over the country, praising her for her courage and thanking her for what she'd done. And among them, most unexpectedly was a card from Tommy Meriton.

I had to write and tell you how much I admire the stand you are taking, he wrote. *I take my hat off to you. You are a brave woman.*

And he added a postscript.

PS Perhaps I shall see you at Cyril's twenty-first.

Good heavens, she thought. Fancy him writing like that. Maybe there's some good in him after all.

'Well that's nice,' her mother said when she read the card. 'It will be nice to see him at the party. I only wish Maud and Ralph weren't making such a fuss over it. You'd think nobody had ever come of age before, the way they're going on. They didn't fuss like that over Emmeline.'

'She had a big wedding,' JJ pointed out.

'And quite right too,' Amy said. 'She was getting married and marriage can be hard work. I'm sure it is in her case. Very hard work. Whereas Cyril never seems to work at all. He just gets sillier every year. And he never visits poor Emmeline and he really should.'

CHAPTER 9

Cyril's twenty-first birthday was just after his finals and it was a grand occasion, just as Amy had predicted. To be fair to him, he did his best to be blasé about it because he was uncomfortably aware that Emmeline's twenty-first hadn't been anywhere near so splendid and because it wasn't the done thing to show excitement. He was a stickler for doing the done thing, although it was actually quite difficult because the Pater had organised a frightfully grand supper with dancing and champagne and everything, and invited all his friends down from Oxford, which was rather sporting of him, so he had to be the man of the hour whether he wanted to or not — and of course he *did* want to, very much indeed. But privately of course.

Tommy Meriton had come of age in January and said it was 'all a fearful bore, old thing,' but it had to be done, which steadied him. A real chum, Tommy Meriton. Always knew the right thing to say.

At that moment, the two of them were sitting in the conservatory among palms and ferns, underneath the grape vine and the frangipani waiting for the guests to arrive, smoking cheroots like the men of the world they were and lounging in the new rattan chairs with their long legs spread before them. In his three years at Oxford Cyril had developed from a gangly — and often spotty — youth to a self-possessed and really quite handsome young man, sporting a silky moustache and wearing evening dress as to the manor born. Tommy Meriton was as handsome as ever and invariably looked the style in everything he wore and *he* had a splendid moustache curving over his mouth like two blonde wings. But then he'd always been someone special, rowing Blue and President of the Union and everybody saying he'd take a Double First and all that. A dashed fine chap, Cyril thought, admiring him.

At that moment the two friends were discussing the extraordinary behaviour of Miss Octavia Smith. 'I never thought she'd actually go and do it,' Cyril said, flicking the ash from his cheroot with his middle finger in the elegantly correct way. 'Dash it all, Tommy. I mean to say a chap could be compromised by something like this. Bad enough all that marching about she would do and carrying banners and everything. But chaining herself to the railings! It's not done. And now she says she's going to do it again.'

'I think it's top hole,' Tommy said.

'You're not related to her,' Cyril told him. 'It's no joke having a jailbird for a cousin.'

'You make her sound like a burglar,' Tommy said, laughing at him. 'Actually I sent her a Christmas card.'

'Really?' Cyril said, amazed to hear it. 'You are a goose, Tommy. What d'you want to go and do a thing like that for?'

'To congratulate her,' Tommy said. 'Taking a stand and all that.'

'Most unwise,' Cyril said. 'You'll give her a swollen head and she's bad enough without that.' But he couldn't say any more, which was just as well because the door was opening and there was a rustle of silk skirts as Octavia herself came swooshing towards them between the palms and ferns with Emmeline close behind her.

'We've been sent to find you,' Emmeline said to her brother. 'Your guests are starting to arrive. You're to come into the drawing room and greet them.' She looked and sounded extremely haughty in her fine new smoke blue dress, even though she was plump with her third pregnancy and secretly feeling rather uncomfortable — which was another reason to make Squirrel mind his manners. He might have come of age but she was a mother of two and soon to be a mother of three and he would always be her annoying little brother, no matter how old he was. Her own twenty-first birthday party had been very small compared to this one and although a lot of her unmarried school friends had been invited tonight purportedly 'to keep her company,' she had a nasty suspicion they were actually here to provide dancing partners for his silly chums. Her mother would keep telling her what an opportunity it was for them. And that sharpened her manner towards him too.

Cyril didn't move from his seat. 'Who's come?' he asked languidly.

'Emma Henderson for a start,' his sister said. Emma was one of her very best friends and should have been greeted properly.

'Oh she's a good sort,' Cyril said. 'She won't mind waiting. Tell the Mater I'll finish my smoke and then I'll be along.'

'Oh no, Squirrel,' his sister said firmly. 'That won't do.'

Octavia stood among the foliage and observed, partly because it amused her to watch the antagonism between Emmeline and her brother and partly because it gave her a chance to assess Tommy Meriton. She hadn't seen him since his clumsy visit to her back in the summer but he *had* sent her that card, which was kind, in a way, and she was interested to see if he'd changed at all. He's still very handsome, she thought, looking at the curve of his mouth under that luxurious moustache and the long pale fingers holding that cheroot.

There was another swish of silk and Aunt Maud appeared, very stylish in a long swirling gown of grey chiffon over dark blue silk with a great deal of intricate embroidery across the bodice and round the hem. She wore dark blue gloves to her elbows and her usually untidy auburn hair was severely pinned in place but she moved in her usual precipitous way and looked as though she expected to become dishevelled at any moment. 'Cyril my dear,' she said, almost timidly, 'your friends are in the hall.'

'Right ho, Mater,' Cyril said, making a face at his sister, and he stood up at once, stubbed out his cheroot, brushed invisible dust from the velvet lapels of his jacket, adjusted his bow tie and offered his mother his arm. Within seconds he and Aunt Maud and Emmeline had gone and Octavia found herself alone in the musty half-light with Tommy Meriton, with the peppery scent of the palms filling her nose and the arriving guests buzzing in the drawing room behind her.

'You won't mind if I finish this, will you?' he asked, holding up the cheroot for her permission. 'He can manage without me for a minute or two I daresay.'

His self-assurance made her feel unsettled, so she sat down in the chair her cousin had been occupying and occupied herself in arranging her dress so that it didn't crease. It was a pretty rose pink silk, which was a daring colour to wear with her gingery hair, and she was rather afraid the bodice was cut too low. There seemed to be far too much of her neck and bosom exposed to be proper. At the final fitting, two days ago, the dressmaker had assured her that it was cut in the latest style and that she had the perfect figure for it, but that could have been because there wasn't time to make any alterations. It worried her quite a lot now that she was wearing it, especially as she couldn't hoist it higher when she was in company.

There was a long pause while she wondered whether she ought to speak first. After all he was a guest and it was only common politeness to look after your guests. But she couldn't think of anything to say, apart from wanting to scold him for the way he'd treated her and she would have to choose her moment to do that. Lounging there in the half-light with all that burgeoning greenery around him he was making her think of Greek gods again, and dryads and fauns. Eventually he spoke to her. 'Did you get my card?' he asked.

'Yes,' she said, pushing the Greek gods from her mind. And then since that sounded rather abrupt and she had to be polite, she added, 'Thank you.'

There was another pause. Then he ventured. 'Are you well? You look well.'

'Thank you,' she said again. What else could she say? She *did* look well. She'd lost her prison pallor within weeks of coming home.

'Bully for you!' he said, drawing on his cheroot. And when she looked at him, wondering what she could say in answer to that, he added, 'I think you're extremely plucky, damn if I don't. I said so to Squirrel. I couldn't have done the half of it.'

'I do what has to be done,' she told him seriously. 'If a thing is right then you must do it.'

He looked at her quizzically. 'Always?'

'I think so.'

'No matter what the consequences?'

'No matter what.'

'My word, you're a corker,' he said and there was no doubt about the admiration on his face. 'I hope you're sitting next to me at supper. Bags I the first dance anyway.'

The conversation was slipping out of her control. She hadn't been anywhere near cold enough to him. They were talking as if they were still friends. 'I'm sitting next to Emmeline,' she said, trying to be discouraging.

He wasn't discouraged in the least. 'Bags I the first waltz, then,' he said.

Oh dear, Octavia thought. Now what could she say? That she didn't want to dance? No, she couldn't say that. It would be a lie. That she didn't want to dance with him? No, that wouldn't be true either. Not if she were honest. She *did* want to dance with him. Oh for heaven's sake! What was the good of being able to read people's expressions if you can't think what to say to them?

'That's settled then,' he said. 'Now I'd better join poor old Squirrel. Moral support and all that.' He stubbed out the remains of the cheroot in the nearest pot plant and stood up, giving her that odd courteous bow of his. 'After you, Miss Smith.'

Octavia walked ahead of him into the crush in the drawing room feeling cross. She'd handled that so badly. What was the use of planning to put him down if she just talked to him as if they were friends? But really he was impossible. She had *tried* to be cold and he should have noticed. He just wasn't sensitive enough. That was the trouble.

He was also impossibly persistent. She'd no sooner sat down at one of the long supper tables than he was drawing up a chair beside her, in exactly the same way as he'd done at Emmeline's wedding.

'Got moved out,' he explained. 'Shove up, Cyril. Make room for a little'un.'

And he *was* good company. Even allowing for the fact that she was mellowed by champagne. They talked and talked, about Oxford and University College, and the theatre, and universal suffrage.

'Can't for the life of me see why they don't just give you the vote and have done with it,' he said. 'They'll have to give in to you sooner or later. Stands to reason.'

'You should be a politician,' she told him. 'We need people in the House with your opinion.'

'Fat chance of that,' he said, holding up his glass to a passing waiter for more champagne. 'And more for the lady, there's a good chap. No. My career's mapped out, I'm sorry to say.'

He'd spoken as though he was joking but there was more regret on his face than he knew and that intrigued her. 'Why are you sorry about it?' she asked. 'Isn't it what you want?'

He shrugged his shoulders, carelessly, as though it didn't matter. 'It's what the Pater wants,' he said. 'He's had it planned since I was in prep school. I'm to follow him into the diplomatic corps. That's why I've been travelling so much. Had to see the territory and all that.'

'And I thought you were just gadding about.'

'Oh I was gadding about too,' he admitted. 'All work and no play and that sort of thing. Got to stop now though. He's arranged my first post.' And he grimaced.

She admired his honesty. She couldn't help herself. And she enjoyed the grimace. He doesn't like having his life arranged for him, she thought, and he doesn't know how to avoid it. 'When do you start?'

'Too soon,' he said.

Somebody was banging on the table. It was time for the speeches.

They went on interminably but Octavia didn't listen to them. She was too busy digesting what she'd just been told. Imagine having your life planned out for you, she thought, and not being able to refuse it or do anything about it. I should hate that. It made her see Tommy Meriton in quite a different way. Maybe he wasn't quite as bad as she'd thought. He certainly had a lot to put up with. And he didn't complain about it. She admired that in him. He'd been jolly unkind to her, there was no denying that, but maybe he hadn't meant to. Sitting there beside her he didn't strike her as someone who would be deliberately unkind. She looked across the table at her father, who gave her one of his lovely smiles, and she smiled back, glad he was allowing her the freedom to choose whatever career she wanted. Then she looked at Tommy again. And he winked at her and pretended to yawn. Oh why do speeches take such a long time, she thought. There was so much more she wanted to ask him. But she had to sit politely and pretend to listen and then to her disappointment, as soon as the last speech had been made, the tables were cleared to make way for dancing and the guests stood up and began to mingle and he was gone.

It wasn't until he came to claim the first waltz, bowing before her and saying, 'My dance I think,' that she got the chance to talk to him again.

'Haven't you ever wanted to plan your own life?' she asked.

'Waste of time,' he said lightly. 'When the Pater's made up his mind to a thing, that's that. This is a dashed fine party don'tcher know.'

His face was closing so she knew she had to let him change the subject and they talked theatre again and he told her he'd seen 'Arms and the Man' and thought it was dashed good.

After that they danced far more dances than was strictly proper and when they waltzed he held her so closely she was afraid he would feel how stupidly her heart was beating. It's the champagne, she thought. It probably speeds up the heartbeat. But it was very pleasant just the same, even if she did feel dizzy.

Towards midnight when more champagne was being served and the dancers had tumbled into sofas and armchairs to rest, he appeared at her side with two flutes filled to the brim and signalled that she was to follow him. By that time, what with the fun of the party and all that good food and so much champagne, she was in the easiest of moods and followed him without demur. They eased past the sprawl of masculine legs and feminine skirts and slipped through the drawn curtains into the darkness of the conservatory.

'Here's to the Cause, Miss Octavia Smith,' he said, and he put one of the flutes into her hand and raised the other in salute. 'May you march to victory.'

'To the Cause,' she said, and drank, looking up at him across the rim of the glass.

He drank too. Then he took her glass away from her and set it down on the little cane table with his own alongside. 'They can wait for us,' he said, and put his arms round her waist, just as he'd done so often in her dreams, bent his head towards her and kissed her full on the lips. She was so surprised it took her breath away. I'm dreaming, she thought. This can't be happening. He can't be... But he was and oh so softly and tenderly. And it was delicious, making her lips tingle and her breasts tingle and sending currents of pleasure from the top of her head to her fingertips. Champagne and pleasurable sensation and amazed disbelief swirled together in her brain. And she kissed him back. She simply couldn't help it.

'I could love you very easily, little suffragette,' he said, looking into her eyes. And kissed her again. This time she simply surrendered herself to the pleasure of it.

Someone was scuffling and making an odd squeaking noise. She pulled away from him at once, alert and anxious. There's someone here, she thought. What if they've seen us? And she turned her head to see her cousin sliding to the floor and pulling someone else down with him. She recognised Emma Henderson's blue gown as it swirled about his legs and remembered how he wouldn't go out to greet her. Well he's greeting her now, she thought, and no mistake. Then she realised that he was drunk and watched as Emma disentangled herself from his grip and struggled to stand up again.

'Squiffy!' Tommy said striding over to hoist his friend to his feet. 'Put your arm over my shoulder, old man. Steady as she goes!'

Cyril was giggling and trying to speak but his words were so blurred that Octavia couldn't understand him. 'Too mush,' he said thickly. 'Wash a shtr... strah... Lemme...' And giggled again.

'Oh dear,' Emma said. 'I didn't think he was going to fall

over. I thought we were going to sit out here and talk. Is he all right do you think? Should I go and fetch someone?'

There was no need. The door to the drawing room was opening, the curtain being pulled back. Loud male voices were demanding to know what was going on. There were hoots of raucous laughter and sardonic cheering as Cyril was hauled back to his party, legs trailing. 'Superfluity of champers!' they chortled, thumping him between his sagging shoulders. 'Tight as a tick, damn if he ain't.'

It was an ignominious end to Octavia's first love scene. Trust Squirrel to butt in, she thought. But it *was* a love scene just the same. He'd kissed her and told her he could love her. It wasn't a dream. She shouldn't have allowed it, of course. She knew that. But she *had* and she'd enjoyed it.

'Disgraceful,' Emmeline said, coming up to stand beside her. 'Nobody fell over drunk at my party.'

'And they won't at mine,' Octavia said, glad of the chance to be disapproving.

It took a long time and a lot of black coffee to steady Cyril sober and Tommy was in charge of the operation. It wasn't until the party was breaking up and the guests were milling around in the hall saying goodbye, that he had a moment to talk to Octavia again.

'Your cousin is a pest,' he said. 'No sense of timing. We never got to finish our champers. I suppose you wouldn't like to come to the theatre with me. There are all sorts of things on and you wouldn't have to worry about catching trams or anything. I could drive you there.'

She was impressed but tried not to show it. 'Could you?' she said and teased, 'What in?'

'It's only a Tin Lizzie,' he said, with deliberate modesty. 'The Pater bought it for me. Cheap and cheerful sort of thing. It's all right for starters. When I'm an Ambassador I shall run a Silver Ghost. So what about it? Tomorrow maybe.'

'Just you?' she asked. 'Or you and Cyril?'

'It's no good talking about Cyril,' he said. 'He'll have a thick head for days. No I thought just you and me. There are some good things on.'

Which there were and over the next two weeks they saw most of them, travelling into London in the Tin Lizzie, which was great fun and made her feel very special even if it *was* bumpy over the tramlines, and driving home in the darkness when they had the suburban streets to themselves. She was impressed by the way Tommy drove and the care with which he tucked her into the passenger seat and shut the door beside her. 'So's you won't fall out. Can't have that.' Their evenings quickly took on an easy pattern, stalls in the theatre or the music hall, supper wherever she fancied, a short drive home and a long time kissing goodnight. And on Sundays they 'tootled off' into the country and went for long circular walks talking all the time and stopping for kisses when there was no one in sight. And oh it was wonderful to be kissed so much and so often.

At the end of the third week and on an unbidden impulse, she asked him if they were courting.

He answered with a question. 'Would you like us to be?'

'Not particularly,' she said. She spoke defensively because that wasn't the answer she'd expected. 'I like being unconventional. I don't see why people should get married just because it's expected of them. Only I thought that what we're doing would probably be seen as courting. By other people I mean. Our families for example. And I wondered what you thought about it. That's all.'

He cupped her face in his hands. 'I could love you very easily,' he said. 'I told you that at the party. But the thing is I can't ask you to marry me. Not yet anyway. I've got to serve my apprenticeship. Juniors in the diplomatic corps aren't expected to marry. They think we're too young.'

That accounts for why he hasn't said anything, she thought.

In Jane Austen the heroes never say anything to the heroines until they're free to propose. It's what drives the plot. She'd written an essay on that very thing less than a year ago. 'Social conventions in the novels of Jane Austen.' She just hadn't expected social conventions to drive her life too.

'How long is this apprenticeship?' she asked.

'Three years, maybe more.' He grimaced. 'It scuppers a chap's chances, I can tell you.'

'It needn't scupper ours,' she told him. 'I don't want to get married. Not for ages anyway.'

'Then why did you ask?'

'Curiosity, I suppose,' she said. 'Wanting to know what you thought. And yes, I know what you're going to say. Curiosity killed the cat.'

He put his arm round her waist, drew her towards him and kissed her. 'You're a brick, Tavy,' he said. 'An absolute brick.'

AFTERWARDS, lying awake in her quiet room, she pondered the wisdom of what she'd said to him. She'd told him she didn't want to marry him because she'd felt she ought to comfort him. She'd responded to that odd grimace of his — which she understood just a little too well now — and without really considering what she was saying. She really didn't know whether she wanted to marry him or not. She enjoyed going out with him and being kissed by him and it was wonderful to think how unconventional they were being. But wanting to marry him was another matter. If she could be sure of a marriage as rich and trusting as her parents', then maybe she did. But what if it were to turn out like Em's? And how did you know what sort it would be? Em had been so happy on her wedding day, so sure that what she was doing was right, and now she was burdened with babies and hardly had a minute to herself. And then there was the Cause. She could hardly pull out now. Not when the next demonstration was planned and she was committed to it. But if they were to marry she would have to go and live with him wherever he was — they could hardly be married and live in two different countries — and then she would *have* to pull out. It was all very difficult. And her next visit to the theatre made it worse.

They were clapping the end of the second act and the stalls were astir with people getting ready to head off to the bar, so at first she wasn't sure she'd heard what he said and she had to ask him to repeat it.

'Sorry about that, old thing,' he said. 'Too much racket in here. I said I'm off to Belgrade.'

It was what she'd thought he'd said, what she didn't want to hear him say. But she kept calm and simply asked, 'When?'

The answer was a shock. 'Next Thursday.'

'But that's a week tomorrow.'

''Fraid so,' he said, standing up and beginning to thread his way along the row.

She followed him, her heart beating anxiously. 'How long will you be away?'

He waited until they'd reached the gangway and were standing side by side. It was as difficult as he'd feared it would be. She looked really stricken. He tried to speak lightly. 'Two months, I'm afraid. I've got to apply for a job there and sit tests and have interviews and all sorts. The Pater's set it all up for me. Sorry about that.'

She made a great effort and tried to be sensible. 'Oh well,' she said, 'it will give me a chance to visit Emmeline and get on with my work for the Cause.'

He put his hand under her elbow and steered her towards the bar. 'I'll write to you,' he promised. 'Every day.' And when she gave him her most doubting look. 'Honour bright. See it wet, see it dry.' Which made her laugh. But it was a horrible moment even so.

They went out together every evening for the next seven days and stayed out late on every one of those evenings kissing until their lips were sore. And on the day he left, she was so unhappy she had to hide away in her room so that she could cry. But the next day she gave herself a talking-to and got on with her life.

The first thing she did was to phone her cousin and ask what would be the most convenient day for her to come to visit.

'Wednesday,' Emmeline said at once. 'He goes to his club on Wednesdays.'

So Wednesday it was. It gave them a long stretch of time together without fear of interruption and meant that Emmeline could dress in comfortable clothes. If Ernest had been at home she'd have been required to dress in the latest style, pregnancy or no pregnancy, so the weekly informality was a treat. On their first afternoon together she chose an old cream-coloured blouse, softened by much washing, and a blue pinafore dress with a skirt that opened at the front to reveal her petticoat, and put carpet slippers on her feet to rest her swollen ankles.

'Do try one of those macaroons,' she said, pouring a second cup of tea for them both. 'They're cook's speciality. Oh it *is* so nice to have tea *tête-à-tête*. I never seem to get a chance to talk to people these days. Not at length anyway. You can't count dinner parties because nobody talks at dinner parties. They all just make noises, don't they? It can be really trying sometimes.'

Octavia attended all her father's dinner parties now and was dazzled by the talk around his table, but she didn't tell her cousin that. There was something about Emmeline's expression that made her feel concerned and she sensed that an argument would be unkind.

There was a diffident knock at the door and one of the nursemaids came in, carrying Eddie and leading Dora by the hand. 'We're just off to bed, Mrs Thompson,' she said. 'Come to say goodnight.'

Emmeline took little Eddie in her arms and shifted in her seat so that Dora could climb into what was left of her lap. Her face was transformed at the sight of them, rounding and softening and losing the peaky anxiety that had been disquieting her cousin. 'Aren't they just two little ducks?' she said to Octavia. 'Yes, you are, my poppets. Two dear little ducks. Give your Mama a big big kiss.' The children put up their plump arms and clung about her neck to kiss her and she laughed and giggled and tried to disentangle Eddie's fingers from her hair. 'We will all go up together,' she said to Octavia, 'and you shall see them in their pretty nightgowns.'

So they finished their tea and fed both babies morsels of macaroon and angel cake and let Dora take sips from her mother's cup of milky tea, and presently they all trooped upstairs together, the nursemaid carrying Dora and Octavia carrying Eddie, and arrived in the night nursery which was pink and white and rather claustrophobic and smelt of baby powder and starched linen. There was a little white crib for the baby set beside the night nurse's white bedstead and a little white cot for Dora that has so many fluffy toys heaped up on its embroidered coverlet that there was barely room for her to lie down, and long frilled curtains to enclose them in their comfortable domain and to keep out the darkness of the world outside.

Emmeline was quite girlish again, sitting in her nursing chair by the fire and kissing her babies as she washed their hands and faces. 'What song shall we sing?' she asked gaily.

'Diddle Dum-ping,' Dora said, clapping her hands.

So it was 'Diddle, diddle dumpling' and 'This little piggy went to market' on all four sets of toes and much tumbling and cuddling until Dora had to be rocked to quietness on her mother's lap while the baby was given his evening bottle. Then the gas was lowered and both children were settled under the covers, thumbs in mouths, and the cousins tiptoed out of the room.

'Aren't they just ducks?' Emmeline asked as she waddled down the stairs.

Octavia agreed that they were dear little things and very pretty, which was true enough for they both had huge brown eyes, button noses and their mother's pale auburn hair, Dora's in a halo of thick curls and Eddie's in a cherubic fuzz, and Dora at least was sturdy and full of mischief. But her brother was a pale little thing and, to Octavia's admittedly inexperienced eyes, looked rather small for eleven months and oddly apprehensive, jumping and turning his head at the slightest sound behind him and looking up sideways at them, like a startled fawn, as if he wasn't sure how they were going to treat him.

'Dear little man,' Emmeline said as though she knew what Octavia was thinking. 'You wouldn't call him a milksop, would you?'

'He's a baby,' Octavia said, watching her cousin's face. 'Babies are milky by nature. I think he's a darling.'

They were at the bottom of the stairs by then and on their way back to the breakfast room. 'It's just...' Emmeline began, but then waited until they were both inside the room and the door and its muffling curtain were closed behind them. 'It's just that Ernest is so keen for him to be manly,' she confessed, as they resumed their seats by the fireplace. 'He's on about it all the time. He'd be quite cross if he knew how we've been romping. In fact between you and me we only have a romp when he's not here. He says they've to be shown how to behave properly and romps make them overexcited. I'm sure he's right but a little fun once in a while...' Her face was peaked with anxiety again.

She's frightened of him, Octavia thought, and she struggled to find something helpful to say. 'They're only little,' she offered. 'Pa used to toss me in the air when I was little. I can still remember it.'

Emmeline was surprised. 'Did he really?'

'Often. And we played bears. He made a wonderful bear. He used to put the hearthrug over his back and I used to ride him.'

'I can't imagine Ernest ever doing a thing like that,' Emmeline said and her face looked wistful. Then she made an effort and changed her tone and her expression. 'But it takes all sorts doesn't it and he's very kind to us. He's a wonderful provider. I can't fault him. We don't want for anything and we've got all the servants we need. I'm to have a second nursemaid when this baby is born. I hardly have to do any housework. It's just...'

Octavia waited, looking encouraging, and there was a thoughtful pause.

'It's just I wish he wasn't quite so stern at breakfast,' Emmeline confessed at last. 'He will have the children take breakfast with us and he's on at them all the time, not to talk — and you know how Dora likes to babble — telling them to sit up straight and eat up their food, and if Eddie cries he gets in such a rage. He says he's a sissy and he'll grow up a milksop. It does upset him, poor little man. He can't bear being shouted at and I don't think he *can* sit up straight. Not yet. He's too young.' She sighed and smoothed her petticoat over her belly. 'But then I suppose he knows best,' she said. 'After all he *is* their father.'

Her meekness annoyed Octavia. 'And you're their mother,' she said. 'Don't you know best too?'

'Well yes,' Emmeline said. 'I suppose I do, in a way. When he's not here. It's just I don't like to upset him. He gets upset so easily, you wouldn't believe. I have to make allowances.'

You're nothing more than a servant yourself, Octavia thought, living round the edges of his temper. And it's not right. But for the first time in her life she didn't speak out. There was something pathetic about poor Emmeline's expression that made her feel protective and she had a suspicion that she might make matters worse if she said what she thought. But if this is what marriage is like, she thought, I'm glad I'm not getting married. I wonder if Tommy *will* write to me.

His first letter arrived the next morning, looking very foreign with its odd stamp and even odder postmark. He had arrived in good order, he said, and was missing her very much. The first interview was tomorrow morning, 'so I will have had it by the time you get this. I will write and tell you how I get on.' And he signed it, 'Yours with love.'

She sat on the edge of her bed with the letter in her lap and cried because she missed him so much. Then she washed her face and put on her hat and walked off to the suffragette shop, determined not to be silly. There was always work to be done, thank goodness.

CHAPTER 10

July and August that year were the longest months that Octavia had ever had to struggle through. There was plenty to keep her busy what with her work with the WSPU and constant visits to Emmeline and her babies but the time dragged. The only bright patches in her day were when the postman brought another letter from Tommy or she was sitting in her bedroom composing an answer. She tried to persuade herself that it was ridiculous to miss him so much, that she was an adult now and should behave like one, that in any case there was nothing she could do about this parting except endure it, but she missed him miserably despite her most earnest persuasion.

How much longer have you got to stay in that horrible Bucharest? she wrote at the end of July. *They must have made their minds up about you by now, surely.*

His answer wasn't encouraging.

I've been offered the position, he wrote, *but there's a sort of testing period, to see if I really suit I suppose, so I'm not likely to be back before September. Not to fret, old thing. We shall see one another soon and I'll give you a big kiss to make up for being away so long.*

September! she thought. That's months away. How can I wait all that time until I see you again? Not that she had any option. It was horribly frustrating. It might have been easier if she could have told someone how much she loved him. And she did love him. There was no doubt about that now. But she could hardly talk to her parents about him, except in a general way as Squirrel's friend. It did occur to her sometimes that her mother was beginning to have suspicions but that was all the more reason *not* to talk to her. And her friends were unaware of what had been going on, which was her own fault because she hadn't told them anything. In ordinary circumstances, it might have been possible to confide in Emmeline, but Emmeline's circumstances weren't ordinary. As her third confinement edged closer she grew more and more anxious and depressed.

'I shall have a bad time with this one,' she said to Octavia.

'You can't know that, Em,' Octavia said, trying to be reasonable.

Her cousin was beyond reason. 'Yes I do,' she said. 'I can feel it. It's going to be awful. Oh Tavy, I wish I wasn't expecting. It's so miserable to be all fat and blown up like this. I feel like a porpoise. I probably look like one. I do, don't I? Go on, be honest. Did you ever see such a fright in your life? And I've got the backache and my legs hurt and look at my ankles.'

'It'll soon be over,' Octavia said, hoping to cheer her. 'It's only a few more weeks.' But Emmeline wept all over again and said she knew she was going to have a bad time, and what if she died?

It was a great surprise to everyone in the family when she gave birth easily. It was another daughter and she called her

Edith and said she was a little duck and seemed quite herself again within hours of the baby's arrival.

'I've never seen such a transformation,' Octavia said to her mother when they were walking home after their first visit. There'd been no letter from Tommy that morning and she was feeling irritable. 'Yesterday she was saying she was going to die. And now look at her.'

'We all feel like that when our time's due,' Amy said, sagely. 'I know I did. I was weepy for days.'

'Well I shan't,' Octavia said. 'All that fuss and crying. It's no way for a grown woman to carry on. After all it was what she wanted. Lots and lots of babies. She always said so.'

'So she did my dear,' her mother said mildly. 'But it's different when you're carrying. As you will find out in time I daresay.'

'No,' Octavia said mutinously, 'I shan't because I'm not going to get married and I'm not going to have babies. The whole business is too ridiculous. Oh look at all that horrible cloud. Now it's going to rain. We'd better walk a bit faster or we shall be drowned.'

The next day the weather improved dramatically and so did her mood. The sun shone in the most soothing way and she had two letters at breakfast time, a loving one from Tommy, saying how much he missed her, which was just what she wanted to hear, and an official one from the University of London to tell her that she had been awarded a Bachelor of Arts degree with first class honours.

'It's no surprise to me, my dear,' her father said, beaming at her. 'What did I always say?'

'I must phone Maud,' Amy said. 'She'll be so happy for you, Tavy. And she must have heard Cyril's results by now too.'

Cyril's results had come out a week ago and it turned out that he hadn't done at all well. 'Only a third I'm afraid,' Maud said. 'I was going to tell you but Em's confinement put it out of my head. It put everything out of my head to tell the truth. I'm so glad it's over.'

I wonder whether Tommy knows his results, Octavia thought. I shall ask him when I answer his letter.

His reply was laconic.

Result was a double first as expected, he wrote, *so the Pater has something to show off about. They are pleased at the Consulate. At any rate, they tell me my appointment's in the bag. I've no doubt the Pater will show off about that too. However, once everything is signed and settled, I have some leave owing. I can hear you saying 'and about time too'. I have to spend a fortnight in Italy first but after that I shall be home for six weeks.*

It was the best news she'd had since he went away. Home in two weeks. Maybe I'll tell Em now she's in a better mood.

But Em was exploding with news of her own. 'You'll never guess what they've done now,' she said, and before Octavia could ask who, she plunged into a complaint. 'Cyril's going to Italy for a holiday. Isn't that sickening? He got a third — did you know that? — lazy thing! — and they're paying for a holiday as if he'd covered himself with glory. It's Meriton Major behind it, naturally. Apparently he wrote to Cyril saying would he was off on some trip or other all round Italy and would he like to come with him. He's going for a fortnight. Isn't it sickening?'

'Yes,' Octavia said with feeling. 'It is.' It should have been me, she thought, angrily. Why didn't he write and ask me? I'd have gone with him like a shot and I've earned a holiday. I worked. 'It's unfair.'

'I knew you'd agree,' Emmeline said with great satisfaction. 'It's scandalous the way they spoil him. Well I hope they do the same for Podge when it's his turn, that's all. I shall have something to say if they don't.'

Octavia laughed at that. 'I'm sure you will, Em,' she said, 'and I'll second the motion.'

But for the moment neither of them could do anything except grumble, which Emmeline did every time Octavia came to visit, all through the fortnight. She was still grumbling when the two young men suddenly appeared in her garden. It was a quiet sunny afternoon and she and Octavia had been taking tea beside the fishpond, with the new baby asleep in her bassinet beside them and Dora and Eddie playing on a rug in the shadow of the apple tree. And without a word of warning there they were, striding across the lawn, looking tanned and foreign, carrying a lot of odd shaped parcels and smiling as if they expected a welcome.

'Good heavens above!' Emmeline said. 'Look what the cat's brought in!'

''Lo, Sis!' Cyril said. 'We've brought you some presents. There are some super things in Italy. Look at this, Dotty Dora. This one's for you.'

'And this is for you,' Tommy said, standing in front of Emmeline and bowing to her in his old-fashioned way. 'Sweets to the sweet!' And he handed her a box of bonbons. It was tied with an elaborate striped ribbon and looked rather grand and very foreign, with its odd colouring and its strange curlicued writing. 'First present we bought, wasn't it, Cyril.'

'What?' Cyril said, and then noticed that Tommy was giving a hint. 'Oh yes, I suppose it was.' But it was plain to Octavia that he didn't mean it because he was fidgeting with eagerness to give one of his presents to Dora, who was clinging to his legs and bouncing with excitement.

'Well thank you very much,' Emmeline said, opening the box. 'It's very kind of you, Tommy. I didn't expect presents. Oh look at these lovely sweeties, Eddie. Shall we have one? Or shall we keep them until after dinner?' If Ernest had been at home there would have been no choice. The box would have been put away at once, sternly, and temptation removed. But because it was mid-afternoon and he was away at work, they could do as they pleased. She pinched one of the little chocolates to see if it was soft centred and as it was popped it into the little boy's mouth. 'Try that. It's delicious.'

'This one is for you, little Dotty Dora,' Cyril said and handed her one of the odd shaped parcels.

Being a sturdy two-year-old, she insisted that she could open parcels 'Misself!' and did so, although very slowly and with some difficulty. The toy that emerged from the wrapping paper was worth the struggle. It was a camel made of rough sand-coloured cloth with black button eyes and thick fur eyelashes, wearing a splendid saddle caparisoned in crimson and gold.

'He's come all the way from Venice,' Cyril told her. 'Do you like him?'

'Much,' the child said and flung her arms round her uncle's neck to prove it.

The lawn was littered with wrapping paper, for there were presents for everybody, even the baby. All three children had muslin dresses from Milan, Eddie had a hobbyhorse from Rome, the baby, who had slept through homecoming and present giving and all the noise and movement around her, snug in her bassinet, was given a wooden rattle 'for when she got bigger'.

'And this is for you,' Tommy said, handing his last parcel to Octavia.

It was very soft and felt squashy under her fingers, so she knew it was cloth of some kind, but for a second she felt too confused to open it. From the moment he'd come striding into the garden looking so handsome and carefree, she'd been torn by such conflicting emotions that she hadn't been able to find a word to say. It was wonderful to see him again. She was flooded with love for him, aching with it, but she was cross with him too. He ought to have taken *her* on holiday with him, not Cyril.

Even if he'd been minding the conventions, which *was* possible, she had to admit, he should at least have asked her and given her the chance to make up her own mind about it. He was sensitive enough when it came to Emmeline's feelings — she'd actually been quite touched by the way he handled Squirrel, so the least he could have done was...

'Open it, Tavy,' Emmeline urged. 'Don't keep us in suspense.'

'Go on,' Tommy said. 'Open it. It won't bite you.'

It was a paisley shawl, rather old-fashioned and intricately beautiful, woven in shades of pink, lilac, buff and smoke blue and heavily fringed.

'Lots of colours,' Tommy said, 'so it'll go with anything.'

'It's gorgeous,' she told him. And that was nothing less than the truth. 'Thank you very much.'

'Cyril got a kiss for his camel,' he teased her.

'That,' she told him steadily, 'is because Dora is two and can kiss whom she pleases.'

'I thought you were unconventional.'

She was recovering her balance by then and could tease. 'Only in matters political.'

'Well now,' Cyril said, 'what shall we do with the rest of the afternoon? Tell you what, let's go on the Heath. I haven't been on the Heath for two whole weeks, I hope you realise.'

'And who's fault's that?' his sister said sternly. 'You shouldn't have gone rushing off all over Europe.' But she agreed that a walk in the fresh air would do them all good and went off at once to summon her nursemaids and have the new perambulator prepared for the baby. 'Button boots for Eddie and Dora, if you please, Mrs Greenacre, and their reins of course, and we'll take the old perambulator to get them there.'

They left the house in procession, first the nursemaids pushing the two prams with the bonneted toddlers sitting in one and baby Edith now wide awake in the other, then Emmeline and Cyril, walking together in an almost friendly way, and bringing up the rear, Octavia, in her splendid new shawl with Tommy beside her. As they reached the end of the street, he offered her his arm, daring her with those dark eyes, and since it was a family outing, she took it.

They dawdled until they were out of earshot of the others. 'Have you missed me?' he asked.

'Now and then,' she said lightly. 'I've had a lot to do with the Cause and Emmeline and everything.'

'I've missed you every single day,' he said. 'It's super seeing you again. I haven't kissed you for months, I hope you realise.'

'Two months, one week and three days,' she said, 'to be accurate.'

'Rebuke taken,' he said. 'You're a corker, Tavy. Supper tonight?'

'Come on you two slowcoaches,' Emmeline called. 'Catch up. We're going to see the swans.'

So they saw the swans, and Cyril took off his shoes and socks and rolled up his trousers and took Eddie and Dora paddling in the ponds, while Em fed the baby in the discrete shade of a tree, and they found a 'Stop me and Buy One' and bought ice creams and Sno Frutes, and both the children got extremely sticky, and Em said she couldn't think what their father would say if he could see them.

'Just as well he can't then,' Cyril said. 'Eh, Tavy?'

'Oh,' Em said, 'this is such fun!'

'I've thought of a good wheeze,' Cyril said to his sister when the heath had been trodden to exhaustion, and they were wandering slowly home again. 'What d'you say we all go down to Eastbourne for a seaside holiday like we did in the old days? You and me and the babies and Tommy and Tavy. And Podge too. He could come down at weekends. All of us. My treat. High time you had a holiday, Em. Swimming, donkey rides, that sort of thing. How would you like that, little Dotty Dora?'

'You've just had three years' holiday,' his sister said. 'Not to mention a fortnight in Italy. Life's one long holiday with you.'

'It'ud be fun,' he urged. 'You'd come with us, wouldn't you, Tavy?'

'Yes,' she said. 'I'd love to.' Which was true, especially if Tommy was coming with them. 'But you'll have to let me pay my way.'

'And you too, Tommy?'

'Rather!' Tommy said, grinning at Tavy. 'With the same proviso of course. I'm all for donkey rides and Pierrots on the pier and all that sort of thing.'

'A holiday!' Emmeline said longingly. 'Do you think Ernest would allow it? I haven't been away from home since I got married.'

'Tell him it will be good for the children,' Octavia said practically. 'He might be glad to see the back of them for a week or two.' And it would do them good to get away from *him*, poor little things.

So it was agreed and the impromptu holiday was booked. In fact Cyril wrote to their old landlady that very afternoon and posted the letter on his way home.

'There you are,' Tommy said to Octavia as he drove her back to South Park Hill. 'Five weeks holiday together. What could be nicer?'

'Five weeks holiday alone together,' Octavia said. 'We shall be ankle deep in babies and nursemaids. We shan't have a second to ourselves.'

'Leave that to me,' he said. 'I've got plans.'

'What sort of plans?' she asked. He had the most devilish expression on his face.

'You'll see,' he said.

So THEY ALL went on holiday, Em and the babies and the nurse-maids by train with Podge and Cyril to escort them and to lift the prams out of the guard's van, and Tommy and Octavia following in his car with any bits of luggage that hadn't been sent by 'passengers luggage in advance'.

Emmeline said a five week holiday was such a luxury that she couldn't believe it. The boarding house was smaller than they remembered it, so small in fact that when Tommy arrived he unpacked the bags, took one look at the room he'd been allocated and drove off at once to find a bigger room for himself in a hotel, pointing out that Cyril always took up ninety per cent of the space in any room he occupied and that he'd got to leave some room for Podge. But apart from this unaccountable shrinkage, nothing else had changed at all. The donkeys were still there, standing in the same patient lines on the beach or stolidly plodding the same well-worn hundred yards of sand, the band played its usual afternoon medley in the bandstand, and the Punch and Judy man still set up his stall at the top of the beach, this time to squeals of delight from Dora and little Eddy. And the weather was superb. Even when there was a shower, as there was that first afternoon, the rain fell quickly and thickly and then passed on, and the sun was so strong that the promenade was dry again in minutes. All three babies took to their new seaside existence as though they'd been born under water; their nursemaids were there to watch over them while their Mama slept in a deckchair; Uncle Squirrel was much in demand for sandcastles and treats; and Uncle Podge, fourteen years old and blushingly diffident in his school boater and a new striped blazer, was a willing slave for piggybacks and paddling. Within that first day a pattern had been established that suited all of them. Or nearly all of them.

On the second afternoon, Tommy announced that he needed a nice brisk walk. 'Can't sit around all day,' he said. 'I need a bit of exercise or I shall get stout.'

'Oh!' Emmeline said, squinting up at him from her deckchair. 'Do you want us all to come with you?'

'Good lord no,' he told her. 'You stay where you are and have a rest. Cyril'll look after the babies, won't you, Cyril? Tavy'll keep me company. We shan't be gone long.'

They climbed to the top of Beachy Head, where a strong breeze was blowing and they could see for miles along the coast. As soon as they were on their own and out of sight of the path, he put his arms round her waist, pulled her close and began to kiss her.

'Sweet,' he said, holding her ardent face between his hands. 'Sweet! Sweet! Sweetheart!'

'Am I?' she asks, drowsed with the joy of being kissed again.

He stroked her lips with his mouth, languorously, enjoying the delicate touch as much as she was and delighted to see that he was making her tremble. 'Of course.'

The breeze was so strong it pushed her old straw hat right off her head and pinned her new summer dress immodestly tight against her legs. But she didn't care. It was a beautiful, richly-coloured, dizzying, magical September day and she was so happy to be back in his arms that she wouldn't have minded if she'd been swept off her feet. Which in one sense she was.

'Oh, my darling Tommy,' she said, when he lifted his head to look down at her. His eyes were dark with desire and so beautiful she had to shut her own eyes for a second to shield herself from their impact.

'Good to have me home?' he asked, knowing the answer.

'Wonderful.'

'Have you missed me?'

She was too caught up in sensation to tease or prevaricate. 'Yes.'

The breeze threw a giggle of voices towards them. 'There's someone coming,' she said, pulling away from him.

He smiled at her, pretending to be annoyed but still holding her round the waist. 'Drat!'

'No, hush!' she said, removing his hands. Two bonnets were

bobbing into view on the slope of the hill followed by a rather splendid striped boater. 'We must be sensible.'

'I don't see why,' he pretended to complain. 'If we were in Paris on the boulevards we could kiss whenever we wanted to and nobody would raise the slightest objection.'

'But we're not in Paris,' she said, pulling her hat onto her head again and walking on. She had to push against the wind and her dress flicked behind her like a sail.

'More's the pity,' he said, walking beside her and doffing his hat to the newcomers. 'Tell you what. How would it be if we went down to the Grand for an hour or two? We could be really private there. I've got a capital room.'

The suggestion made it difficult for her to breathe. 'Do you mean — stay there with you?' she asked. She couldn't say what she was really thinking. She hadn't got the vocabulary. But they both knew what he was proposing. This was what he'd meant when he'd told her he'd 'got plans'.

'Well not overnight, naturally,' he said, smiling down at her, enjoying her flushed cheeks and startled eyes. 'That *would* put the cat among the pigeons. But we could go there in the afternoons, when we're supposed to be out walking. Don't worry, it'll all be perfectly proper. You won't get nasty looks or anything like that. They're expecting my wife to join me. I told them as much when I booked.' And when she gave him a quizzical look he explained, 'Had to, old thing, or they'd have wondered why I wanted a double room. I said you were looking after your cousin — well that bit's true at any rate — and you'd join me when you could. It's a nice room. You'll like it. Just right for a Mr and Mrs. There's a sea view and everything. I've got you a ring to wear so it'll all be perfectly proper.'

'No it won't,' she told him seriously. 'It'll be a lie. I could put any number of rings on my fingers but it wouldn't mean anything. We're not married.'

'No,' he said equally and passionately serious. 'We're not. But if you come with me now, we'll be something better. We'll be lovers.' And since the strollers had disappeared over the brow of the hill, he pulled her towards him and kissed her long and lovingly. 'You will, won't you, Tavy? Oh my lovely, lovely Tavy, you will.'

It wasn't sensible, or proper. The sensible thing to do would be to wait until they could get married and have a wedding with flowers and bridesmaids and interminable speeches like Em... (oh for heaven's sake, like Em!). This was foolish and dangerous and unconventional. Oh wonderfully, exhilaratingly, temptingly unconventional. 'Yes,' she said. 'I will.'

He held her so tightly he made her breathless all over again. 'You won't regret it,' he said. 'I promise you.'

The walk to the hotel was slow and amorous for they were arm in arm and stopped for kisses whenever the street was clear. And it was a very grand hotel indeed, with a uniformed doorman and a hall porter to give them their key and a curved flight of softly carpeted stairs to lead them the way.

'Heavens!' Octavia said, as they walked into the room. It too was thickly carpeted and very luxurious, with a pretty washstand, an enormous bed, beautifully curtained windows overlooking the sea, everything a visitor could possibly want or need. It was so richly decorated that at first glance, it looked more like a rose arbour than a room. There were roses everywhere, patterning the carpet and the curtains and the wallpaper, stencilled on the washstand, arranged in a plump vase on the little round table by the window in all their natural beauty. 'What luxury! It's downright decadent.'

'And so it should be,' he said. 'It's our love nest.'

She took off her hat and threw herself backwards onto the bed, sinking into the softness of it. 'Heavens!' she said again. 'It makes my bed at Mrs Norris' feel like a plank.'

'Sleep with me,' he promised, removing his blazer, 'and you shall have feather beds for the rest of your life.'

CHAPTER 11

'Have you seen the news this morning, Tavy?' Cyril asked. He was sprawled in his usual deckchair in his usual place on the beach, basking in the last of the September sun, with his feet propped up on Dora's tin bucket. 'Right up your street.'

'We don't want to be bothered with news,' Emmeline told him, handing the baby back to Mrs Greenacre. 'We're on holiday.'

Octavia held out her hand for the newspaper. She was languid with love, sprawled in her own deckchair and feeling as if she could sleep for a month, but something in his mocking expression told her that this was news she ought to know.

'*Suffragettes in Birmingham being force fed,*' the headline said. She was instantly alarmed and read on, thinking, what do they mean 'force fed'? How can you force someone to feed? The article gave her more information but it didn't answer her questions.

It was confirmed in the House of Commons today, it said, *that several of the nine suffragettes in prison in Winson Green in Birmingham have been force fed. The announcement came in response to a question from Labour MP James Keir Hardy, who was told the Home Office authorised the action to prevent the women killing or harming themselves through self-starvation.*

Oh what nonsense! As if they'd do a thing like that!

'Was I right?' Cyril said.

'Yes,' Octavia said shortly. 'You were. I must write to Mrs Emsworth and find out what's happening. It sounds terrible.'

He was grinning at her, almost as if he was gloating. 'They're treating 'em rough,' he said, 'and not before time. Serve 'em right. Now perhaps they'll see sense and stop making a nuisance of themselves.'

'They're standing up for the right to vote,' Octavia told him crossly. He really was very obtuse. 'It's a matter of principle and they're being extremely brave.'

'That, dear coz,' he said, 'is a matter of opinion. Some people would say they're being extremely stupid and making a nuisance of themselves.'

'Then some people would be wrong,' Octavia said. 'Oh come on, Squirrel, be fair. Men have the vote so why shouldn't we?'

'Because you're women, old thing,' Cyril said. And yes, he *was* gloating.

'Where's Tommy this morning?' Em said, intervening before this could develop into a row. It was much too pleasant out here on the beach for anyone to be quarrelling. 'He *is* a slugabed. He'll be late for lunch if he doesn't come soon. The sun's high already.'

'He's on the promenade, ma'am,' Mrs Greenacre said. 'Waving.'

As he was, and after a few long legged strides he came crunching down the pebbles towards them.

'Where have you been?' Emmeline said. 'We've been worrying about you.'

'No you haven't,' Cyril corrected her, determined to make mischief one way or another. 'You said he was a slugabed.'

'Been to London, old thing,' Tommy said. 'Bought myself a flat.'

'What, there and back?' Emmeline said, blinking in disbelief. 'All that way? This morning?'

'Drove like the clappers,' he told her. 'Aren't you going to ask me about the flat?'

So they asked him and he unfolded a deckchair, sat down in it and told them. It was in Kensington, no distance from the tube station, unfurnished, 'so I shall have to look slippy and see to that before October' and not particularly well decorated, 'so I suppose I'd better see to that too.' But the views were top hole and there was a garage for the car and restaurants all over the place and Hyde Park just over the road and he could get to the West End and back in seconds, so all in all he thought he'd got a bargain.

'I thought you were going back to Bucharest,' Cyril said rather sourly. 'I can't see the point of a flat in London if you're living in the embassy in Bucharest.'

'Got to have somewhere to come home to, old thing,' Tommy told him easily. 'Place of my own and all that sort of thing. I shan't stay in Bucharest when I'm on leave.' And he turned his head to smile at Octavia.

The little movement wasn't lost on Emmeline. So I'm right, she thought. They *are* walking out. She'd suspected it ever since that second afternoon and now she was sure. He'll ask her to marry him and they'll live in the embassy while he's working and come home to the flat when he's on leave. Very sensible. 'It all sounds splendid,' she approved. 'I shall expect to be invited to tea as soon as it's ready for occupation.'

'And so you shall be,' Tommy promised.

Octavia didn't comment. That could wait until they were alone together. She was glad to think he'd got a flat and that he intended to come home when he was on leave and live in it, but she didn't think much of wasting their last few days together choosing furniture.

'Tell you what,' Tommy said, 'let's have fish and chips for lunch to celebrate.'

'Chip!' Dora said rapturously.

So that was settled, although Emmeline said she didn't know what Ernest would say if he could see how they were all going on.

LATER THAT AFTERNOON, when Octavia and Tommy were lying relaxed and easy in their comfortable feather bed, she asked him if he was really going to spend time rushing about buying furniture. 'We've very little time left now,' she said. 'I don't want to waste a minute.'

'No more do I, little Tikki Tavy,' he said, kissing her hair. 'And no more we shall. That was just a cover to fool your cousin. Once we're all back in London I want them to think I'm fully occupied. Don't worry. I've been to Waring & Gillows and picked what I wanted and they're going to deal with it. And I've hired the decorators. It's all taken care of.'

It sounded decidedly civilised — if a trifle devious. 'Oh Tommy,' she said. 'I do love you. And I shall miss you.'

'Don't let's think about that now,' he said. 'Time enough when the time comes.'

But it was rushing down upon her like an express train, all unpleasant noise and obscuring steam and unnecessary speed. In four days their interlude in Eastbourne would be over and she would be back at home; in just over a fortnight he would be on the boat train and on his way back to Europe. There were moments even in those last few joyous days by the sea when she thought she couldn't bear it.

In their last week, they spent as much time as they dared in his grand new flat and when the final miserable day arrived she went to Victoria station to see him off and kissed him lovingly as he leant out of the window of the train. It was certainly improper and she was probably making a spectacle of herself but she was too anguished to care.

'I'll write to you,' he called as the train creaked him away.

She ran along the platform, so that she could keep sight of him for as long as possible. 'Every day!' she called.

'Promise,' he called back. 'See it wet, see it dry.'

His first letter arrived the very next morning, written in Calais and at length, telling her how much he loved her and how much he missed her and promising that he would cadge a few days leave as soon as he could.

I might not be able to get back to London, he wrote. *But I could wangle a day or two in Paris and you could meet me there, couldn't you?*

Oh yes, she could. She would. And wrote back by return of post to tell him so. Then and rather guiltily she walked to the WSPU shop to find out what was happening to the prisoners in Winson Green. She'd never written that letter to Mrs Emsworth and now she felt ashamed of herself for such an oversight. It wasn't like her to forget things.

What she heard was horrific. 'They'd gone on hunger strike,' Betty Transom reported, 'and apparently the Home Office decided they'd got to be fed whether they would or no, so this is what the authorities are doing. They tie them to a chair and push a rubber tube down their throats and pour the food down it.'

Octavia was appalled. It was disgusting, obscene. 'What sort of food?'

'Soup I suppose,' Betty said. 'Mushy things. It would have to be wouldn't it, or they'd choke them.'

'It's barbaric,' Octavia said. The mere thought of it was making her heave. 'Bad enough to think of such things but to actually go ahead and do them. We're supposed to be one of the most civilised countries in the world and we do this! Words fail me.' But now that she'd started asking questions, she went on until she'd heard the whole story. 'Why were they on hunger strike?' she asked.

Mrs Emsworth knew the answer to that. 'They'd been down-graded,' she said, 'from category A to category C, which means no books or writing paper, as you know, among other things. So they made a formal protest, pointing out that they were political prisoners and should be treated accordingly and when that was ignored, they refused to eat.'

'And now they're being tortured,' Betty said. 'Because that's what it amounts to, doesn't it. The group in Birmingham say they're really ill.'

'I'm sure they are,' Octavia said. 'We must write and tell them how much we support them and admire them.'

'We write every other day,' Mrs Emsworth said and there was rebuke in her tone. 'We've done it ever since they were sentenced.'

'Of course,' Octavia said, and was ashamed of herself again, thinking, I was speaking out of turn. Naturally they've written. As I would have done if I'd been here. 'Do you know when they are likely to be released?' she asked, trying to be helpfully practical. 'Perhaps we should send a deputation to greet them. What do you think?'

THEY ARRIVED HOLDING flowers and wearing their most impressive clothes, neat and bright in the sooty darkness outside the prison gates. A pervasive rain was falling and the October sky was wintry.

'I hope they'll be on time,' Betty Transom said. 'My feet are like ice already.'

But the appointed hour arrived and passed and nothing happened. They were joined by two more groups of women and a quiet couple with a pale young man in tow, who arrived in a cab, which was told to wait, and they all stood together on the cobbles, side by side for warmth, their breath pluming before them in the chill air.

'Why are prisons so grim?' Betty Transom said, looking at the blackened walls and that forbidding oak gate.

'They're designed that way,' Octavia told her. 'They're supposed to deter us.'

And then suddenly a small door in the forbidding gate was inched open and there they were, four pale women, holding on to one another and advancing towards them, very very slowly. They gave them a cheer and walked towards them equally slowly with their flowers outstretched and offered. The pale young man was the first to reach them and now Octavia saw that he had a notebook in his hand and realised that he was a reporter. 'Mrs Ainsworth?' he said. 'Mrs Laura Ainsworth?'

One of the prisoners detached herself from her friends and answered him. 'Yes,' she said. 'I am she. I haven't the energy to stand for long but if you would care to come home with me I will tell you all you need to know.' She was trembling but impressively calm.

I hope I can behave like that when my turn comes, Octavia thought, because it would come, sooner or later. She couldn't put it off forever. But the sight and smell of the prison was deterring her where she stood and she wasn't at all sure how resolute she would manage to be when she was put to the test. Or how strong.

· · ·

THAT NIGHT when she was back home after her two long journeys, she wrote a letter to Tommy describing everything she'd seen and analysing everything she'd felt. It was rather a disappointment when his answering letter hardly mentioned what she'd said. But she forgave him when she read the PS.

I shall be in Paris on Saturday week, for three days. I told you I'd swing it, didn't I? Write and let me know what train you are catching and I'll be at the station with bells on. Can't wait to see you again. Txxxx

To see him again, and so soon! It was wonderful news. Oh wonderful! But it presented her with a problem. A trip to Paris had to be explained to her parents and she could hardly tell them she was going to visit Tommy, much less that they were going to stay in a hotel together. They were broadminded, but not that broadminded. She would have to think about what she told them and chose her words very carefully. But however she phrased it, the explanation was bound to be a lie. And oh she did so hate the thought that she would have to tell lies. This is what comes of loving someone, she thought. It makes you dishonest. Or perhaps I ought to say this is what comes of loving someone in a society that won't accept a loving couple unless they are married. If you ever heard of anything so illogical.

In the end she told them she wanted to go to France to meet up with a group of suffragettes who were staying in Paris. Her mother was most concerned.

'All that way, Tavy,' she queried, 'on your own? Do you think that's wise?'

'I shall be met at the station,' Octavia said. That much was true at any rate.

'So you may be, but it's a long journey. What do you think, JJ?'

Fortunately her father thought it was a capital idea. 'Paris is no distance these days,' he said. 'You go, my dear, and enjoy yourself. Just don't go getting arrested.'

'No Pa,' she said, bowing her head in mock obedience. 'It's not that sort of meeting.'

'No,' he said, grinning at her. He had a really devilish grin sometimes. 'I rather thought it wasn't.'

So she travelled to Paris on her own and was met at the Gare du Nord by a beaming Tommy, who pulled her into his arms and kissed her, there and then, out in the street and nobody seemed to mind. He'd been right about that, she thought. But then he was right about so many things, her dear, dear Tommy. They spent the next three days visiting the city, arm in arm and stopping to kiss whenever the spirit moved them, as it often did, and the next four nights making luxurious love. By the time they parted again at the Gare du Nord, she felt as if she'd been with him for weeks.

'When can we come here again?' she asked, as she climbed into the train.

'As soon as I can wangle it,' he promised.

'I do love you,' she said.

'Likewise,' he told her.

I COULD HAVE STAYED HERE FOREVER, she thought, as the train rattled her through the Parisian suburbs. But there was work to be done in London and she couldn't and shouldn't avoid it, much though she wanted to at that moment.

The debate about violent protest had been fanned into a rage by the forcible feeding of the hunger strikers. In October the now renowned Laura Ainsworth took the prison authorities to the High Court and although she lost her case, it was rumoured that there was going to be an enquiry into the whole business of forced feeding. In November, a group of militants broke into the Lord Mayor's banquet and threw stones at the assembled worthies.

'It is the wrong tactic,' Octavia said, over and over again at one meeting after another. 'We lose public sympathy every time we are violent and we need public sympathy if we are to prevail. I know the authorities are being extremely violent to us, but we should show our supporters a better way than throwing stones and hurling insults. We must go on pressing for proper democratic change, and that must come eventually through a bill in Parliament. We cannot bully our enemies into giving us what we want.'

Many agreed with her, but they all knew that something would have to be done to persuade the men who made the law and drafted the bills and none of them could think what it could possibly be. Mr Keir Hardy, MP, was the staunchest of allies but there were times when he seemed to be the only one. 'He's a voice in the wilderness,' they said sadly.

If it hadn't been for her infrequent visits to Paris, that winter would have been a very difficult time. She spent four days there at the end of November, when mist rose from the surface of the Seine and the city was dank with rain, and nearly a week in the middle of December, when the streets were brilliantly lit, the shops were crammed with Christmas treats and the pavements crowded with elegant shoppers, the women snuggled into fur trimmed coats and hats like Russian Cossacks, the men in well-cut overcoats and leather gloves, escorting them in and out of shops and hotels, gallantly attentive. She was glad to be in their company. 'They look so cultivated,' she said to Tommy.

'Like us!' he said, putting his arm round her as they walked along. 'You, my lovely Tikki Tavy, are the most cultivated woman in the city.'

His lightness of tone sustained her. When she was with him, she could joke and flirt, as if the world were an easy, comfortable place, and no one had ever thrown stones or smashed windows or been spat at or force fed. It was only in London that she had to be serious all the time. And as the months went by there was more and more to be serious about.

The New Year brought a piece of rather alarming news. It was tucked away in the middle pages of the newspaper and she wouldn't have seen it at all if she hadn't been scanning the pages for a report on the latest WSPU meeting.

'Britain could face a serious shortage of horses should war break out, it was reported yesterday. The National Horse Supply Association was told that 170,000 would be needed immediately on the outbreak of hostilities, the same number being replaced every six months. Germany and Austria spent £200,000 each annually on horse breeding, Britain less that £5,000.'

'Have you read this, Pa?' she said, passing the paper across the breakfast table.

He glanced at it and said he had. 'There was something similar in *The Times* yesterday.'

'It sounds as if they are expecting a war,' she said. 'That's not right surely.'

'We live in an age of empire, little one,' he said, 'and empires are belligerent by their very nature. They are won by armed force, don't forget, and maintained by occupying armies.'

'But there's no reason for us to want to fight anyone now,' she persisted. 'Surely to goodness. We're the biggest empire in the world.'

'All the more reason,' he told her. 'The biggest empire has the most to lose.'

It was a sobering thought. I shall write to Tommy, she decided and see what he has to say about it.

It upset her that he seemed to agree with her father.

I daresay we shall put up a fight sooner or later, he wrote. *Not to worry your head about it. If it comes, it comes. I shan't be in Paris*

until May but then I've got a whole fortnight's leave. Good or what?
I'll take you to Versailles and show you the Sun King's palace.

Which he did and very charming she found it. 'The French are so civilised,' she said. 'They're not talking about a war coming.'

'Everybody's talking about a war coming,' Tommy told her lightly. 'You should hear them in the embassy. It's all they ever do talk about. That and the warring tribes. I can't tell you how boring it is. Don't let's waste *our* time on it.'

Fortunately the newspapers gave them something else to talk about the very next day. King Edward VII was dead. 'Well how about that!' Tommy said. 'I hope they let us home for the funeral. I shall put on a black tie and look sorrowful and ask them. It's about time we got back to our flat, don't you think.'

The black tie and sorrowful expression paid off. This time it was a month's leave and he came straight back to London to enjoy it. 'The king can die any time he wants,' he said to Octavia on their first afternoon in the flat. 'It suits me to a T.'

'I'm sure he did it to suit you,' she teased. 'All the papers keep saying what a diplomat he was.'

'Come to bed,' he said.

IT WAS a summer of good meals, family picnics on the river with Cyril and Em and the three children, frequent and cheerful visits to the theatre, occasional sorties out into the country on their bicycles, and all of it spiced with the most passionate and satisfying lovemaking. By this time Em was speaking quite openly about them 'walking out' but Octavia didn't mind. She explained to her cousin, privately of course, that she and Tommy had got to be patient because they couldn't marry until he'd finished his apprenticeship and naturally Em passed on all her news to her mother, who naturally passed it on in her turn to her sister Amy.

'I knew there was something in the wind,' Amy said to JJ. 'All those letters he keeps writing. And now he's home there's never a day goes by when they're not together. He'll be speaking to you soon, JJ, I shouldn't wonder.'

Her husband made a grimace and returned to his newspaper.

'Maybe I'll say something to Tavy,' Amy said. 'When she comes in tonight.'

But when Octavia came in that night she was bursting with such good news she couldn't wait to tell them what it was. 'They've formed a conciliation committee, Mama,' she said. 'Isn't it wonderful.'

'Who have?' Amy asked. 'What for?'

'Why, the MP's,' her daughter said. 'They're going to draft a women's suffrage bill and Keir Hardy's going to steer it through the commons. It's going to be called the Conciliation Bill. We're going to get the vote at last!'

'I couldn't get a word in edgeways,' Amy said to JJ as they were preparing for bed. 'I don't think I've ever seen her so excited.'

The excitement was short lived. Despite Keir Hardy's most passionate efforts the bill was defeated. And so was the second a year later, and the third, when Em was expecting her fourth baby, a year after that. The movement was more demoralised than it had ever been and Octavia more angry. It was no surprise to her when a group of furious women stormed into Oxford Street on a mad March day with hammers hidden in their muffs and smashed as many plate-glass windows as they could before they were arrested.

I know so exactly how they feel, she wrote to Tommy. *I never thought I'd say this but I could do it myself.*

But of course the result of their actions was a police raid on the headquarters of the WSPU and the arrest of Christabel Pankhurst and the Pethick Lawrences. They were tried for conspiracy and sentenced to nine months.

Sometimes I think the whole world has gone mad, Octavia wrote, *for such people to be sent to prison as if they were common criminals is tantamount to lunacy. To say nothing of the way the government is treating the miners and the dockers. They are making it a crime to ask for a living wage. Is it any wonder there are riots?*

The one bright moment in that crazy spring was the arrival of Em's fourth baby. It was another little boy, born on March 20th and as pale and fragile as his brother Eddie. She called him Richard and even though she was wearied by his birth was instantly enamoured of him. 'Dear little man!'

As there was no hope of seeing Tommy again until the summer, Octavia spent a lot of time with Emmeline and her brood during the next three months. Dora was now a pretty little girl who had her fifth birthday four days after her new brother's arrival and was given a special party by her mother because she'd been so good. Eddie was still pale and undersized for a child who was nearly four and had a decidedly nervous air but he loved his Aunty Tavy and crept happily into her lap for stories whenever she appeared. And as to baby Edith she was so plump and cheerful it was a joy to see her.

'Four babies,' Octavia said to her cousin, who was sitting on her sofa with the new baby across her knees and Edith cuddled against her side. 'You're like the old woman in the shoe, Em.'

'Who had so many children she didn't know what to do,' Emmeline laughed. 'I feel like her sometimes, especially when they're all crying. But I love them so much I wouldn't be without them.'

'They were your dream,' Octavia said.

'And the Cause was yours,' Emmeline said. 'How oddly dreams turn out, don't they. They seem so easy and straightforward when you're young but when they come true everything's so complicated it's a different matter altogether.'

'Mine is a bit of a nightmare sometimes,' Octavia admitted. They were talking so openly to one another that a confession was possible. 'We've been campaigning for such a long time and we're no nearer to getting the vote than we were at the beginning.'

'Don't you ever want to give up?' Emmeline asked, stroking the baby's downy head. 'Leave it all behind you and marry Tommy.'

'No,' Octavia said. She was quite certain about it, bad though things were. 'We must go on now. There's nothing else we can do.'

'Even if it means being sent to prison and force fed?'

Octavia's heart contracted at the thought but her answer was steadfast. 'Even if it means that.'

'You're very brave,' Emmeline said. 'I don't think I could stand it. It must be terribly painful.'

'You've had four babies,' Octavia said. 'Now that's what I'd call brave. And painful.'

'Having babies is natural,' Emmeline said sagely. 'It *is* painful — very painful, I'll grant you that — but when it's over you soon forget it and you've got a baby to show for it. Being force-fed isn't natural by any stretch of the imagination. That's the difference. I couldn't stand somebody doing that to me.'

And I will have to, Octavia thought. I can't go on avoiding action forever.

CHAPTER 12

The moment Octavia had been dreading arrived so unobtrusively that it had begun and the whole terrifying chain of events had been set in motion, before she was aware enough to realise it.

It was a blustery morning in March, not long after baby Dickie's first birthday and she and Betty had gone up to London to help at the national headquarters, as they often did when there were committee meetings there and one or the other of them had been delegated to attend. They'd been the first to arrive that morning and had settled down to work at once while they waited for the others. Betty had gone straight into the inner office to do some filing while Octavia stayed in the outer office and started to open the mail. She was slitting open the second letter when an odd fluttering movement caught her attention and, turning her head, she saw that there was a sparrow frantically trying to get out of the upper window, throwing itself at the unyielding glass over and over again, its wings in perpetually baffled motion.

It must have been shut in all night, poor thing, she thought, and she took her chair over to the window to climb up and let it out. It was in such a panic she was afraid it would do itself a mischief before she could release it, so she pulled her clean handkerchief out of her pocket, shook it out, and after a brief struggle managed to catch hold of the bird and soothe it until it was still. She could feel its heart beating wildly through the white cloth, poor little thing. 'Hush! Hush!' she said, speaking to it as if it was a baby. 'You'll be free soon. I've got you.' It wasn't easy to hold a bird with one hand and open a window with the other and she was still struggling to lift the sash when she heard footsteps and voices coming up the stairs towards her.

'There's one of them!' a man's voice called. 'Look there, sir!'

And another said. 'You girl! Get down! Get down at once!'

Alarmed by the noise, the sparrow tried to struggle out of her handkerchief. 'Don't be stupid,' she said, aiming her words at the speaker but not taking her eyes from the bird. She was irritated to be called a girl, which she most certainly was not. 'I shan't fall. I'll get down when I've got the window open and let this...'

'She's throwing something out the window,' the voice said. 'Grab her legs!'

Then everything happened at once and in an odd disconnected way as if time had been fractured. The window gave and she pushed it up at last and eased the bird out into the air giving her handkerchief a shake to set it free; someone seized her legs — how dare they! — she was being pulled backwards off the chair and kicked out instinctively to disentangle herself from his objectionable hands and stop herself from falling. She was aware that there were other women in the room, and that one of them was asking, 'Do you have a warrant for this intrusion, Officer?' And she looked down and found she was staring into the reddened face of a policeman. He was rubbing his ribs so her kick had obviously landed. Good!

'You're under arrest,' he said.

She was appalled. 'What on earth for?'

'Obstructing a police officer in the execution of his duty. Go an' see what she threw out the winder, Fred. It could be evidence.'

The idiocy of the man! 'Try not to be more of a fool than you look,' she said. It was probably risky to speak to him like that but really, he *was* asking for it. 'It was a sparrow. That's all. A bird. I was...'

He didn't believe her. She could see that from the mocking expression on his face. 'You wanna watch your lip, young lady,' he said, and his tone was threatening. 'You got a lot too much to say for yourself, you ask me. Won't do you no good, all this argy-bargy.'

The words were as insulting as his expression. She had to fight back the urge to hit him again. But she could see Betty standing in the doorway, slightly out of focus, shaking her head and miming that she shouldn't say any more, and she hesitated long enough to notice what was going on around her and to feel angry at that instead. One of the policemen was scooping all the letters off the table into a sack and another was collecting all the leaflets. Dear God! she thought, we're being raided. I *have* been arrested. But really it was too absurd.

The second constable tossed the last of the leaflets in the sack and stepped up to take her by the arm. She still felt bemused and aggrieved at what was going on but she followed him almost obediently. It was pointless to make a fuss at that stage. It would all be resolved when they got to court and the magistrate heard what she'd actually been doing. She might even get an apology.

She got six weeks, for resisting arrest and attacking a police officer. It was totally, hideously unfair. The objectionable policeman made a great to-do about his 'bruised ribs' and the magistrate didn't believe a word she said. Afterwards, sitting in the Black Maria as she was driven away to Holloway Gaol, she tried to make sense of what had happened, but it was as if her mind had been switched off, like one of the new electric lights, as if she'd been suddenly plunged into darkness. There was a terrible inevitability about what had happened, almost a pattern, linking the frightened bird beating its wings against that high window, to the prisoner she had become crouched in her cell with its own high filthy window and its chokingly remembered smell, beating the wings of her mind, endlessly and uselessly against the injustice of it.

She had been admitted as a category C prisoner, with no rights, no books and no means of writing, told that she would work sewing mail bags, that she was allowed to write and receive one letter a week and warned that they 'wouldn't stand no nonsense from her'. Then she was left on her own. Trying to be practical, she decided that her first letter must be to Tommy. She knew she ought to send a message to her parents, because they were bound to be anxious, but he was expecting her in Paris at the end of the month, and would have to be told that their plans had been changed. The trouble was that she had no idea when she going to be allowed to write it and that made her feel bleak and lost. Oh Tommy, she thought, what a long way away you are. Then since there was no one there to see her, she put her head in her hands and wept. It was weak of her but she couldn't help it.

The conflict began that evening when a tray full of unappetising food was pushed through the flap into her cell and she told the warder, very calmly and politely, that she wasn't going to eat it. 'I am a political prisoner,' she said, 'and should be treated as such.'

The warder wasn't impressed. 'You eatin' it or ain'tcher?' she said.

Octavia's hands were shaking but she spoke firmly. 'When I am reassessed as a category A,' she said, 'I will eat my meals. Until then I will not.' And she repeated her reason. 'I am a political prisoner and should be treated as such.'

'You're a blamed fool,' the warder said, 'and you'll live to regret it. If you won't eat, you won't. We give yer four days, that's all. Then you'll pay fer it. Don't say I didn't warn you.'

They were four increasingly anxious days during which Octavia sewed the mail bags they'd given her, as well as she could which was extremely clumsily because the sackcloth tore her fingers, wrote a long careful letter to Tommy telling him what had happened, and tried not to think about the horror to come. On the third day she felt so hungry she had pains in her stomach and on the fourth the pains were so bad it was all she could do to sit up, let alone sew. And the next day they would feed her by force.

This is a fearful place, she thought, as the room darkened and the fourth night began. And so cold. It's March outside but it feels like January here. There were perpetual frost flowers on the high window and the small square of sky was the sort of dirty grey that usually led to snow. She was shivering even though she'd gone to bed in her clothes and was lying with her blanket tightly wrapped round her. Up and down the corridor, feet tramped and stamped, keys rattled and the women were banging the walls with their mugs, ting, ting, ting, sending their nightly defiance into the chill air, like a tinny Morse code. 'We are here! You might have locked us up but we're still here.'

She slept very little that night and when a grey dawn finally lightened the window she was wide awake and terribly afraid. I don't want to be here, she thought. I want to get out and walk in the fresh air and breathe to the bottom of my lungs. I want see Tommy again. Oh Tommy, Tommy, I do miss you and it's such a long time since we were together. Weeks and weeks. She pulled the memory of that last time into her mind, aching for comfort, remembering how they strolled along the Boulevard St Michel arm in arm, stopping for coffee and croissants at one of the little cafes, spinning out the time until they could take possession of the room he'd booked for them. Oh the aroma of that coffee!

The sharp rough smell of the French cigarette he was smoking. The sharp rough scent of his skin as he pulled her towards him to kiss her. Oh Tommy, Tommy. But the remembered ache of desire was no proof against her present terror. She was in a place dedicated to punishment and about as far away from the tenderness of love as it was possible to get and she was so afraid that her stomach was shaking. She knew exactly what was going to happen to her and that nothing she could say or do would prevent it, apart from giving in to them and eating, which wasn't an option. It was a matter of principle. She had to make her stand the same as all the others had done. Being force-fed was almost part of your imprisonment these days. If only she wasn't so terribly aware of what it would entail.

By midday her fear was so extreme it had swollen her tongue and blocked her ability to think. The long unexplained waiting was making everything worse. She couldn't speak to them now even if she wanted to. The only thing left was to endure. So that is what she did, all through the afternoon and into the evening, trying to control the shaking and to ignore the pangs of hunger that were knifing her stomach. Supper was pushed through the door at her as usual. She didn't eat it, as usual. It was taken away. The waiting and the pains went on.

And then just as she was beginning to hope that they'd forgotten all about her, there was a clatter out on the corridor, the cell was unlocked and within seconds was full of strange people crowding her view — two warders, one she recognised, three men in dark suits, a skivvy in an apron and someone else behind her standing in the shadows. They smelled of sweat and vomit and their faces were hard, their eyes glaring. They hate me, she thought, and her stomach shook again.

'This is yer last chance,' the strange warder said. 'Make yer mind up to it. If you won't eat we'll 'ave ter feed you by force.'

'No good talking to 'er,' the second warder said. 'She's a hard case. Best get on with it.' And before Octavia could speak or think, they all moved at once, coming at her from all directions. She was pushed into her chair and gripped there as though she was in a vice. Her legs were tied to the legs of the chair with a rough towel, her arms pulled back and bound behind it. She tried to twist her face away from them but they were too strong for her. One grabbed her head from behind, pulling it backwards as though he wanted to break her neck. 'Keep still!' he ordered when she struggled again. 'Keep still or it'll be the worse for you.'

Then they were pushing a sheet of rubber under her chin and she could see the instruments of torture being held above her, the long rubber tube that would be pushed down her throat, the clamp that would hold her jaws apart. Oh dear God, she thought, I can't bear it.

They paused for breath, looking down at her, their faces full of that dreadful hatred. One bent to look at her mouth. She wondered if he was a doctor. He looked as though he might be, in his fine suit and waistcoat and that clean white shirt. She noticed that he was wearing expensive cufflinks, that his hair was well cut, his nails manicured. A doctor. Surely not. Would a doctor be so cruel?

'Open your mouth,' he said.

She shook her head, clenched her teeth, prepared herself to fight.

He repeated his order. 'Now come along,' he said, talking down to her as though she were a naughty child. 'You don't want your teeth broken, do you?'

She tried to swallow and couldn't because her mouth was too dry. Will they really break my teeth? she thought. They looked as though they could. Would it be better to open my mouth and just get it over with? Indecision made her lips tremble and seeing the involuntary movement the doctor had his fingers on either side of her jaw at once, pressing and forcing. Her mouth opened even though she struggled with all her might to prevent it and the clamp was wedged in place so tightly and brutally that it made her bleed. She could taste the blood in her mouth and instinctively tried to lick the wound but her tongue was held down and she couldn't move it. The tube was forced between her lips, past the clamp and down her struggling tongue. It made her retch, and at that it was withdrawn a little and forced again. This time it was pushed into her throat. The pain of its pressure was excruciating, the smell of rubber filled her nose, she was screaming inside her throat but she couldn't make a sound, she retched again, heaved to vomit, arched her back, but they were holding her, pushing at her, forcing their hideous tubing down and down. For a second she felt herself sliding away into unconsciousness, then another searing pain pulled her back to awareness. They were pouring something down the tube, something hot and evil smelling. It was in her throat swelling the tube, in her nose, falling hard and hot into her stomach. She was struggling for breath now and mortally afraid. They will kill me, she thought.

They held the tube a little higher, looking down at her, and she managed to pull some air into her lungs. Then they resumed the torture, pouring their abominable liquid into her silent screams. Oh stop! Stop! Or I shall die.

It went on and on without pause or pity. She retched and groaned but they paid no attention to her. When they finally pulled the tube from her throat, she was totally exhausted and in so much pain she didn't notice as they untied her fetters, gathered their instruments and left. She slid from the chair to the concrete floor and lay there panting and retching, unable to move. Even when she was sick — and she was *so* sick — all she could do was turn her head to one side and wait for the vomiting to subside. She felt as if she was heaving up her heart.

She lay on the floor for a very long time, drifting in and out of consciousness, sore and sick and defeated. The room darkened. After a while, the sounds of the prison impinged on her senses, a door banged, feet clumped along the walkway, someone was shouting, and she was reminded of where she was. She got up with a great effort, moving slowly like an old woman and crept to her bed. All she wanted to do was to lie down and sleep.

But once she'd fallen onto her unyielding mattress, sleep was impossible. Thoughts buzzed in her brain as the hours passed achingly by. She wondered if they'd done her any lasting damage. There were traces of blood in her vomit. She could see them even in the half-light. But there was nothing to be gained by wondering about it. If they had injured her there was nothing she could do about it. It's done, she thought, it's over, and the thought encouraged her. I've stood up to them. I've lived through it. They haven't won.

But she was wrong. It wasn't over. They left her alone for three more days, offering food, which she refused, and water which she drank eagerly, while the pains in her stomach became a dull perpetual ache and the agony in her throat eased from knife sharpness to a painful prickling as if she'd been grazed.

Then, and with the awful suddenness she remembered from the last time, the trolley was rattling outside her door and the torture team were in the cell and binding her arms and legs. This time she had less energy to fight them, although she struggled as hard as she could, desperate to avoid that searing pain. This time they pushed the tube into her throat with such force that blood rose into her mouth and spilled out onto their abominable rubber sheet. This time they left her barely conscious and she took a long time to come round. I can't bear it, she thought, as she crawled back onto her bed and tried to wrap herself in the blanket. If they're going to do this to me every four days for the rest of my six weeks, I shall have to give in. She tried to work out how long she'd been inside, but her brain wasn't functioning and she couldn't do it. More than a week, certainly, but less than a fortnight. I can't bear it, she thought. Please God don't let me be tortured any more.

There was a key rattling in the door. Oh God! Now what are they going to do? But it wasn't the trolley. It was the doctor with the neat hair and the manicured hands, followed by the warder with the hard face. He walked to the bed and took her chin in his hands. 'Open your mouth,' he said, and then a little more kindly. 'It's all right. I'm not going to feed you.'

She opened her mouth, fearfully and painfully. He produced a torch from his pocket and shone it down her throat. 'Yes,' he said. 'Discharge.' Then he and the warder turned away from her and left.

Her heart was juddering with alarm. What did he mean, 'discharge'? Had her wounds turned septic? Was that what it was? And if they had shouldn't he be doing something to treat them? She understood enough about wounds to know that if a septic wound was left untreated you could get blood poisoning and die. Oh dear God, what is going to happen to me now?

What happened was that the fierce warder arrived in her cell the next morning carrying her clothes. 'Get dressed,' she said. 'You're being discharged.'

It was agony for Octavia to speak but she croaked a question. 'Do you mean I'm going home?'

'Not that you deserve it,' the warder said. 'But yes. Doctor's orders.'

Tears were rolling from Octavia's eyes. Home, she thought. The very word was a comfort.

THEY RELEASED HER THAT AFTERNOON. There was even a warder to help her totter through the gate. And there was her father, her dear, dear father, standing on the cobbles looking out for her, rushing forward to take hold of her as she stumbled towards him.

'Oh my dear child,' he said, his face creased with concern. 'What have they done to you?'

She was in too bad a state to tell him. It was all she could do to put one foot in front of the other. She had to concentrate because it was so difficult. She was numb to everything except the searing pain in her throat and the utter relief of being out of that awful prison. As the cab rattled them home, she had so little energy left that the first jolt made her fall against his shoulder and, at that, he put his arm round her and kissed her hair and told her she was a good brave girl. It shamed him to realise that he was the one who was weeping and that she was dry-eyed.

Amy had been watching anxiously from the parlour window and came out at once, even before the cab had come to a halt, to ease her poor wounded daughter into the house. She was horrified by what she saw and swept into furious action. Octavia was put straight to bed with a hot water bottle at her feet and the blinds drawn to encourage her to sleep: Mrs Wilkins was despatched to make a pot of tea, with plenty of sugar, and a good beef broth for later: then having attended to her poor patient's immediate needs, she phoned the doctor.

He arrived within the hour and examined the now sleeping Octavia very gently, noting the bruises on her arms and legs, her obvious loss of weight and the telltale shadows under her eyes. Then, apologising that he would have to distress her if he were to make a proper examination, he gentled her awake and put a spatula on her tongue so that he could see how badly her throat had been damaged. She retched and groaned but he examined her carefully notwithstanding.

'She is suffering from a badly lacerated throat and complete nervous exhaustion,' he said to Amy. 'She will need very careful nursing. Very careful nursing indeed. I have to tell you, Mrs Smith, that in all my years in the profession I have never seen a case so bad. Coax her to eat but don't worry her if she can't take anything more than tea. With care, she will improve by degrees.

Keep everything as mild as possible, jelly and junket, broth if it's strained. Plenty of water of course. I will look in again tomorrow, but phone me should you be concerned about anything.'

It was a long and gradual convalescence. To start with Octavia spent most of her time asleep, relieved to be back in her own comfortable bed in her own familiar room. She ate what she could, although even eating a junket felt like swallowing needles, and from time to time she tried to speak. But her voice was so husky her mother couldn't always understand what she was trying to say.

'Rest, my darling,' she said. 'Save your poor voice. It will come back more quickly if you don't use it.'

So the days passed into weeks and the weeks were endured for a month. Tommy sent her several letters but although they asked how she was, they were mostly about the *warring tribes* and what utter fools they were and how *they ought to have their stupid heads knocked together* and she set them aside. She would write to him when she had more energy.

One morning her mother arrived in her bedroom with a vase full of freshly cut lilac. The heavy double-headed blossoms filled the room with the fragrance of spring. 'From the garden, my darling,' she said.

Octavia was talking by then, although her voice was still croaky. 'Is it spring?' she asked.

'Come to the window and see,' Amy said. 'I'll get your dressing gown.'

It was like a return to life, to sit in her chair by the window and look out at the garden, at the cherry tree foaming with white blossom and the grass so green and the borders dappled with wallflowers, all bright reds and yellows and purples and browns.

'Oh!' she said. 'It's so good to be home.'

Returning strength reminded her that she had friends — and a lover — who ought to be told how she was. That afternoon she sat at her desk and wrote to them all, to Mrs Emsworth and Betty reporting on her return to health, to her friends at the shop describing the conditions in Holloway Gaol, because she knew that was what they would want to know, and to Tommy to tell him she'd been released from prison and was back at home. She decided not to say anything to him about the forced feeding. There would be time enough for that when they were together.

I am sorry I have not written to you before, she said, *but letters were restricted, as you probably know.*

Then she added a postscript.

PS I can't wait to see you again.

His answer was rather odd. He was glad she was out of gaol and at home again but he couldn't say when he would be eligible for any leave.

Since the Balkan league decided they'd stop killing each other and attack the Turks instead, the situation has been extremely complicated. Warring tribes and all that. Now there is talk of a possible conference to be held in London, some time in May, which the Powers fondly imagine will solve all problems here. Personally I take leave to doubt it. However, the upshot of all this warmongering and manoeuvring is that we are all kept hard at it preparing reports on the current situation and until the conference has sat to everyone's satisfaction all leave is cancelled. I wish I could say otherwise but that is the situation.

The businesslike tone of the letter upset her. She needed tenderness and loving messages or at the very least an assurance that they would meet as soon as it could be arranged and this brusque talk of warring tribes and conferences made her feel bleak. For several days she left his letter unanswered, while she came downstairs and took her first breakfast at the family table, went for her first short walk on the Heath, sat up late one evening to play Bezique with her father, and finally had tea with Emmeline and her little ones who had walked across the heath to visit her and were overjoyed to be allowed into her bedroom to see how she was.

'You must be very good and not trouble your Aunty,' Emmeline warned them as they climbed the stairs.

But Octavia held out her arms to them as they peered round the door and soon they were all sitting on her bed and feeding her crumbs of madeira cake and she was laughing and saying she felt like a baby bird.

From then on she felt stronger every day. She took to reading the papers to see if anything was being said about Tommy's conference and, once she had started reading again, rapidly regained her appetite for news and information, to JJ's delight.

'On the road to recovery, my little one,' he said.

She agreed that she was although in one respect she knew she would never recover. For what she had been facing during the weeks of her convalescence was the fact that she was a coward. She knew beyond any doubt at all that she couldn't go back to prison and face being force-fed ever again. Somehow or other she would have to find a way of putting herself beyond the reach of any more lawbreaking and the only way she could think of was to take a job, something that would pay her a wage and expect her loyalty in return, or at least her presence at a workplace every day. If she did that, she simply wouldn't be available for any more civil disobedience and couldn't break the law even if she wanted to. Eventually she mentioned it to her father.

'What would you say if I told you I should like to go to

work?' she asked, keeping the question as light as she could make it.

'There are plenty of positions you could occupy with your qualifications,' he said. 'What do you have in mind?'

She didn't really have anything in mind. Just a job. But pressed she admitted that she might be able to teach.

'There are plenty of positions available at the moment,' he told her. 'It's the time of year for new staff. I will look out some of the advertisements for you. Were you thinking of university or school?'

She said 'school' because a university post might be more than she could manage in her present state. So school it was.

Four days later, when the papers were full of the London conference that was going to solve the conflict in the Balkans, she had her first letter asking her to appear for an interview. Eight days later she had been hired to teach in a London elementary school. It was all remarkably easy. It occurred to her to wonder what Tommy would say when he heard about it, but as his letters had grown shorter and more distant as the weeks has passed, she didn't write to tell him. Something was wrong but she didn't have the energy to find out what it was. It could wait until they met again, she thought — and wondered, sadly, if they ever would. How much your life can change in a short time, she thought. And it was a short time. March to the beginning of June. Oh Tommy, Tommy, she mourned, if only I could see you again. I don't know where you are or what you're doing. If only you weren't such a long way away.

CHAPTER 13

Tommy Meriton was sitting at his desk in his ornate office in the British embassy in Bucharest, with his feet on a velvet stool, his backside on a velvet chair and a pen idle in his hand, trying to think of something to say to Octavia. All he'd written so far was '*Here I am, still among the warring tribes*' and then he'd had to stop because he'd run out of inspiration. What he really wanted to do was tell her what a bore it was to be stuck out here in the Balkans but that was out of the question. It wouldn't be the done thing, as he was a member of the embassy, not diplomatic and all that, and in any case he was beginning to suspect that she wouldn't be interested. She rarely answered what he told her, and if she did it was in an offhand sort of way. In fact there were times when he was beginning to think that their affaire was over and he'd have to find someone else. Which would be easy enough. She ought to think of that sometimes. The world was full of women and most of them had beds. It wasn't as if he didn't put himself out to say the right thing when he was writing to her. All that rot she'd told him about some silly woman who'd thrown herself in front of the king's horse at the Deby and got herself killed. Emily Something-or-other.

What did she imagine would happen? Stupid woman. Four pages she'd written about that and he'd made a really good fist of answering. Said how sorry he was and how sad. Perfect diplomacy. Couldn't have bettered it. So it wouldn't hurt her to pay attention to what he was telling her for a change. Was that so much to ask?

He sighed, feeling weary and sorry for himself. In three minutes, he thought, checking his watch, Frankie Marlborough is going to stroll in through that painted door, adjust his eyeglass and ask me if I'm ready, and then I'll have to leave this and go off to some God-forsaken battle ground somewhere and write some God-forsaken boring report about it. Supposed to keep an eye on what's happening. And how the hell can we do that? How could anyone, when it's just a collection of stupid warring tribes settling old scores and grabbing up as much land as they can get away with and taking revenge on one another under cover of driving out the Turks. All that rot about the London Conference and how their precious armistice would bring a lasting peace and what happens? Lasts three weeks and then they all start up again and now we've got to have another stupid conference here. I've no patience with 'em. They're all as bad as one another and someone should move in and bang their stupid heads together.

Frankie Marlborough's predicted head appeared at the door, eyeglass and all. 'All set?' he asked. 'Ready for the off?'

It was a long journey and although the first part was pleasant enough because they were travelling by train across the gentle plain south of the Danube, when they reached Sofia they were in much more hostile territory, surrounded by bleak mountains that loomed in upon them in a brooding darkness and poorly dressed men who glowered at them with suspicion. A chauffeured car and an interpreter were waiting for them outside the station, but neither were encouraging. The car was an ancient black saloon which looked as though it would be jolly uncomfortable, the interpreter a bearded man with a wall eye, who spat a stream of chewed tobacco onto the pavement before he greeted them and then spoke at length but so incomprehensibly that neither of them could understand a word he said.

'This is a damned fool idea,' Frankie Marlborough complained as they rattled out of the town, 'chasin' about the country in the middle of the night. We shall be black and blue before we get there, you mark my words, and our interpreter's a fool and it'll all turn out to be a wild goose chase, same as it was last time. Three dead soldiers and a pile of guns. Game ain't worth the candle. I don't know why we bother.'

'I wouldn't mind so much if the geese were to fly over better terrain,' Tommy said. 'Don't they have *any* roads in this country?'

'Ain't seen one yet,' his friend sighed, 'and I've been here a sight longer than you have. We'll stop for supper in a little while.'

Supper was unpalatable, darkness impenetrable, the roads they were travelling now little better than dirt tracks, and the car was murderously uncomfortable and extremely cold. It would have been better if they could have settled to sleep but sleep was as impossible as the terrain and after several grumbling hours even breathing was difficult. After a while, it smelt as if they were driving through a bonfire and when they looked out of the window, they could see clouds of smoke and a distant dance of sparks.

'What is it?' Tommy asked the interpreter.

He shrugged. 'Is Turk. No good.'

'We'd better take a look,' Frankie decided. 'It might give us something to report back.'

So THEY STOPPED THE CAR, found their torches, checked their revolvers and set out to reconnoitre.

They were in a narrow country lane and once they were out of the car they could see that there were fires burning about half a mile away. Houses by the look of it. Or huts. No sound of gunfire but they could hear the crackle of the flames. 'Approach with caution,' Frankie ordered.

It was a village of sorts, or what was left of it, and even before they reached the burning houses it was obvious that there'd been butchery there. The earth path was heaped with slaughtered cows, lying stiff-legged in dark congealing pools of their own blood. One was still alive, although her belly had been ripped open. She mooed plaintively at them as they passed and struggled to stand. Now they could see the outline of a church immediately ahead of them and more dark shapes lying on the ground, smaller shapes, sheep maybe? But the light of their torches revealed that these were not livestock but children. Little girls lying spreadeagled where they'd been dropped, their rough clothes torn and bloodstained.

'Christ Almighty!' Tommy said. Little girls no older than Dora and Edith, raped and murdered. What sort of people would do a thing like this? As he turned his torch he saw that one of the poor little things had had her throat cut. She was drenched in blood. The smell of it was overpowering.

'Christ Almighty!' he said again. 'Christ Almighty!' Horror had stripped him of the power of speech. He was stuck with that one disbelieving oath, repeating it over and over again. He'd heard about rapes and murders, naturally, there were always rumours and some of them pretty lurid, but until that moment it had just been words. Not this. Oh God, not this! Then the gall rose into his throat and he had to turn aside to be sick.

Frankie walked on, the beam of his torch wavering before him, a small white light among the lurid red and sulphur of the flames. The church seemed to be steaming. There was a grey-white vapour rising from the roof and the west door was badly burnt and, as they discovered when they tried to open it, locked from the outside. It took their combined strength to turn the key and neither of them spoke because they could smell the horror that was waiting for them inside.

The place was full of charred corpses, lying against the remains of the pews, piled on top of one another, old men, toothless and wrinkled, women with burnt hair, tattered children, barefooted and filthy with the grime of the fire. It was terribly obvious what had happened to them. They'd been herded into the church and burnt alive.

There are prayers you have to say for the dead, Tommy thought, but he couldn't remember them. His mind was stiff with shock and pity. He stooped to the nearest dead child and closed his eyes, gently as though he was still alive and could be hurt by the touch. Then he began to weep, hot angry tears of outraged pity for the suffering of these tangled corpses. The men who had done this were not mere warring tribes — thinking that was glib and silly. This was something much, much worse. These men were murderers, rapists, torturers, appalling, evil, cruel, despicable. If there was any justice in the world, they should be hunted down and shot like the mad dogs they were, an eye for an eye, a split skull for a split skull, a death for a death. They should be shut up in another church and burnt alive like their victims.

The interpreter was standing beside him, chewing another wad of tobacco. How can he chew tobacco at a time like this? Tommy thought. 'Who did this?' he asked.

The interpreter shrugged. 'Turk. Yesterday they come through. Two, three days.'

'This is terrible,' Tommy said. It was inadequate and he knew it but he felt impelled to say something.

The man shrugged again. 'Is war,' he said calmly. 'Is what happen. They kill. We kill better. We kill much better. We cut throat, we take women.' Underlit by the torch, he looked as though he was gloating, his face brutal. 'We are Bulgar! We kill good.'

'He speaks as though such things are normal,' Tommy said as he and Frankie walked back to the car.

'They are,' Frankie said. 'These people are like animals. All as bad as one another. This won't be the last atrocity you'll see, you mark my words.'

'But even so…' Tommy said.

'Best not to think about it too much,' Frankie advised. 'Best just to write our report and get back to civilisation as quickly as we can.'

They wrote the report on the return journey to Sofia, using their torches to light the pages. By the time they were back in the embassy again it was mid-morning, they'd filtered the incident into diplomatic language and they were drained of all energy.

Tommy's letter to Octavia was still lying on the desk where he'd left it. The sight of her name made him ache to be in her arms, with a tearing, agonising yearning to be loved and comforted and as far away from this nightmare region as he could get. It was a powerful sensation and not one he'd ever felt before. Was it only yesterday that he'd sat at that desk writing 'Warring tribes' Dear God! How could he have been so naïve? Only yesterday and yet everything had changed. Standing there in that baroque office, he knew so exactly what he wanted and what he needed. It wasn't a series of easy conquests. Had he really thought that? How could he have been so trivial? That was petty and selfish. What he needed now was honesty and the chance to say what he truly felt, and the only person who could cope with that was his lovely, outspoken, determined Tikki-Tavy. He screwed the offending paper into a ball and threw it away. Then he wrote a simple message.

Sweetheart, I shall be in Paris as soon as it can be arranged. Please, please meet me there. I will write again with details as soon as I can. I cannot wait to see you again. I miss you more than I can say. Your ever-loving Tommy.

'I MUST GO TO PARIS, MAMA,' Octavia said, folding his letter and putting it neatly back into its envelope. Her mother raised her eyebrows so she felt she had to explain. 'My friends have invited me to stay for a while.'

'Oh dear!' her mother worried. 'Are you strong enough, my darling? It's a long journey. I wouldn't want you getting ill again.'

'It's a Channel crossing, Mama,' Octavia said. 'I might get a little seasick but no more than that.' The urgency of his letter was too obvious not to be answered. That and the revealing pressure of that redoubled plea. He needed her and that was enough. After all these months of wanting to see him and wondering whether they would ever meet again, after all those puzzling, distant letters, he'd written to *beg* her to come to Paris. She would go no matter what her mother said.

'But even so...' Amy said. 'You were so ill when you got back from that funeral. I wouldn't want you to suffer another setback.'

'It wasn't a setback, Mama,' Octavia said rather crossly. There were times when her mother's concern, loving though it undoubtedly was, could be decidedly trying. 'I was tired, that was all. It was a very moving occasion. We were all tired.' She was remembering her fatigue as she spoke, the ache behind her knees as the great cortege wound through the streets, the staring crowds lining the pavements, many of them moved to tears, the dizzying scent of the flowers they'd carried, the white lilies and purple irises, the impact of so many women all wearing the suffragette colours, and marching with such strength. She'd felt so proud marching behind the hearse in the place of honour with all the other hunger strikers, wearing her silver arrow for the first time. Her pride had carried her along, that and the strength she'd felt at being in such a powerful crowd, following such a courageous martyr. 'In any case,' she said to her mother, 'even if I was tired, it was the right thing to do. I wouldn't have missed it for the world.'

'I don't think you need to worry, my love,' JJ said to his wife, interceding before his two darlings could quarrel. 'As far as I can ascertain, the waiters on the cross-channel ferries are not yet force-feeding their passengers. Given a fair wind and a strong tide, I think she will be safe.'

'It is all very well for you to make light of it, JJ,' Amy rebuked him, 'but health is a serious matter.'

'And Octavia takes it seriously,' her father said. 'Do you not, Tavy? When do you intend to go?'

'In a few weeks I expect,' Octavia said. 'They will write and tell me.'

But the situation in the Balkans was so difficult that it was August 10th and after the Bucharest Conference before Tommy could wangle the leave he wanted so much.

How beautiful Paris is, Octavia thought, all those chestnut trees heavy with high summer and the city so at ease. Of course, it was the month of the *fermiture annuelle*, so it was deserted by its inhabitants and their usual bustle and left to the amble of visitors. The Gare du Nord was full of them when she arrived, most of them British, and as heavily laden as the chestnut trees, talking excitedly in their now foreign language. Outside in the sunshine along the Rue de Dunkerque, the touts and taxi cabs waited in line for their custom and the café tables were set out on the opposite pavement under their bright scarlet awnings primed to tempt them.

Their clarion colour was the first thing Octavia saw as she walked out of the station, sniffing the familiar air. The second was her darling Tommy, striding across the road, elegant in a cream summer suit, dodging the traffic and watching the road. Then he saw her and stretched out his arms towards her. It was such a yearning, loving gesture she ran to answer it, calling his name. It would have been hard to say which of them was more in need of the other. They tumbled into an embrace, oblivious to the smiles and nods of the passers-by, and clung together kissing hungrily. 'Oh my darling, darling Tommy!' 'Sweet, sweetheart!'

'How husky you are,' he said, surprised by the timbre of her voice. 'Have you taken a cold?'

She had grown so used to the change that she hardly noticed it. It was improving gradually and didn't really concern her. 'No,' she assured him. She would have to tell him what had happened to her, but eventually, not at that moment. 'I am quite well,' she said, smiling into his eyes. 'It is nothing. Kiss me again, my darling.'

So he ignored her husky voice and raised an imperial hand to call a taxi. They kissed all the way to the hotel, where they registered with such impatience that the receptionist could barely conceal a snigger and the concierge looked askance at them. And at last they were in their room and alone together and could satisfy the aching sharpness of their desire, this new, driving, painful desire to be loved and comforted. After such a rapturous greeting they knew it would be a blissful coming together. But it wasn't. It was a disappointment to both of them. He was too rough and too quick and was demoralised to have felt so little, she was left unsatisfied and puzzled. Worse, instead of lying lazily beside her and lighting his usual cheroot, he got up again and went to stand by the window where he looked down at the boulevard, stroking his moustache and frowning.

She sat up among the tumbled bedclothes. 'What is it, Tommy?' she asked. 'What's the matter?'

'This is such a beautiful city,' he said, looking at a fashionable couple who were strolling along the pavement below him, he suave and handsome in well cut grey and a jaunty hat, she tall and slender and dressed in style in a wide-brimmed hat, an elegant rose-pink suit with a long straight skirt and a belted jacket and the prettiest pointed shoes. It was a lifetime away from the mud and squalor of the Balkans. 'People look so — oh I don't know — intelligent I suppose, sophisticated, cultured, like people you can understand, people you can trust.'

'And that makes you sigh?'

'Yes,' he admitted and tried to make a joke of it. 'Potty isn't it?'

She left the bed, put on her glasses and joined him at the window, aware that there was more to the sigh than he'd told her. The sun streamed in through the casements to light the opulence of the room, the high bed, thick carpet, heavy furniture. It was such a solid unchanging room, a place to depend on, in a city they could trust. But her instincts roared that the world was changing for both of them. 'What *is* the matter, my darling?' she said.

He told her about the massacre, detail by appalling detail, speaking quietly and not looking at her, but gazing down at the boulevard, one hand resting on the heavy tassel of the velvet curtains. It wasn't how he'd intended to tell her but once he'd begun he had to go on until the whole horrible business had been described. She was so appalled by the horror of the things he was saying she listened without moving. 'Oh Tommy!' she said when he'd finished. 'That's dreadful.'

'War is the most terrible thing,' he said, turning to look at her at last. 'It brings out the hatred in people, which God forbid you should ever know anything about.'

'I know it already,' she said. And because it was exactly the right moment, she told him what had happened to her in Holloway gaol, at first speaking quietly and sensibly but soon growing tearful at the memories she was stirring.

He put his arms round her as she wept and they clung together for comfort. 'Don't cry, my darling,' he soothed. 'You're all right now. You're with me. I'll look after you. Oh my dear darling, don't cry.' He was roused to the most protective tenderness. How dare they treat her so? Torturing her and making her ill and husky. Oh how he loved that huskiness now. I shall marry her, he thought, kissing her tousled hair, I shall marry her and look after her. She can't go on facing horrors like that all on her own. He hadn't thought about marriage until that moment but it seemed the natural and obvious thing. He led her back to the bed and gentled her to sit down. He must start looking after her at once. 'Dear Tikki-Tavy,' he said. 'You've suffered enough for this cause of yours. Don't you think so? You must stop. You really must.'

They were being so honest with one another she told him the truth about that too, wiping her eyes and her glasses. 'I've stopped already,' she said. 'I've taken a job. I shan't have the time for demonstrations and hunger strikes. Or not so much time anyway.'

He approved. 'Well good for you.'

'No,' she said, sadly. 'It's not good. It's cowardly. I wouldn't tell anyone but you, but I'm afraid it's the truth. I can't face being force-fed again. I'm going to work so as to get out of the way.' She was torn by her cowardice, deeply, deeply ashamed of it. 'Things are going wrong, Tommy. It's only two months since Emily Davison died. Only two months. We had that wonderful funeral procession for her and there was such sympathy for us. I thought we'd made our point at last, that people understood what we were saying. But I was wrong. They're treating us like criminals again, Mrs Pankhurst is ill, Sylvia's in Holloway, we've had three suffrage bills put through Parliament in the last three years and they've defeated every single one. We haven't made any progress at all. I feel we're going backwards.'

He kissed her. 'And what is this work you've taken?'

'I'm going to teach in a National School,' she said. 'I start in September.'

A job's no bad thing, he thought. It doesn't matter why she's taken it, it'll keep her occupied and out of prison until I can leave Bucharest. 'I only have six more months to serve,' he told her, 'and then I shall come back to England and marry you. How would that be? At Christmas if you like, or in the summer. You've only to say the word. And then when I've got my next appointment you can come and live with me, wherever it is. It might by Paris. That would be all right, wouldn't it? What do you think?'

She was so surprised that for a moment she couldn't think what to say. If he'd proposed to her after that first amazing summer at Eastbourne, she would have accepted him without a second thought, but so much had changed now that she wasn't sure. She'd adapted herself to this disjointed life of theirs, accepted that he couldn't marry until his work and his father allowed it, grown accustomed to the deceptions that had been necessary to hide their meetings, even down to wearing a wedding ring. Most important of all, she was committed to teaching now. It would be unfair to take on a position at the school and leave it after a term. She steeled herself to tell him they must delay.

'I would rather wait for a couple of years,' she said. 'Until the summer after next perhaps. We don't have to rush things, do we?'

'Dash it all, Tavy,' he said, feeling rather put out, 'I thought you'd like to get married. Most girls do.'

'It's not that I don't want to marry you,' she explained. 'I do. Very much. I always have. It's just… If I marry, I shall have to leave my job — they don't allow teachers in National Schools to be married — and I'd like to do it for a little while at least. To prove that I can. We can go on as we are, can't we?' It was a genuine question because he was looking so disturbed she needed to be reassured.

'But you do love me?' he said and that was a real question too.

'More than ever.'

'And you'll marry me in two years' time?'

'Of course.'

'Always providing there isn't a war I suppose.'

That sounded alarming. 'There isn't going to be is there? I thought it had gone quiet. *The Times* said the London Conference had arranged an armistice.'

'I'm not talking about the Balkans,' he said. 'The armistice didn't work. They're fighting again already. It's all they ever do. No, it's not the Balkans.'

She was suddenly alarmed. What was he trying to tell her? That everything was worse than she thought? 'What then?'

'There could be a war between England and Germany,' he said. 'Our ambassador says he can see it coming. You must have heard rumours.'

She had, of course. Her father's dinner guests had talked about the possibility of it, and there'd been an article in *The Times* about how many horses would be needed if a war broke out — she'd been appalled at the huge numbers they'd estimated for — and when the old king died, all the newspapers said his diplomacy would be sorely missed and hinted that a war with Germany was imminent. But she'd assumed it was rumour and no more. People were always talking about wars of one kind or another.

She got up and walked back to the window, needing a pause

to get her thoughts in order. 'Yes,' she admitted. 'I have heard things. But it's only talk, isn't it? It can be avoided, surely.'

'There's no knowing,' he told her sadly. 'The Balkans is full of bloodthirsty maniacs and they're all scared stiff of one another so they've made alliances with every major power in Europe — Great Britain, Germany, Russia, the Austro-Hungarian Empire, everyone. It's a powder keg down there. It only needs a spark to set it all off. Anything could happen.'

Below the window the chestnuts shifted in the afternoon breeze and the taxis darted about like water beetles on the shining blue of the boulevard. 'Then we must hope it doesn't,' she said.

She looked so sad and bleak he was stirred to pity for her all over again, and pity triggered desire. 'Come back to bed, Tikki-Tavy,' he said. 'It wasn't good last time was it? I mean...'

It was so nearly an apology and so very unlike him to offer one she was quite touched by it. 'No,' she said. 'It wasn't but we've got a month to make up for it.'

'Starting now?' he hoped.

She walked back to the bed and stooped to kiss him. 'Starting now,' she said.

'Oh Tikki-Tavy,' he said. 'I do love you.'

CHAPTER 14

On that damp September morning when Miss Octavia Smith faced her very first class for the very first time, she knew at once that it was going to be a challenge. After three weeks in Paris with Tommy, which had been luxurious in every way, the sight of her pupils was a shock. It was a very big class, much bigger than she'd expected. Forty-two nine-year-olds, so the headmaster said. They stood ranged before her, two by two beside their narrow desks, nineteen boys and twenty-three girls, most of them filthy dirty and all of them standing bolt upright as if they'd been nailed to the floor.

The sight of them was daunting enough but the smell was worse. It was the first time in her life that Octavia had been nose to nose with the enclosed stink of poverty and she found it nauseating. The headmaster didn't seem to notice it. He introduced her, told the class to stand up straight or it'd be the worse for them, strode out of the room and left her to it, but she felt too sick to speak. She stood before her new charges, swallowing hard and analysing the smell as a way of forcing herself to cope with it. It was, she decided, a combination of ammonia, stale sweat, coal dust and rancid frying fat, with traces of unwashed bodies, smelly feet, filthy hair, and rain-damp clothes, most of which were reach-me downs impregnated with the work-stink of their previous owners. It was so strong it stung her eyes.

After a few seconds, she pulled herself together and told them to sit down, which they did noisily, their rough boots clomping on the floorboards.

'Now,' she said, making another effort and remembering to smile at them, 'I want you to take out your slates and your slate pencils and write down today's date. I've written it on the blackboard for you. There it is. Monday September the first, 1913.'

They obeyed her, some quietly, some grudgingly, and for a few minutes there was no sound in the room except for the scratch of their pencils. It's such an ugly room, Octavia thought, looking round at it. It reminded her of Holloway gaol with those green walls and those awful green tiles, and the windows were repressive in the same way, tall enough to let in plenty of light, but too high for children to see out of. She remembered Wordsworth's lines, 'shades of the prison house begin to close upon the growing boy/ but he beholds the light and whence it flows,' and was full of sympathy for her smelly pupils. Then she noticed that one of her growing boys was gazing round the room. It was the one with the squint and the shaven head.

'Have you finished?' she said to him, kindly.

He closed one eye and looked up at her. 'Yes, Miss.'

'Then bring your slate to me.'

He clomped to her rostrum and held up his slate for her inspection. He had drawn a line of loops.

'What's this?' she said to him.

'Please, Miss, it's me pothooks, Miss.'

A girl in the front row enlightened her. 'That's what he does, Miss.'

'All the time?' Octavia asked.

'Yes, Miss. He don't know nothink else.'

I must see about that Octavia thought as she sent him back

to his seat. Then she walked round the room to check what her other pupils had been doing. It wasn't encouraging. About a third of them had copied the date more or less accurately, the rest had made a stab at it and obviously hadn't understood what they'd been writing. 'Can you read that to me?' she asked one tousled haired girl.

The child twisted her apron in both hands. 'Yes, Miss.'

'Go on then.'

But it was beyond her. She just sat and stared at it and after a long pause she explained, 'Please, Miss, I got summink in me eye, Miss.'

She can't read and she can't write, Octavia thought. What a lot of work there is for me to do. I shall start with reading. If they can't read, they can't do anything. I must sort out which of them *can* read and which can't and then I shall start from the beginning and teach the backward ones their letters. Meantime there was a headmaster to obey — more or less — a timetable to follow and some rather peculiar lessons to be taught.

She looked down at the timetable, which she'd pinned on her desk to remind her of the things she was supposed to do, and wondered how on earth she would manage to do them. Half the subjects listed there were incomprehensible. What was 'drill' for example? The headmaster has written an explanation of sorts alongside the word — 'this is for the relaxation of mental strain' — but that didn't tell her what it meant. And what was free arm work? Or mechanical poetry? She had a vision of a tin robot barking out verse when she wound it up, probably with a drill in its free arm. And that made her want to giggle. 'Arithmetic now,' she said, to steady herself. That would be simple to teach if nothing else and it would give them a break from all that dreadful slate scratching. According to the headmaster, their arithmetic books were in the cupboard, or should be. 'Come up and get your book when I call out your name.' It was a long process but they didn't seem to mind and it gave her the chance to learn a few names. 'Now let us start with adding up. I will put ten sums on the board for you.'

As she'd expected, half of them could add up, more or less accurately, and half couldn't, even though they were counting their fingers and chewing their lips for all they were worth. She walked among them observing their efforts and feeling sorry for them. It didn't take her long to see what was wrong.

'Stop work,' she said to them, and waited until they were all looking up at her. 'Arithmetic can be difficult sometimes, can't it?' Much nodding. 'Very well. What I am going to do is to teach you a trick to make it easier.' She drew six boxes on the board. I must take this slowly, she thought, and give them time to digest it. So she began to fill in the boxes, very slowly and one figure at a time. 'One box for one figure,' she said. 'Do you see? As if we're putting them in little cages. They'll have to behave themselves if we put them in cages, won't they. There'll be no slipping away from us now. One box for one figure. Remember that. It's the golden rule for adding up. One box for one figure, tens on that side, units on this. There's our sum and there are the empty boxes waiting for our answer. Now open your books and look at the page. Can you see the boxes?' Some heads were shaking. 'No? Look again. They're there. It's not lines in an arithmetic book, is it? What is it?'

Several hands were raised at that and an answer attempted. 'Squares, Miss.'

'Well done,' she said. 'Quite right. It's squares. Lots and lots of little squares. Lots and lots of little boxes. All drawn up and ready for you to use. Can you see them now? Well done. Fill in this first sum and then we will solve it together.'

It was a quiet success. They hadn't all understood but many were working almost happily and there was far less lip chewing. Billy Pothook looked completely baffled but she was beginning to suspect that this was his perpetual expression.

If this is teaching, she thought, watching their small hands at work, I believe I can do it. Even if I don't know what drill is. The word leapt at her spitefully. It was the next thing on the timetable.

There was a disturbance at the door and a young man came in. He introduced himself as Mr Venables and said he'd come to show her the ropes. 'Hand in your books,' he said to the class. 'Who's the monitor?'

'Please, sir, ain't got one, Sir.'

'We'll choose someone after drill,' he said. 'Whoever's best. All stand.'

They obeyed, standing two by two beside their desks the way they'd done at the beginning of the morning, but they were looking sullen again. Whatever this drill is going to be, Octavia thought, they don't enjoy it.

'Arms in the air!' Mr Venables shouted. 'On the command — Up! Down! One two, one two. Put some more beef into it.' They raised and lowered their arms as well as they could and Octavia wondered if they'd ever eaten beef in their lives and decided it was unlikely.

'Sideways bends,' Mr Venables said. 'On the command, to the right. One, two, three. Left, two three.'

The robot bent left and right in Octavia's imagination and she remembered the nursery rhyme, 'Click, click, monkey on a stick,' and wondered why they couldn't go out into the play-ground if they needed exercise and simply play. Whenever suffragette marches had taken her through the East End, she'd seen riotous games going on in the street — hopscotch, tag, swinging on the lamp post. If they needed to use up some energy for — what was it the headmaster had written? — 'the relaxation of mental strain', what happier way to do it? Not that she could start arguing with the headmaster on her first day in his school.

It was a long day. Longer than she expected, for after the children had been released at four o'clock there were the next day's lessons to prepare, alone in her deserted classroom. She found the window pole and opened the high windows as far as they would go to let in some fresh air. And was annoyed to discover that she was letting in the smell of the local brewery.

'POVERTY IS ALL PERVASIVE,' she told her father at dinner that night. Even after a long soak in a warm bath and a thorough wash with scented soap, she could still smell the awful stink of her class. It must have got into her hair. 'When you think how they live and what shabby clothes they wear and how little they have to eat, it's a wonder they can concentrate on anything at all and yet some of them try so hard.'

'I believe you have found your cause, my dear,' her mother said. She was very relieved to think that her daughter had joined a profession at last. Of course, she would have preferred her to teach in a nice comfortable grammar school, but any kind of teaching was preferable to that awful suffragette movement, which was altogether too dangerous.

'Tavy will find causes all her life,' JJ said happily. 'It is dyed in the wool, is it not, Octavia? You must tell our Fabian friends about all this on Thursday. They will be deeply interested.'

As they were. But not until they'd talked about Bernard Shaw's latest play which was being premiered in Berlin prior to a London production in April. It was called 'Pygmalion' and was about a professor of phonetics who trained a flower girl to speak like a duchess and then passed her off as a member of society.

'And this from a man who would ban all schools,' Mrs Bland teased, 'and holds that education is evil incarnate.'

'So it is,' Mr Shaw agreed, beaming at her, 'for there isn't an iota of freedom within it either for teacher or taught. Education today is a matter of prescription and control, and that never did any good to anybody, which is what my hero discovers by the end of the play, when he has created his duchess and doesn't know what to do with her. I might add that she doesn't know what to do with herself either. It is all vastly entertaining.'

'But does it argue the need for educational reform?' Mr Bland wanted to know.

'It argues a good many things,' Mr Shaw said, 'and I daresay my audiences will discover even more argument in it than I intended, as they usually do.'

Octavia felt she could venture a question. 'Do you really advocate the closure of all schools, Mr Shaw?'

'Since most schools are instruments of social control,' the great man told her, 'in my opinion they are too harmful to be allowed to stay open. However few politicians would agree with me, I fear, other than the enlightened company around this table.'

The compliment was enjoyed with smiles and nods from all eight guests and their hosts. 'But if schools were closed, Mr Shaw,' Amy said, 'what would you put in their place?'

'Why nothing at all,' Mr Shaw told her. 'I would allow our children to run free.'

'Would you not be afraid that they might run wild?'

'That would be my most devout hope,' Shaw said wickedly. 'Every child has the right to run wild, the right to its own bent, the right to find its own way and go its own way.'

'But some sort of control surely...'

'Let me ask you a question, my dear Mrs Smith,' Shaw said. 'Why should one human being impose his view of life upon another? There is no justification for it beyond greed, profit and imperialism, all of which are intolerable vices. Nobody knows the way a child should go, except the child itself. All the ways discovered so far have led to the horrors of our existing civilisation, which no thinking man would wish to perpetuate. Very well then. If we are to change these horrors we must first make changes in the manner in which we educate our children. In my opinion we should give them autonomy and release them from the tyranny of the National Schools.'

'Octavia could tell you what is going on in a London National School,' Professor Smith told his guests. 'She started work in one this very term.'

'How very interesting,' Mrs Bland said, turning to Octavia. 'Is it as bad as Mr Shaw makes out?'

'Every bit,' Octavia said with feeling. 'We control them every minute of the day, poor little things.' And she told them about drill and mechanical poetry. 'They spend hours copying off the blackboard and hours chanting — prayers, tables, even poetry — and most of them haven't got the faintest idea what it all means.'

'Then change it!' Mr Shaw boomed.

'I intend to,' Octavia said.

'We will give you all the help we can,' Mr Bland promised. 'Will we not, Edith. Have you seen our latest pamphlet on education? No? Then I will send you a copy.'

'I will do better than that,' Mr Shaw said, all wickedness and bristling beard. 'I will give you my advice. If you seriously intend to change the system — and I must warn you that you will suffer for it if you do, for the establishment is deeply suspicious of any change that might curtail its own wealth and power — but if that is what you seriously intend, you must leave the National School, no matter how noble your work there may be, and transfer to a grammar school. That is where reform is most needed, because that is where you will find the next generation of teachers.'

It was sensible advice and very tempting. It would be wonderful to change a generation of teachers. 'I will think about it,' Octavia promised. 'But not yet. I must see the year through.' And after that I shall be married.

The table was ringed with approving faces, bright-eyed and soft-skinned in the candlelight. The conversation turned and continued; eloquent hands emphasised witty words; there was the occasional discreet flash of jewellery, the occasional waft of expensive perfume, wine winked as the decanter was lifted, the cloth was snowy white, the epergne hospitably laden with fruit. But Octavia was thinking of stained pinafores and reach-me-down dresses, of collarless shirts, dirty waistcoats, cut down trousers and the all-pervasive, shaming stink of poverty. What these children needed in their school lives was colour and a bit of fun. I shall draw a set of alphabet cards, she decided, and buy a lot of coloured pencils and they can colour them in and hang them on the walls. Big A, little a and a picture of an apple. That sort of thing. Then I'll see if I can find something that will be more fun for them to do instead of that awful drill.

The alphabet cards were a great success. 'Cor, Miss,' her pupils said. 'D'you mean we can colour 'em in all by ourselves?' and reassured that this was exactly what she did mean, they set to at once, faces bright with activity. It took a very long time. In fact the timetable was saying 'mechanical poetry' and they were still filling in outlines and admiring results. Eventually after much pencil licking, much happy chatter and some boldly peculiar colouring, they handed the cards in. 'Ain't we done 'em lovely, Miss,' they said.

Miss agreed and tried not to look askance at the purple horse. 'It don't matter do it, Miss?' the artist said. 'We run out a' brown an' that's ever so lovely.'

Even the headmaster admired the display and said it was a credit to her. She didn't tell him that she was allowing her pupils to walk about the classroom to 'borrow' pencils when they were colouring in, nor that she was telling them stories instead of reading from one of his dull school books, nor that they were playing skipping games in the playground instead of waving their poor little skinny arms about beside their desks. It was enough that he seemed to realise that she was teasing them into beginning to read.

'That's a C,' she said. 'Do you remember colouring it in? You did that one didn't you, Ethel? C for cat. And that's an aitch. Can you tell me what H is for?'

''Orse,' they said, happily. 'Haitch fer 'orse.' Confusingly purple and non-aspirant he might be but a horse he most certainly and recognisably was.

That night Octavia wrote a long letter to Tommy telling him what a revelation Bridge Street School had been and how much she was enjoying her new life there. He read it twice and found it rather alarming. All this talk of learning and teaching seemed a little too permanent for his liking. After all, it was only a stopgap until they could get married. He didn't want her getting used to it. That wasn't his idea at all, by Jove it wasn't. He wrote back carefully, saying it all sounded quite extraordinary to him, and adding *'I'm glad you enjoy it. That's the ticket.'* Then he spent the rest of the letter detailing arrangements for his Christmas leave. Not being able to see her in term time was a great disappointment and he meant to make the most of the holiday.

I've got a charlady coming in to heat the place up, he wrote, *so it won't be cold for us. I shall book tickets for all the best shows the first thing I do when I get back. You must tell me what you fancy. Can't wait to see you again.*

Then he added a postscript, just to make his feelings clear.

PS I hope you haven't forgotten me.

'*How could I?*' she wrote back. Although privately she had to admit that there were times in her teaching day when she hardly thought of him at all because she was giving so much attention to her pupils and the progress they were making. Worse, she'd barely given a thought to the suffrage movement either, certainly not since the term began. I must visit the shop, she thought, and see how they're all getting on. I haven't been near them since the funeral and that's months away. I suppose I ought to resign from the committee. She felt that she was deserting the Cause and that made her feel ashamed of herself. But of course it *was* what she was doing. It was why she'd taken the job. I owe them an explanation, at the very least, she thought. I shall go down and see them at the next committee meeting.

It was a delicately handled occasion, for she was being careful not to upset them by appearing to be critical of what other suffragettes were doing and they were mindful of the illness she'd suffered since she was released from that dreadful gaol and wanted to treat her gently.

'We're so proud of you, my dear,' Mrs Emsworth said, when they were sitting round the table in the committee room. 'To have run such a risk for our Cause is admirable beyond words.'

But there *were* words and Octavia had to speak them. 'I would be less than honest if I let you think I'm of the same mind now as I was when I was arrested,' she said. 'The truth is that being ill for such a long time has given me pause to think and I have to say I'm not at all sure that deliberately breaking the law and facing the punishment is the most effective way to further our Cause. In fact, I'm afraid we are losing the support of the public the more violent we become — and the more violent our opponents are towards us — and unfortunately public support is something we must have if we are to prevail.'

'But what else can we do?' Betty Transom said. 'We've marched our feet off and they don't take any notice, we've petitioned, we've written endless letters, what other way is there?'

Octavia had to confess that she didn't know. 'It must be democratic,' she said. 'I'm sure of that. It must be within the rule of law even though it's the law we want to change. I shall give it as much thought as I can, I promise, and I shall keep in touch with you all even if I'm not your secretary any more. I haven't deserted the Cause. I should hate you to think that. I shall march whenever the march is legal, and I shall write letters and sign petitions until my arm falls off. It is just that I can't break the law again.'

She was surprised by how sympathetically they understood. They are good women, she thought, as she walked home. They deserve the vote if anyone ever did and I shall do everything I can to make sure they get it. Then she felt she ought to correct herself, *that we all get it*, and was ashamed to realise that she had distanced herself from all these good women who had been her allies for so long. It was a relief to turn her attention to the next day's lessons.

THE AUTUMN TUMBLED her along in a chorus of letters learned. Soon it was November, London was muffled and snuffling in the first fog of the winter and gangs of scruffy children stood at bus stops and alongside underground stations with their straw stuffed effigies propped against the nearest wall, begging, 'Penny fer the Guy!' Octavia's new method of education continued and expanded. She drew a huge Guy Fawkes sitting on a bonfire and a display of exploding fireworks to stick on the wall above his head and her pupils coloured all that in too and sat enthralled while she told them the story of what happened to the real Guy Fawkes. By November 5th the class and the classroom were transformed.

'I think,' she said to her parents one fog-clammy evening over dinner, 'that I have found the secret of teaching.'

'That you must like your pupils?' her father smiled.

'That of course,' she agreed. 'Although I must say most of the teachers I've met so far don't seem to like them very much. They're always saying what a poor lot they are, which isn't true at all. They're lovely when you get to know them and so willing. No, the other secret, the one I'm talking about, is that it's no good just telling them things and shouting at them to understand, you have to coax them and make them laugh. You have to allow them to do things and to enjoy what they're doing. It has to be fun.'

Amy had been letting her mind wander as she usually did when the conversation turned academic but she caught the word 'Fun' and latched on to it happily. 'Just so long as you're enjoying it, my darling,' she said. 'That's the main thing. I wouldn't want you to do anything you didn't enjoy.'

'That's rather a sybaritic point of view my love,' JJ teased. 'Would you not be better to urge her to strive for striving's sake?'

'Striving is all very admirable,' Amy told him, 'but I don't see any reason why you shouldn't have fun while you strive.'

'My point exactly, Mama,' Octavia said.

'Changing the subject,' her father said. 'I had a letter from Tommy Meriton this morning. He wants to know if he can — now what was it he said? — *be granted an interview with me*, when he comes home on leave. You wouldn't happen to know what that's about, would you, Tavy?'

To her horror Octavia could feel herself blushing. She pretended to drop her napkin so that she could duck her head below his line of vision as she picked it up. For heaven's sake! She was acting like some stupid heroine in a romance. 'No,' she said, as calmly as she could, folding the napkin across her knees so that she could keep her head down and not meet his eye. 'Obviously something he wants to talk to you about.' And she tried a joke. 'Perhaps he's taking up mathematics.'

Her father gave her his most wicked grin. Really there were times when he was as bad as Bernard Shaw. 'Ah well,' he said. 'All will be revealed in time I daresay.'

· · ·

THE INTERVIEW WAS ARRANGED as soon as Tommy got home and JJ found it fascinating, if prolonged. He was intrigued to see this handsome, confident young man so obviously ill at ease, and to wonder what words he would use when he finally got to the point. He was taking long enough to get there in all conscience. They'd talked about the weather — endlessly — and some of the shows that were running in the West End, including the one he and Octavia were going to see that evening, and even the possibility of a war with Germany, which he said was looking extremely likely. Surely he should broach the main topic soon.

'I gather you had something rather particular you wanted to say to me,' he said at last.

'Yes, sir,' Tommy agreed. 'Rather.' But then words failed him and he sat silent, his hands on his knees.

'Something about Octavia perhaps?' the professor prompted.

'Rather. Oh I should think so. Yes indeed.' But he still couldn't say so and he was still looking at his knees.

'In my limited experience,' the professor prompted again, 'I believe the correct form of words is something in the order of *"I have the honour — or may I have the honour — of asking for your daughter's hand in marriage."'*

'By Jove, yes,' Tommy said, looking up in relief. 'I mean, rather. She's such a corker you know, sir, but she does need looking after, what with the suffragettes and everything. Not that she's weakly or anything like that. I'm not suggesting that. Far from it, as you know, sir. Very far from it. What I mean to say is I'd like to look after her, sir, being she's such a corker. I can provide for her and all that. Might have to live abroad now and then but she would live well, you have my word. Wouldn't want for anything.'

The thought of his darling living abroad stabbed at JJ's heart. 'So when were you hoping to marry?' he asked, carefully calm.

'Not till the summer, sir. August I hope. I'm taking up a new appointment in September. In Paris. But it depends on

Tavy. She wants to see the year out at this school of hers. Says she'll get the sack if she marries. Sounds absolute tosh to me but I daresay she's right. Anyway, she wants to wait until the summer. I'd marry her now if it were up to me. Like a shot. But there you are, sir, it's her decision, and I'm bound to honour it.'

There was a pause while both men wondered what should be said next. Then Tommy ventured. 'Do we have your blessing, sir?'

JJ smiled at his prospective son-in-law. 'Of course,' he said. 'If that is what you need. Although I would have thought good footwork might be an advantage too. Octavia is an affectionate young woman but her determination can be prodigious.'

Tommy grinned. 'I know, sir. That's why I love her. May I go and tell her now?'

JJ watched as the young man strode from the room. There was such strength in that walk and, now that he'd made his declaration, such happy confidence, as if his life were charmed. And so it is, he thought, if he's going to marry my Tavy. He could hear her running down the stairs and Tommy's voice murmuring to her. They are lovers, of course, he thought. He'd never seriously believed in Octavia's 'suffragette friend' who had to be visited so often and at such length and was never invited back to meet her parents, although he'd never admitted as much to Amy, who needed to believe it for her own peace of mind. The young are not the same as we were at their age, he thought, and hoped for all their sakes that this marriage would be a good one. We know so little when we set out, he thought, and life is full of hazards.

But then Tavy and her mother were in the room and both talking at once, and Tommy was standing behind them, beaming so widely it was a wonder he didn't crack his jaw, so they all had to be gathered into a circle round the fire for the delightful business of drinking champagne and making plans.

'Now for a start,' Amy said happily, 'we could have an engagement party on New Year's Eve. How would that be?'

It would be wonderful, as the engaged couple were happy to tell her.

'Oh I'm so happy for you, my darling,' Amy said to her daughter, for the third time since she'd heard the news. 'What a splendid way to start the New Year. You must lay in plenty of champagne, JJ. It isn't every day of the week your daughter gets engaged.' She was into her full planning stride now and thoroughly enjoying herself. 'We must have a cake and a band for dancing and a buffet supper. It's all going to be perfectly splendid. I can't wait to tell Maud and Emmeline.' Although of course Emmeline had known there was a romance ever since that holiday at Eastbourne.

'And after that you must choose a date for the wedding,' she went on, 'and we can start organising that.' She gave them both a rapturous smile. 'Have you any ideas?'

The engaged couple answered at once, but not with the same voice. Tommy said, 'First Saturday in August,' eagerly, Octavia offered that there was no rush.

'She don't meant that,' Tommy said. He spoke as if he was joking but there was an edge to his voice. 'Do you, Tavy?'

'Well actually, I do,' Octavia said. 'I'd rather like a second year at the school. What if we say the August after next?'

'But that means waiting nearly two years!' Tommy said. 'Oh come on, Tavy, you don't mean that.'

'I wish you'd stop telling me what I mean and don't mean,' Octavia said and now it was her voice that sounded sharp.

JJ intervened before they could quarrel. 'You don't have to make your mind up here and now,' he said. 'Take your time. There's no rush. We're happy to go along with whatever you decide.'

'The first Saturday in August would suit us fine,' Tommy

said, but when Octavia glowered at him, added, 'but we'll do as you say, sir, talk it over and all that sort of thing.'

'And now you have a theatre date, I believe you said,' JJ smoothed. 'We don't want to lose you but it wouldn't do to be late.'

So they wrapped themselves up in coats and scarves and hats and gloves, kissed Amy good night, and stepped out into the cold air. They were obviously still arguing as they walked down the path towards his car.

'Whatever's the matter with Tavy?' Amy said as she and JJ returned to the fire. 'I've never known her so tetchy.'

'Nerves?' JJ offered.

'She never has nerves.'

'Determination then,' her father said. 'I think she wants to go on teaching for a bit longer.'

Amy sighed. 'That's always been her trouble,' she said. 'Determination. She's got a darn sight too much of it. The sooner she's married and settled, the better, if you ask me. Now then, I must draw up an invitation list for the party and after that I must telephone Maud and Emmeline. Oh what a day this has been!'

CHAPTER 15

Tommy and Octavia bickered all the way to the theatre. And all through the interval. And all through a rather good dinner, which they wasted. And all the way back to his flat, where being alone at last they exploded into a full-scale quarrel.

'Dash it all, Tavy,' he said, as he opened the door, 'what's the matter with you? I thought you wanted to marry me. I came hot foot to London. You've no idea what a journey it was. Hot foot. And I saw your father the very first thing. I couldn't have done it better if I'd tried. I thought you'd be grateful.'

'I am,' Octavia said, throwing her hat and gloves in the nearest chair.

'You're not. How can you say that? You turned me down. In front of your own father. I said August and you turned me down.'

'I didn't turn you down,' Octavia said, unbuttoning her coat. 'Don't exaggerate. I said a bit later. That's all. You're making a mountain out of a molehill.'

'Oh that's lovely!' he said, furiously. 'You get a *bona fide* proposal and you call it a molehill. A molehill! That just shows you don't want to marry me.'

'Yes I do,' Octavia said, throwing her coat across the chair. 'I keep telling you. I do. It's just that I want to go on teaching too. I thought you'd understand *that* at least. It's important to me.'

'Oh yes,' he mocked, 'I can see *that*, all right. It's more important to you than I am.'

'No it's not. I didn't say that.'

'Yes it is. You think about it. If I was important to you you'd marry me. You wouldn't put me off and say "later, later, later" all the time. You'd say "yes, Tommy, August would be ticketty-boo".'

'I don't say ticketty-boo. It's childish.'

'Don't split hairs,' Tommy said. 'You know what I mean.' He was shivering and that annoyed him too. 'What's the matter with this damned place? It's like ice in here. What's happened to that damned fire? They were supposed to keep it in for us. Oh God! I wish I'd never come back.'

Octavia went to look at the fire, glad of a chance to move away from the quarrel. 'It's still alight,' she said. 'I'll fix it if you like. Have you got a newspaper?'

'Don't ask me,' he said crossly. 'I don't light fires.'

She looked behind the coal scuttle and found a copy of the *Daily Herald*. It wasn't really big enough but it would have to do. At least it fitted over the grate. She held it there tightly to draw the embers back to life, while Tommy watched her and scowled. It took a few minutes before the coals began to roar and by then the centre of the paper was turning brown.

'Drop it, Tavy!' Tommy said, growing anxious at her daring. 'You've done enough now. Drop it. I don't want you burning yourself.'

She held on a little longer. 'Give it time to take,' she said. 'I know what I'm doing.' And with that, the newspaper burst into flames.

He'd snatched it from her hands, thrown it on the hearth and was stamping on it before she could catch her breath. And then she was in his arms and being kissed with such relief and passion that she was breathless all over again. 'Come to bed,' he begged. 'I've missed you so much. Don't let's quarrel any more. Come to bed.'

So it was a happy homecoming after all, if a trifle sooty. Afterwards as they lay warmly together in their familiar bed while their once recalcitrant fire burned strongly as if to make up for its earlier shortcomings, they put their quarrel behind them, talked like the married couple they were to be and gradually found a compromise. He said he couldn't understand for the life of him why she should want to go on teaching but could see that she did. She told him that she knew quite well that he wanted to marry her in August and in ordinary circumstances that's when she would have married him but she did so hope he would wait a little while longer. And eventually they agreed that Easter 1915 would be a sensible time. It didn't really satisfy either of them, of course, but they were both love calmed by then, and wise enough to know that mutual dissatisfaction is the nature of a compromise.

'We'll buy the ring tomorrow,' Tommy said, as they got dressed ready for her return home. On this at least he could get his own way.

It was a rather grand diamond and he gave it to her at the start of their party on New Year's Eve, to the assembled delight of their relations, who'd been rather surprised to hear that the wedding wasn't until the Easter after next and had spent the first part of the party telling one another how odd it was to have such a long delay.

'I mean,' Mrs Meriton said to Amy, 'it isn't as if there's anything to stop them, when all's said and done. I can't think why they're being so long-winded about it.'

But it was a splendid party, they were all agreed on that, and when Tommy and Octavia kissed one another at the stroke of midnight, right there in the middle of the room before them all, they were misty eyed at the romance of it. 'Long life and happiness,' they called as they drank their champagne and were confident that there was nothing that could possibly stand in the way of either.

THE NEXT EVENING in the House of Commons David Lloyd George gave a speech in which he described the build-up of armaments in Western Europe as 'organised insanity'. Few newspapers reported it and, even if they had, the partygoers wouldn't have paid any attention to it. They were too busy discussing the party over dinner or were lurking in their rooms nursing the remains of their champagne hangovers. The governments Lloyd George was castigating ignored him too and went on amassing guns and bullets, and training soldiers to use them.

In March, while Octavia's pupils were cheerfully colouring in pictures of wild flowers and Tommy was moping in the embassy in Belgrade, miserable for lack of her, the Russian government announced that their standing army was to be increased from 460,000 to 1,700,000, Admiral von Tirpitz declared that the German navy had ordered fourteen new warships and, not to be outdone, Mr Winston Churchill, the first Lord of the Admiralty, asked the British government for two and a half million pounds to speed up the production of battleships and aircraft. The race to war was gathering momentum.

It began on a sunny day at the end of June in an obscure corner of the Balkans, just as Tommy had predicted it would, and two rapid pistol shots were enough to set it off. The first was aimed at the Archduke Franz Ferdinand, who was heir to the throne of the great Austro-Hungarian empire, and was visiting Sarajevo as its southernmost outpost. It hit him in the neck and killed him ten minutes later. The second killed his wife instantly with a wound to the stomach.

For several days there was confusion, as rumours circulated, were contradicted and reiterated. The assassin had made no attempt to get away, had been arrested immediately and said he'd carried out the killings to avenge *the oppression of the Serbian people*. It was rumoured that he was a member of a secret society of Serbian army officers called the Black Hand. In Berlin the Kaiser made a point of reaffirming the strength of the German alliance with Austria; in St Petersburg, the French president arrived to visit the Czar: in Vienna students took to the streets to demonstrate against the Serbs and to demand vengeance; there was confusion and anger throughout the Austro-Hungarian empire from Prague to Sarajevo.

Three weeks later, Austria broke off diplomatic relations with Serbia and in rapid succession, the Serbian army was mobilised, and the British embassy in Belgrade was cut down to a skeleton staff. Two days later Tommy was back in his flat in London and that afternoon he was sitting outside Bridge Street School in a swanky new car waiting for Octavia to finish work and come out and join him. Her pupils were owl-eyed at the sight of him and deeply impressed when she climbed into the car and they drove off together.

'I shall never hear the end of this,' she laughed, looking back to wave at them. They were standing in the road to watch her go but were too overawed to wave back. 'They thought my ring was wealth enough, now they'll think I'm royalty.'

'So you are. To me anyway.'

'Oh it's lovely to see you,' she said. 'I thought I was going to have to wait until we broke up. Are you home for good?'

'So they tell me. Till the war ends anyway.'

'So there is going to be a war.'

'Looks like it,' he said, laconically. 'Foregone conclusion as far as I can see. They're mobilising all over Europe. Got my commission last week.'

She was aghast. 'What do you mean, got your commission? You're not in the army.'

'Am now, old thing,' he said.

'But why?'

'Time of war,' he said. 'It's expected of a chap. It's what you do.'

'But you might get hurt.'

'Tell you what,' he said, turning the car and the conversation equally deftly, 'what say we go to the music hall tonight. I don't fancy the theatre.'

She didn't fancy the music hall much either. It was too light-hearted for her sober mood. But she didn't argue. It was enough to sit beside him in the dusty stalls and sing the familiar songs. She could find out about the commission later.

She found out at the end of the week, when he told her with the studied flippancy that she was beginning to recognise as a mask for something serious, that he had 'to pop off to Salisbury plain for a spot of training'. She was very upset for by then there was no doubt that war was imminent. Every day brought fresh news, now fully reported in every newspaper — of another ulti-matum, another threat, more mobilisation. People were jittery with the uncertainty of it.

On July 28th Austria declared war on Serbia and the next day the Czar responded by mobilising his enormous army. On July 30th Kaiser Wilhelm sent the Czar an ultimatum saying that Germany would mobilise too unless Russia stopped its own mobilisation at once. The threat was ignored and the mobilisa-tion continued. Things were now moving almost too quickly to be reported, diplomatic messages being sent between the great powers one after the other. The Kaiser contacted Paris asking what the French government intended to do, and having received no reassurance from that quarter, promptly declared war on Russia; the Royal Navy was mobilised; the Italian government declared its neutrality; and London sent a message to the Kaiser pledging to 'guarantee Belgian neutrality and protect the French coasts'. But it was already too late. On August 4th the German army invaded Belgium and by the end of the day Britain and Germany were at war.

From that moment everything changed. It was as if a fever had passed, or an ugly boil been lanced. The long months of anxiety and uncertainty were over. The war had begun, the time for action and decision had come. Now it was all excitement and a joyous, uplifting, wonderful sense of relief and importance. Crowds came out onto the streets to shout and cheer.

In Paris they thronged the Boulevard Haussmann from the Opera House to the Place de la Republique, throwing their hats into the summer air and shouting 'A Berlin! A Berlin!' as though they were ready to march on the enemy there and then. In London they gathered in Parliament Square to hear the declaration, their summer boaters bobbing like pale flowers above the green lawn of the central garden, or they marched down the Mall, waving paper flags, as though it was the Jubilee all over again, and stood before the gates of Buckingham Palace, flushed with patriotic fervour, singing 'God Save the King!' Oh what splendid times to live in! Every day brought a new thrill.

Within days, young men were volunteering in their thousands all over Great Britain, glad of the chance to leave their dull lives and prove themselves heroes. Everybody said the war was going to be short and decisive, 'over by Christmas' according to Sir John French, so they had to be quick about it. By the time Tommy returned from his training, in the full uniform of a second lieutenant and looking extremely handsome, the British army had doubled in size, the British Expeditionary Force had landed in France and the war was under way.

He got back just in time for a celebration. Cyril and Podge

had enlisted on the first day of the war and their proud parents had followed their training day by day, commiserating with them for the lack of tents and provisions and consoling their impatience as the weeks grumbled past. Now they were organising a family party to give them a proper send off.

'Such good brave boys,' Maud said to her sister. 'Heroes the pair of them.'

Amy was sorting out a pile of bunting, which was in such a tangle it was harder work than she expected. She had to pause for a minute to catch her breath. It was something she often had to do these days. 'You will miss them when they go,' she said.

'Oh I shall,' Maud agreed. 'But I wouldn't have it any other way. I'm so proud of them. Especially when they're in uniform. They look so splendid! They wear it all the time you know, even when they're on leave.'

'So does Tommy,' Amy said. 'And you're right, it does make them look handsome.'

'Do you think we ought to invite his parents?' Maud asked. 'Tommy's I mean. Now he's home. After all he is part of the family and he'll come to the party, won't he. It would be rather nice. A combined send-off.'

So the guest list was extended to include Tommy's family and friends, and extra catering was ordered, and even though it all had to be done in a matter of days, it was a great success. By then Tommy's brother James had enlisted too, so there were four soldiers to be petted and toasted and told they were heroes, even if young Jimmy wasn't in uniform yet. In fact, they had so much champagne urged upon them that Podge, who wasn't used to quite so much praise nor quite so much alcohol, became incoherent and giggly. When the time came to make a speech he could barely manage a sentence and every word in it was slurred, although he was applauded to the echo. And Jimmy was little better, saying, 'Thank you. Most kind. King and Country and all that,' and then sinking back into his seat to happy cheers and laughter.

Having reached the maturity of twenty-six, Cyril and Tommy could take as much drink as they were offered and still retain their eloquence. Tommy thanked his guests for their good wishes and told them he considered himself the luckiest man alive to be part of the great British army *and* to have persuaded Octavia to be his wife, 'which took some doing, I can tell you!' Cyril surprised everybody by quoting poetry.

'It's a sonnet by Rupert Brooke,' he told them. 'You know. The feller from Cambridge. Jolly good stick by all accounts. Anyway here it is. I think it speaks for us all.' And he cleared his throat and began.

> 'Now God be thanked who has matched us with
>   His hour
> And caught our youth, and wakened us from sleeping
> With hand made sure, clear eye and sharpened power
> To turn, as swimmers into cleanness leaping,
> Glad from a world grown old and cold and weary.'

It was done with such style that his guests broke into admiring applause. 'Bravo that man!' they called. 'Well said!'

'I don't mind telling you,' he admitted, a touch bashfully. 'It speaks for me too. I was getting to be absolutely stifled in the bank before this happened. Sorry about that, Pater, but it's the truth. Banks are a dashed good idea and all that but they ain't for everyone. I feel like a free man now. Absolutely top hole. Off to do my duty and show the Hun what's what. They may think they've got everything going their way, invading poor little Belgium and all that rot, but you wait till we get there. It'll be a different story then.'

That was applauded too. 'That's the style!' his guests called. 'You show 'em, Squirrel!'

'Didn't I tell you he was a hero,' Maud said to her sister. 'My dear brave boy.'

'And I'll tell you something else,' her hero went on. 'If there are any chaps out there who haven't enlisted yet, you'd better tell 'em to jump to it or it'll all be over before they're trained. I give it till Christmas.'

Later that evening when the drinking and dancing were done, Tommy walked Octavia home across the quiet Heath. They strolled together in the moonlight, dreamily, his arm about her waist, stopping for kisses that roused them to the sharpest desires, kissing again and again, aching and unsatisfied.

'You will come to the flat tomorrow,' he urged.

'Yes,' she said between kisses. 'Yes. Of course, my darling, darling.'

'If we were married we could go there now,' he complained. 'All this observing the proprieties is such a bore.'

'I know,' she soothed. It wasn't the time or the place to argue, for the heath was tranquil about them and the western sky already greened by the approach of dawn. Trees and bushes rustled in a sudden breeze as if they were sharing secrets, the grass was dappled with mysterious shadow, the white stars studded in their familiar patterns, aloof and watchful.

'Will it be over by Christmas?' she asked.

He was kissing her neck and in thrall to sensation, so it took him a minute to answer. 'Who can tell?' he said. 'Wars ain't predictable.'

'What do you think?'

'I prefer not to think about it at all,' he said. 'I'd rather take you to bed and love you all night.'

'There's not much of the night left now,' she told him. And teased, 'You're running out of time.'

He was suddenly and unnervingly serious. 'We're all running out of time,' he said, bitterly. 'That's the truth of it. Squirrel and Podge and me, all of us, running out of time, running away from our homes and the people we love, running, all of us, running headlong into a war and we don't know what it will do to us, or what we shall see, or anything about it. Blind fools, the lot of us.'

She was riven with pity for him, remembering that dreadful massacre and how she'd felt when she heard about it. He was right. It was all very well people saying it would all be over in six months but how could they possibly know? War was unpredictable. He was right about that too. There was no knowing what he would have to face in France, no knowing how monstrous the battles would be, and there were bound to be battles. It occurred to her that she was being selfish, thinking of herself and her job when he was going away to war. She ought to have agreed to marry him in August and not made him wait till Easter. Maybe she ought to do it anyway, now, quickly, before he leaves, while there's still time.

He was walking on, his arm still round her waist, as the trees whispered above them. I will speak to Papa, she decided, and see what he advises. Tomorrow, at breakfast.

SUNDAY BREAKFAST at South Hill Park was always a leisurely meal, with plenty of time to read the papers and discuss the news. JJ said it was the one moment in the week when they could relax and be themselves. 'When I retire,' he promised, 'we shall have Sunday breakfast every day of the week. How will that suit you?'

'I shall be married by then,' Octavia told him, making her opportunity. 'In fact, to tell you the truth, I'm beginning to wonder whether I ought to be married now.'

'Now?' her father asked, laughing. 'Today do you mean?'

'Before he goes to France.'

Her mother was alarmed. 'Don't think I'm trying to discourage you, my darling,' she said, 'but it would give us very little time to prepare. We would do it of course, if that is what you truly want but it's very short notice.'

Her father was looking at her quizzically. 'I thought you had decided on next Easter,' he said. 'Is this a change of heart?'

She answered him seriously, 'No, Pa,' she said. 'A change of obligation. He is going to war and I'm staying here. I shall be safe at home and he'll be in the thick of it. He could be wounded — or even killed.' It made her shudder to think of it. 'Perhaps I ought to marry him before he goes. It's what he wants.'

JJ became serious too. 'I see,' he said. 'But what of your work in the school?'

'That is the problem.'

He considered for a few minutes before he spoke again. Then he said, 'Would you be happy to leave it now? Have you achieved all that you hoped to?'

'Oh no,' Octavia said earnestly. 'I've barely begun. I've learnt a great deal over the year but there is so much more I need to know.' And as her father's expression was encouraging her, she began to elaborate, exploring ideas as they came into her mind. 'There are so many educational practices I don't understand. For example, why do we tell children the same things over and over again and make them learn everything by heart? The other teachers say it's because children can't learn without endless repetition and reinforcement, but that isn't true. I know it isn't. When they're happy in what they're doing, they learn easily and only need telling once — or at most twice. I've seen it on so many occasions.'

The pins were falling out of her hair, as they always did when she was agitated but she didn't notice. It was such a relief to be able to speak like this. She'd never been able to tell Tommy what she felt about teaching. He'd never seemed interested. He was a darling and she loved him passionately but he didn't care about her work at all. Now with her father's intelligent face approving what she was saying, her ideas pressed in upon her so hard she could barely contain them. 'And there's another thing,' she said. 'Why do people think it's necessary to shout at children so much? You don't have to shout at them. When they're happy they will listen to a whisper. There are times when I think the others just want to punish the poor little things, they shout so much and cane them for so little. You would hardly believe what small transgressions merit the stick. But then again, to imagine teachers as sadistic is rather harsh. Too harsh to be acceptable, anyway. I have to admit that. Sometimes I suspect that they're just doing what they've always done, without thinking about it. And they should think about it. If I could find a way to make them think, I should have lived to some purpose.'

There was a strand of hair in her mouth and she stopped to remove it. 'But then there are other matters too. Most of our children are underfed and poorly clothed, many are ill. They have head lice and adenoids and toothache. When the weather's bad they cough all the time. And they truant. If they're girls and their mother goes to work they have to stay at home to look after the little'uns. If they're boys and their father is working he takes them along as an extra pair of hands. And who can blame him? They need the money. Mr Shaw is quite right. We should be attending to all their needs, for food and clothing and some-where to live, not just making them chant their tables. And that's another thing...'

'Stop! Stop!' JJ begged, holding up both hands in mock alarm. 'You are making my head spin.'

'Yes...well...' Octavia said and grimaced at him. 'I'm sorry, Pa. I have gone on a bit but you *did* ask me.'

'You have answered my question,' he said. 'Don't you think so?'

It was true. She had. Her work was too important to her to be left. But knowing it didn't stop her feeling selfish and when Tommy's embarkation leave was over and she went to Victoria station to wave him goodbye, she felt worse than she'd ever felt in her life. She stood on the platform among all the other wives and mothers, watching as the long train snaked away from her, khaki arms waving from every window and grieved to think how badly she had treated him. My poor dear Tommy, she thought. I should have married you. I was wrong to put the school first.

CHAPTER 16

L ife was very quiet after their soldiers had gone and it seemed a long time before their first letters home began to arrive.

'At last!' Octavia said when Tommy's letter was delivered and was annoyed to see that her hands were shaking as she opened it. To her disappointment, he hardly said anything at all. He'd arrived 'in good order', couldn't tell her where he was, 'they censor everything', hadn't seen anything of the others, hoped she wouldn't forget him.

'The others' were equally terse. According to Emmeline, 'Podge sends picture postcards and doesn't say *anything* and all Squirrel ever says is that he's ticketty-boo or in the pink and please send another parcel and can he have some more jam. Although he *did* say he hoped we were missing him. Soppy thing. As if we wouldn't.'

Her children missed him terribly. Dora and Eddie, being seven and six years old, were grown up enough to understand that he'd gone to France and that it was a long way away and he couldn't just come back when he felt like it, but Edith, who was only just five and often very babyish, fretted to see her uncles every time she came to visit Grandma and refused to be comforted, no matter how hard her mother tried to explain things to her. Two-year-old Dickie was too young to understand, of course, which was just as well, for Emmeline was now heavily into the seventh month of her fifth pregnancy and too weary to cope with tears and tantrums.

'It's all very well for people to say when you've got four you don't notice another one,' she complained to Octavia. 'I do. My back's killing me and I notice it every day.'

In September, Octavia started her second year at Bridge Street School and was soon enjoying it even more than she'd enjoyed the first one. She'd been given her old class in a different classroom. 'It is a special dispensation you understand, Miss Smith,' the headmaster told her. 'In view of the good work you did with them last year.' The children knew nothing about dispensations. They simply welcomed her back like an old friend. 'Billy said you was gettin' married, Miss,' one little girl confided, 'but we knew you'd never.' Octavia was touched by their confidence even though it renewed her guilt about the way she'd treated poor Tommy. She tried to assuage it by writing to him every day and as an extra sop to her conscience, she took to visiting Emmeline every Thursday to help with the children and swap such news as they had.

It would have been easier for them if the news had been good. But it wasn't. It had been bad from the beginning, when what had been reported as a great victory at a place called Mons turned out to be a retreat, and as the weeks passed it got worse. The Germans overran Belgium and neither the French army nor the BEF seemed able to stop them, there were battles at places they'd never heard of, the casualty lists were terrifying, and as if to underline how appalling they were, there was an official call from the government for another 'half a million men.'

'If they go on killing one another at this rate,' Octavia said to her father, 'we shan't have any men left.'

On October the 19th, when baby Johnnie slid, red-faced and bawling, into their darkening world, there was a battle at a place called Ypres. The casualty figures were the worst yet. That night when Octavia wrote to Tommy to tell him about the new baby, she asked him how things really were.

His answer was no help to her at all.

Can't tell you, old thing, he wrote. *Blue pencil and all that rot.*

Christmas came and was celebrated quietly. None of them had the heart for parties now, although Amy did volunteer that she'd try to organise something if JJ thought she should.

'And what about your wedding, my darling?' she said to Octavia, as they sat about the fire on Boxing Day. 'Easter isn't far away now. Will you still go ahead with it?'

'I doubt it, Mama,' Octavia said. 'We chose Easter because we thought the war would be over by then. Now… No I think we'll probably wait until it really is over and plan it then.'

'That would probably the best thing,' her mother agreed, with evident relief. 'Everything's so uncertain these days.' And she tried a little joke to lighten the conversation, because it was really extremely sad to be talking about postponing her Tavy's wedding, especially when they'd all been looking forward to it for such a long time. 'I don't suppose you could even be sure he'd get leave for it, could you. And we could hardly have a wedding without the groom. Perhaps it will be over by the summer.'

'Perhaps,' Octavia said, although privately she was beginning to think that even the summer was unlikely. It was going on so relentlessly and, reading between the lines of what the newspapers were reporting, it seemed to have reached a stalemate, because the armies were digging themselves in. By the end of

January, there were reports of soldiers living in trenches all along the front line, and so many men were in the army that there was a chronic shortage of manpower back at home. More and more women were working in munitions and it wasn't long before they began to appear in the streets of London, cleaning windows and delivering bread and coal. But in February, at long, long last, Tommy came home on a week's leave.

He was so changed that when he arrived at Octavia's doorstep to collect her for their first evening out, she could hardly recognise him. All his lovely thick hair had been cut back to a stubble, his face was lined and there was a long scar on his left hand.

'Oh Tommy!' she said, as they walked down the path together. 'What have they done to you?'

'Fortunes of war, old thing,' he said lightly.

'It's bad isn't it,' she said.

'It's no picnic,' he agreed but she could see from his closed expression that he wasn't going to talk about it. He opened the car door for her and gave her his old courteous bow. 'Hop in,' he said. 'Let's go and have fun.'

They spent as much time together as they could, given that she was at work and they '*had fun*' every evening. She found it exhausting and perplexing, for although it involved a nightly trip to a theatre or a music hall, which was pleasant enough, it also meant some very heavy drinking, most of it whisky, which was a taste she'd never seen in him before, and that wasn't pleasant at all. Too much drink made him rough when they finally got to bed, and she was used to gentleness. It was almost a relief when his leave was over and they were kissing goodbye at Victoria station again.

'Tootle-pip,' he said, in his laconic way. 'See you again soon. DV.'

It wasn't until she was home again that she realised they hadn't talked about her work at the school. Not once, in the entire week. And they'd never mentioned their wedding either, so she'd been right to say it had been postponed for the duration. The war's taken him over, she thought. He's not interested in anything else. It was understandable, given how awful it must be out there, but it hurt her feelings to be marginalised. It's just as well I've still got a job to keep me occupied, she thought. And returned to it with renewed enthusiasm.

Two weeks later she found an advertisement in *The Times* that made her sit up and take notice. It was asking for applications from *'Teachers of English Language and Literature'* for a position at a local Grammar School. She passed it across the breakfast table to her father.

'I've half a mind to apply,' she said, taking care to sound casual. 'What do you think, Pa?'

He thought it an excellent idea. 'Bernard Shaw would be delighted,' he said. 'Has he not always maintained that you should be training the next generation of teachers?'

'Indeed he has,' she agreed. 'He maintains it with steady regularity. But if I do apply, it will be for my benefit and not that of the great dramatist.'

He laughed at that. 'Then you must do it for your benefit — and the benefit of your pupils,' he said.

So the application was sent. And in the rush of the school week, quickly forgotten. It was an exceptionally cold week, with flurries of snow most playtimes and frozen pipes in all the lavatories. 'Makes yer life a right misery,' the school keeper complained. 'Mussen grumble though, not when you think of our poor fellers out there in them trenches.'

Octavia thought of them every day, when she sat at her desk to write to Tommy. It was no good asking him to tell her how he really was — she'd learnt that now — but that didn't stop her from telling him how anxious she was for his safety.

I think of you every day, she wrote, *and hope you are well and haven't been hurt, you and Squirrel and Podge and Jimmy. If I could send you each an invisible shield to protect you I would.*

But as things were, all she could do was write, and worry, and try to read between the lines of his laconic answers. Revelation, when it came, was at a moment when she least expected it and she was shattered by it.

There were four letters for her that morning, delivered to the breakfast table in the usual way by Mrs Wilkins and she looked at them in the usual way to see whether one was from Tommy — postcard from Emmeline, letter from the WSPU, something official by the look of it, and a letter from the front. But it wasn't from Tommy. It was from Cyril. She opened it and spread it out in front of her to read while she ate her toast.

Dear Tavy, it said. *I hope you will forgive me for writing to you like this but I have to tell someone what is happening here or I shall go mad and I can't tell Mama or Emmeline, they would never understand.*

Life here is hell. There is no other word for it. We are not supposed to tell anyone about it for fear of breaking morale and every word we write is censored, so I've arranged to send you this with the help of a girl in a local estaminet behind the lines. It would be all blue pencil if I posted it in the normal way. We officers talk to one another, of course, but it's mostly chaff. No one wants to lose face I suppose. We mustn't say anything in front of the chaps. That's absolutely forbidden. We're supposed to keep up their spirits, though they must know what we think, and how you can keep up anyone's spirits when you could all be killed the next time you go over the top is beyond my comprehension.

Yesterday was the worst day since I came out here. The worst day of my life to tell you the truth. We were supposed to be out of the line for a couple of days because we'd just finished our stint and we were resting in a trench a few miles back, but we were woken at three, so we knew there was something up. Not much for breakfast just bread and cheese and pretty hard tack at that. But that's standard. We're often on short rations. I've known days in the line when we were out of food and water altogether. I don't know how we'd manage sometimes if it wasn't for your parcels. Pretty soon word came down the line that the Germans had broken through and we were to proceed to the forward trenches. So I got my platoon in order pretty sharpish and we marched off in good order. When we got to the railway line it was full of refugees, all scared stiff, running away from Ypres as fast as they could, heading for Dickesbusch. It was ten kinds of chaos, people in a terrible state, rushing at us out of the darkness, old women hib-hobbling along, children in filthy clothes pushing carts piled so high with mattresses and chickens and pots and pans they couldn't see where they were going, women with babes in arms, and all their livestock with them, cows, goats and kids all covered in mud and bleating and baaing and kicking up a racket, and everybody shouting and crying. We knew something bad was going on but we couldn't make out what they were saying so we left them to it and just pressed on. It really put the wind up some of our lads, the locals running away and us marching into it.

When we got there we could see that the forward trench was still in our hands, which was one good thing, but we'd hardly arrived before the barrage started up. Big one this time and the noise enough to shatter your eardrums. Our gunners hadn't got their range and a lot of shells were falling short which made us jittery, although we all tried to hide it. It's no joke being out in no man's land and being fired on by both sides. Bad enough being fired on by the Hun. Then the order was given and we had to go over the top. I don't know how I'm going to tell you what happened next. It is making me cringe to think of it. But I must tell someone or my nerve will crack entirely, which would never do. An officer has to keep up his morale for the sake of his men. Only, after yesterday, I feel so much worse, I don't think I can do it for much longer. If people back home knew what is going on out here they would do something to stop it. Only how can we tell them? I can barely find *the words to tell you. It is all too enormous and beastly and brutal and inhuman. Every time I get back to the line I feel as if I'm stepping off the edge of the world. The line goes on for ever. You cannot see the end of it. They say it runs from the Channel to Switzerland in a long strip ten miles wide and everything in it is blackened and destroyed. There is nothing where I am but mud with the stumps of trees sticking out of it and bomb craters full of foul water and the twisted corpses of men and horses, everywhere you look, lying in heaps, decomposing. We bury our dead whenever there is a lull and the stretcher bearers can get out to gather them in but the next push leaves the place full of dead and dying all over again and the horses lie where they fell, all twisted and distorted with the rats eating their flesh. You only have to look at them to see what pain they were in when they died. The stink of dead bodies is dreadful. It fills your nose and throat and makes everything taste bad. It is worse than a nightmare. At least a nightmare stops when you wake up but this goes on and on, day after day and month after month, getting worse and worse and worse. I am sorry to write to you like this, but it is the truth.*

I was going to tell you about yesterday, wasn't I? You see how it is, your mind gets twisted up in this place and you forget what you were going to say. We went over the top at dawn with the bombardment going on all round us. Appalling noise, shells screaming overhead, explosions, men screaming when they were hit, the Huns' machine guns rattling. The machine gun is the most efficient killing machine known to mankind. It can kill fifty men a second, and does. It just rattles on and on, spitting red hot metal and our chaps drop like flies. They were falling all round me. I could see that there were fewer and fewer of us still running. Although you can't see very well what with the smoke and the mud being thrown up by the explosions and men falling everywhere. I must have gone about twenty yards when the soldier in front of me was hit. I was going so fast I fell over him. Knocked the wind out of me. And the spirit. I should have got up and run on but I didn't. Oh my dear Tavy. I hardly know how to tell you this but in the end I have proved a coward. That's what I am. A miserable rotten coward. I just lay there in the mud, playing possum, praying not to die, trying to scrabble into the filth to find somewhere to hide. I couldn't stand up and get shot. The man I fell over was groaning and calling for his mother and I didn't even crawl over to help him. I was stuck to the spot. A yellow-bellied coward. I don't know how long I lay there in that shameful way. The man stopped groaning so I assumed he was dead but I didn't go to see. In the end I heard whistles and someone yelling that we were falling back and then I got up and ran hell for leather until I was back in the trench. The same trench. Back where I'd started. There were only three of us left alive and unharmed from the entire platoon. All that suffering and all those lives lost and that poor devil lying out there in the mud and me not helping him and all for nothing. I should have gone to help him. I know it. It was shameful. They were my men and I let them down. Shameful. Well now I have something to expiate.

Please don't let any of our parents see this letter. It is for your eyes only. I'm sorry to be such a coward and I shan't be surprised if you write back and tell me never to write in such a way again. If you do I shall obey you of course. You can tell them I am not wounded. Not wounded in body anyhow, although I fear I am shamefully wounded in spirit.

I am your loving and most miserable cousin,
  Squirrel.

Octavia folded the letter and tucked it back inside its envelope carefully, keeping her head down and her expression under control and moving in the calmest way she could as though it was one of Squirrel's usual cheerful missives. The shock of what she had just read was making her heart shudder but, if she was to be true to her cousin and guard his secret, she had to hide what she was feeling. She was glad that her father was absorbed in *The Times* and wasn't looking at her and that her mother was complaining about the price of bread. 'Up again, JJ. It can't go on. A large loaf costs eightpence. And it was fivepence ha'penny when the war started. I think it's scandalous.'

'We *can* afford it, my dear,' JJ said from behind the paper.

'But what of the poor?' she asked, blue eyes earnest. 'They can't and they'll have a hard time of it. Especially in this weather. It's those awful profiteers, that's the real trouble. The government should do something about them.'

Outside the windows of their coal-warmed room, the sky was leaden with impending snow. But inside it was an easy luxurious place. Octavia looked at the voluptuous patterns of Mr Morris's wallpaper behind her father's head, the familiar painted roses on the teacup in her mother's hands, the shine on the white damask tablecloth under her fingers, the flames flickering above the coals, the gleam of the fire irons, the expensive watercolours in half shadow on the walls, the *chaise longue* with its pile of tumbled cushions welcoming in the window bay, and she felt cosseted and protected, ashamed to be living so well when her cousin was suffering so much.

'Who are your letters from?' her mother asked mildly. 'Is that a card from our Emmeline?'

Octavia read the postcard to bring herself back to the reality of the morning and to prevent her mother from asking about Cyril. 'She wants me to go to tea with her this afternoon instead of Thursday,' she reported, glad that what she was saying was so mundane.

'Shall you?' her mother asked.

'I expect so.'

'Are they all well?'

'She doesn't say.'

'So we may presume that they are,' JJ said. 'Amy my dear, could I trouble you for another cup of tea. Is there any in the pot?'

The difficult moment passed and Octavia could turn her attention to the rest of the morning's mail. After Cyril's letter it would be hard to take much interest in it but she was dutiful about her correspondence and there would be sufficient time before she had to catch the tram to work for her to answer the most important. Which was perhaps just as well for the official letter was from St Barnaby's High School for Girls.

'Well, well, well,' she said to her parents. 'You remember the job I applied for last week. The one at the grammar school. They've asked me to go for an interview.'

'So they should,' her father approved. 'When it is to be?'

'Friday week.'

'You must have a new hat,' her mother decided, planning the event at once. 'And a longer skirt, I think. Those new short skirts of yours won't be at all the thing in a grammar school.' The length of Octavia's skirts had been a sore point ever since the new style came in. In her opinion — frequently given and as frequently rejected — any woman showing her ankles was unladylike.

For once Octavia didn't argue about it. She just said, 'Um, well, we'll see,' in a vague way, as if it wasn't important, which of course it wasn't, not after Cyril's letter. Then she went on opening her mail, still keeping calm. The last one was from the WSPU and contained a piece of news that gave her an outlet for the anger she'd been holding in check. 'Oh!' she cried. 'How disgraceful!'

Her father set *The Times* aside and smiled at her affectionately. 'What is it, Tavy?' he asked. 'Who has the ill fortune to be out of your grace this morning?'

'Listen to this,' she ordered, glaring at the letter. 'Mrs Pankhurst is organising a march to demand — what is it she says? — women's right to serve in this awful war. She has the backing of Mr Lloyd George, so it says, and is hoping for "a demonstration of at least forty thousand women."'

'And that displeases you?' her father asked.

'Yes it does,' she said firmly. She had to be displeased about something. 'Our movement was organised to demand the vote, not to kowtow to politicians.'

'Kowtowing to politicians might be exactly the way to get what you want,' JJ said. 'Your Mrs Pankhurst is a very shrewd lady. A patriotic march could sway public opinion in your favour. The next time you ask you might be heard with more sympathy. Which would be no bad thing surely?'

Octavia was in no mood to be reasonable. 'It's dishonest,' she said. 'We should be campaigning for what we want, not organising a patriotic parade. Oh I can see what they're up to. Lloyd George wants more women to work in munitions now that the men are away at the war and we're a big organisation so he's enlisted us to help him. We shall be waving white feathers next. It was a great mistake to stop the campaign when the war began. We should have gone on and pushed them when they were weakened. I thought so then and I think so now.'

'So you won't be taking part in this parade?' her father asked.

She answered firmly, from the rigid determination of fear and anger. 'No I will not.' Then she gathered up her letters and went to answer the easiest ones. Cyril's would have to wait until the evening when she could write at length and gently.

On the way to Bridge Street School, as snow swirled about the windows of the tram and her fellow passengers coughed and snuffled and complained to one another that the weather really should be improving 'bein' it's February. I mean ter say, it can't go on much longer' she thought of her cousins and her dear Tommy, out there in the cold facing up to horrors she would once have said were beyond imagination and could now imagine only too well. It was as if Cyril's terrible letter had been etched into her brain. She could remember it almost word for word, the terror and pain of it, his needless, heartbreaking shame at what he called his cowardice. As if anyone could blame him for wanting to stay alive. At least she could reassure him about that. Who better after the way she'd behaved when they let her out of Holloway that last awful time? She thought of what he'd said about telling people what was really happening, about how necessary it was to tell the truth, and how it couldn't be done, how even her friends in the WSPU were compromising themselves because of this war. Their kowtowing march was planned for the summer so the politicians obviously thought the war would still be going on then and for all she knew it could drag on into next winter too. It's only four months since Podge and Squirrel and Tommy had their farewell party, and now they're facing death every time they go over the top and we live in dread of the casualty lists. What will become of them? It seemed to her, sitting there, cold-footed on her uncomfortable wooden seat, as the tram jerked along the rails and the snow tumbled against the window that the world was changed beyond hope or redemption and that all three of her darlings would be killed.

The woman sitting next to her was patting her arm. 'Bad news is it, duck?' she asked, her lined face full of concern.

'No,' Octavia said, trying to smile and failing. 'Not really. Not the worst.'

'That's it, duck,' the woman said, acknowledging the half smile. 'Gotta keep cheerful ain'tcher, or where would we be?'

'Bridge Street,' the conductor called. 'Anyone fer Bridge Street?'

Thank God for work, Octavia thought, as she trudged off towards the school. At least I've got something to keep me occupied. If I had to sit at home waiting for news I should go mad.

Two of her pupils were waiting for her at the school gate, hopping up and down to keep warm. They were very excited, waving at her as she approached, and as soon as she reached the gate, they told her their news. 'We got our own colourin' pencils, Miss. Look! Ain't they dandy! We gonna do our colourin' in today, Miss?'

She admired the pencils. 'Very nice,' she said. 'Aren't you lucky?'

'Our Mums give 'em to us,' the taller of the two confided. 'We got new boots an' all, *an'* I had roast beef Sunday. It ain't half good now they're on munitions.'

It's taken a war to improve their lives, Octavia thought, as the snow dropped lacy curtains between them. 'Come on,' she said, taking their hands. 'Let's get inside in the warm. It's too cold by half out here. Where's your friend, Minnie?'

'Not here, Miss. Her aunty got the telegram.'

They were the worst words in the language. Another death, Octavia thought. Poor woman. But now she knew what sort of death it had been and the pity of it was too great to be contained. Tears spilled from her eyes before she could stop them.

'Ne'er mind, Miss,' the child comforted, squeezing her hand. 'Me Mum's gone over ter look after her. You got ter look after one another, ain'tcher.'

CHAPTER 17

Octavia went to her interview at St Barnaby's High School still troubled by difficult emotions, guilt at the way she had treated Tommy, anguish at how poor Squirrel was suffering, doubt as to whether she ought to be leaving her children at Bridge Street when they were making such progress, but from the moment she walked into the building she knew she had made the right decision. It was such a clean, cultured, well-ordered place, the pupils neat and presentable in gym slips and white blouses, the floors well cleaned, the walls hung with prints of the great classical pictures. She noticed 'The Hay Wain', 'The Laughing Cavalier' and 'When did you last see your father?' as she was escorted to the staff room by one of the school prefects.

There were four other candidates, all of them women and all excessively genteel, talking of anodyne subjects like the weather and the price of bread and saying nothing about themselves or their applications. Tea was served in china cups and they sipped it politely, then they waited to be called, in alphabetical order, naturally, which meant that Octavia was the last to go.

The headmistress's study was like a middle class parlour, with a carpet on the floor, pictures and books on the walls, a fire in the grate, two comfortable armchairs and an imposing desk in the middle of the room. The headmistress herself was small, dapper and bespectacled but her questioning was skilled. She wanted to discover how well her applicants knew their subject and whether they had other skills that could be of use to the school.

'We teach a wide curriculum here, Miss Smith,' she explained, when she and Octavia had talked at length about nineteenth century novelists and the Lake poets, parsing and clause analysis, 'and however well qualified they may be, many of our staff do not restrict themselves to their chosen subject.'

Octavia supposed that she could teach arithmetic to the juniors and the fact was noted.

'There is however one thing that I must make clear to you,' the headmistress continued. 'Your predecessor has been prevailed upon to join the army, which is why this position was advertised, and when he returns he will naturally expect to resume his post, so this is by way of being a somewhat temporary position, for the duration of war, you might say. Would you be prepared to accept it on these terms, should it be offered to you?'

Octavia agreed that she would and the interview was concluded. When she got back to the staff room the school secretary was sitting among the other candidates and obviously waiting for her.

'The headmistress thought you might care to walk in the grounds while you wait for her decision,' she said to them all. 'Penelope will come and collect us.'

So they put on their coats against the chill, for although the snow had thawed it was still cold, and walked in the grounds, nervously, but still contriving to make polite conversation. Watching her competitors, Octavia thought how nerve wracking it was to know you were being judged and that only one of you would succeed and four of you would be found wanting. This, she thought, admiring the holly bushes there being very little else in the wintery garden to admire, is how children must feel when they have to take an examination and are afraid they are going to fail. The talk and the walk went on and finally, Penelope, who turned out to be the Head Girl, appeared on the terrace to say that she'd been sent to ask Miss Smith if she would be so kind as to return to the Headmistress's study. It was a moment of such relief and pleasure, Octavia was quite surprised by the strength of it. She'd got the job. It might only be 'for the duration' but she'd got the job.

'The war affects everything we do,' she said to her parents that night, after she'd told them her good news. 'Even a teaching post can't be offered without a proviso nowadays.'

'If the government can alter the drinking laws with impunity,' her father said, 'which I have to say they seem to have done — even the King is teetotal now according to *The Times* — then no aspect of our lives is beyond their reach. We must be thankful they are not legislating on the amount of sleep we need.'

'But how wonderful to be a grammar school teacher, my darling,' Amy said. 'Just think of all the good work you will do there. When do you start?'

'Not till after Easter,' Octavia said. 'The start of the summer term.'

Amy was disappointed. 'That's a long time to wait,' she said.

'Not really, Mama,' Octavia said. 'I have to hand my notice in at Bridge Street and give them time to find a replacement. And then I shall have to study the syllabus and prepare lessons. There won't be enough hours in the day.'

'It can't come quickly enough for me,' her mother said. 'I think it's wonderful news. A real step up. I wonder what your Tommy will think.'

He didn't seem particularly interested.

Well bully for you, he wrote. *Just don't forget me while you're teaching your precious pupils.*

I could never forget you, she wrote back, *as you know very well.*

The exchange upset her. It reminded her of their awful quarrel and how rough he'd been on that awful leave. And it renewed her guilt. This damned war changes everything, she thought, even the most tender, private things. But is it any wonder when they're out there in those awful trenches, facing death every day of their lives, like our poor Squirrel. Not for the first time, she grieved for the insanity of what they were being ordered to do. All those young men being sent out to that hell hole in France to kill one another, young brave, idealistic young men, and all for what? How did we ever get involved in such a hideous business in the first place? It was lunacy. No matter what the quarrels had been, they should have been settled by treaties and conferences and compromises, not by killing our young men. Thank God I've got my work to keep me busy.

During the rest of that spring term she kept herself extremely busy, coaxing her Bridge Street children by day to make as much progress as they could before she had to leave them and pouring over the syllabuses by night to ensure that she would know what she was doing when she took up her new job. By the time she said goodbye to her tearful pupils on the last day of the spring term, she was exhausted.

'You push yourself too hard,' her mother rebuked, noting her pale face and the shadows under her eyes. 'I hope you will rest up over Easter. I don't want you getting ill.'

But none of them were able to rest up that Easter. On Easter Friday Amy had a phone call from her sister Maud that took all the colour from her face and left her looking so ill that JJ was alarmed for her and shouted for Octavia.

Amy waved them both away, her hands fluttering like white

moths in the half light of the hall, while she went on listening to the voice on the other end of the line. 'It's Maud,' she whispered to them eventually. 'She's got the telegram.'

'Oh dear God!' Octavia said. 'Which of them is it?' But she knew already. She'd been dreading it ever since she got that letter. It was Cyril.

'I'm on my way over, darling,' Amy said, reaching for her coat. 'I'll be with you as soon as I can get there.'

They walked across the Heath together, all three of them, holding on to one another's arms for comfort. None of them spoke. What was there to say? The ultimate horror of this appalling war had reached out to stun them, just as it had stunned thousands of others. In the face of death there is nothing anyone can do except weep.

Emmeline wept uncontrollably, with her head on her mother's shoulder. 'Oh my poor Squirrel!' she said over and over again. 'My poor dear Squirrel.'

But Maud was stuck in a terrible, necessary disbelief. 'They must have made a mistake,' she said to Amy. 'They must have mustn't they, Amy? It can't be Cyril I mean to say, he's always so strong. They'll write to us presently and say it was a mistake.'

A letter did come, two days later, but it was from Cyril's commanding officer and there was no mistake.

Dear Mr And Mrs Withington, he said. It is with the deepest regret and sorrow that I write to sympathise with you on the death of your son Lieutenant Cyril Withington. He was a fine officer and much loved by his men. I am sure you would want to know of the heroic way in which he died.

He and his platoon had been detailed to take out an enemy pillbox, which they accomplished successfully after many hours of fierce fighting and after taking many casualties. The last man to fall was a member of your son's platoon, a soldier well-known to him and for whom he was responsible. Since he lay directly in the line of enemy fire, and the battle was still going on, he could not be reached by the stretcher-bearers. Without regard for his own safety, your son immediately ran out into No-Man's-Land to rescue him. He was shot by enemy machine gun fire as he was carrying the injured soldier back to the nearest trench. It might be some comfort to you to know that he died instantly and did not suffer. Most of all I am sure you will be proud to know that he died a hero's death, laying down his own life to save a comrade in arms.

Maud passed it round the family that afternoon and although she was tearful she said she was glad to know that he'd died a hero's death. 'My poor boy.' But Octavia was thinking of what he'd said in that letter of his, *'I have something to expiate'* and knew with a numbing certainty that he'd thrown his life away.

'We can't even have a funeral,' Maud was saying. 'Or do they send their bodies home, do you know? No how could they? There are too many of them. Oh my poor Cyril.'

'We can have a memorial service,' Ralph said. 'Lots of people do that.'

So it was arranged but it really didn't comfort any of them because it was totally unreal, as if everything and everybody had been altered. Even Ralph's fine white house was changed, subdued by a yellowy half-darkness because every Holland blind had been drawn against the sun. The servants moved in and out of the parlour, soft shod out of respect and silent as fishes, and Emmeline and her mother sat in the armchairs on either side of the fireplace, weeping into their black-edged handkerchiefs as though they would never stop. It was as if grief had cast a pall over the house and everyone in it. Now and then a breeze trilled the blind until it lifted and a shaft of bold sunlight knifed into the room. Now and then a blackbird sang with melancholy yearning from the unseen blossom of the apple tree out in the innocence of the garden. Now and then Aunt

Maud sighed and said, 'Oh my poor dear boy! My poor, poor dear boy!' But Emmeline crouched between the arms of her chair too pained to move or speak and when Octavia bent over her, she clung to her hand for comfort and said nothing. All the frantic, disbelieving, terrible things had been said. Now there was nothing but loss and the aching void of extreme grief.

Eventually there were murmurs out in the hall and the guests began to return. JJ and Amy were the first to venture into the room, and while JJ coughed and tried to find an unobtrusive corner in which to stand, Amy knelt beside the chair and took her sister in her arms. There was tea to be served. Should she attend to it? Should Annie bring it in?

'A cup of tea, my dear,' she suggested. 'You *must* take something or you will be ill and what would Emmeline and your poor Ralph do then?'

'I can't eat,' Maud said. 'I simply can't. You don't know.'

'I do, my darling. I do.'

The parlour maid was lurking outside the door with her tray and they could hear the next group of arrivals talking quietly in the hall. They might not have had a funeral but a funeral tea must be served nevertheless, the rituals of the lives that remained after this appalling death must somehow be observed. Octavia watched as the rest of the family made their entrances, clumsily concerned, awkwardly embarrassed, and she was torn by anguish all over again. There was no end to this sorrow and no escape.

Her uncle and his brothers talked gruffly about how well the service had gone, all things considered, and how kind the Reverend Allen had been. Teacups were rattled round to all the guests. Delicate sandwiches were offered and accepted. Aunt Maud made an effort to speak to those who were standing near her. The talk gathered into a paean of praise for their dead hero.

'Fine chap,' his uncles agreed. 'Greater love hath no man and all that sort of thing. You couldn't ask for a better end.'

His father said, 'I always knew he had it in him. Valiant, you see, even as a little lad. Soldier of the King.'

'Bred in the bone, old thing,' his uncle John said. 'Breeding always tells.'

'Made of stern stuff,' his uncle Albert agreed. 'Good stock, that's what breeds heroes. Good stock. That and a good education, of course. You made a good choice there, Ralph. Fine school. Fine tradition. All the best values and all that sort of thing.'

'Terrible time of course,' John said to his brother. 'Feel for you and Maud and all that sort of thing.'

'But he made a good end,' Albert pointed out. 'Mustn't forget that, eh? A brave end. Something to be proud of. Greater love hath no man and all that sort of thing. He was a fine chap your Cyril. A hero. A cut above all the riff-raff you see about these days. Made of sterner stuff. Not a cowardly bone in his body. That's the truth of it.'

How can they stand there saying such stupid, fatuous things? Octavia thought. Her chest was so tight with irritation she was finding it hard to breathe. If they had to talk, they should try to say something truthful.

But now that they'd moved into myth-making there was no stopping them. 'A fine chap,' they said, nodding agreement with one another. 'Good moral fibre. Straight off to save another feller. Not a thought for his own safety. A hero you see. Not an ounce of fear in his entire body. Simply didn't feel it.'

It was too much. She couldn't stand quietly by and let them say such damaging things. It was as if they were burying him all over again, covering him with their warped view, changing him into an icon, hiding the real person as if he'd never existed. And the real person had been ten times better than this meaningless, fearless hero. She stepped towards them, her face flushed.

'No!' she cried. 'You're wrong. Quite, quite wrong.' Her voice was loud in the hushed room. Faces turned towards her in the gloom, round-eyed, shocked and anxious. She knew she was upsetting them but she couldn't stop. The words tumbled from her in an ecstasy of grief and anger. 'He wasn't fearless. He was terrified. That's the truth. He told me. He sent me a letter and told me all about it. They're all terrified, every single one of them. You'd be terrified if you were there. Look at the casualty lists. Imagine it. It's a nightmare and they have to endure it. Think of *that* if you must think of something. They endure it, day after day, on and on and on. They're not fearless. They're made of flesh and blood the same as everybody else, the same as you, the same as our poor Cyril. You diminish him when you say he hadn't got an ounce of fear in his entire body. Don't you understand? He was paralysed with fear but he went ahead just the same. He did what he had to do even though he knew exactly what it would cost him, exactly what sort of death he was going to die. Even though he was frightened. That's real courage. He was *truly* brave and he had a conscience. That's what killed him. The need to ato...' But no! She mustn't tell them that. That was his secret. She stopped talking with an effort, swayed on her feet, gulped to prevent herself from uttering another damaging word. She was aware that they were all listening attentively, cups still poised, that her mother was reaching out towards her, that her father had a restraining hand on her arm, but she shook him off and wouldn't look at him. She ran headlong out of the door and across the hall to the sanctuary of the drawing room.

It was warm in there because there were no blinds to draw across the long French windows and, although the curtains were closed, it had been roughly done and sunshine was streaming through the gaps between them. She opened the nearest pair and stepped into the forest of the conservatory. Oh such white truthful light flooding through the high thick glass above her head, oh such peaceful plants, all so fleshily green and alive and polished by sunshine, oh such easy, soothing colours out there in the garden. And her dear brave murdered Cyril would never see any of it again. She put her head against the doorjamb and wept.

Presently there was a disturbance in the air behind her and her father appeared. 'Are you all right?' he asked.

'I'm so sorry, Pa,' she said. 'I shouldn't have spoken like that. Are they very upset?'

'They will understand,' he assured her, putting his arm round her shoulders and leading her to the nearest wickerwork chair. 'Grief takes us all in different ways.'

'It was the letter you see,' she said. 'He sent me a letter.'

'I rather gathered he had. That was what you were referring to, wasn't it.'

'It was a terrible letter, Pa. He told me exactly what it was like out there and it was horrible. I promised him I wouldn't let anyone else see it, but I suppose it doesn't matter now he's... I'll show it to you when we get home. It was a terrible, terrible letter.'

'I should like to see it, my dear,' her father said, 'if you could bear to show me.'

'I'm sorry about the way I went on in there,' she said again and tried to explain. 'It was the way they were talking. As if he was someone different, someone inhuman. I've been standing here remembering him at his twenty-first. Do you remember that? All giggly and happy and so drunk he couldn't stand up. That was the real Cyril, rushing into things, hero-worshipping Tommy, dreaming of being an explorer, playing bears with Dora and Eddie, bringing us presents when he came back from his tour. Full of life. A person. And they stand there talking nonsense about him. I couldn't bear it.'

'I don't think they were talking at all,' JJ said in his gentle way. 'They were making sympathetic noises, that's all. It's the best some of us can manage when we're grieving. The most some of us want. Human beings can only take a limited amount of truth.'

Eased by his gentle support she began to recover. 'But if you don't tell the truth,' she protested, 'you lie.'

'You see things in such black and white terms, my Tavy,' her father said. 'Truth is rarely absolute and opinions vary, as you know. Do we not teach our pupils to examine every possibility, to be open to shades of opinion, to respect the fact that others might not think as we do?'

All this was correct and she accepted it.

'Facts,' JJ went on, leaning back in his chair, 'that one man will accept as entirely true from his limited knowledge and experience will be — shall we say — questionable from the point of view of another man with wider information at his disposal. You see that too, I am sure. They vary, as opinions do.'

'Cyril thought he was a coward,' she remembered. 'That's what he said in his letter. And that certainly wasn't true. Fact or opinion. I knew that when I read the letter. I think he was brave. Amazingly brave.'

'Exactly so,' JJ said. 'So we are of one mind.'

'Possibly,' she admitted. 'But not entirely. I still think it's important to tell the truth.'

'I might go so far as to say that most truth is relative,' her father said, coaxing her away from grief by way of philosophy. 'I might go so far as to say that one man's truth is another man's prevarication. That knowledge and experience influence every fact we know or think we know. That all facts need constant re-examination and all opinions constant readjustment. Then again, there are occasions when we don't tell the whole truth in order to protect someone we love. There are times when I protect your mother by half-truths, as you know. And I daresay there will be times when Tommy will protect you in exactly the same way.'

That she couldn't and wouldn't accept. 'I sincerely hope not,' she said. 'If we are to make a go of our marriage we've got to be truthful. All the time.' But hearing his name reminded her of him just a little too powerfully and her mind drifted, as it so often did when somebody mentioned him. She wondered where he was and what he was doing and whether he was thinking of her. She knew where he was going. He'd told her that on their last leave together. He and his company were sailing to Gallipoli to fight the Turks. In fact, the last letter she'd had from him, in which he'd apologised for missing Squirrel's memorial service, had been posted in Egypt. Oh dear Tommy what a long, long war this is.

JJ watched her reverie with pity. 'You are right,' he said. 'You and Tommy must discover your own way. But I think we should rejoin the others, don't you, my dear, and be sociable.'

She didn't want to be sociable. She would rather have stayed where she was and thought about the things he'd just said to her. But she did as he suggested because he was so plainly expecting it. Dear Pa, she thought. You always say exactly the right things to me. You know me so well.

'We will go in together,' he said and offered her his arm.

CHAPTER 18

I n the long weeks after the funeral service, Octavia lived in a
half world, missing Cyril and fraught with worry about
Podge and Tommy, even though both of them sent fairly regular
letters and postcards to report that they were well and unhurt.
Even a letter a day wouldn't have been enough to reassure her
now. She was far too aware that they could have been killed
after the mail was sent, could be lying dead even as their
messages were being read. Her world was thoroughly out of
kilter. Nothing was what it had been. She started work at St
Barnaby's High in a dream, as if she'd been anaesthetised, and
although she worked hard and took some comfort from what
she was doing, she was often ashamed to think that she wasn't
responding to her new pupils as well as she ought to have done.

'There are times,' she said to Emmeline, as the two of them
were taking tea at the end of a wet school day, 'when I think that
the only thing that's normal nowadays is having to prepare
lessons and teach classes and mark exercise books.' Raindrops
wept down the windowpane, soundless and incessant.

Emmeline was trying to spoon a mash of rusk and milk into
the reluctant mouth of her youngest. 'Come along, Johnnie,' she

coaxed, 'one more teeny-weeny mouthful for Mama. Be a good boy.'

Johnnie screwed up his face and turned his head away from the jab of the spoon, waving his hands defensively in front of his mouth, fingers splayed like starfish. One of them caught the edge of the spoon and tipped the mash down the front of his bib.

'Now look what you've done, you naughty little thing,' Emmeline said in exasperation. 'Your Papa is quite right about you. You're impossible.'

The baby began to cry, his mouth square with distress. Octavia felt quite sorry for him. 'Let me try,' she offered.

Emmeline handed over the baby spoon. 'He won't take it,' she warned. 'He's always troublesome at mealtimes. I don't know what to do with him.'

Johnnie was sucking his fingers for comfort. 'Maybe he'd suck a dry rusk and get it down him that way,' Octavia said. 'Shall we try that?'

'Try anything you like,' his mother said wearily. 'I'm sick of him.'

Octavia removed the offending bowl and put a dry rusk on the baby's tray. She didn't offer it to him but just left it, lying there. 'You haven't found another nursemaid, then,' she said to her cousin.

'No,' Emmeline said. 'You can't get servants for love nor money these days. They can earn so much more in munitions, that's the trouble. We've still got our Dolly, bless her, and she's very good. She gives the others their tea and puts them to bed and everything but she can't handle Johnnie. I'm at my wits' end with him some days, especially since Squirrel was killed.' And she began to cry too.

The baby had recovered from his scolding and was picking a small piece of mash from his bib. He placed it carefully on the tray alongside the rusk, and considered it with solemn gravity, patting it with the palm of his hand. Then he put it in his mouth and ate it.

'There! You see!' Emmeline wept. 'How can he be so aggravating?'

'Maybe he wants to feed himself,' Octavia said, watching him.

'He's not old enough.'

Johnnie went on feeding himself. He was completely absorbed.

'There are times when I wonder why I ever said I wanted babies,' Emmeline wailed. 'I must have been mad. If I'd known how difficult they were going to be I'd have said something quite different. Oh quite, quite different. Or not had so many. Not that there's anything you can do about that. You just have to take them as they come, don't you? Oh Tavy! Everything's so impossible.'

It was an opportunity to help, a chance to give poor Emmeline some much-needed practical advice, something Octavia had thought about on many occasions when she'd seen her cousin weary with childcare. Until that moment she'd always been restrained by delicacy or the presence of too many sharp-eared children, but now, the combination of Emmeline's distress, Johnnie's happy concentration and her own ingrained determination to tell the truth, gave her the daring she needed. 'You don't have to just have them these days,' she said. 'There are things you can do.' And then blushed at the thought of what she would have to say next.

Emmeline stopped crying and blushed too, staring at her, her blue eyes still tear-washed but wide-open with embarrassment and curiosity. 'What things?' she asked. Surely they're not going to talk about 'that'! Nobody ever talks about 'that'.

Octavia pushed her glasses up the bridge of her nose, her own embarrassment having made them slip. 'I've got a leaflet about it,' she said. 'It's quite straightforward.'

Emmeline waited, ducking her head to hide her blushes.

'There have always been things that men can use if they don't want babies,' Octavia explained. She was hot with embarrassment by then and the more deeply her cousin blushed the hotter she became. She knew she couldn't talk about the things men use, that would be just too embarrassing for words and it was words she needed and hadn't got. It was going to be difficult enough to find a way to talk about birth control for women, but now that she'd started she felt she had to go on. Emmeline had been overburdened with babies for far too long. 'Well,' she said, 'nowadays there are things for women to use too. The leaflet explains about them. It's written by a doctor called Marie Stopes, so it's all perfectly proper. I could lend it to you if you'd like.'

Emmeline knew she *would* like but it took her a little while to pluck up the courage to say so and the effort made her cough. 'I don't know what Ernest would think,' she said. 'He says babies are a gift from God. It's odd really because he doesn't like them a bit. He's always shouting at them to behave and telling them how dreadful they are.'

'If I were you I'd just read the leaflet and not tell him about it,' Octavia advised. 'You don't have to.'

'How did you find out about all this?' Emmeline wanted to know.

'They were talking about it at one of Pa's Fabian dinners,' Octavia told her. She had recovered her balance by then and could speak calmly. 'I asked Mrs Bland afterwards.' Then she paused, remembering what a long time ago it had been. Back in that lovely summer, just after she and Tommy had started their affair.

'Heavens!' Emmeline said. 'I wouldn't have dared. And *I'm* married.'

Johnnie was still happily picking up bits of mash so the two women returned to their own tea. The information had been given. They could move on to an easier topic now, if they could find one.

'Do you remember how we used to sit in your garden and plan our lives?' Emmeline said. 'Under the cherry tree. On the little seat.' They both remembered — for several quiet seconds and with consuming sadness. 'I said I wanted lots and lots of babies and Squirrel was going to be an explorer — poor Squirrel — and you were going to change the world. What innocents we were! And now here we are in the middle of a war and nothing's the same. Everything's changed.' Tears welled into her eyes again.

'Not quite everything,' Octavia said, speaking quickly to forestall any further weeping. 'I still want to change the world.'

'Votes for women, do you mean?' Emmeline said, blinking. 'I thought that had all gone quiet.'

'So it has,' Octavia agreed. 'We called off the campaign for the duration. But no, that's not what I mean.' And when her cousin looked surprised, she went on, 'Don't misunderstand me. I'm sure we should be given the vote and I shall go on campaigning for it, but I think it will happen now, one way or another, once the war is over.'

Emmeline was impressed by how knowledgeable her cousin was. 'Do you? What makes you say that?'

The reason was obvious and had been for some time. Mrs Pankhurst's prescience was being justified. With so many young men killed or too badly wounded to work, more and more women were doing men's work and making a very good fist of it and they would have to go on doing it, even when the war was over, because there would be very few men left to replace them. It was becoming plain that once people understood what had happened, it would be hard for the government to ignore the WSPU's demands. But she couldn't say so, not now Cyril had been killed. She would have to choose her words with care or she would upset her cousin all over again and she couldn't bear to do that. They'd passed through grief and embarrassment together and now they needed the sort of talk and thought that would calm them.

'Before the war,' she said at last, 'most women were at home. That was the way things were. Only a handful were out at work and most of them were indoors somewhere, fairly well hidden, in a school or a hospital. Now they're out in the streets, where everyone can see them, driving trams and delivering coal, working on the railways, cleaning windows, even sweeping chimneys. Lloyd George is a shrewd man, too shrewd not to realise he'll have to give way. I think he'll pass a bill quietly, once the war's over, and open the door to us when our opponents aren't looking.'

'So you'll have won,' Emmeline said.

'We were bound to in the end.'

Emmeline smiled. It was her first smile since the conversation had begun. 'So what will you change next?' she said and her tone was teasing.

Octavia wasn't quite sure where to begin because her ideas were still at the pondering stage. She looked at the baby who had picked all the bits of chewed rusk from his bib and was searching his tray for more. 'There you are, Johnnie,' she said to him and absent-mindedly put his dish on the tray with his baby spoon beside it. Then she turned her attention to Emmeline again. 'The thing is, I've been wondering why some children find learning easy and others don't.'

'That's obvious,' her cousin said. 'Some are clever, like you, and some aren't, like me.'

'That's an oversimplification,' Octavia said, 'and besides, it isn't true. I've watched you doing your household accounts and you're every bit as clever as I am.'

Emmeline grimaced such an idea aside. 'That's different.'

'I don't think it is,' Octavia said seriously. 'In fact I'm beginning to think we're all quite capable of being "clever". It all

247

depends on what we're asked to do and how we're asked to do it. The teachers at Bridge Street used to say that, apart from the handful they were coaching for the scholarship, the children there were dumb and couldn't learn anything. But they were wrong. They were all perfectly capable of learning, all of them, even the boy who drew pothooks all day. What was getting in their way and making them look unintelligent was boredom and being asked to do things that didn't make any sense to them. Once they saw the sense of what they were doing there was no stopping them. My girls at St Barnaby's are the same. Some of them leap into any new task I set them and really enjoy it, but the others are bored. They don't say so, because that would be complaining and they don't complain. They're all much too well brought up for that, but I can see how hard it is for them. And I want to do something about it.'

'Heavens!' Emmeline said. 'So what will you do?'

'I don't know,' Octavia told her honestly. 'I shall think about it, try things. I have a feeling that part of the problem is never giving them any choice. Think how it was when we were at school. Did we ever have a choice about anything we did? I can't remember a single occasion. We simply sat at our desks and did as we were told and that was all there was to it. That's the way the system works, the way it's always worked, all right for those who enjoy it, misery for those who don't.' She was warming to her subject now, speaking with more passion. 'Well I don't think it works well, even for those it seems to suit. In fact, I've started a little experiment. I've given my first form the freedom to choose. I started this week. Instead of setting one essay for the entire class, the way we're supposed to, I've given them half a dozen different titles and let them choose the one they like best.'

Emmeline laughed. 'I thought it was going to be something revolutionary,' she said, 'and it's only essays. You *are* funny, Tavy.'

'It is a revolution,' Octavia told her seriously. 'It may not look like it but it is. You should have seen their faces when I told them they could actually choose what they wanted to write about. They were all smiles and disbelief, just like my Bridge Street children were when I told them they could skip and play tag and hopscotch instead of doing that awful drill.' And as Emmeline was still looking baffled, she joked, 'Anyway, it gives me something to think about.' Apart from this dreadful war and whether Tommy and Podge will survive it and whether it will ever ever end.

'Will you look at that baby,' Emmeline said. 'Now just you tell me that isn't naughty.'

They both looked at him. He had put the little spoon in the centre of his bowl and was packing it with mash, piece by piece and very delicately, patting the mixture down with great deliberation. It took a long time but finally he was satisfied with it and holding the spoon in his plump little fist began to steer it with great difficulty towards his face. Most of the mash fell out as he lifted it but there was still enough left to make a solid mouthful which he sucked off the spoon with great relish. He was feeding himself.

'I despair of him,' Emmeline said. 'All that fuss when I tried to feed him and now look at him. He's just a naughty wilful little thing.'

'Yes,' Octavia agreed. 'He's certainly wilful but ... well maybe that's a good thing, Emmeline. Perhaps he wouldn't let you feed him because he wanted to feed himself. Perhaps that's the start of learning.'

'If that's learning,' his mother said, wrinkling up her nose at his efforts, 'I don't think much of it. He's making a fine old mess.'

'Yes,' Octavia had to admit. 'He is. But the point is, he's feeding himself and he's getting better at it. If you were to let him feed himself every day he'd get the hang of it in no time.'

'No jolly fear,' Emmeline said. 'I'd be forever scraping food off the carpet. I've got enough to do in this house without that. Experiments are all very well in a school but a nursery is not the place for them.'

And Johnnie, having completed his own experiment, looked up at the sound of her voice and gave her a rapturous smile.

LETTERS AND CARDS from the Front continued to arrive, the news bulletins were always bad, the casualty lists always terrifying, summer drudged by. Food was in short supply and very poor quality. Bread was ten pence a loaf, to Amy's consternation, and poor adulterated stuff, gritty with chalk. Tommy came home on leave but was so irritable and preoccupied that their ten short days together left Octavia feeling dissatisfied and bereft.

The Battle of the Somme went bloodily on and was still a stalemate. In August the newspapers reported that 700,000 men had been killed at Verdun and 650,000 on the Somme and that many more had been wounded. And one of the casualties was Podge, who wrote to his mother to say that he'd been gassed but 'it wasn't too bad' and they'd be sending him 'back to Blighty' any day. When she first read his letter Maud was distraught but after a while she recovered and tried to cheer her family up by saying that at least he hadn't been killed, poor boy and urging them to be thankful for small mercies. He spent a month in hospital and she visited him every day but he was extremely ill and when he finally came home he was thin and withdrawn, and sat in the conservatory all day coughing endlessly and reading the papers.

Octavia hadn't seen him while he was in hospital because visiting was limited to wives and mothers and she was appalled by the change in him. He looked like an old man, not a boy of twenty, with his nails blackened and broken and all that ginger hair cut short. What sort of life had he got to look forward to?

They should stop this war now, she thought, before any more young men are killed. But, of course, they didn't. They just let it go on and on and the death toll rose inexorably. The parks were full of wounded soldiers in their pale blue uniform, taking what air they could and the casualty lists were a daily horror.

In October Tommy was sent to Salonika and wrote more and more infrequently and with deepening pessimism. She wrote back to him as often as she could, urging him to take care of himself and telling him how Podge was getting on, because she thought he ought to know.

It seems such a wicked waste, she said. *A senseless, wicked waste.*

It was only at school that there was hope of better sense and a chance to improve things. When the autumn term began she felt more at home in the place and started to study her pupils more intently and to make careful notes. Soon she began to make changes too — offering a choice of class readers and the freedom for every girl to read on her own and at her own pace, acting out a scene from the prescribed Shakespeare play instead of reading it round the class, teaching parts of speech much more slowly and in smaller groups, moving from the known to the new by gentle degrees. Her fellow English teachers started to complain — politely — that she was dominating the text-books and that her method of offering four books to her classes instead of the normal one, meant that four sets of twenty books were now diminished to four sets of ten, which were too small to be used by anyone else. So that experiment had to be modified to a choice of two schoolbooks and the reassurance that, if they wished, her pupils could read novels they had brought from home.

At the end of her second spring term the Headmistress called her in to tell her that experimentation was all very well but that she mustn't do anything that would jeopardise the girls' chances in their public examinations. She agreed that nothing damaging would ever be done and promised — keeping her fingers crossed behind her back — that that year's examination results would be as good as ever, if not better.

Every evening after dinner, she wrote up her lesson notes, sitting at her desk in the window of her bedroom overlooking the heath and watching as another subdued summer inched into bloom. It grew apologetically, as if richness and light-hearted colour were inappropriate to the sorrow of the time. And no matter how hard she worked, Octavia was subdued too, living from day to day and from letter to letter. There were times when she felt rather lonely and wished there were other teachers who thought as she did. There must be some somewhere. She couldn't be the only one. In fact if it hadn't been for the complications she was making for herself at St Barnaby's High School and the regular stimulus of her father's dinner parties, her life would have been rather miserable.

As the weeks passed, she found she was looking forward to their Thursday evenings as the highlight of the month, seeing it as a time when the darkness would lift and hope and good sense return. The Fabians were stoical about the war, turning their attention away from the slaughter, which they deplored but over which they had no control and no influence, and concentrating instead on how international affairs should be conducted when the fighting was finally over, which was a great deal more positive and a great deal more pleasant to consider.

'I see your friend Wells is still advocating a Peace League,' Edith Bland said to Bernard Shaw, one mellow evening in late October in the third year of the war. She was making eyes at him, knowing how the two men quarrelled and daring him to rise to the bait she was setting. 'He had an article about it in the New Statesman this week.'

'I read it,' Shaw said, ginger whiskers bristling. He gave her his most devilish grin and answered the dare. 'Not too closely, mind, his style being anathema to careful reading, but with sufficient attention to know that he is in the right, for once. Whatever else he may be, he is a gifted thinker. It is manifestly the sort of organisation we shall need.'

'Could it be set up, do you think?' JJ asked, offering more wine to his neighbour. 'I can foresee prodigious difficulties.'

'Since President Wilson is expounding a similar idea,' Shaw said, 'I should say it stands a fair chance. A league of nations gathered together to give protection to small states and pause to aggressive ones could be a powerful force for peace. It would have my blessing.'

'Anything to prevent another war like this one,' Amy mourned. 'It is all very well to say that this is a war to end all wars but we are killing off an entire generation.'

'We must hope that President Wilson will persevere with his idea,' Edith Bland said, 'and that he will persuade others to support him. I must say there are some excellent notions coming out of the United States at the moment. I read of another only this morning. An educational idea. It would interest you, Octavia.'

Octavia was already interested. 'Indeed?' she asked.

'Apparently there is a school in New York that is trying out a most interesting educational experiment. They call it — What was it? Let me think — the Dalton method, and it sounds extremely sensible. As far as I can see from the article, they allow their pupils to choose what lessons they will attend and when they will do their work. They say there is no true learning without the freedom to learn at one's own pace. It seems rather similar to the attitude you are taking to your pupils at St Barnaby's.'

Octavia was intrigued. 'I should like to know more about it,' she said.

'I will send you the paper,' her mentor promised.

'High time you were a headmistress, young woman,' Shaw

told her. 'Influencing a single class of infant minds is all very well, and I'm sure you do it splendidly, but you should have a school of your own where you can put all your ideas into practice. Education will be more important than ever when this war is over. You may smile, but this is a piece of highly valuable advice, which I've given you before, free, gratis and for nothing. I daresay I am wasting my breath, for I don't believe you were listening then any more than you are listening now.'

'On the contrary,' Octavia told him returning his grin. 'I am all attention. All I need is the opportunity. I only hold my present position on sufferance. I shall lose it when the previous holder comes back from the war.'

There was a murmur round the table and then Sidney Webb leant towards Octavia and joined the conversation. 'As it happens,' he said, 'the LCC are looking for a headmistress at this moment. There is an old pupil teacher centre in Hammersmith that they are planning to convert into a local secondary school. They need a graduate with teaching experience and plenty of energy and enthusiasm, so they say. I think you would be admirably suited. Would you like me to recommend you? It would be a challenge. I should warn you of that. It's an old building and completely unequipped. You would be starting from scratch.'

But she would be starting and it would be *her* school. 'Thank you, Mr Webb,' she said, keeping her excitement under control. 'I would like that very much indeed.'

Mrs Wilkins gentled into the room to remove the dirty dishes and, at a signal from Professor Smith, to turn up the gaslights, which bloomed into golden haloes on either side of the fireplace. Light, Octavia thought, admiring it. Beautiful, necessary, truthful light, which is what education should be about. Understanding what is true and good and seeing it clearly.

Later that night, when the guests were gone and she and her

parents were sitting round the fire in her father's study discussing the evening's events, her mother returned rather tentatively to Mr Webb's offer.

'Do you really want to be a headmistress, Tavy?' she asked.

'Very much, Mama.'

'It would mean a lot of work,' Amy said in her worried way.

Octavia tried to reassure her. 'I'm not afraid of work, Mama.'

'No,' Amy agreed. 'That is true. You are not. I never knew anyone work as hard as you do, my dear. But then again, there is Tommy to consider. He might not approve of it.'

'I suppose that is possible,' Octavia admitted. 'On the other hand he might say it's a capital idea. There's no knowing what he might think.'

'Perhaps you should write and ask him,' Amy suggested.

That sounded too much like asking his permission. 'There's no point,' Octavia said. 'If I do, he will either agree to it without thinking about it, or tell me not to do it, without thinking about that either. Being in action is such an overwhelming business they haven't got the energy for anything else. We will talk about it when the war's over and he's back home. Time enough then.' And as her mother was looking upset, she tried to explain. 'War changes people, Mama. It is changing us all. When he comes home I shall have to get to know him all over again.' She looked at Amy closely, noticing how much *she* had altered in the last three years. Her hair was completely grey and, even when she was sitting, her shoulders stooped and she tucked her shawl about her like an old lady.

'I still think you should write and tell him,' Amy said.

'I'm sure she will,' JJ smoothed. 'When the time comes. She has yet to be offered this position. It is not in Mr Webb's gift.'

'Quite right,' Octavia agreed, smiling at him for his intervention. 'Anything could happen.' Here in Hampstead, in Hammersmith, in Salonika — which God forbid — anywhere. 'We can't be sure of anything.' Except that she would apply for this headship, no matter what Tommy might think. He'd probably be as dismissive about it as he'd been about her present position, and to be realistic, there was little real hope that she would actually be offered the post, or even asked for interview — she was only a class teacher after all and hadn't even run a department, which was the usual prerequisite for a headship — but she *would* apply because she knew she could do it and do it well and because it was the right thing to do. The end of the war and marriage to Tommy had receded further and further into the distance all through that awful year.

CHAPTER 19

The last months of 1917 limped miserably by. It was dark and cold, the news was always bad, there were far too many people in mourning, houses were shabby for lack of paint and food was in parlously short supply. There were even shortages of bread and potatoes despite the fact that there were nearly a quarter of a million women working on the land and, as the lean weeks passed, there was talk of rationing being introduced and teams of women were gathered to cope with the paperwork. There could be no doubt in any politician's mind that whatever their opinion of women's suffrage might once have been, women had become too crucial to this war to be ignored. They were in France nursing the troops, they worked in munitions, they'd even been given a special dispensation to join the armed forces.

'They will have to give us the vote when this is over,' Octavia said to her father.

But when would it be over? The stalemate in the trenches continued endlessly, the casualty lists grew more horrific by the day and the fighting in Flanders went bloodily and muddily on over the same few soured and cratered miles, which were now such a quagmire of mud and filth that if a soldier lost his footing on the duckboards and fell into it he was drowned. Elsewhere the fortunes of the war seemed to vary with the territory. In Italy the Italian army was overrun by the Germans, in Palestine Jerusalem was captured from the Turks by the British, on the Russian front there was a revolution and the Russian troops took off and marched home, refusing to fight the Czar's wars for him any longer. The British press was considerably alarmed, pointing out that if there were to be a new government in Russia it might make peace with Germany and that would be disastrous because it would release all the German troops on the eastern front to fight in the West.

Their fears were realised in November, when the British troops in Flanders were being annihilated at a place called Passchendaele and German Zeppelins were dropping bombs on the East End of London and the Isle of Sheppey. By that time there was a new popular leader in Russia by the name of Lenin and the Czar and his family had been sent to Siberia, where, so the newspapers said, they were being well looked after. And just as the West had feared, peace talks between Russia, Germany and Austria were opened just before Christmas.

Tommy wrote about it to Octavia quite sourly.

The one thing you don't want in a war is for your allies to go sloping off and leaving you, he said. We've got enough on our plates without that, fighting Johnnie Turk, who is much worse than the Jerries, I can tell you.

Like so many of his letters it was full of complaints. There wasn't enough food and what there was of it was poor tack, the guns were in a foul state, they were running out of ammunition, half the army was in the sick bay with dysentery and cholera and other noxious diseases, German spies sat on the quayside in Salonica, bold as brass, and made notes on every arrival.

Far too many damned incompetents around, that's the truth of it, he said. *If I survive this lot, I shall join the Foreign Office and show them how things should be run.*

But for once Octavia wasn't paying attention to his letters or to the politics of the war, because two momentous things had happened, one public and extremely quiet, the other personal and quietly public.

In January the House of Lords finally approved Lloyd George's Representation of the People Act and married women over the age of thirty were given the vote.

'It's not enough,' Octavia said to her father. 'It's a start. I'll grant you that. But they should have given it to all women over the age of twenty-one, married or not. The Campaign will have to continue.'

However she didn't have time to think about the Campaign because two days later, an advertisement for the headship she'd been advised to apply for appeared in the papers and ten minutes after she'd read it, she was busy composing a detailed application. It seemed obvious to her that a newly formed, small school would be just the place for her to put her newly formed large ideas into practise and she meant to make out the case for them as persuasively as she could. It took her the best part of a week to get her thoughts in order.

I believe, she wrote, *that learning should be pleasurable and should bring its own reward. I believe that lack of pleasure in what we ask our pupils to do impedes their ability to do it. A baby learning to feed himself or to stand and walk is utterly absorbed in what he is doing. He doesn't fear mistakes, since mistakes are one way of learning, he doesn't tire, he is never bored and when he finally succeeds he is quite rapturously happy. If we could find some way to translate that experience into the teaching situation we should revolutionise the lives of our pupils. I have made a start at St Barnaby's by allowing choice, offering praise and endeavouring to use understanding instead of resorting to punishment, but there is much more that could be done. My pupils are much happier than they would have been under a more rigid regime but they are still under pressure because mine is the only subject which offers them freedom of choice. As a headmistress and with a carefully chosen staff, I could extend this freedom to all my pupils in all the subjects they were studying.*

It was the most demanding piece of writing she'd ever put together and even after she'd posted it she was still remembering other things she felt she should have included. By then, of course, there was nothing she could do except return to her work and try to put it out of her mind — which couldn't be done. During the day she was kept busy by her pupils but at night she thought and hoped and planned. Oh if only they'd give her an interview. Just an interview. That was all she needed.

IT CAME at the beginning of February, on a cold wet day that chilled her to the bones. The fire was slow to take that morning and she and her parents ate their limited breakfast, wrapped in their dressing gowns and shivering. In fact, when Mrs Wilkins came limping in to deliver the letters, Octavia left hers by her plate until she'd drunk a little tea to warm her. But then she opened the third one with a shriek of pleasure.

'Oh Pa!' she said, 'Mama look! I've got an interview. What do you think of that?'

'You must have a new hat,' her mother said, predictably.

'Nobody dresses up in wartime,' Octavia told her.

But her mother prevailed and Octavia wore her new felt hat with her old cloth coat when she took the tram to Hammersmith. As she was led into the interview room, she was so excited her hands were shaking.

There were three people in the room, one elderly man with

a splendid set of white whiskers, who introduced himself as Mr Gillard, Chairman of the Governors, and two well-dressed women in rather grand hats. They were sitting on the opposite side of a long table facing the chair that had been centrally set for the candidates and they all smiled at her as she sat down.

'We were all intrigued by your application, Miss Smith,' Mr Gillard said. 'It was quite a credo, was it not? Would you care to tell us why you believe as you do?'

She told them at length, stressing that everything she now believed had grown from her observations of the children she'd taught at Bridge Street and was currently teaching at St Barnaby's High and that the methods she used had been evolved by trial and error. 'It has been a learning process for me too,' she said. 'We've all been learning together. It's been something of an experiment.'

'And now you are looking to extend the experiment from a single classroom to an entire school,' the older of the ladies said. 'Would I be right in that assumption?'

There was no point in denying it. That was exactly what she was doing.

The questioning went on. Did she expect to find other teachers with the same views?

'I would hope to find other teachers who would be sympathetic to what I've been trying to do.'

'They would be rather exceptional I fancy?'

'Very exceptional but I am confident I could find them, given the right advertisement.'

'Which you would compose with the same care you devoted to your application form.'

'Exactly so.'

'It would be a very small school to start with,' Mr Gillard told her. 'We estimate about fifty pupils, all girls, and a staff of five including yourself.'

She would have preferred more teachers but agreed that five would be sufficient to make a good beginning.

The interview continued. They asked about the sort of staff she would hire and she told them she would need a science teacher, and a mathematician, someone to teach History and Geography and someone else for French and Latin if possible, and if she could find one, a teacher prepared to take PE and Cookery. The younger of the two women wanted to know how and when she would punish her pupils.

'I deal with whatever happens as it occurs,' she said, 'and would hope to continue with the same approach as a headmistress. If a child has done something wrong or unacceptable, she needs to know as soon as possible and to face the consequences.'

'Which would be?'

'It would depend on the offence. If someone has been hurt by it, then there must be an apology and an attempt to make amends. That is essential. If it is caused by bad temper, the reasons for the temper must be discovered and dealt with, if it is laziness, the child must be helped towards greater effort, if it is misery she will need cheering. I suppose what I'm saying is that it is necessary for me to understand the cause of the offence if I am to deal with it adequately. There are always reasons for bad behaviour and that's what I try to tackle.'

'What if you can't find the reason though, Miss Smith?' Mr Gillard asked. 'What would you do then?'

'I would try harder,' Octavia said.

He laughed out loud. 'By Jove, she would too,' he said.

Eventually they asked her if she had any questions for *them*. She had of course and asked them at once. 'If I were to be appointed,' she said, 'how soon could I advertise for my staff.'

'How soon would you want to advertise?' Mr Gillard said.

'As soon as possible,' Octavia told him. 'It might take quite a while to find the sort of teachers I would be looking for, and finding the right staff would be extremely important if we are to make a success of our venture.'

'I see no reason why you shouldn't advertise as soon as you were appointed,' he said. 'But where would you interview them? That could present a problem could it not?'

'Could I use the school building? It is currently empty you say.'

'Empty but extremely dirty.'

'I could take a broom.'

He laughed again, looked round him at the other two and closed his notebook. 'I think that will be all, Miss Smith,' he said. 'If you have no further questions. No? Then would you be so kind as to wait in the reception room.'

The reception room, to which the secretary led her, was just along the corridor. It was comfortably furnished with a good fire in the grate and armchairs for six people but they were all empty. How odd, she thought, where are the other candidates? Or do we have a room each? There was no one to ask, so she walked across the room to the window and stood looking down at the cars and trams that were clattering their way through Hammersmith Broadway. I should like a car, she thought, and imagined herself down there among all the others, manoeuvring among the trams.

A movement at the door, the secretary had returned, she was being asked to rejoin the committee. That was quick, she thought, glancing at her watch, and feared that they were going to turn her down.

But she was wrong. The job was hers. Her relief and delight were so strong she knew she was grinning like a fool but she simply couldn't control her face. I've got it, she thought. I'm twenty-nine and I'm going to be a headmistress. I must be the youngest head they've ever appointed. 'Thank you,' she said. 'I hope I shall be worthy of the trust you are putting in me.'

'I will send you a broom,' Mr Gillard said and shook her hand warmly.

Oh wait till I tell Ma and Pa.

'CHAMPAGNE!' her father said. 'We've got one bottle left and what better time to open it. Don't you think so, Amy?'

'I think it's perfectly splendid,' Amy said. 'When do you start?'

'In September,' Octavia told her, 'and I can't wait either. Just think, Mama, I can have a place of my own, a nice little flat somewhere near the school.' Oh the possibilities were endless! 'I shall have to go house hunting.'

Her mother's face fell markedly. 'There's no rush is there, my dear?' she said. 'I wouldn't want you to buy something that didn't suit. You need to take your time over a house.'

'Don't worry, Mama,' Octavia said, reassuring her. 'I shan't rush into anything. I've got plenty of time. September's a long way off. I shall choose something really suitable, you'll see.'

But Amy didn't want her to choose anything. There was no necessity for it. She should stay at home with us and be looked after properly, not go rushing off on her own. 'You might be married by then,' she pointed out. 'You never know. And then you'll be setting up house with Tommy.'

That looked very unlikely now but Octavia decided not to argue about it. Mama was anxious and it was better to drop the subject — for the time being. She could stay at home for the first year and let her get used to the idea. 'There's plenty of time,' she said. 'And there are so many things to be done. I think I shall keep a journal, Pa, like you do.'

'You shall have my spare one,' he said, relieved to see that the difficult moment had passed, and went off at once to get it.

She began it that evening, in her best handwriting because only the best would do for such a document and feeling so inordinately proud of herself that she was afraid she was getting conceited. I must guard against conceit, she thought, as she dipped her pen in the inkwell. It wouldn't do to get swollen-headed. So she began soberly.

February 1918.
Today I have been appointed headmistress of a new secondary school for girls in Hammersmith. I truly believe I am setting out on my life's work.

But then her pride in this achievement reasserted itself and she went on,

I am sure it is going to be a great adventure. I cannot wait to see it. My own school!

She visited her own school on the following Friday evening and, although she was loath to admit it, her first sight of it was not encouraging. She stood in the empty playground for quite a long time while she assessed it — dark brick, three forbidding storeys high, with a sternly separate floor for infants, girls and boys. The entrance marked 'Girls', which she'd been told led to her floor, was narrow and dark and not at all welcoming. She would have to do something about that come September — a bright notice board perhaps, with a red arrow to show her new pupils the way. Something eye-catching. Inside there was the usual flight of concrete stairs, which led to five more, which took her eventually to the top floor and the rooms she had been allotted.

There were eight of them, five surrounding a hall full of broken furniture and old exercise books, and three more along the corridor, one of which had obviously been a cookery room. They were all half tiled in the usual dark green and impossibly scruffy, the dark green paintwork peeling and the floorboards stained and covered in dust. Being positive she noted that they were well lit, with the usual long high windows, and plenty big enough for the sort of classes she was expecting. Spot of paint'll work wonders, she thought, that and a good scrub down. At least there were plenty of cupboards. She checked them out one by one — broom cupboard, smelling of disinfectant and beeswax polish, PT cupboard heaped with hoops and ropes and with an antique horse pushed into the corner, much scuffed, three stock cupboards full of books, most of them as old and tattered as the horse. Oh dear, oh dear. Then she went to check the room that would be her study.

It was in the corner of the hall and it too was full of broken furniture, chairs with three legs, two broken easels and a cracked blackboard, two boxes full of tattered books and broken cups, even a pile of old coats. Where did *they* come from? It'll take months just to clear it, she thought. But that's where she would have to start because this room was where she would hold her interviews. I will write to the board and tell them what I want, she decided, and the sooner the better. She stood in the dust, took her notebook from her handbag and began there and then, determined not to be downhearted.

My study must be completely cleared and thoroughly cleaned. That is a priority, for this is where I shall be interviewing my staff. I shall need a good sized desk, several comfortable armchairs, similar to the ones in your waiting rooms, a large bookcase, a small tea table, curtains and a carpet.

Then she went back home to write the letter and to compose the advertisements for the teachers.

By the end of the following week, to her public delight and private surprise, she had received five applications.

'Isn't that encouraging,' she said to her parents at breakfast. With a constant flow of good news, breakfast was becoming the best meal of the day, despite the chill of the room and the poor quality of the bread.

'I don't mean to nag you, my dear,' her mother said, 'but have you told Tommy yet?'

In the excitement of planning her campaign, she'd forgotten all about him. 'No, I haven't,' she admitted. 'But he wouldn't be interested if I had. All he ever thinks about these days is the war.'

'Isn't that a letter from him?' Amy asked, looking at the envelope beside her daughter's plate.

'Yes, it is,' Octavia said and was ashamed to think that she'd set it to one side until she'd read the applications. Poor Tommy. 'I've left it till last,' she felt she should explain. 'I'll read it to you if you like. It'll be all about how many men are sick and how atrocious the food is and how he hates the German spies and what a lot of fools the commanders are.'

In fact it held a surprise.

There's a rumour we're pulling out, he wrote. *If I'm any judge we shall be back in Flanders before Easter, ready for the next big push. Might even get a spot of leave. God knows I've earned it.*

'Good heavens,' Amy said. 'Does he say when it will be?'

'No,' Octavia said, reading on, and felt ashamed again because she knew she was hoping it would be after she'd chosen her teachers. 'Soon I should imagine.'

'That'll be nice,' her mother said.

But Octavia was thinking of the car she meant to buy.

IT WAS a little black Ford and she was totally enamoured of it from the moment she sat in the driving seat. It came with a book of instructions so it didn't take her long to learn how to start it and put it into gear, speed it up and slow it down.

Steering round corners made her arms ache until she got used to it but that was a small price to pay for the convenience of being able to drive to school exactly when she wanted to without standing in line for a tram. Her pupils were very impressed to have a car-driving teacher. 'That's never been known before, Miss Smith,' they said, and came out into the playground in inquisitive groups to admire it.

'The time will come,' she predicted, 'when all your teachers will drive cars. It will be as normal as riding on a tram.'

But for the moment, of course, it was unusual but then so was being a headmistress designate at the age of twenty-nine. She decided to treat herself to some new clothes as well as the car. If she was going to interview staff and parents — for she'd be bound to be interviewing parents when the school was officially opened — she needed to look the part.

She was in Derry and Toms, trying on dresses, when Tommy came home on leave, two days earlier than she'd expected him.

'Not to fret, Mrs Prof,' he said to Amy. 'I'll just stick around here and wait for her, if it's okay by you.'

Amy gave him her permission and made him a pot of tea but he had a long wait. It was over an hour before Octavia's little black Ford drew up behind his big black Packard and then she was so hung about with hat boxes and huge carrier bags that he could hardly see her.

'My stars, Tikki-Tavy!' he said. 'Have you bought the shop?'

She *had* bought rather a lot, she had to admit. A summer dress in white cotton with a stylish scarlet jacket with a long white shawl collar to match, a pale green linen suit and a brown felt hat, decorated all over the crown with the prettiest pale green leaves, gloves and silk stockings, a fine pair of button boots in tan leather with louis heels, even a boater with a blue and red ribbon to match the scarlet jacket. But she had a bigger surprise for them than her new clothes. She grinned at her mother, took off her old hat and threw it into the nearest chair. Her long frizzy hair had been cut into a short frizzy bob.

'Oh Tavy!' her mother said, ready to reprove.

But Tommy was speaking at the same time and his tone was all delight. 'My stars, Tavy,' he said. 'You're a corker, damn if you ain't. What say we go to the pictures? See this Charlie Chaplin feller they're all talking about. You look just the ticket for a night at the pictures.'

So they went to the pictures and the theatre and the music hall, wined and dined at expensive restaurants, none of which seemed to have heard of meatless days, and returned to his flat at frequent and delectable intervals. And for eight of his ten days they were ridiculously happy together. Like everyone else he too was hoping that this last big push that was being planned would actually drive the Germans back.

'If we can once do that,' he told her, as they were driving off to another picture palace, 'it'll be the beginning of the end. Break their morale. That's what we need. Should have done it years ago. Break their morale and then back to Blighty. And about time too.' The feeling he ought to compliment her on her appearance, 'Is that one of your new dresses?'

'Good heavens no,' she said. 'This is ever so old. You must have seen it dozens of times. I wore it in Paris.'

He pretended to remember. 'Then when am I going to see the new ones?' he asked.

'Not for a long time,' she said. 'They're my Sunday-go-to-meeting suits. I bought them to wear at my interviews.'

He was disappointed because he was sure they'd been bought to please him. 'What interviews?' he said.

She didn't notice the tetchiness in his voice so she told him — exactly.

He was very cross. 'Oh come on, Tavy,' he said. 'You don't want to be a headmistress now. That's all over and done with. Once the war's over I shall come home and join the Foreign

Office — it's almost certain, did I tell you? You've no idea the strings I've been pulling — and then we can get married. We'll have such a life together. I've got it all planned. We'll choose a house for starters. Something rather grand, don't you think? There are bound to be all sorts of parties, dinner parties, cocktail parties, diplomatic parties. I can just see you playing the hostess. You'll be top hole. We shall be in our element.'

'No,' she said angrily. 'You'll be in your element. My element is a school.'

'You don't want to bother with that,' he said, pursuing his own thoughts. 'I shall earn good money. Very good money. You'll never have to work again. We'll have holidays in the South of France, run a Rolls Royce. Oh we shall live in style, I can tell you. You don't want to mess about being a headmistress. You can leave all that.'

'I'm a headmistress already,' she told him.

'Then write and tell them you've changed your mind.'

'It may have escaped your notice, Tommy, but it's what I want to be.'

'Not when the war's over, surely to God. Once we've done with all this fighting, you can marry me and live the life of Reilly.'

It was too much. He wasn't listening to a word she was saying. 'Stop the car,' she said. 'I want to go home.'

He was genuinely surprised. 'What do you mean, want to go home?'

'Stop the car.'

He obeyed her, looking puzzled, and watched as she struggled to open the door and got out, very ungracefully. By that time he was cross.

'I thought we were going to the pictures.'

'Well you thought wrong.'

'Shall I ring you tomorrow?'

She was already walking to the tram stop. 'Do as you please,' she said. 'Just don't live my life for me.'

He didn't ring until his last day and then it was to suggest that she might like to say goodbye at Victoria, 'the way you used to' and as he was going back to the fighting, and it would have been unkind to let him leave unkissed, she went.

It was a bittersweet farewell, for it occurred to her as they kissed that this could be the last time she would ever see him. 'Oh Tommy,' she said. 'I'm sorry we quarrelled. I do love you.'

'Likewise,' he said. 'Don't worry, Tikki. I'm like the proverbial bad penny. I'll turn up again before you know it.'

She waved goodbye feeling sick at her stupidity and unkindness, wishing they could have his leave all over again and live it differently. But it was done and he was gone and on Tuesday she would be interviewing her first set of applicants.

It was the middle of the Easter holiday before she had chosen all the staff she wanted and because it had taken so long and been such a delicate difficult procedure, she decided to hold a tea party at Hammersmith to celebrate. She wore her new green suit, her new felt hat and her new button boots, and took a picnic basket full of carefully packed tea things — Mrs Wilkin's homemade seed cake, a bottle of milk, a small bowl of her precious rationed sugar, a small tin of biscuits.

It was more than three weeks since her last interviews and a lot had changed. The walls were newly painted and exactly as she'd specified, in a neutral cream that lightened the darkness of all those green wall tiles and would make it easier for pictures and notices to be seen. The hall had been cleared, and now she could see that it was a good size, with a clock on the wall at one end and a raised platform at the other. There were rows of new benches too and a piano for assemblies, and between the high windows, three sets of new wall bars for PT lessons. And down in the right-hand corner her study had become a very pleasant room, with everything in it that she'd asked for, a carpet on the floor, a desk set at an angle to make best use of the light and a nice warm fire in the grate with five easy chairs placed in a circle around it. The tea table was set for tea and there was a welcoming note from the school keeper, tucked between the cups to say:

Dear Miss Smith, Ring when you want the Tea or if there is anythink else.
HE Turner.

She took the seed cake and the sugar and biscuits from her basket and arranged them among the cups and filled the milk jug from her bottle. Then she went to inspect the classrooms.

They too were much improved and were now clean and well-ordered with new desks and new blackboards and plenty of bookshelves. Some of the new stock she'd ordered had arrived, and was standing in the rooms waiting to be unpacked, which pleased her. Not all of it, of course. She made a note of the missing deliveries in her notebook. Then she walked through the hall to inspect the cookery room.

She'd just reached the door and had her hand on the door-knob when she heard feet trudging up the stairs and the murmur of several voices. Her staff had arrived and spot on time.

There were three of them walking across the hall, all young, all carefully dressed and all nervous, smiling guardedly. She greeted them by name, introducing them to one another. 'Miss Fletcher, our Cookery and Needlework teacher, good to see you again. Miss Genevra, who will be teaching French and Latin. Did you have a good journey? Miss Gordon, History and Geography. Your new History books have arrived, you'll be glad to know.' They relaxed a little, but were still guarded as they followed her into the study.

'Mr Turner's got a good fire going for us,' she said. 'We'll have some tea first, shall we? And then you can have a look at your form-rooms.' And she rang the bell for the school keeper.

The combination of hot tea and seed cake, blazing fire and warm welcome gradually made them relax. They started to talk shop, tentatively at first but with more confidence when she approved of what they were saying, and presently the fifth member of staff arrived, Miss Fennimore, the oldest and most experienced, who was to teach Science and Mathematics.

Looking at them all as they sat around the fire, Octavia felt suddenly and entirely happy. The breakthrough may have begun, she thought, there didn't seem much doubt about that now, but the war's still going on, food is still short and there are far too many people catching that awful Spanish flu, but we five have turned our lives in a new direction. We five have the chance to build a better world. She looked from face to face, at Alice Genevra's china doll prettiness with her fluffy fair hair and wide blue eyes — and fierce intelligence — at Morag Gordan's motherly presence in her long wool cardigan and sensible shoes — how reassuring she will be to all our new girls — at Elizabeth Fennimore's severity, her dark hair pinned so tightly into its bun, her pince-nez dangling on her white blouse, her suit so impeccable tailored — and caught the warm smile that gave her stern appearance the lie — at Sarah Fletcher's loving ugly face with its long nose and small grey eyes and touching eagerness, and she knew that they were all cheerful eccentrics and that she had chosen well.

'I give you a toast,' she said, raising her teacup. 'Here's to our school. May we all be very happy teaching here.'

CHAPTER 20

It was a grey November day on a grey Hampstead Heath but because it was peacetime at last, a few hardy couples were out for a stroll, returning to normal despite the weather, doing their best to ignore the mist that clouded the denuded branches of the trees, the chill of the sodden air and the total lack of colour in the sky. They were well cocooned against the cold, with furs and scarves mounded about their necks and gloves tightly buttoned, and they walked briskly, while their dogs trotted at heel, damply and obediently, their ears drooping.

Only one couple was walking slowly, and even stopping from time to time to face one another. They were so deep in conversation that they were oblivious to the chill, the fading light and the curious stares of their fellow strollers. They made a striking pair, he with his military bearing and his military moustache, dapper in a fashionable grey overcoat, neat kid gloves and a light grey trilby, she striding tall and slim beside him, in her pretty leather boots, elegant in a russet brown cloth coat with a fox fur collar and cuffs and a Cossack hat to match. Neither was aware of the stir they were causing among the other passers-by, for what they were saying to one another was paining them so deeply they needed all their energy and attention to cope with it.

'Dash it all, Tavy,' Tommy said, in exasperation. 'We can't go on drifting forever. You must see that. I mean to say. There's no excuse for it now. The war's over. Everyone's expecting us to tie the knot. It don't make sense to keep putting it off. I thought a wedding at Christmas would be just the thing.'

'It would,' Octavia said, her face fraught. 'Other things being equal. I'd marry you tomorrow if I could be married and go on teaching. But it isn't possible. They don't allow it. You know that. Married women have to resign.'

'Let's cock a snook at 'em,' he suggested, trying to dare her. 'Marry and be damned. How about that? You'd like to get the vote, now wouldn't you? And you won't get that if you're a spinster.' He felt quite pleased with himself to have pulled that particular rabbit out of the hat. It had to be a clincher. Surely.

She took his arm and walked on, aching to find an answer that would help them through their impasse and quite unable to do it. 'I'm afraid it would turn out to be marry and be fired,' she said and tried to sound as though she was joking.

It was a vain attempt. They'd been over this stale sad ground so many times and his face was taking on the sullen look she recognised just a little too well. 'You don't love me,' he said. 'That's the truth of it.' Behind him the dome of St Paul's rose from the distant fog like the boss of an ancient shield and the spires of the lesser churches around it were sharp as spears. 'I've been four years in hell and now I want to start work at the Foreign Office and be normal again, get married, settle down, bit of comfort in my life, place of my own, children, warm bed, warm wife, that sort of thing. I've earned that surely to God. Still, if you say it's unreasonable...'

'No, no,' she said, reassuring him quickly. 'It's not unreasonable. I never said that. It's perfectly natural.'

He stopped again and took both her hands, cupping them

between his own, the way he'd so often done before. 'Then marry me,' he pleaded, 'and have my babies. You're not too old for it, and you want children, don't you?'

'I've got children,' she told him. 'Hundreds of them.'

'Don't be flippant,' he said crossly. 'I'm not talking about them. I mean real children.'

She ignored that, knowing that if she argued it would side-track them and cast him down. She's been casting him down a great deal too much over the last few days and it hurt her as much as it was hurting him. 'If we *were* to marry,' she said, care-fully, 'if we went ahead with it, and then I got fired and didn't have a job, I would make you a very poor wife.'

He was hopeful again, almost eager. 'Let me be the judge of that.'

'No,' she insisted. 'We must think about it now. It will be too late once we're married. I would be a poor wife. I'm not made for domesticity.'

He was still urging her. 'You'd come round to it. Women do you know.'

She knew they did, but whether they ought to or not was another matter. She thought of Emmeline, worn out by chil-dren, and still turning herself inside out to placate that awful Ernest. 'I might not,' she said. 'We have to think about it. I might not be the sort of wife you want. I might make you very unhappy.'

'You don't know the sort of wife I want,' he said.

But she did. She'd known it with sharpening clarity ever since that awful leave when he came home from Salonika. He wanted a hostess for the dinner parties he meant to give once he was at the Foreign Office, someone who dressed well and spoke well but was never out of order, a mother for his children, a woman always at home and always at his beck and call, someone subservient and obedient, like all those little dogs trot-ting along in the cold and hating it. What was it he'd just said?

'Warm bed, warm wife.' The very words disturbed her, spreading irritable ripples through the dark pool of her mind. That was not the sort of woman she was or ever could be. She had to be true to her nature and follow her calling. And she knew too well that if she did that, she would make him unhappy.

He was sighing. 'I don't understand you, Tavy,' he complained. 'All this fuss about a job of work. I can't see the sense of it. I mean it's not as if it's anything special, now is it. Teaching. I mean anybody can teach.'

She'd held on to her self-control for so long that the effort was making her chest ache. 'That's what people think,' she said, struggling to be patient. 'But they're wrong. It takes a special person to teach. It's an art.'

He shrugged. 'If you say so. I should have said they're all much of a muchness. Boring and dull. At least the ones who taught me were. Positive ditchwater the lot of 'em. Couldn't wait to see the back of 'em.'

'It's an art,' she insisted. She felt she *must* make him understand but his incomprehension was as impenetrable as a wall. 'If it's done properly it isn't boring. It doesn't bore the teacher or the taught. It's fascinating. And I mean to do it better and better. Once I've been to New York...'

He groaned. 'Oh God, Tavy! Not New York again. We've been all through this before. You don't want to go to New York. Not now anyway. And certainly not to see some stupid school. Wait till the summer and I'll take you. We can travel as man and wife, eh? I'll give you a first rate time there. Leave all this school nonsense. There are plenty of other people to do that.'

I'm wasting my breath, Octavia thought. He hasn't understood a word I've said. He doesn't see what this is about at all. 'There aren't plenty of other people, Tommy,' she said. 'I'm the only one. I'm not replaceable. At least not yet. Others will follow me, I'm quite sure of that, but I'm the one who has to lead and I have to lead now. The war is over and the time is right. It's what I have to do. I can't turn my back on it. I would regret it for the rest of my life.'

He didn't understand her reasons but he could see their implication. 'So what you're telling me,' he said wearily, 'is that you've made your mind up. You're not going to marry me. That's it, isn't it? Not now and not ever.'

It was an utterly miserable moment but she answered him honestly. 'Yes, I'm afraid it is, Tommy. I'm so sorry.'

The cold was making her nose red and behind the severity of those round glasses her grey-blue eyes were swimming with tears. He was caught by such an overwhelming surge of love for her that it was all he could do not to pull her into his arms and kiss her. But it was too late for kisses and they both knew it. They had parted. Their affair was over. 'I shan't see you again,' he said, gruffly. 'Wouldn't be wise.'

She nodded and agreed. 'No.' And paused, waiting for him to say something else. But he didn't. 'What about my ring?' she said. 'Do you want me to give it back?'

'No, no. You keep it.'

'Thank you.' Oh how banal this is!

'You will explain to your parents?'

'Yes.'

For a second he dithered before her, although they both knew there was nothing more to be said, then he straightened his spine, turned and walked away, self-consciously but steadily. He didn't look back. She watched as his figure dissolved in the mist, first his striding feet, then those long, long legs, then the sturdy bulk of his greatcoat and finally his dear, fair, stubborn, uncomprehending head. She felt as if he was being taken away from her piece by piece and the thought made her shiver. Already loss was scrabbling in her belly and filling her throat with tears. I shall never see him again, she thought, never lie in his arms or wake to find him beside me, never share a meal with him, never watch him shave, never hear him laugh, never smell him. But what else could I have done? I couldn't leave my job. Not now. Oh how cruel it is to force a woman to choose between marriage and career. Cruel and wasteful. Utterly, utterly wasteful. Anger rose in her and she let it rise because she knew it would sustain her. She could feel her strength returning to her already. Something will have to be done about it, she thought. We can't go on wasting talent forever. I shall put my mind to it. Then she too turned and headed for home.

Now she would have to tell her mother and father that there would be no wedding and the sooner she got it over and done with the better.

IT WAS MORE difficult than she imagined for her mother seemed determined to talk about trivial things and did it all through dinner, with a nervous intensity that Octavia found horribly disquieting. It wasn't until they were sitting round the fire drinking their ersatz coffee that her father finally rescued her.

'I think, my dear,' he said gently to Amy, 'that Tavy has something she wants to tell us.'

'Well I hope it's the date of her wedding, that's all,' Amy said. 'We can't go on hanging about for ever, Tavy.'

'There isn't going to be a wedding, Mama,' Octavia said. 'The engagement's over.'

Amy made a grimace. 'I noticed you weren't wearing your ring,' she said.

'No.'

'And that's final is it?'

'Yes.'

'Well it's a great pity if you ask me. You won't get another offer anywhere near as good.'

Octavia felt so irritable that for a second she couldn't find the words to answer. But her father stepped in again.

'She has found her life's work, my dear,' he said to Amy. 'I think it deplorable that she is forced to choose between work and marriage — if the world were a better place that would not have been necessary — but nevertheless she has made her choice and it is an honourable one. We must wish her well, must we not?'

'I do,' Amy said. 'You know that, Tavy, don't you. I do with all my heart. It's just…'

'Yes, Ma,' Tavy said. 'I know what "it's just" and it's very *unjust.*'

'Shall you go to New York now the war's over?' JJ asked, apparently changing the subject.

'When the weather's better,' Octavia told him. 'Easter probably. I don't fancy crossing the Atlantic in the middle of winter.'

'I don't fancy doing anything much in the middle of winter,' her father said. 'I am getting altogether too long in the tooth for extremes of temperature. I shall retire before the next one, I give you fair warning.'

And I shall start house-hunting, Octavia thought. It's high time I had a place of my own.

But first they had to get through the winter that was looming down upon them and that season had some terrible things in store, although it began with a small triumph.

JUST BEFORE CHRISTMAS WHEN OCTAVIA, her staff and her pupils were happily hanging the classrooms with paper chains and singing carols at every assembly, Lloyd George held the General Election he'd called as soon as the war was over. The new women voters were much in evidence at the polling booths and there were several pictures of them in the papers, smiling shyly at the cameras as they cast the vote for the first time.

Octavia devoted an assembly to it and wore her precious silver arrow around the school all day, with great pride. 'When you get the vote,' she told her girls, 'as you will sooner or later, either when you are thirty or when the government wakes up to its responsibilities and awards it to all women over the age of twenty-one, but when you do, be sure to use it. The franchise is too valuable not to be used. Never forget that.'

And they beamed at her cheerfully and turned the pages in their hymn books ready for the next carol.

It was a cheerful Christmas. Maud and Ralph brought their entire family to Amy's Boxing Day tea, with the exception of their son-in-law who was busy with his papers, according to Emmeline.

'It's his loss,' she said to Amy. 'I *did* tell him he was invited. My stars but that's a pretty dress!'

And our gain, Octavia thought, as his children sat up to the table and had napkins tucked under their chins to protect their clothes. 'Wouldn't do for them to go home covered in chocolate,' Emmeline said. 'Would it, my poppets?'

They made a very good meal, to Amy's delight, the adults happy to be in such entirely cheerful company, the children happy to be spoilt and petted. Dora and Edith, who were very grown up now they were nine and eleven, tried pickled onions for the first time and said they were *'scrumptious'*, Johnnie, who was a plumply ebullient four-year-old, ate so much plum pudding it gave him hiccups, their Uncle Podge put away a really good meal for once and hardly coughed at all, and even Eddie and Dickie, who came to the table pale and anxious in case they were going to be scolded, gradually discovered that in this house they were permitted to pick at their food and could eat what they pleased and actually began to enjoy it.

When the cloth was cleared, they sat round the fire and ate roasted chestnuts and played Pit.

'It's like old times,' Emmeline said. 'Do you remember how we used to play Pit when we were little?'

'Speak for yourself,' Podge said, shifting Johnnie into a more comfortable position on his knee. 'You never let me play anything. It was always you and Tavy and Squirrel. You said I wasn't old enough. It didn't matter how old I was, six, ten, sixteen, I was never old enough.'

Emmeline chortled with delight at the memory and denied such an accusation at once — because it was true. 'The tales you do tell, Podge. It's all fairy stories children. What shall we play next?'

It was charades, by universal acclaim, and Podge was the star of the show to make amends for the terrible way he'd been treated when he was little.

'It's been a lovely Christmas, Aunt Amy,' Emmeline said, when the clock had struck midnight and they were finally leaving. 'What a difference peace makes.'

'Let's hope it will be the first of many many more,' Amy said, kissing her. And she held out her arms to the children. 'Come and kiss your old Aunty and then you really must get home to bed.'

And so on to the last excitement of the day, which was being driven home by their Aunty Tavy, all five of them squashed together on the back seat of her car, with barely room to breathe. Oh it was lovely!

'Although,' Emmeline said, looking over her shoulder at them and pretending to be stern, 'what your father would say if he could see you I dread to think.'

AFTER THE EUPHORIA of the party and the unaccustomed luxury of good food, the New Year brought them back to reality with a palpable shock. It was cold and dark and the streets were full of ex-servicemen, standing in queues for what little work was on offer and looking much older than their years, their faces lined and war-weary. No one had given any thought as to how they should be treated once they were out of the army and few jobs had been kept open for them, although because so many had been gassed or wounded they couldn't have coped with the sort of hard labour they'd endured before the war, even if it *had* been available. The impact of so many suddenly unemployed men could hardly be ignored but the weeks went by and the politicians had little idea what could be done about it.

It was the Glasgow trade unions that came up with a possible answer. What they suggested was a statutory forty-hour week for all manual workers, without loss of pay, to create extra jobs for returning soldiers. It was a simple and obvious expedient but the employers were opposed to it. Why pay two men to do a job when you can get it done at half the price by one? In the end the dispute came to a general strike and, according to the newspaper reports, things got nasty. 20,000 demonstrators massed in George Square, bottles were thrown, the police charged and forty men were injured.

'Disgraceful,' Octavia said angrily. 'It was a good idea. They could at least have given it a try.' In the last two months she'd been carrying a niggling, useless anger with her wherever she went, at herself for having treated Tommy so badly, at Tommy for not understanding, at society for its stupid rules and regulations, at all the follies and idiocies of their war-torn times. Nothing was right with the world. She was living in an unexpected and cramping limbo, needing change and a new impetus to carry her forward but unable to reach out for it, missing Tommy so much that the lack of his presence was a physical pain, feeling guilty because the pain was self-inflicted. 'There are times when I despair of people, I really do.'

She despaired again later in the month when the disinfectant teams began to appear on the trams and buses. The Spanish flu had broken out again even more virulently and the authorities were hiring ex-servicemen to spray disinfectant in various public places, in a vain attempt to contain it.

'It's like King Canute,' she said to her father at breakfast time. 'What earthly good do they think a little disinfectant will be? It won't stop people coughing all over one another and that's how flu is spread.' This time there was fear in her anger for so many people were falling ill and the death rate was alarming. 'They're talking about closing the schools if it gets any worse.'

'And colleges,' her father told her.

'That would be no bad thing,' she said. At least it would keep him at home and out of harm's way. He was too old and too dear to her to be risking this awful disease because he still had to go to work. 'The sooner you retire the better.'

'At the end of the academic year,' her father promised. 'You have my word.'

'You know my feelings on the matter,' Amy said. She was afraid of this awful flu too. 'It can't come too soon.'

What came a mere three days later was a terrified telephone call from Emmeline. Octavia had just got in from school and was standing by the hallstand unpinning her hat when the phone rang so she took the call.

'Oh Tavy!' Emmeline's voice said. 'I'm so glad you're home. You couldn't come over could you?'

She sounded so distraught that Octavia was alerted at once. 'Something's the matter,' she said.

'It's Eddie,' Emmeline explained, and now she sounded tearful. 'He's really ill and Ernest won't have the doctor. He's says he's not to be a milksop. And he's not. I know he's not. He's really ill. He keeps on cough, cough, cough all the time and that's not like my Eddie. I'm at my wit's end. I've phoned Ma three times and I can't get her. I think they must be out. You couldn't come and see him could you?'

'I'm on my way,' Octavia said. 'I'll be with you in five minutes.'

And was.

Eddie was lying on the *chaise longue* in the drawing room, limp with fever and looking very ill indeed. His skin was clammy to the touch, there were two red fever patches on his poor pale cheeks and although he managed to open his eyes when Octavia felt his pulse, he was too ill to focus them.

'Get the doctor,' Octavia said.

'What about Ernest?' Emmeline worried.

'I'll deal with Ernest,' her cousin said grimly. 'You phone the doctor.'

Emmeline was dithering with worry. 'Oh dear, Tavy,' she said. 'You don't think it's the flu do you?'

'Get the doctor.'

He came with remarkable speed and his diagnosis was instant. Yes, it was the flu, he was sorry to say. The child should be put to bed and given plenty of water to drink and a blanket bath to bring down the temperature, and kept away from his brothers and sisters. That was imperative. He would require careful nursing. Would Emmeline be able to manage or did she need assistance? He couldn't promise her much help because the district nurses were run off their feet but he would do his best.

Emmeline was calmer now that she knew the worst. 'I shall manage,' she said. 'My cousin will help me, won't you, Tavy? And my mother. We will look after him, poor little man.'

She and Octavia sat up with their patient all night, as he tossed and sweated and coughed. They gave him a blanket bath in the hope of making him cooler but it didn't seem to do much good. In fact he coughed more after it than he'd done before. At one in the morning Ernest came clumping home from wherever he'd been all evening, stamped up the stairs and disappeared into the master bedroom banging the door behind him. At a little after two, Eddie began to sleep more peacefully and Emmeline told Tavy to go to the spare room and catch a few minutes' sleep herself. 'I'll call you if I need you.' But at four she was at Tavy's bedside saying the child was worse and could she come.

Octavia got up at once, buttoned her blouse, put on her boots and her cardigan and was in the corridor in minutes. But as she headed for Eddie's sickroom, the door to the nursery opened and Dolly came out in her dressing gown looking worried.

'Oh Miss Octavia,' she whispered. 'What a blessing you're here. Could you come and see Dickie for me? He's just been sick and I don't like the look of him at all only I don't want to worry poor Mrs Freeman if it's nothing.'

The horror that Octavia had been dreading ever since she heard about Eddie was happening. The sickness was spreading. They had another patient. Within an hour she had taken charge of the household, carrying Dickie back into his own bedroom and settling him as well as she could in his own bed, phoning the doctor, sponging both her patients down, insisting that Emmeline should eat breakfast with her other three children and then take a nap — 'Or you'll be no good for anything and that won't do' — and finally, when the doctor had visited them and confirmed their fears, phoning Aunt Maud and breaking the news to her.

'I'll be straight over,' Maud said. 'Oh my poor Emmeline! What a dreadful, dreadful thing!'

Only Ernest took the news with calm. He came down to breakfast at his usual time, dressed and ready for work and was annoyed when Octavia told him that Emmeline wouldn't be joining him because two of his sons were ill.

'They will pull through,' he said.

'Your sons,' she corrected him furiously, 'have an illness that is killing people in their thousands. They are very seriously ill.'

'I will trouble you not to talk nonsense, Octavia,' he said coldly. 'My sons don't die.'

'I have never talked nonsense in my life,' she told him, anger growing. 'I am renowned for telling people the truth. If you chose not to believe it, that is your prerogative and your folly.' And she took her cup of tea and went back to the better company of the sickroom. 'I'm off to school now,' she said to Emmeline. 'You'll be all right, won't you, now Aunt Maud is here. I'll be back at tea time.'

Emmeline had been crying but she dried her eyes to kiss her cousin. 'Take care of yourself,' she said. 'I don't want you falling ill too.'

The one who should fall ill is Ernest, Octavia thought as she walked out to her car. It would do him good to suffer a bit, nasty pompous creature.

But the devil took care of his own and Ernest stayed pompously fit as his sons struggled with the fever that was inching their lives away. And nobody could do anything about it.

Dickie was the first to slip away, dropping out of his short life as gently as a leaf dropping from the tree, and two hours later while his mother was still too stricken with grief to move away from his bedside, Eddie stirred back to consciousness, tried to look at her, coughed, gave a deep sigh and followed him.

Emmeline was felled by grief, defeated, lost. 'They were my babies,' she wept, crumpled on the floor between their two beds. 'Such dear good boys, such dear, dear good boys, and so young. Oh Tavy, what did they ever do to deserve this? It isn't fair. It really isn't. They were such good boys, always trying to please their father and do the right thing. And it was so hard for them and they went on trying and trying. Such dear good boys. It's not fair. And after that lovely Christmas too and your mother saying may it be the first of many. It's not fair.'

'No,' Octavia said. 'It's not. There's no justice in the world at all.'

'Haven't we suffered enough,' Emmeline wept, 'with that awful war and Squirrel killed and Podge in such a state and all those millions and millions killed and wounded. I used to say I believed in God but I don't now. If there really were a god he wouldn't allow such things. Oh my poor dear boys! They were my life, Tavy. What shall I do without them?'

It was a bleak and anguished time. And the funeral with its two pathetic white coffins lying side by side in the grave was more terrible than any of the family could bear. Octavia stood beside her cousin and held her poor trembling arm all through the service and wished with all her heart that there was something she could do or say to comfort her and knew there was nothing. And Dora and Edith and little Johnnie clung to their grandmother's skirts and cried with grief and confusion. For how could this be happening? How could their brothers be gone? Ernest stood apart at the foot of the grave and revealed no feelings at all, and glancing at him Octavia couldn't help wondering whether he was cloaking his emotions with that stern expression or simply being heartless. If it had been Tommy, she thought, and he'd lost a child, he would be weeping. And despite herself she yearned to see him again.

What she saw, six weeks later when they were beginning to ease away from the first and most terrible anguish was an announcement in *The Times*.

Mr and Mrs HE Drewry... were pleased to announce the engagement of their elder daughter, Elizabeth to Major Thomas Meriton...

It was unexpectedly and exquisitely painful. Oh Tommy, she thought, staring at the paper, we only parted in November and you're engaged to someone else. How could you? But then she thought about it and decided to be sensible and was ashamed of herself. If he'd found someone else she could hardly complain. He'd made it quite clear that was what he wanted. 'A warm bed and a warm wife.' And I chose my career. Well, it's no good sitting here feeling sorry for myself. That's a fool's game. I must get on with my life. There are things to be done.

'I think,' she said to her parents, 'it is time I booked my passage to New York.' And after that she would start house-hunting.

CHAPTER 21

The SS *Olympic* eased her storm-dishevelled grandeur towards the port of New York, obedient to the bark of the tugboat, engines throbbing. Most of her first class passengers were standing at the rail watching as the great city rose into view, pointing and exclaiming. It had been an unusually difficult crossing, for they'd hit a force 9 gale in mid-Atlantic and most of them had been extremely seasick, but now they were within sight of land and their six-day water torment was nearly over. And what land it was, this brave new world, this teeming incredible continent of new inventions and new men and new ideas. It made Octavia catch her breath simply to look at it. Such magnificent buildings, she thought, scanning the skyline, and so tall, and so many of them. They're like a great cliff face. She couldn't wait to be walking among them, seeing the city at first hand, but for the moment she stood quite still, elegant in her russet coat and her Cossack hat, contained and steady, because her unexpected happiness was so great she was afraid it would spill and be lost if she made the least movement.

She felt exactly as she'd done on her first release from

prison, set free to enjoy her life again. I'm here, she thought, at last. She could see the Statue of Liberty so clearly she could pick out the spikes on her crown, and the closer they got to shore the more shipping they encountered, ferries and tugs and cargo ships, all following their allotted paths across the choppy water, each leaving a froth of foam in her wake and a frisson of excitement in the *Olympic*'s watching passengers.

'How's that for a skyline honey?' the woman beside her asked.

'It's extraordinary,' Octavia said, with perfect truth.

'You staying long?'

After six days afloat Octavia had grown accustomed to the outspokenness of her American fellow travellers. At first it had worried her to be asked personal questions by total strangers but after a day or two she'd realised that what appeared to be rudeness was simply natural curiosity and that it was invariably friendly. Now she answered happily. 'Just for the Easter holiday, I'm afraid. I wish it could be longer.'

The interest continued, brightly. 'Where are you staying? Have you made a reservation?'

'With a friend,' Octavia said. 'She's coming to meet me.' And wondered how on earth they would find one another among the crowd of passengers who would be disembarking.

She needn't have worried, for there was a small slender woman in a blue suit standing at the foot of the gangplank with a placard held in front of her proclaiming 'Miss Octavia Smith,' in letters a foot high. It made Octavia feel like a celebrity. She was blushing as she stepped forward to greet her new friend.

'Connie Weismann,' the lady said, introducing herself. 'I'm so glad you could make it. Did you have a good crossing?'

The quayside was full of noise and movement, hemmed in by massive cranes and jostled by swarms of porters in heavy jerseys like sailors yelling 'Carry yer bag lady?' and striding forcefully up the gangplank as the passengers tottered gingerly down still feeling the swell of the sea. Horse-drawn carts stood stolidly in the traffic or inched through the confusion, wheels creaking; honking cars and taxi cabs fidgeted and throbbed, emitting a strong sharp smell of petrol; and a chorus of voices called and shouted in a bewildering variety of accents, raucous as gulls. It was an excitement simply to be standing in the middle of it. But it made hearing difficult.

'I've gotten us a cab,' Miss Weismann shouted at her. 'If you'll just follow me.'

The luggage was loaded, the cab rattled away, faces passed the window jerkily and out of focus like pictures from the cinema, they were edged into a street crowded with vehicles and picked up exhilarating speed. Now images jostled upon Octavia with kaleidoscopic irregularity, here a group of young men, hats at a jaunty angle, dodged across the road between the cars, missing their approaching bumpers by inches, grinning and shouting, there a man sat in a huge chair casually smoking a cigar and reading a newspaper while a bootblack crouched before him buffing his shoes to a gleam, here a pair of delivery boys wobbled their bicycles between the traffic, there an elegant lady walked a white poodle with a blue ribbon tied in a bow between its ears.

Octavia answered Miss Weismann's questions as well as she could, explaining that her journey had been 'quite eventful' but making light of the storm, while this amazing city racketed and roared around her. Inside her head, her thoughts shifted and intermeshed like cogs. It seemed to her that all the experiences of her life were culminating in this visit — the easy lessons she'd learnt at school and at home, the hard ones forced on her as a suffragette, the rich talk around her father's Fabian table, the hesitant speech of her first and youngest pupils, being secretly loved and publicly unmarried, even the anguish of Cyril's death, the distress of seeing Podge crippled by that awful gas, the agony of watching Emmeline's two poor little boys succumbing to that awful influenza, the dragging misery of refusing Tommy and knowing she would never see him again. These things, good and bad, had been her education and had brought her to this invigorating city and the questions that would soon be answered. Oh yes, yes! The questions that would soon be answered.

AFTER THE BUSTLE of the city, Aristotle Avenue was like an oasis, wide, tree-lined and already leafy, traffic-free and gently quiet. The Dalton School was a large white building at the corner of the road and that was quiet too, although, as Octavia saw at once, every classroom was full of pupils.

The Principal was waiting in the foyer to welcome her. She was an impressive lady with iron-grey hair, a very straight spine and a disarming smile, who introduced herself as Amelia Barnes and, having settled Octavia's luggage in the school office and handed her hat and coat to the school secretary, set off at once on what she called 'a short tour of inspection' explaining that Octavia would just have time to see a few studies at work before they adjourned for lunch.

'The study period is the core of our system,' she said, as they walked along a corridor, 'as I believe I told you in my letter, so I felt sure you would wish to see it at the first opportunity. Let us start with an English study, shall we, since that is your subject.' And she opened the door to the nearest classroom.

Octavia was prepared for something out of the ordinary but even so she was surprised by the impact of this room. For a start it was full of cheerful voices, not gossiping or chattering, as she could see and hear, but deep in earnest discussion. So much for the doctrine of *sit up straight and stop talking!* she thought and remembered how very unpleasant she'd found that instruction the first time she'd heard it. Then as she continued to look around, she saw that the pupils were of all ages, from serious fifth formers who went on reading as though there were no interruption, to inquisitive first formers who looked up at her as soon as she entered the room. They seemed perfectly at ease and not at all put out by her arrival. She smiled at them but hesitated in the doorway uncertain as to whether it was in order to walk in, steadying herself as if she was about to embark on another long voyage.

Miss Barnes gentled to the front of the class, treading lightly, her skirts silkily a-swish. 'This lady is Miss Smith,' she said. 'She is the headmistress of a grammar school in London and she's come all the way from England just to visit us, which is a great honour.' Even the fifth formers looked up and smiled at that. 'I'm sure you will answer all her questions and show her the work you are doing. And I'm sure she will answer your questions in her turn. Is that not right, Miss Smith?'

Octavia agreed that it was and edged to the nearest desk, as quietly as she could. There were two small girls sitting side by side with their heads close together discussing the essays they'd just written. They were very friendly and stopped to explain what they were doing. 'It's full stops, ma'am. We have to be sure they're all there.'

The teacher in Octavia took over. 'I know a useful trick for full stops,' she told them. 'Would you like me to tell you about it?'

They would. So she did. 'You use a full stop to show you when to breathe when you're reading out loud,' she said. 'That's what it's for. I expect you know that. If one of you were to read, the other would hear when she was breathing. If it's a little gulping breath it might be a comma but if it's a nice long breath, it's sure to be a full stop.'

They tried it at once and were delighted to find that it worked. And Octavia was delighted too because she had made a good start to this visit and given before she began to take. She smiled at the two girls and moved on to another group, this time a pair who looked like third formers and were working through a page full of adverbial clauses. The variety of work being done in the room was impressive — studying poetry by Longfellow, reading *David Copperfield*, *Emma* and *Julius Caesar*, parsing and clause analysis, writing essays — and so was the ease with which the teacher turned from one pupil to the next as girls arrived at her desk with their queries.

Later, over lunch, she asked the English teacher how she managed to cope with such variety. 'It's much the same as coping with the difference between lessons, I guess,' the teacher said. 'Only quicker. As long as you're well prepared and have all the material you need to hand, you can cope with pretty much anything and of course if you don't know the answer you can promise to find it or suggest that you find it together. They quite enjoy doing that.'

This begged the first of the questions that Octavia had planned to ask. 'How long does it take to gather all the material you need?'

'When we first began,' Miss Barnes told her, 'we allowed ourselves six months in which to prepare and we needed every second of it. Now we aim to keep half a term ahead of ourselves — more if possible. We give every girl a syllabus of work in every subject, a month at a time for the first two grades, half-termly for the others, and we check and change at regular intervals so as to keep up to date. You can't afford to rest on your laurels when you operate this system. So yes, to answer the question you haven't asked, it means a lot of work. But the rewards far outweigh the effort.'

'Tell me,' Miss Weismann said, leaning forward across the

table. 'What roused your interest in our system in the first place? Was it a particular concern or just general curiosity?'

They get to the heart of things so quickly, Octavia thought, and answered carefully. 'It was a combination of things,' she told them. 'Having heard about you from the Fabian Society started me thinking, as I told you in my first letter, but there were worries too, about the efficiency of what we were doing, about the lack of impact our teaching was having.' Miss Barnes was looking a question at her, so she continued. 'I've been aware for quite a long time that many of our pupils are bored, no matter how hard we try to inspire them, and sometimes I only have to read their written work to see how little of what I've said has actually gone in. Some have understood and made great strides, others have tried hard but missed the point and some are floundering.'

'Exactly so,' Miss Barnes said. 'Because you have been teaching them at one speed and one speed cannot possibly suit an entire class. Once you give them the freedom to work at their own speed, in their own time and to ask for your help when they need it, you will notice an enormous change. There is no reason, when you think about it, why all children should learn at the same rate. Some will come to understanding slowly and after much discussion, sometimes with their friends, sometimes with their teachers, as you've already seen, but given encouragement and time they will all get there in the end. Not scrappily and unsure whether they understand or not, but completely and happily. There is nothing quite so happy as a child who has learnt and understood.'

'I saw that this morning,' Octavia said. 'Happy and sociable. I don't think I've ever been in a classroom that was quite so friendly.'

'Exactly so.'

'You will see more of it this afternoon,' the art teacher said. She wore a rather gorgeous Indian shawl over her shoulders and had hair so black it looked blue in the sunshine that streamed in upon them through the high windows of the staff room. 'I hope you will visit my studio and see what a joy painting can be.'

Octavia visited the studio, a French study and a Science one, in a lab full of retorts and Bunsen burners and the usual faint smell of gas, and then went on to the gymnasium where a group of juniors were climbing the ropes, leaping a horse and exercising on the wall bars.

'Gym and Games are the only lessons on the curriculum with no studies attached,' Miss Barnes explained, as they stood amid the twirling bodies. 'Much enjoyed, as you can see.'

'Could they opt out if they wanted to?' Octavia asked.

'Indeed yes. Some do, on occasions.'

'What do they do instead?'

'Join a study group,' Miss Barnes said, 'visit the library, go to the studio to paint or make pots, or the cookery room to bake cakes. There's always plenty to do in a Dalton school. The choice is theirs.'

'Which is the essence of the system,' Octavia said. 'You give them the freedom to plan their own lives. Rather as one does at university.'

'Exactly as one does at university.'

There was only one more question that needed asking — at least for that afternoon. 'How many lessons do they have to attend?'

'It varies,' Miss Barnes said, 'depending on the age of the girl and the number of subjects she wishes to study. As a rule of thumb, the juniors have about fifteen lessons a week, one or two in each subject including gym and games and religious instruction of course, and the seniors have about ten or so. It works out at two a day, which gives them plenty of time for private study. And fun.'

The word sang in Octavia's head. She smiled happily at her new friends. 'You believe in fun too.'

They all did and smiled and nodded to prove it. 'High days and holidays,' Miss Barnes said, 'are the icing on the cake. Christmas and Santa Claus, Thanksgiving and turkey, Easter for eggs and bonnets. We have an Easter parade to mark the end of the spring term, which you will see in two days' time. Every girl makes an Easter bonnet and they wear them for the end of term assembly. It's a great occasion. They love it. Why aim for a dull life when you can have a life full of richness and variety? It's the great moments we remember, is it not, and the richer the ritual the more keenly we look forward to it.'

Octavia was remembering the Queen's Diamond Jubilee and all those splendid horses stepping in line, the little fat Queen in her red and gold coach and the massed choristers in full song on the steps of St Paul's and she was uplifted simply by the memory. 'Exactly so,' she said.

It wasn't until much later that evening when she was settling to sleep in Miss Barnes' blue and white spare bedroom, her thoughts spinning with all the impressions and information she'd been gathering, that she recognised the feeling that had been growing so strongly in her ever since she arrived. It was the sense that she had come home.

DURING THE NEXT five days of her visit she learnt so much she began to be afraid she would forget it all before she got back to England. Miss Barnes gave her five copies of a booklet which she said would give her staff an outline of the system but there was so much more, the extraordinary number of high days and holidays for example, the lack of supervision in the grounds, which Miss Weismann told her was unnecessary 'because the girls are happy there, I guess,' the way textbooks were provided in cupboards at the back of every classroom, to be readily available. Every question she asked provided her with almost more information than she could digest. The only thing to be done was to take notes, which she did copiously.

The Easter parade was a splendid occasion with every hat trimmed to excess, and the final assembly that followed it was more cheerful than any school gathering she'd ever seen. 'We always sing the same hymns,' Miss Barnes explained. 'It's one of our traditions.' And on the last day of her visit there was a party for all the staff at Miss Barnes' house 'to celebrate an excellent term,' and that seemed to be an Easter tradition too.

By the time Octavia was being driven back to the quayside for her return journey she felt she'd known these forthright, eccentric women for years.

'You must write to us,' Amelia Barnes said, as they kissed goodbye, 'and let us know how you are getting on. Don't forget. And if there's any way we can help you, you have only to ask. Have a safe journey home.'

It was a very busy journey for, the Atlantic being relatively calm, she made use of the time to arrange her notes in the most intelligible order and to write up her impressions as clearly as she could. She had no doubt at all that this system was entirely right for her and her school and she wanted to present it to the others as positively as she could.

The summer term was well under way by the time she rejoined the school and her staff had been hard at work, teaching her classes as well as their own, so she was loath to burden them with yet another chore until she had settled back to work among them. But they were all keen to know how she had got on and what she thought of the system, so after a little persuasion, she handed them all a pack of prepared material and suggested that they should discuss it at the staff meeting at the end of the week.

It was a lively meeting for, although they were all in complete agreement that the system would suit them and should certainly be tried, there were two distinct opinions as to how they should go about it. Alice Genevra was all for starting it in September at the beginning of the school year.

'I know it would mean a lot of work,' she said, 'but we're none of us afraid of work, are we, and it would make much better sense to begin at the beginning of the school year. Our new first formers could be Dalton girls from the word go.'

Morag Gordon supported her. 'I know they said — what was it? — *In our opinion it takes at least six months to prepare for such a change.*' But that would be for a full sized school, would it not? Ours is small, so there would be less work. I think we could do it. In fact I would go so far as to say I think we should. I agree with Alice. It would be good for the first formers to start off the way they are going to go on and we must consider our present third formers too. I know there are only fourteen of them but what a difference it would make if they could be taught in this new way for two full years before they take their Lower Schools Certificate.'

Miss Fennimore put her pince-nez to her eye and consulted her copy of the leaflet. 'At least six months is considerably more than we would be allowing ourselves if we want to be ready by September,' she pointed out. 'We are well into April now and the new term starts in the first week of September don't forget. We would be looking at twenty-one weeks. I don't think that would be anywhere near enough. I should hate to start the term unprepared and in a rush. I suggest we defer the start until the New Year and give ourselves eight and a half months to do the thing properly.'

Sarah Fletcher was the last to speak and, rather to Octavia's surprise, she opted for caution. 'I'd like to make a really good job of it,' she said. 'I'd like to see our third formers getting the best we can give them, I agree with you on that, Morag, but would we be able to do it if we were rushed and ill prepared?'

The debate went on for nearly an hour and they were no

nearer to a decision. The only thing they were agreed on was that they wanted to make the change and they wanted it to be a success. Eventually Octavia told them she would have to use her casting vote, and that as she too felt it would make better sense to start at the beginning of the school year with the new first form, she voted for September. 'Although I know what a lot I am asking of you,' she said. 'It will be a formidable task. We must work together and help one another all we can.' And she thanked them for having studied the pack so closely and for giving their opinions so honestly, and declared the meeting closed.

Once they'd left her, she realised that she would have to delay her house-hunting, yet again, and the thought wearied her. There never seemed to be a moment when she could actually get down to finding herself a home. But she couldn't have allowed personal considerations to influence her when they'd been discussing something so important and all in all she felt she'd probably done the right thing.

ALICE STARTED work on her French syllabuses that evening. And so did Elizabeth Fennimore because she was well aware of the enormity of the task they'd now set themselves. Octavia spent the evening writing to her friend and ally Mr Gillard.

She told him about her visit to New York and what an inspiration it had been, she detailed the change that she and her staff were now proposing to make and what a lot of work it would mean for all of them, she said she was sure they would have his full support in the great experiment they were undertaking. Then, turning from the philosophical to the practical, she suggested several ways in which the task could be made easier for them.

It would help the entire school if we could have a school secretary, she wrote. *It would release me to supervise classes and assist my staff in drawing up the new syllabuses and ordering the extra stock that this method requires. It would also help the entire school, both now and in the future, if we could expand our staff. At present we have no art teacher and no music teacher and Miss Fennimore although she does not complain, is considerably overloaded as a teacher of Science and Mathematics. I think we shall find that two new members of staff would be more than justified by our rising numbers.*

She wasn't sure whether her numbers would rise that autumn, that had yet to be revealed, but it was at least likely. Their popularity was growing.

Then she signed herself, '*Yours hopefully.*' And took the letter to the post.

Mr Gillard was a valuable ally. His answer came almost by return of post. A school secretary was an excellent suggestion. He'd been thinking along the same lines himself. She could advertise for one as soon as she liked. The matter of two new teachers would have to be discussed with the board but it would be done at the earliest opportunity and he would write to tell her the outcome as soon as he knew it.

His next letter was delivered along with ten applications for the post of School secretary. The two new teachers she had asked for had been approved. He suggested an advertisement be put into *The Times* to ensure a high calibre of applicants and as soon as possible to ensure that the successful candidates would both be free to start work in September.

Octavia sent the advertisements to the paper that very morning. After being stuck in the doldrums for so many miserable weeks, her life was suddenly moving and at such speed it was making her feel quite dizzy. Now she had more work in a day than she could comfortably do in two, but the pressure was exactly what she needed. It sharpened her perceptions and made her daring. The English Literature syllabuses that she drew up late at night in the quiet of her bedroom were full of inspired cross-references and quirky pairings. Her present third formers would love them. She couldn't wait to teach them. But in the meantime there were staff to appoint, and the first of them was her secretary.

She pared the list of applicants down to four, all of them middle-aged and well qualified, with clear handwriting and excellent references, and then almost on a whim, she added a fifth. Her name was Margaret Henry and she hardly seemed qualified for the work at all, because she was only eighteen and had little experience, but there was something about her letter that spoke directly to Octavia's sharpened senses, and she was curious to see whether the young woman matched her word.

She was small, pale and skinny, and she sat before Octavia's desk clutching her handbag in her lap and looking anxiously apprehensive. But her answers were just what Octavia was looking for, honest, open and forthright. No, she didn't have experience of working in a school, but she was a hard worker and willing to learn. Yes, she would be prepared to work long hours. She knew that staff worked on after the children had gone home and would have to be in school before they arrived. That stood to reason. She thought being part of an experiment would be wonderful. 'Most of the work in offices is very ordinary. You could do it with your eyes shut.'

That made Octavia laugh. 'So you need work that will open your eyes,' she said. 'Is that what made you apply for this particular job?'

'Well, ma'am,' the girl said, 'to be truthful I didn't know it was going to be part of an experiment. The thing is, there's a girl in my office who used to come here. She was in your fifth form last year. Penny Morrison. So I've heard a lot about the school. She's always talking about it. She says it's the only school she's ever been in where the girls liked the teachers. She says she was fond of you, ma'am. And I've been listening to her and thinking, I wish I could have gone there. So when I saw your advertisement...'

It was a perfect answer. A clincher, as Tommy would have said. 'Were I to offer you this job,' Octavia said. 'When could you start?'

She began work a week later and, just as she'd promised, she was a very hard worker and learnt quickly. Within days she was Maggie to all the staff and had befriended all the children who appeared in her office. Within a week she was sending out appointments to all the parents who'd applied for their children to join the school in September and typing and duplicating the new syllabuses, neatly and accurately, as if she'd been dealing with such things all her life. 'A treasure,' Elizabeth Fennimore said.

But it was nearly the end of May and they only had three more months to get everything ready and there were still two new members of staff to appoint and all the stock to order to say nothing of the day to day teaching, which was never easy in the run up to examinations, and was especially difficult that year because they had ten candidates for Lower Schools and all of them were anxious.

'We shall never get it all done,' Sarah Fletcher said.

'Yes, we will,' Octavia reassured her. There was no point in worrying now. They were committed. 'In two weeks' time we shall have two new members of staff.'

'But when will they join us?' Sarah said. 'If it isn't until September they won't be much help to us now.'

Their new Art teacher, Phillida Bertram, started work in the middle of June, on the day a reluctant German delegation finally signed the Treaty of Versailles and the Great War was officially over. She was a considerable help, even though her own syllabuses were, as she was the first to admit, probably the easiest to compile. The teacher of Maths and Biology, an amiable lady called Mabel Ollerington, came in to help Miss Fennimore as often as she could, which wasn't anywhere near as often as they would both have liked, but was better than nothing, according to Elizabeth. 'We must work through the summer holidays, I'm afraid,' she told her new colleague and was relieved when Mabel said, 'Of course.'

Octavia worked in every moment she could find, sitting up late at night to get things completed, and staying on after school for several hours every evening, with Maggie to help her. For besides all the new work at school, she also had to make time for Emmeline and Johnnie and the girls. She'd taken them out every weekend since she got back from New York, for trips to the Zoo or Madame Tussaud's or a walk across the Heath or a visit to the cinema. She felt it was important to give them things to enjoy, to make their lives as normal as possible, and Emmeline was still grieving so terribly and recovering so very slowly that she simply couldn't do it.

There were days when she felt so tired she could have slept where she stood, nights when she was so tired she couldn't sleep at all, private moments of anxiety when she began to doubt her own judgement in choosing September.

But September came and they were all more or less ready, with most of the stock in the cupboards and all the work planned for the first half term, if not longer, and the considerably enlarged school were sitting before her at their very first assembly of the new school year, eager to be told what it would be like in this new Dalton school of theirs. And glancing round at them all she felt so proud of them it made her chest ache.

'Today,' she told them happily, 'is the start of an adventure. We — you, me, Miss Genevra, Miss Gordon, Miss Fennimore, Miss Fletcher, Miss Bertram, Miss Ollerington and Miss Henry — are pioneers. Not just teachers and a school secretary and school pupils but pioneers. It is a splendid thing to be a pioneer. You must be proud of yourselves and of what we are beginning, for great things will come of it. We are going to be the very first people in this country to use a completely new method of education and there will be people watching us to see how well we shall do it.

'Now I will tell you a little more about it. When you get back to your classrooms you will each be given a folder. Take great care of it, for this is where you will keep the syllabuses of all the work you will be doing in the coming half term. Every girl will get a syllabus for every subject she is going to study and every syllabus is a guide. It will tell you what you are going to learn, which books and equipment you will need and when your written work has to be handed in. You will not be going to lessons all the time, as they do in other schools, so it will be up to you to decide when you do your work and how you will do it. For example you may find some subjects quite easy and, if that is the case, you might like to do all the tasks you have been set in those subjects in the first few days after you get your syllabuses. Other subjects will be more difficult and you will find you need to spend more time on them and take them step by step. Your teachers will be in their rooms to help you and that's where you will find all the books you need too.

'In the first few days it will probably be a bit puzzling but after a while you will get used to it and begin to see what freedom our new system will give you and what fun it will be. If you are confused, don't battle on alone. Ask for help and it will be given. We shall expect great things of you and I know you will not disappoint us.'

She opened her hymn book ready for their first hymn and smiled round at them before she gave Miss Fletcher the nod to start playing the opening bars. 'Good luck!' she said.

WITHIN A WEEK she was recording how easy the transfer had been.

Most of the girls have taken to it like ducks to water, she wrote in her journal, *and those who are confused have the good sense to ask for help. There has been a certain amount of muddle at the start of the study periods when the first formers weren't sure where they ought to go, and some study rooms were full, but that was to be expected and it was pleasing to see how quickly the older girls came to their assistance. It is very encouraging.*

CHAPTER 22

John Algernon Withington was heartily sick of being called Podge. Not that there was anything he could do about it. The family habit was too firmly entrenched. He'd had words with Em about it once, but that was a long time ago — four years at least, must be — just after he was invalided out of the army and when he was feeling dicky. Anyway he'd spoken to her — several times actually — and she *had* promised she would try to remember but it didn't do the slightest good, even though he'd scowled at her every time she forgot and she'd put her hands over her mouth and made apologetic faces. The name kept slipping out, and usually on embarrassing occasions, like Uncle JJ's retirement party.

True to his promise, although somewhat belatedly, Professor Smith retired at Christmas, having agreed to stay on for one more term to ease his successor into the post.

'And not a minute too soon,' Amy said, brushing invisible dust from the lapels of his dress suit. 'I was beginning to despair of you.'

'I think your timing is perfect, Pa.' Octavia laughed. 'Now we can have a proper retirement party. If you'd done it any earlier I wouldn't have had the energy for celebrations, even for my father.'

'In that case, I'm glad I didn't discommode you,' JJ said, adjusting his bow tie. 'I would not have wished to have been given an improper party.'

It was a splendid occasion and a very happy one with all his old colleagues there to salute him and his entire family around him to congratulate him. Even Podge cheered up after a glass of champagne and Dora and Edith, who were allowed half a glass to mark the occasion, were soon giggling with the best.

Emmeline said it was the first time she'd really enjoyed herself since her babies died. 'Which is not to say I haven't been glad of all the outings you've arranged,' she said to Octavia. 'I wouldn't want you to think that. It's just that my heart hasn't been in them.'

'I know my darling,' Octavia said. 'Nor has mine sometimes.'

'But it *is* now, isn't it,' Emmeline said. 'For both of us. Because it's family I suppose. That makes the difference. Doesn't your Pa look well?'

He made a sparkling speech, as they all knew he would, thanking his guests for their presence, his family and colleagues for their unfailing, and sometimes incomprehensible, understanding and support. Then he turned to Octavia and told them 'by way of a closing remark' that he was handing on the torch of learning to his daughter, 'confident that whatever fuel she might use to keep it alight, it will burn freely and brightly if — shall we say — occasionally unexpectedly. My advice to you would be, watch for fireworks over Hammersmith.'

'Quite right,' John Algernon said, grinning at his cousin as the laughter died down and the drinking was resumed. 'We shall be lucky if the entire place doesn't go up in flames.'

JJ's friends were a little surprised by such a blunt criticism, and showed it.

'Ignore him,' Octavia advised. 'He's my cousin, Podge. He's renowned for hyperbole.'

'What an unusual name!' they said, looking at his skinny wrists and his gaunt cheeks, as people always did when they heard it for the first time. 'How did you come by that?'

He explained, as *he* always did, but it was very tedious and he found himself glancing at his watch as soon as he'd finished, wondering when he could make his excuses, thank his aunt and uncle for their hospitality and slip away. The *palais de dance* was waiting for him and so, with a bit of luck, was Olga. Absolutely top hole place the *palais*. A lifesaver. Saved his life on innumerable evenings in the last year, especially when another God-awful day at the bank had bored him crazy. Couldn't wait to get there most evenings if the truth be told. Although he had to find excuses for his mother and that could be tricky. Couldn't let on to *her* where he was going. That would never have done. She'd have hated the idea. She said dance hall girls were common. Which they probably were. But good fun, common or not.

They were dancing the quickstep when he arrived that evening and for a few seconds he just stood at the edge of the dance floor and wallowed in the sight of them. They were so young and brightly coloured and alive, a million years from the blood and slime and mud-stiff khaki of the trenches. It did him good just to be with them, listening to the band and letting his feet tap in rhythm, while his eyes adjusted to the yellow half-light from all those art deco wall lamps and his lungs coughed their first protest against the blue fug of the cigarette smoke. It made him cough every time, but what the hell, it was worth it. And there was Olga, waving to him, wearing her red dress with its short skirt showing her lovely long legs and its low neck showing her lovely brown back, and her painted mouth as red as her dress.

'Algy!' she said as she walked off the floor towards him.

'You're late ain'tcher. I thought you wasn't coming. Where you been?'

They were playing the next dance and it was a waltz. 'Dance?' he hoped.

She slid into his arms, all artificial silk and cheap perfume and tempting flesh, and he bent his head to kiss her as he walked her backwards onto the floor.

'Now look at the state of you,' she pretended to scold. 'Mucky pup. You're all over lipstick. Stand still.' And she took a handkerchief from her little bag, spat on it and rubbed his mouth clean where they stood. Oh she was delectable. She could rub his mouth with her hanky any time.

'There's ever such a good picture on up the Ritz,' she told him as they danced.

He took his cue at once. 'Would you like to see it?'

She made eyes at him, her black eyelashes spiky with mascara. 'I might.'

'Tomorrow?'

'I never knew a bloke like you,' she said. 'You can't wait five minutes fer nothing.'

'No,' he admitted happily. 'I can't. Tomorrow it is then.' And he put his hand on the small of her lovely naked back and pulled her body towards him, lusting at the touch of those delicious titties and that luscious curved belly. Tomorrow they would be sitting in the back row at the pictures and he could take even more liberties. I'm twenty-three, he thought, and I'm alive and that lousy war is over and I'm going to live all I can.

'You never said where you was,' she said languidly as they shifted their feet to the music.

'Only some boring old party,' he told her, too lost in sensation to remember it.

· · ·

311

THE BORING OLD party was still going on, although Emmeline and her children had gone home to bed and some of the academics had retreated too. JJ was sitting on his ancient sofa talking to his brother-in-law, who had just confessed that he was going to retire too, probably in the summer.

'A very good idea,' JJ said. 'If this is retirement I can't recommend it too highly.'

'I thought the end of July,' Ralph told him. 'That will make forty-four years I've worked for the firm, and forty-four years is enough.'

'I would have said it was more than enough,' JJ agreed. 'Have some more brandy?'

'What will you do now that you're a gentleman of leisure?' Ralph asked, holding out his brandy glass.

'As little as possible, I daresay,' JJ said, filling it generously. 'I've promised my womenfolk that we shall have a Sunday breakfast every morning.'

'I can't imagine Tavy taking a leisurely breakfast,' her uncle said. 'She's always in such a rush.'

'That's what comes of being a headmistress.'

'Is she happy?' Ralph asked.

JJ gave it thought. 'She's busy,' he said, 'and that's tantamount to happiness where Tavy is concerned.'

'Is she still working for the Suffragettes?'

'Not as often as she used to,' JJ said, 'but now and then. She's more interested in the League of Nations at the moment.'

OCTAVIA HAD great hopes of the League of Nations and followed its progress in every newspaper. Buoyed up by her success at Hammersmith Secondary School, and with a new year coming and a new and peaceful decade, she was in the mood to be hopeful, even if she still hadn't got round to buying a house. This proposed League seemed a sensible organisation since it was restricting its activities to the prevention of war. In fact its sole reason for existence was to prevent them from breaking out in the first place and they intended to do it by dealing with disputes between nations by diplomacy and compromise — although it had to be admitted that there was a war being fought in Russia even while the plans were being formulated.

'Which I am sure they will deal with the moment they are fully organised,' she told her father. 'We can't expect them to start work before they are ready. That would be unwise.' Didn't she know it?

Life at Hammersmith was still burdened with work. The teachers were busy preparing their second and third syllabuses, and learning how to handle a study group by daily trial and error and, what seemed to them, far too many mistakes. And as if that weren't pressure enough, they also discovered that they were suffering from a troubling shortage of books. Now that their pupils were allowed to read as widely and as often as they liked, they were getting through textbooks and subject libraries much more quickly than their teachers had originally estimated they would.

'We should have ordered three times the number of Science books,' Miss Fennimore said to Octavia. 'I've never seen such an appetite.'

'That's a triumph,' Octavia told her, 'and a result of your good teaching. I hope you will take it as such.'

Elizabeth wasn't placated. 'Shortage of books is a disaster,' she said.

Octavia went cap in hand to Mr Gillard, but this time he couldn't help her. 'We are running over budget as it is,' he said. 'I will do what I can but I'm not promising anything. Not till after April in any event.'

So they had to find a way to make do, partly by advising their pupils to join the public library and partly by setting up a rationing system, which didn't please any of them, for the girls didn't like waiting, especially when it was for the one book they really wanted to read, and the staff all said it was defeating the object of the exercise if they had to ask their pupils to defer the pleasure of finding things out just at the very moment when they'd started to discover how pleasurable that could be.

Octavia did what she could to cheer them up by organising an Easter parade for the last assembly of the spring term, and prevailing on Phillida Bertram to help all the girls who wanted to take part to design their Easter bonnets, which since they were mostly cloche hats was easily done with coloured cardboard and crepe paper and discarded ribbons and trimmings. But April was a long time coming even so.

The newly formed League of Nations was having a hard time of it too, despite having been inaugurated at St James' Palace. The civil war in Russia went on and they didn't seem to be able to do anything to stop it.

'Although,' as Octavia said to her father, 'the solution is staring them in the face. They should use their influence to stop foreign powers sending troops and arms to help the Whites and just let the Russians sort it out for themselves. And yes, I know what you're going to say, the foreign powers are America and Great Britain, but the principle should be the same whoever they are.'

'Unfortunately, you are talking about wealthy capitalists,' her father said, 'and they are not open to persuasion, British or American. A communist government would affect their trade.'

'So young men have to be sent to another war so that they can go on making money, is that what you're saying? That's scandalous.'

'It is,' JJ agreed. 'But there is a worse scandal, I fear. The ruling class are not above calling out the troops to attack their own workers if they come out on strike, even in this country. There are plans already laid for the use of the military against strikers. It won't just be police with batons next time. They've got tanks and machine guns waiting and ready.'

'That,' his daughter said, 'is downright disgusting. It shouldn't be allowed.'

'It is the way our society is organised,' JJ said.

'Then we should change it,' his daughter said trenchantly. 'We should use the ballot box and change it. Being rich shouldn't give a man the right to dictate to his fellow creatures and he certainly shouldn't be allowed to send them to their deaths or call out the troops to attack them if they ask for a living wage.'

'We shall see you in Parliament yet,' JJ said, laughing at her.

'Oh I do hope not,' Amy said, pouring more tea for them both. 'They work all night in Parliament. We should never see her.'

But for the moment Octavia was fully occupied in changing her school.

IN THE SUMMER term the visitors began to arrive, most of them teachers who were curious to see for themselves what this new system was like, so as well as writing her own syllabuses and helping her staff with theirs, chasing the books that hadn't been delivered and badgering the governors for more money, Octavia had sightseers to escort round the building and endless questions to answer. She was proud to think that her new ideas were acquiring a reputation and it pleased her to show how well the system was working, even in their rather cramped quarters and with inadequate stock, but it left her with too little time for her family. Her outings with Em and the children often had to be cancelled at the last moment because there was school work that just had to be finished.

'I'm a poor cousin, these days,' she apologised to Emmeline.

'You can't help being busy,' Emmeline told her. 'But you will help me with Pa's party won't you. You're so good at organising parties and I'd like him to have one as good as Uncle JJs.'

It wasn't quite as good because there were fewer people who were able to attend it and bank clerks don't have quite the same ebullience as eccentric academics, so the conversation was limited, but they made a great fuss of him and drank a great deal of champagne and he said it was the best party he'd ever had and told them all he was looking forward to his retirement and then sprang a surprise.

'Now that the war is over and I haven't got to work anymore I mean to enjoy my life to the full,' he said. 'I shall take a few risks for a start because that's something I've always wanted to do and you can't take risks when you work in a bank and have a family to support. Not that I'm complaining about having a family. They have been the great joy of my life. Nor about my work, which has always been dull but secure, exactly as my teachers told me it would be. It would be the end of civilisation as we know it to run risks in banking, as my colleagues will bear me out. But now I can. So what am I going to do? I'm going to buy a car and Maud and I are going to travel the country. There are so many places we want to see and now we can.'

'Good heavens, Ma!' Emmeline said turning to her mother during the buzz that followed. 'Did you know about this?'

Maud was twinkling. 'I had an inkling,' she said. 'He's been talking about it for a long time.'

'Where are you going first?' Emmeline called to her father.

'Scotland,' Ralph said. 'And then we can bring you back some Edinburgh rock.'

They set off three weeks later, on the day the Turks signed their peace treaty with the Allies and lost eighty per cent of their once great Ottoman empire. But none of them except Octavia and her father took any notice of things that were happening so far away. Ralph was impatient to get started. The luggage was packed and stowed in the boot and he'd mastered the art of driving his new toy and could steer well enough to keep out of the way of any other cars he might meet on the road and could even get into reverse gear, which his grand-children thought was quite amazing. The entire family turned up to wish them *bon voyage* and even Algernon-Podge waved his encouragement before slipping away for his date with Olga.

'Who would have thought it?' Emmeline said as the car rattled round the corner and disappeared from view. 'I always thought my Pa was such a sober man. I never imagined this for a minute. Oh I *shall* miss them.'

'How about a trip to the zoo?' Octavia said, aiming her question at the three children who were looking rather cast down. Now that the term was over she had time for trips — at last — and like her uncle she meant to make the most of it.

They had an excellent summer holiday, each in their own way, JJ and Amy reading and relaxing in their garden, Algernon-Podge in the dance hall and at the pictures with Olga, Octavia arranging treats for Emmeline and the children, a river trip to the Tower of London, a picnic on Box Hill, and finally a fort-night at Eastbourne, enjoying all the old familiar delights of the seaside, and missing Tommy a lot more than she'd expected to. And Ralph and Maud motored about the Scottish Highlands.

They didn't come home until the new school year had begun and eleven-year-old Edith had joined her sister at the North London Collegiate School and seven-year-old Johnnie had started at his prep school, despite considerable misgivings on his mother's part and considerable opposition on his own.

'Everything's changing,' Emmeline mourned, 'and they're not here to see it. You'd think they'd at least come home to see my poor little Johnnie off to school. After all, poor little man, it's a big step to take. But no. Apparently they're off to Inverness, of all places. Why would anyone want to go to Inverness? It's right out in the wilds. I had a postcard yesterday and you should see how wild it looks. I tell you, Tavy, I'm beginning to forget what they look like.'

They came home halfway through September looking quite unlike themselves. They'd both put on weight and were both wearing new clothes and they'd brought all sorts of strange presents for the children — lengths of tartan and odd hats called tam-o-shanters and the most peculiar sweets.

'You're just a pair of old gadabouts,' Emmeline scolded, 'away all this time. I don't know what's to be done about you. I hope you're going to stay at home now with the winter coming on and everything.'

But her mother giggled and her father said he'd got plans for a trip to Norfolk next, to see where Nelson came from.

'I don't know what's got into him,' Emmeline complained to Octavia. 'I really don't. They'll catch their death of cold rushing about all over the place like this. It isn't natural.'

'We're in the twenties now, Em,' Octavia said, 'and lots of people are driving. I saw six cars on the road only yesterday on my way to school. Six. Imagine that.'

'Well I wish they'd take theirs off the road and start behaving like grandparents again,' Emmeline said. 'That's all I can say. It's going to be a cold winter and I don't want them driving about in it.'

IT WAS CERTAINLY A DIFFICULT ONE, as the newspapers were constantly saying. The economy had been in decline for nearly two years and now a slump had set in and prices were falling disastrously.

The price of coal had fallen particularly sharply and the mine owners, fearful because their profits were falling too, proposed a cut in the miners' wages. According to the *Daily Herald*, colliers, who were currently earning £4 9s 3d, were now being offered a mere £2 13s 6d, which, by any standard, was a pittance on which to feed, house and clothe a family. It was no surprise to Octavia when they came out on strike. And no surprise to JJ when the government declared a State of Emergency and began to mobilise troops.

Octavia was horrified. And her horror grew when a deputation of London Mayors, led by no less a person than George Lansbury, marched to Downing Street, to request an interview with Lloyd George, with several thousand unemployed men marching behind them. It was a peaceful demonstration but for some unaccountable reason the police suddenly decided that Whitehall had to be cleared and ordered a mounted baton charge.

'It's exactly what they did to us,' Octavia remembered. 'They didn't agree with what we were saying so they hit us with sticks. Oh Pa, nothing ever seems to change. It was brutal and unnecessary then and it's brutal and unnecessary now. Violence like that makes matters worse. I shall write to the paper and say so.'

Meanwhile Maud and Ralph were continuing their travels, writing home rapturously to Emmeline about how they were exploring Norwich, *which is such a lovely old-fashioned place* and rejoicing at how cheap everything was. *We can get bed and breakfast for half a crown. Imagine that.*

Emmeline wasn't impressed. 'I shall be glad when they come home and stop all this gadding about,' she said. 'It's nearly November. High time they'd had enough if it, I should have said.'

It was more or less what the delectable Olga was saying to her brother, only in a rather different setting, in rather different vocabulary and for an entirely different reason. 'Ain't you 'ad enough, Algy?'

'No,' Algy whispered, nuzzling into her neck. 'You're too beautiful.'

'You're too greedy,' his beloved said, shaking herself free of him. Necking could be uncomfortable sometimes, cramped in the back row. 'That's your trouble. I never knew such a greedy guts.'

'Marry me, then,' Algy said. 'And then I really will get enough. All this stopping and starting and never getting anywhere's enough to drive a chap bonkers.'

But at that point the couple sitting in front of them turned round to shush them, so he had to stop what he was doing and make himself respectable again. It didn't stop the yearning though nor the thought that the cure for it was to get married. If only she wasn't so dead set against it.

'It'd be fun,' he urged, over and over again. But her answer was always the same.

'Maybe fer you. It wouldn't be no fun fer me. I like a bit a' life. Besides you don't get married in the winter in all this rain a' sleet an' everything.'

'I'll ask you in the spring then,' he promised. 'That's got to be better.'

THE SPRING WAS WORSE than the winter had been. In February 1921 the Germans were reeling under the news that their government had been fined 200 billion gold marks as reparation for the damage their army had done in France. In Great Britain there were a million unemployed in Great Britain and ex-servicemen were selling matches and bootlaces on the streets to earn what little they could — and the miners' strike went on and on. In April the miners' leaders pressed their allies in the Triple Alliance to set a date for their supportive strike and the government stepped up its military preparations for an all-out conflict. Soon there were tanks and armoured cars on the country roads and armed troops on standby in every garrison town.

'Wales this year,' Ralph told his daughter. 'We want to see the valleys, don't we, my love.'

Maud agreed that they did, adding that she'd heard they were very pretty. 'We'll send you postcards,' she promised Emmeline, as they kissed goodbye.

'What about Easter?' Emmeline asked.

'We'll be back long before then,' her father told her. 'We'll bring you some Welsh Easter eggs.'

'I don't want Welsh Easter eggs,' Emmeline complained to Octavia. 'I want them at home.'

The arrival of a nervous police constable on her doorstep late on a cold afternoon at the beginning of April, was almost what she expected. 'It's that stupid car, isn't it,' she said to him. 'It's broken down.'

'Well no, Mrs Thompson,' the young man said, diffidently. 'I'm afraid it's a bit worse than that. They've had a crash.'

'I knew it,' Emmeline said. 'Are they all right?'

'Well no,' the constable said again. 'I'm afraid they're in hospital. I've got the address for you.'

Her throat was instantly full of panic, but she took the little paper from his hands, and kept her self-control until he had gone. Then she ran to the telephone to call her cousin. 'Oh Tavy, what am I going to do?' she wept. 'They're in hospital.'

'Pack an overnight bag,' Octavia said. 'I'll be with you in half an hour. Your Connie will look after the children, won't she? Try not to worry. I'll drive you straight there. Have you told Podge?'

'No. I suppose I should have. It's just…'

'It's all right, Em,' Octavia said. 'I'll do it.'

But the person who answered the phone was Aunt Maud's one and only servant and she said she had no idea where Mr Algernon was. 'Out somewhere, Miss,' she said. 'He's always out somewhere. Can I give him a message?'

'Tell him his mother and father have had an accident in their car,' Octavia said. 'Emmeline and I are going down to Wales to see them. I'll phone him later when I know how they are.'

It was a long journey, across country through Oxford and Cheltenham and Gloucester and all along the Severn estuary, as darkness gathered forebodingly around them and the gloom thickened. Emmeline cried nearly all the way. 'Are we nearly there?' she asked, over and over again. 'Oh poor Pa. Poor Ma.'

The hospital was dark too, all red brick and tall bare trees, and what light there was from the long windows flickered like candles. They were directed to a woman's surgical ward, where they found Maud, with both her hands bandaged and her face bruised and patterned with ugly stitches, lying in a narrow bed, too deeply asleep to be woken. Emmeline wept again at the sight of her but Octavia went off to find a doctor.

It was a woman doctor, small, neat and brisk to the point of brusqueness. Yes, she said, consulting her notes, Mrs Withington had been admitted that afternoon with two broken wrists and cuts and contusions, and had since developed concussion. The car she was travelling in had been involved in a head on collision with an armoured vehicle. 'It was a very serious accident,' she said. 'She is seriously ill. Are you a relation?'

'How seriously?' Octavia asked. But she knew the answer before it was given. The familiar nightmare was beginning all over again. First Cyril and then the boys and now this.

'The prognosis is not good.'

'You mean she might die?'

'As I said, the prognosis is not good. We haven't told her about her husband of course, because of the shock.'

'He is ill too?' Octavia asked.

'Haven't they told you?' the doctor said. And when Octavia shook her head. 'He was dead on arrival I'm sorry to say. There was nothing we could do for him.'

Oh dear God! Octavia thought. My poor Em. But she remembered to thank the doctor for her information and to ask how long they could stay on the ward.

They stayed all night because Emmeline said she couldn't leave her mother until she'd seen her open her eyes. She never did. By four o'clock in the morning Emmeline was broken by the knowledge that she had lost both her parents.

She allowed Octavia to lead her out into the hospital grounds and then she railed against everything and everyone, against her father for coming to this awful place and her mother for coming with him. Against that stupid, silly car — hadn't she always said it was dangerous? — Against the army — what were they doing driving an armoured car along an ordinary road? Against the doctors and the nurses for not saving them, and the weather and the police and that stupid, stupid, silly car, until she ran out of targets and descended into terrible tears. And Octavia held her and tried to comfort her and felt that she was being totally inadequate.

Afterwards there were things to be done and as Emmeline was incapable of doing anything at all except weep, Octavia took over and, as soon as the new day had begun, made all the arrangements that were necessary. She phoned Podge and her mother and the school, registered the deaths, arranged for an undertaker to transport the two poor bodies back to Highgate, and finally drove her weeping cousin home. It was late on the following evening before they arrived and they were both completely exhausted.

The next week passed in a muddle of arrangements and grief. There were friends and relations to inform, a funeral to attend, and finally Ralph's last will and testament to be found and read. It was short and simple. He left all his savings, after the funeral expenses had been paid, to his son John Algernon Withington and his daughter Emmeline Elizabeth Thompson. The house and its contents were to be sold and the monies realised shared between his said son and daughter.

'I don't want money,' Emmeline wailed. 'I want them alive again.'

'Don't worry,' her husband told her. 'You don't have to do anything about it. I will invest it for you.'

'That's not what I meant at all,' Emmeline said, anger flaring again.

But Algernon-Podge was glad of the money. It was an opportunity. Heaven sent. 'Actually,' he said. 'It's come in the nick of time for me. Sort of thing.'

They looked at him curiously, wondering what on earth he was talking about. Has he got into debt? Octavia thought. Surely not. Or is he more ill than he's let us know? He certainly looked ill but that could be because he was wearing his black suit. She was upset to see how thin he looked and noticed that his hair was receding and that there wasn't a trace of colour in his face.

'I want to go "down under",' he explained. 'To Australia. This is my chance to do it. Heaven sent, sort of thing. It's not the right time to tell you, I know that, but it's what I want and I shall do it sooner or later, so it's better you know now. There's nothing for me here.' Olga was never going to marry him. She'd made that clear all along and now that he'd lost his parents, he could see it. He could see a lot of things now he'd lost his parents. That the bank wasn't the place for him. That Olga wasn't the right girl for him either. His mother had been right about that, poor old dear. That he needed a different life. No, it was better to go. Make a clean break and start again somewhere else. 'I'm going to join this government scheme they've got going. Try my hand at farming or something. Out in the fresh air. Give the old lungs a chance.'

So many changes, Octavia thought, catching the sadness on Emmeline's plump face. But he's right about the fresh air. It could be just what he needs. If only he hadn't told us now.

. . .

THAT EVENING she sat at her desk in her quiet bedroom and wrote up the events of the last awful week while they were still fresh in her mind.

'It seems to me,' she wrote, 'that these deaths are all interlocked, as if one has followed almost inevitably from the causes of the previous one. They all seem to me to be the result of the war. Cyril's certainly was and in a way so were Eddie's and Dickie's, for the flu came at a time when we were all exhausted and hadn't got the energy or the will to fight against it. And now this last, which wouldn't have happened if there hadn't been an armoured car on the road, and that was only there because the mine owners and the government had decided to wage war against the miners. It is always war and fighting, the illogical and non-proven belief that one human being can prevail over the wishes or needs or beliefs of another by hitting him or bullying him with guns and tanks.'

CHAPTER 23

Octavia went back to school after the funeral in her most rigidly determined mood. Changes would have to be made. How well she knew that now. She set about making them at once.

'By next September,' she told her staff at their next meeting, 'I should like us all to be in a position to provide syllabuses for the full school year. This will be our third year as a Dalton school, so writing syllabuses should be a great deal easier than it was at the beginning. I'm sure being thoroughly prepared will make things easier for us as the year progresses.'

'I don't doubt that,' Elizabeth Fennimore said, surprised by the tone Octavia was taking, 'but it's a tall order. We're well into May now and the state examinations are almost upon us. I doubt whether we could write syllabuses for the entire year in three months. For half a year, maybe, but not a year.'

The others began to agree but their headmistress was all brisk determination. 'We have to move forward,' she said and there was something so implacable about her tone that dissent was quashed — for the time being.

'What on earth's the matter with her?' Morag said when she

and Elizabeth were alone in the cloakroom afterwards, putting on their straw hats. 'I've never known her ride roughshod over us before. Have we done something wrong?'

'It could be grief,' Elizabeth said sagely. 'It takes people in all sorts of odd ways. But we mustn't let her do it, no matter what the reason might be. It isn't sensible to put us all under pressure, especially at this time of year.'

The pressure was maintained. The next morning there was a notice on the staff notice board detailing the dates by which each syllabus should be completed.

'Good heavens!' Alice Genevra said. 'She's given us our marching orders.'

'Then we must subvert them,' Elizabeth said.

The orders continued. The next morning it was a list of instructions for the invigilation of the examinations. 'Totally unnecessary,' Morag said. 'They're exactly the same as they were last year. Nothing's changed. We can invigilate them in the same way.'

The next morning it was a list of the senior forms that would be required to take assembly together with the dates on which the assemblies would be.

'We do this by consultation,' Morag said. 'Not dictat. It might not be convenient for a form to take assembly at the time she's specified. Mine certainly couldn't. They've got Geography that day and I want them fresh for it. I shall go and see her.'

It didn't get her anywhere. The headmistress was adamant. It was, as Morag reported to the others, as if she'd become a different person.

'What are we to do about it?' Mabel Ollerington wanted to know. 'I can't possibly get a year's syllabuses ready by September. I've only just found out how to write them.'

'We will have a staff meeting without her,' Elizabeth said, 'and decide which of her suggestions — we will assume that that is what they are — which of her suggestions we are prepared to agree to.'

'And then?' Mabel asked.

'Then I will see her again and tell her what we have decided.'

'Would you like company?' Sarah Fletcher offered.

'No,' Elizabeth said. 'It would be better if I were on my own. I'm the oldest member of her staff, so she would expect me to take the lead.'

Even so she found it daunting to face her transformed head-mistress with such a task in hand, and could feel her heart quailing when she admitted that they had called a meeting without her.

'Really?' Octavia said. 'That is a little extraordinary surely.'

'We are in an extraordinary situation.'

Octavia let that pass. 'So what decisions have you made? Since I assume that was the purpose of the meeting.'

'We are not at all happy about having to prepare a year's syllabuses by September,' Elizabeth told her. 'It's very short notice and none of us think it can be done, or at least, none of us think it can be done to our satisfaction, which is what we would all like to do. Half a year's syllabuses would be possible, a year's no.'

'I see. Is that all?'

Now that she'd begun, Elizabeth was finding it easier. 'No,' she said. 'We discussed the invigilation timetable too and would prefer to work to the old one, the one we used last year. It worked very well and we're familiar with it. And we'd like to draw up the rota for assemblies between us, so that we don't ask too much of our girls at exam time.'

'Anything else?'

'No,' Elizabeth said, adding, rather stiffly, 'If there were any way we could accede to your requests we would have found it. Unfortunately there is not.'

Octavia was angry. She couldn't deny it. And although she

did what she could to control it, her anger was clear in the tone of her voice. 'I would have thought my requests, as you put it, were perfectly reasonable,' she said, 'and well within the bounds of acceptance. I intend to draw up my own syllabuses by September. I'm not asking you to do anything I am not prepared to do myself.'

They were being so coldly distant with one another that Elizabeth lost her temper too. 'It's all very well for you,' she said. 'You are superhuman. We are mere flesh and blood with clay feet. We can't keep up with you and it is, if you will forgive me for saying so, unrealistic of you to expect us to.'

'I have never claimed to be superhuman — as you put it,' Octavia said. 'I am merely looking for ways to make our lives easier and that seemed an obvious way.'

'To you perhaps, but not to us.'

It was a quarrel and they'd reached stalemate. 'Very well then,' Octavia said. 'If that is really your unanimous opinion.'

'Yes, Miss Smith, it is.'

That 'Miss Smith' was just a little too formal not to have been deliberate. It's as if she's putting a barrier between us, Octavia thought, and there have never been barriers between us. 'Then we will consider my suggestion rejected,' she said. 'Personally, I think you are being unwise but this is a democratic school and I will abide by the democratic process.'

Elizabeth pressed on. 'And your other suggestions?'

'I will abide by the democratic process,' Octavia said. 'If you wish to use last year's invigilation timetable that is up to you. I think that's unwise too, but it's your decision. I trust you will inform me as to the matter of the assemblies. And now you must excuse me, I have a telephone call to make.'

So Elizabeth gathered up her papers and left. She might have won her case, but she was extremely unhappy to have done it in this angrily formal way. It hadn't been natural to either of them, as she told her colleagues later in the day.

. . .

ONCE SHE WAS on her own, Octavia realised how extremely upset she was. She was glad she'd been able to maintain her dignity and accept their decisions more or less gracefully, but it was profoundly troubling to have found herself in the middle of a quarrel. It wasn't necessary to call me superhuman, she thought. That was uncalled for. It was almost as if she was baiting me. I can't understand it at all. I'll sound Pa out this evening and see what he has to say.

She chose her moment carefully and asked her question as casually as she could, making a joke of it. 'One of my staff called me superhuman today,' she said. 'Isn't that ridiculous?'

JJ gave her a shrewd look, sensing that she'd been hurt. 'Odd perhaps,' he said, 'but not entirely unexpected.'

'Oh come on, Pa,' she said. 'That's not fair. You're as bad as Elizabeth. I've never claimed to be anything other than ordinary, now have I? I'm an ordinary woman.'

'Ordinary women don't usually get themselves arrested and go to gaol for their beliefs,' her father told her, wryly. 'Nor travel across the Atlantic on their own, come to that. Nor…'

'Ordinary women do all sorts of things when they're in extraordinary circumstances,' Octavia argued. 'But they don't lay claim to anything special about their personalities. Not even Mrs Pankhurst does that. Others do it for her but she is modesty itself.'

'You are not going to claim that you are modest, surely to goodness.' JJ laughed.

'I don't see any reason why not,' Octavia said crossly. 'I never brag. Or lay claim to talents I don't possess. And I don't ask my staff to do anything I'm not prepared to do myself. I don't understand what's got into them.' Then she realised that she'd said more than she intended and stopped abruptly, noticing the quick eye messages that were being sent between her parents.

'Maybe,' Amy said, joining the conversation gently, 'it is something that has got into you my dear. It is just possible you should consider that. You've been like a bear with a sore head ever since Maud and Ralph were killed.'

'That's understandable, surely.'

'Indeed it is,' her mother said. 'But you must remember that we are your family and understand you better than your teachers might be expected to do.'

'We've been working together for four years,' Octavia said. 'And working closely. They ought to be able to understand me by now.'

JJ decided it was time to change the subject. 'Have you any more of that excellent tart, my love?' he said. 'Mrs Wilkins has excelled herself for us this evening.'

'I think I shall go and see Em tonight,' Octavia said, following his lead. 'It's high time I did. She must be wondering what's got into me to leave her for so long.' And escaped.

But she couldn't escape her thoughts and they kept her awake and unhappy all night. That awful word had burned itself into her brain. Superhuman, she thought. It was ridiculous. And unkind. I've never claimed to be anything other than ordinary, no matter what Pa might say, but from the way she was talking you'd think I'd been acting like a dictator, like Herr Hitler or that terrible man Mussolini who's bullying the Italians. You'd think I'd been imposing my will on them instead of working with them. I haven't done that, have I? Or maybe I have. Maybe she was telling me something I ought to hear. Or at least listen to.

But it was hateful to call me superhuman. It was diminishing. It made me sound less than human. It was uncalled for. Especially when all I was trying to do was to make their lives a little easier. That was all it was. Why couldn't they see it? I'd thought it all out, the way I always do, and it was helpful and necessary or I wouldn't have done it. So why did they have to turn down every single thing I suggested? It doesn't make sense. Unless they were bad suggestions. But I don't make bad suggestions. I've never made a bad suggestion in all the years I've been teaching. At least not as far as I know. But then again that could be because nobody's ever told me they were bad suggestions. So they could have been bad, if I'm honest, and I simply haven't known it.

But why did they call a meeting behind my back? They didn't have to do that. It's as if they were afraid of me, as if I were an enemy instead of a friend and ally. Am I an enemy? No surely not. We've worked together like friends. Good friends. I can be a bit dictatorial sometimes, I'll admit that — but not an enemy. What was it Ma said? That I'd been like a bear with a sore head. Was that the sign of someone being dictatorial? Grumpy certainly but surely not dictatorial. Or was it? Have I really lived thirty-three years without knowing myself? It was an appalling thought. But do we ever really know ourselves? Maybe there are corners of our personalities that we shy away from and keep hidden, because we can't bear to face them. Maybe this is one of them. I don't want to think I'm a bully. That's obvious. So maybe I ought to.

If I were still with Tommy, she thought, he'd tell me straight out. He was always so open. It was one of the best things about him. I only had to look at his face to know what he was thinking. And the memory of him suddenly filled her mind, his tender mouth, those passionate eyes, his strength and good sense, and for a few anguished minutes she missed him as keenly as she'd done when they first parted and ached to be in his arms and comforted. Oh my dear Tommy, she thought, if only you were here now, you'd know what I ought to do. But she was being foolish. They had parted and she was on her own, for good or ill, and she must make the best of it. If she had been a bully she must come to terms with it and then do something about it.

But it was all distressingly difficult and when the hall clock struck six, she was no nearer to finding an answer to her questions than she'd been when she went to bed. At that point, she abandoned all hope of sleeping and got up. The house was so quiet it was as if she were all on her own. She put on her dressing gown and walked over to her desk. She was up and wide awake and she might as well make use of her time by writing up her journal. Heaven knows she had enough to write about.

And there, staring up at her from the last page she'd written were her own peculiarly prophetic words. 'It is always war and fighting, the illogical and non-proven belief that one human being can prevail over the wishes or needs or beliefs of another by hitting him or bullying him...'

'Physician heal thyself,' she wrote.

She came down to breakfast obviously tired and with dark shadows under her eyes, which her parents, having talked about her late into the night, were careful not to comment upon.

'Pa,' she said, as she spread butter on her toast, 'you wouldn't say I was a bully, would you?'

JJ smiled at her. 'Is that a statement or a question?' he asked.

Her heart sank. 'In other words "yes".'

'You've always wanted to change the world,' he told her. 'Ever since you were a little thing. You see a problem, a difficulty, something unfair or unkind and you immediately want to change it. Women's suffrage, the education system, war, the state of the country. Nothing is safe when you're on your warhorse.'

'But does that make me a bully?'

'When you have the bit between your teeth, you do tend to gallop.'

'In other words, "yes",' she said again. It was very dispiriting.

'On the other hand,' Amy said, taking a second slice of toast from the rack, 'there are other aspects of your personality that more than make up for it. For a start, you are loving. Very loving. You would never willingly hurt anyone in any way and we all know it. And secondly you admit to your mistakes. You always have. Even when you were quite a little thing and you knocked the tea tray over in the hall — do you remember? — you owned up to it straight away and washed the carpet when your father told you to and never complained. These are great strengths, my darling, and very admirable.'

Octavia got up and walked round the table so that she could put her arms round her mother's neck and kiss her. 'Dear Mama,' she said. It was all that needed to be said for they both understood the subtext underneath their exchange. How well you know me, Octavia thought, looking down at her mother's grey hair, and how sensible your advice is, even if you don't spell it out and you don't know why it's necessary. I shall act on it this morning. It will be the first thing I do. If I have been bullying people, the sooner I put it right the better.

In fact, although she got to school rather earlier than usual, she had another matter to attend to before she could apologise to her colleagues. There were three fifth formers waiting for her in the playground, looking very pretty in their white blouses and their straight short skirts with their hair neatly bobbed and brushed shiny, but rather anxious she thought. Penny Seaward, wasn't it and her two friends, Thomasina and who was the other one? Jane? Joan? They stepped towards her as she walked through the gate.

'Were you waiting for me?' she said.

They were. 'We've got something to ask you, Miss Smith,' Penny said.

'Then you'd better come in.'

'It's like this, Miss Smith,' Penny explained when they were settled in her study. 'We would like to put on a play at our next assembly.'

Octavia approved at once. 'What a splendid idea.'

'The thing is,' Penny said, 'we don't want to make the others think they've got to put on a play too, not at this time of year, with exams and everything, so we thought we ought to do it right at the end of term, if that's all right. Only we know the final assembly is a bit special.'

'The final assembly,' Octavia told her, 'is a ritual. We daren't change it. There would be a revolution. What about the penultimate one?'

That would be lovely.

'Do you know how long it will take, this play of yours?'

'About fifteen minutes,' Thomasina said. 'Would that be all right?'

It would be exactly right. 'That's settled then,' their headmistress said, wishing all problems could be solved as easily. 'I shall look forward to it.' And she shook their hands before sending them on their way.

It wasn't until she was walking down to the staff room that she realised it had provided her with the perfect introduction for what she wanted to say.

'I've just had a deputation from three of the fifth formers,' she said as she walked into the room. 'Wanting to change the date of their assembly.'

Their reaction was upsetting. They looked wary, or worried, or both and Genevra was anxious. Because they're her form, Octavia thought, and she's frightened something's gone wrong. Oh yes, I have been putting them under pressure. They're showing all the signs of it. And she went on quickly. 'They want to put on a play.'

They relaxed a little. They were approving. 'What a splendid idea,' Elizabeth said. 'What is it going to be?'

'I'm afraid I didn't ask them,' Octavia said, smiling at them. 'It was all done in a bit of a rush because I wanted to get down here before registration.' And she told them what had been said and what decision they'd come to, aware even as she spoke that she had broken her own timetable and proved what a bad decision it had been.

They approved of that too.

'Very sensible,' Morag said. 'They're a good lot, our fifth form. I wonder what it's going to be.'

'It's Pyramus and Thisbe from *The Midsummer Night's Dream*,' Phillida told them. 'I've promised to help them with the costumes.'

More approval. Several smiles. Now, Octavia thought, while they're happy. Now I must do it. She realised she was feeling nervous and ashamed. Yes, she thought, I have been bullying them. It was obvious from their reactions and the way she was feeling. 'I wanted to see you before registration,' she said, 'because I've got something I want — something I need to say to you. I'm afraid I've been treating you badly over the last few days. There's no excuse for it. It's in my nature to want change. I need to feel I'm moving forward, achieving things, but that doesn't excuse the way I've treated you. You must have thought I was turning into Signor Mussolini. Last night I was beginning to wonder myself. Anyway what I want to say to you is, I'm sorry for putting pressure on you. And for being so undemocratic. If I could put the clock back and it could all be undone, it would be. My word how ungrammatical!'

They were moving towards her, their faces open and reassuring, speaking at once, Elizabeth leading the way. 'Grief takes us all in different ways, my dear,' she said, 'as most of us know only too well. We do understand.'

'I was angry when my brother was killed,' Sarah Fletcher told her. 'I wanted the whole world to be changed. I wanted to go out and shoot the generals. I still do sometimes.'

'We've all had to face grief for someone,' Morag said gently. 'All of us and sometimes more than once, I fear, as you have. It's never easy.'

Their warmth as they rushed towards her, their understanding and their dear open kindness was too much for her. After a night spent sleepless and worrying she was more vulnerable than she knew. The tears welled into her eyes and rolled down her cheeks. 'I'm so very, very sorry,' she said.

Their concern was instantly practical. Elizabeth put her arms round her, someone else was rubbing her back, Genevra was holding her hand and telling her it was all right, a handkerchief was produced, clean and still neatly folded, and she shook it out and tried to dry her eyes, someone was filling the kettle. She could hear the rattle of the water. 'Oh dear,' she said. 'What a way to go on!'

'You carry formidable burdens, my dear,' Morag told her. 'It doesn't hurt to lay them down now and then.'

'I'm supposed to be taking assembly in ten minutes,' Octavia said, looking at the clock.

'Plenty of time,' they told her. 'Have a nice cup of tea while we take the registers and you'll be right as rain.'

'You are good friends,' she said and meant it. 'I don't deserve you.' She felt relieved and exhausted, as if she'd been standing on the edge of a precipice and they'd pulled her back from it.

'Yes you do,' Elizabeth said as she gathered her bag and her register. 'We deserve each other.'

IT WAS an unusual assembly and not the one that Octavia had planned.

'In this school,' she told her girls, 'your teachers and I make it our business to provide syllabuses and books and equipment and the most interesting lessons we can give you, so that you can all enjoy what you are learning. I think I can probably say that, by and large, you do.' Much beaming agreement from along the benches. 'However there are times when it is life that teaches you and learning from life can be a very different matter. When you learn from life, it can often — not always, but often — be a very hard lesson. So what advice can I give you about learning from life?' She paused and looked round the hall and smiled at her staff.

'Well, not a lot I'm afraid,' she said, 'for we all have to tackle that sort of learning more or less on our own. But you will notice that I said "more or less", so there is hope. It is at the hard times in your life that you need your family and your friends. They are the ones who will support you and help you and see you through. Hang on to your friendships. Treasure them. They are more valuable than any gold.' Friends all over the hall were sending eye messages to one another. 'And now that's enough of a sermon for one morning, I think. Time for a hymn to take us into the day. "Glad that I live am I, that the sky is blue." Miss Genevra.'

So despite her dark night and her anxiety, despite the shame of having to face the fact that she'd treated her good friends badly, the day began well after all and continued better. That afternoon the postman delivered a most welcome letter. She took it down to the staff room at once, with an explanatory note.

This has just arrived, her note said. *It's an official notification that for the first time we have more applicants for next year's first form than we have places to offer them. Sixty-eight applicants for fifty-six places, as you see. Our reputation is spreading, as well it should. I shall write to Mr Gillard to warn him that we shall soon be needing bigger premises. OS.*

THE SUMMER TERM was taken up with state examinations and grew steadily hotter and hotter. Octavia interviewed her new applicants and their parents, and arranged outings for her existing scholars whenever they were possible. And life at Hammersmith Secondary School was good.

In the middle of June Algernon-Podge took ship for Australia and they all went down to Tilbury to see him off — Octavia and her father and mother in the car, Emmeline and all three of her children on the train. It was an unseasonably cold day and very early in the morning and the quays were swathed in mist, which rolled in towards them from the marshes, obscuring and chilling. They stood close together on the crowded quayside, a sad group among a hundred farewells, choked by the smell of dusty steel and stagnant water, assaulted by the swoop and scream of the gulls, shivering in the damp air as the emigrants toiled up the gangplank with their battered luggage. Even their deliberate cheerfulness couldn't disguise the fact that it was a miserable occasion.

'Now be sure to write,' Emmeline urged, tugging at her brother's lapels as if she were pulling the promise from him. 'I shall worry till I hear from you.'

'I'll be fine,' he told her. 'It'll make a new man of me. You see if I'm not right. I shall come back in a few years' time and I shall be such a great fit strapping bloke you won't know me.' But he coughed before he kissed her and when he turned to say goodbye to Octavia his face was bleak. 'Keep up the good work at that school of yours,' he said to her, 'and write and tell me what you're doing.'

'I will,' she told him, torn with the old yearning sense of loss.

They watched him as he struggled up the gangplank and Emmeline hung on to her control and didn't cry until he had disappeared into the black hulk of the ship. Then she crumpled into tears. 'It's one thing after another,' she wept. 'We were such a lovely big family, all of us together going on holidays and everything and now look at us. First Squirrel and then my darling boys in that awful flu, and then Ma and Pa in that stupid car and now Podge. And I know what you're going to say, Tavy.

He's only gone to Australia but what good is that? It's halfway round the world and I shall never see him again. No, there's only you and me and Uncle JJ and Aunty Amy and Eddie and the girls left.'

'And Ernest,' Octavia said. 'You mustn't forget him.' But they both knew he didn't count because she was talking about her family and he kept himself deliberately apart from any involvement with any of them nowadays. Poor Em, she thought. It's very hard for her. I've got the school to go back to but she's only got him.

The school grew more rewarding as the year progressed. On the day that Emmeline got her first letter from Podge and was tearfully happy about it — even though he'd signed it Algy and underlined the name three times — the fifth year assembly finished the Summer term in high style; in August the results of the General School Certificate examinations were so good that they coloured the entire summer holiday; and then it was September and they had ten girls in the Lower Sixth and their new full-sized first year arrived. They took a bit of getting used to.

'There are first formers wherever you look,' Morag said.

'Wait till next year,' Octavia told her. 'We shall have a full-sized first and second year by then. There'll be no stopping us. And think what fun it's going to be with all these little ones.'

The fun that first term was mostly Egyptian. In November an explorer called Howard Carter discovered a cave full of treasures in the Valley of the Kings. It turned out to be the burial chamber of a handsome young king called Tutankhamen and the newspapers were soon full of amazing pictures, of his golden death mask, and his golden throne, of statues and jars and gilded beds and canopies. There was no end to it. Naturally the art classes were soon as devoted to it as the newsmen and by

Christmas the hall was full of golden masks and drawings of strange Egyptian gods.

'What happened to holly?' Miss Ollerington wanted to know.

'They're saving it for the final assembly,' Phillida told her, 'for when they sing the "Twelve Days of Christmas".'

'We must be thankful for small mercies,' Miss Ollerington said.

IN THE NEW YEAR, the school reassembled to discover that their headmistress had bought one of the new radios. It was on a stand in the corner of the hall and she said it could be used whenever there was an item of news that would interest them or whenever Miss Gordon thought it would be helpful to her History classes. Wonders would never cease.

The news was actually rather troubling that year, for in January the French government grew tired of waiting for Germany to pay the reparations they owed and sent their army to occupy the Ruhr and not long afterwards the German currency, which had been struggling for a long time, finally collapsed. Soon German banknotes were virtually worthless and there were pictures in the papers of children using piles of them as building bricks. The sixth form were most concerned about it and asked Miss Ollerington to explain how the value of currency could fall so quickly. She ran three extra classes, all of them well attended, and told Octavia that she'd never expected to find eighteen-year-olds who could actually understand Keynesian economics. 'They'll be a gift to their universities,' she said.

That year they had four girls who were daring to apply for a University place, a fact that Octavia detailed with great satisfaction in her half yearly report to the governors. And in May, when Emmeline's daughter Dora was struggling with the General School Certificate examination and telling her mother it was very very difficult, the list of next year's applicants for the first form at Hammersmith arrived on Octavia's desk. Just as she'd predicted they had more applicants than places for the second year running. In September 1923 they would have eight forms and a sizeable sixth form and they only had eight class-rooms. Octavia wrote at length to Mr Gillard, who wrote back to say that he would scrounge two classrooms from the floor below, 'for the time being' but that what was now obviously needed was a move to bigger premises.

My sentiments exactly, she wrote back. *Meanwhile I shall need three extra teachers by September. Is that within the bounds of possibility?*

At the end of May, Miss Jenny Jones, who came from Cardiff and was small and dark and had a beautiful voice, was appointed to teach Music and Miss Joan Marshall, who came from Battersea and was tall and hearty with strong limbs and the shortest hair cut Octavia had ever seen, was chosen to teach Games. Helen Staples, who was pretty and blonde, joined the staff at the beginning of July to teach English and French. And just before Christmas, when the girls were rehearsing their now customary Christmas play, Octavia got the letter they'd all been waiting for.

The excellent work done by the Headmistress and staff at Hammersmith Secondary School had been noted, particularly in the matter of the General and Higher Schools examination results and the success of the four applicants who had applied to London University. It was felt by all the governors that the time had come for the school to transfer to bigger premises so that its work could expand as they all had every confidence it would. They had consequently made representations to the LCC to that effect. By great good fortune a new secondary school for girls was currently being built in Roehampton to serve the new LCC Roehampton Estate. It was be called Roehampton

Secondary School and was intended to be a three form entry grammar school and would be ready for occupation at the start of the Autumn term 1924. The governors had the greatest pleasure to inform Miss Smith and her staff that this school was to be the new premises of the current Hammersmith Secondary School.

He was, yours most sincerely,
  Edward Gillard.

'Break open the champagne,' Octavia called, rushing into the staff room letter in hand. 'They're giving us a brand new school. Just listen to this.' And she read the letter aloud.

There was instant uproar in the little room. Their efforts in this difficult building were being rewarded at last. They were being recognised, endorsed, praised.

'Success!' they cried. 'We've made it!' 'A brand new school. We couldn't get better than that!' 'Wonderful! Wonderful!'

'If that's not a pat on the back,' Elizabeth said above the din. 'I don't know what is.'

Maggie Henry had been clearing the notice board of all its out-of-date material. Now she stood, drawing pins in hand, transfixed by the celebration that had broken out around her. 'My stars!' she said. 'When do we move in?'

'Well they say the start of the autumn term,' Octavia said, beaming round at them all, 'but let's be generous and say sometime in September.'

'It'll be a red-letter day, whenever it is,' Maggie said.

'Oh it will,' Octavia said.

IT WAS, but not quite in the way she envisaged.

CHAPTER 24

'She's got the weather for it, poor thing,' Maggie Henry said, peering out of the office window.

'Is she all right?' Miss Fennimore wanted to know, putting her class register in the pigeon hole.

'She seems it,' Maggie told her, 'but you wouldn't know if she wasn't, would you. Not today. I mean she wouldn't want to let the side down. Not today.'

'Where is she?'

'Oh, she's in the hall already,' Maggie said, 'watching them file in. She said she wanted to see it for the last time.'

'I'd better bring my lot up if that's the case,' Elizabeth said and went to do it. 'This is quite an occasion, Maggie, no matter what.'

Octavia was thinking the same thing. She sat perfectly still in her high-backed chair on the platform and watched as her pupils filed in for the ninth assembly of the new school year and the last they would hold in that hall. I'm headmistress of Hammersmith Secondary School for the last time this morning, she thought. By this afternoon I shall be Head of Roehampton Secondary School and we shall all be in our brand new building.

344

She'd gone out of her way to look well, choosing her grey suit and her button boots, with her new glasses framing her blue-grey eyes, and her new blue hat jammed onto her frizz of ginger hair like a halo above her long face. The girls grew quiet at the sight of her as they always did, as if her stillness were infectious, and she waited until they were all settled before she stood to address them, as she always did. But despite her calm appearance her thoughts were in turmoil and for once it wasn't the school she was thinking about, as her staff knew only too well.

The events of the early morning tore at her memory, the anguished wait for the doctor's visit, her mother's terrifying struggle to breathe, her father's controlled distress. She could still hear her own voice asking, 'Should I stay at home, Pa? I will if you think it would be best. Miss Gordon would take over for me.'

And her father's sad answer. 'No, Tavy my dear. You must be there. They will expect you to lead the way. In any case there is nothing you can do if you stay. Not with pneumonia. It's as the doctor says. We just have to wait. All of us.' And looking down at her mother, sweating and grey-faced, wheezing at every breath and only half conscious in her white bed, with two unnatural patches of colour on her cheeks and the rank smell of her illness rising from her like a miasma. Oh Mama! My poor dear Mama!

Before she left home her father had promised to phone her if there was any news. Thank God for the telephone. And he was right of course. There was nothing any of them could do, except wait for the crisis and pray that she would pass through it. Even so, Octavia was torn by her lack of care. If only it hadn't been so rapid. How could they have known that a chill would turn to pneumonia so hideously quickly? Four weeks ago she'd been so well, out on the river, picnicking on the riverbank, laughing and talking, enjoying herself. She'd looked frail, of course. She'd been looking frail for years. It was something they all accepted.

A sign that she was getting older, like Pa's white hair and his grizzled beard. Something that made you feel fonder than ever of her. But not ill. No one could have said she looked ill. And then that stupid silly cold. Oh why hadn't they made her wrap up warmer? It was such a stupid stupid thing to let her take cold. Oh if only the crisis hadn't come on this particular day. Oh please, please let her pull through.

The girls were assembled, all one hundred and seventy-four of them. There wasn't a single absentee. They stood before her, in their school hats and blazers, with their bags and satchels at their feet, bright-eyed with expectation. They're such good girls, Octavia thought, looking round at the juniors in their neat gym slips, the seniors in their fashionable skirts, their black stockings, the pretty variety of their white blouses, the hair they'd brushed and combed so carefully for this special occasion. She pulled her mind back to the occasion with an effort and managed to smile at them. And was glad when they smiled back.

There was nothing that needed to be said. Books and equipment were all waiting for them in the new building, the special trams that had been laid on to take them there were due to arrive in three minutes, everything was well prepared. It was just the matter of the carnations. She looked across at Alice Genevra and signalled that was time for the basket to be retrieved. Then she addressed her school.

'This is our red-letter day,' she said and smiled at them all again. 'I hope it will be one that you will remember with pleasure and look back on with pride, for we are starting the next stage of our school's development and great things will surely follow. Now as you leave this hall you will see Miss Genevra at the top of the stairs with a basket of carnations. There is one for each of you with a pin to fix it to your blazer.' She paused to give them the chance to react, as they did in a murmur of surprise and delight, turning their heads and craning to see if they could catch sight of the flowers. 'We shall leave and arrive in style,' she told them, picking up her own basket. 'Good luck to all of us. Lead on, Miss Fennimore.'

It was the happiest procession. Even though they only had a few yards to walk before they reached the tram stop, they stepped out in style, two by two in a long cheerful crocodile, the September sun enriching the colour of their young bright hair and turning the carnations into red stars against the dark cloth of their blazers.

Oh such happy chatter on the journey! Oh such impatience! Oh such excitement as the tram stop was finally finally reached. And then what a rapturous walk to their unseen promised land. At first they tried to be sedate and to behave like young ladies, but that wasn't possible for more than two minutes. Soon the leaders were rushing, red stars bouncing, and the straggling tail of their long crocodile had to run to catch up. And there it was. Their lovely new school. It was absolutely enormous.

They toured the building form by form, sniffing the lovely clean unused smell of the place, exploring and exclaiming from the western end, where there was a music room with a grand piano and an art room with easels and long north facing windows, to the eastern end, where they discovered the cookery room with its gleaming saucepans and its brand new ovens and three science rooms with their rows of workmanlike benches.

Morag Gordon was still stunned by the size of the hall. 'It's like a theatre,' she said to Octavia. 'Look at the size of that stage. If we had some curtains fixed we could put on a play.'

'That would be fun, wouldn't it, girls?' Octavia said. 'We could have a drama festival. Or an annual school play.' Anxiety about her mother was still tying sharp knots in her belly but she'd found that the way to cope with it was to push her mind to respond to every suggestion she heard. Now she thought about the best time for a school play. At the end of the summer term, perhaps, and then they could have a party in the school garden afterwards. She already had plans for a garden in their grounds. There were so many possibilities in this place.

When the bell rang for the dinner hour the tours were still going on and it took a considerable time for the girls to gather in the hall and find the places allotted to them at the dinner tables. Not that anybody was worried. The excitement of eating their very first school dinner in that very grand hall carried them all happily along. They knew it would take time to settle in and Miss Smith had told them there would be no lessons or studies until the last period of the afternoon, when they were to go back to their form rooms. That's what it meant to have a red-letter day.

None of them noticed that their indefatigable headmistress wasn't in the hall with them. The staff, who were dining in the cookery room, were aware of her absence but assumed that there was something that had needed her attention and that she'd gone to deal with it. In fact she was sitting in her study with her back to the window waiting for someone in Hampstead to answer the phone. The insistent *brin-brin* of the unanswered call was tying her stomach into knots of anxiety.

A voice. At last. Mrs Wilkins, giving the number and sounding hesitant. 'No,' she said. 'No change. Your father's with her. Shall I call him?'

'No,' Octavia said. 'Just give him my love. Tell him I'll be home as soon as I can.'

In fact it was well past six o'clock before she finally put her key in the lock and let herself in to the house. All the way home she'd been buoying herself up with hope, that the crisis would be past, that her mother would be improving, at the very least that she would be no worse. When she wakes up, she thought, I'll tell her about my day and how well it's gone. That will cheer her. But the minute she stepped into the hall she knew that things were too bad for the comfort of stories. The smell of the sickroom was so strong it pervaded the house and there was a palpable sense of foreboding. She put her bag by the hat stand, quietly, hung up her coat and hat and tiptoed upstairs.

Her mother was lying propped up by pillows, her closed eyes sunk in their sockets, breathing noisily and painfully through her open mouth. She writhed and moaned in her struggle but was too deeply unconscious to be aware of anyone. The sight of her suffering was more than Octavia could bear without weeping.

'Oh Mama,' she said and sunk to her knees beside the bed, reaching for her mother's limp hand and trying to hold it. But her touch was an irritation and her mother pushed her hand away.

'She's too far gone,' JJ explained with terrible sadness. 'She doesn't know us.'

'Can't they do something for her?' Octavia said, furious at her own impotence. 'There ought to be something they could do. Has the doctor been?'

'Twice,' her father told her, 'and no, there's nothing he can do. Nothing anyone can do. We just have to wait.' His face was seamed with distress and fatigue for he'd been sitting at the bedside nearly all day.

'We'll take it in turns to watch now I'm home,' Octavia said, torn with pity for him. 'Go down and have a bit of a rest. I'll stay with her.'

'She's sixty-eight,' JJ said. 'We've been together for forty-seven years. I'll not leave her now. She might wake and want me.'

So they kept watch together, cramped and uncomfortable in the haunting half-light, with the curtains drawn against the night and one small table light to ease the worst of the shadows, not eating, for how could either of them eat in such a state? And not speaking much either, for what was there to say? The long terrible struggle went on — ten o'clock, midnight, one o'clock, two. Occasionally they cat-napped and woke ashamed to have succumbed to sleep at such a time. And Amy sank deeper and deeper into unconsciousness.

At around half past two Octavia woke with a start to a new sound. Her mother's laboured breathing had changed to a dreadful rattle, low in her throat and very loud, and JJ was leaning towards her, holding her hand and weeping.

'She's going,' he mourned. 'Oh dear God! She's going. My poor darling.'

They sat on either side of her, holding her hands and kissing her fingers, even though they knew it wouldn't do any of them any good. And the death rattle went on. It was an interminable anguish. But at last, at a little after three, Amy gave a short shuddering sigh and stopped breathing. It was over.

Octavia was surprised by how calm she was. She took away the mound of stained pillows, found a clean one and laid her mother's head on it as though she were asleep, she got a bowl of warm water and washed her face and hands, very gently as if she would be hurt by the slightest roughness, brushed her hair and closed her poor gaping mouth. She persuaded her father that he really ought to get to bed and try to sleep. Then and only then she went to her own room and undressed wearily. The triumph of the day was so distant it was almost unreal. I never told her about it, she thought, and she would have been so proud to hear it. She remembered all the other times when she'd come rushing home with some titbit of news to please her. How closely she'd listened. It was an anguish to remember, seeing those gentle grey eyes again, widening as they followed every word. She paid such attention to us, she thought. She set us at the centre of her world, listening to us, praising us, feeding us, worrying over us, but really it was she who was the centre of our world and now the centre is gone. After so many dreadful deaths she should have been used to loss, or at least better able to cope with it, but she wasn't. This grief was worse than any of the others, even what she'd felt for

Em's poor little boys. Oh my poor darling Ma. What shall we do without you?

There was little sleep for her that night, even though she was tired to her bones, and when the day dawned she got up and washed and dressed ready for the inescapable miseries of the day. It was an unbearably perfect morning, the air soft and full of rapturous birdsong, the sky a blue dome above the rich autumnal colours of Hampstead Heath, the sunshine gently warm. She drifted from room to room, through the terrible hush of her bereaved house, gazing down at the heath, out at the garden, along the empty pavements of South Hill Park. Everything she saw made her ache with misery at the unsuitability of such a day. It should be brewing a storm, she thought, or raining commiserating tears, or gathering into a fog, a thick damp demoralising fog to chill her bones and shroud her grief and make her runny nose acceptable. But not sunshine. Oh dear God! Not sunshine. Not today. Not when she enjoyed a sunny day so much. Poor Mama.

There was a figure approaching along the street, a familiar straw hat catching the sun as it bobbed above the hedges. It turned in at the gate and became Emmeline, stout and determined in her old-fashioned button boots and her neat walking costume, with a wicker shopping basket over her arm, pink in the face and puffing after her long walk across the heath. Octavia drifted to the door to let her in.

Emmeline put down her basket and threw her arms round her cousin's poor bowed neck. 'Oh Tavy, my dear, dear Tavy,' she said. 'I'm so very sorry.'

How does she know? Octavia wondered. Did I phone her? Her mind was so embedded in misery she couldn't remember. She could have done. In her present numbed state she could have done anything and she wouldn't have remembered.

'Mrs Wilkins phoned,' Emmeline said, answering her unspoken question. 'I came straight away. Eddie and Edith can go off to school on their own for once. They don't need me to wave them goodbye. Now, are you all right? Is there anything I can do?'

'I think I'm all right,' Octavia said. 'I've got to be, haven't I? The undertakers are coming presently and Pa's in no fit state…'

'Of course not,' Emmeline understood. 'That's why I've come.' She pulled out her hatpin and took off her hat and gloves, setting them neatly on the hallstand, removed her jacket and hung it up. Then she took a white apron from her basket and put it on over her skirt, brisk and purposeful and loving. 'Have you had any breakfast?' she asked. And when Octavia shook her head. 'Now that won't do. You can't go without eating.'

The sense of being cared for made Octavia aware of how desperately lonely she'd been feeling. 'Oh Em,' she said, 'I'm so glad you're here. You're the one person who really knows how I feel.' Then she had to sit down on the hall chair because her control had broken and grief was welling over into terrible tears. 'I'm sorry,' she gasped. 'I shouldn't…'

Emmeline put a loving arm round her shoulders. 'You cry all you want, my darling,' she said. 'Time like this. What else would you do? You just sit down there and have a little cry and I'll trot and put the kettle on. Nice cup of tea. That's what we need. I shan't be long.'

What good will tea do? Octavia thought wildly, as she gulped and sobbed. Even if she made gallons it wouldn't bring Mama back to life. But when the familiar teapot was carried up from the kitchen, with the tea things set out neatly on the tray cloth beside it, three cups and saucers, milk jug, sugar bowl and all, the day jolted into a sort of normalcy and she followed Emmeline into the breakfast room as obediently as a child and drank what was set before her. After a few minutes her father drooped into the room to join them and he drank obediently too. To Octavia's grief sharpened sensitivity, he looked smaller and peculiarly vulnerable, the flesh below his brown eyes puffy with weeping, his beard dull, his white hair not bushy and vital but lying flat and damp on his skull. My poor Pa, she thought.

'It is very good of you,' he said to Emmeline in his quiet courteous way. 'We do appreciate it, don't we, Tavy?'

'It's the least I can do,' Emmeline said, 'after all you've done for me over the years. The very least. You think how Tavy sat up with me when my poor boys were ill. Night after night and then off to school in the morning. And then when Mama was... And Pa. All that way to Wales and looking after me all the time. Oh no, it's the least I can do and I'm very glad to do it. Now could you fancy another cup?'

But there wasn't time to answer because someone was ringing the doorbell and presently Mrs Wilkins edged quietly into the room to whisper that the undertakers had arrived. So Octavia had to go out and attend to them and it wasn't until half past nine that she got back to the breakfast room and by then, what with the misery of seeing her mother's body again, and the strain of her long fast, she was feeling quite faint and had to hold on to the back of her chair to steady herself.

'Porridge,' Emmeline decided. 'Don't you think so, Mrs Wilkins? And then bacon and eggs. We can't have you passing out on us.'

'I ought to phone the school,' Octavia said, remembering. 'They'll be wondering what's become of me.'

But Emmeline was in full command by then and said that she would phone and that Tavy and Uncle JJ were to sit down and have their breakfast and not to worry. And because they were stunned with grief and the day was thoroughly out of kilter, they did as they were told. But as she ate what she could, Octavia thought longingly of her new building and wished she could be there with things to do and the girls' enjoyment to carry her along. She knew it was what she needed but she could hardly say so.

The day passed in a blur of chores and tears. People phoned

and called to tell her how sorry they were, Emmeline ran the household, and at a little after two o'clock Dora arrived to help out too, looking very stylish with her red hair cut in a fashionable bob and dressed in the latest fashion in one of the new cloche hats and high-heeled shoes and a blue skirt so short that Octavia could see her knees.

'I'll wear a long one to the funeral,' she promised, noticing her aunt's expression. 'This is what I wear for the office. I know it's the wrong colour but there wasn't time to go home and change. You don't mind do you?'

'I don't mind at all,' Octavia told her, understanding that she needed reassurance. 'I think you look lovely.'

'That's not what her father says,' Emmeline grimaced. 'You'd never believe the ructions we've had over the length of their skirts. You'd think it was the end of the world the way he goes on about it. That and their hair.'

'He should come to Roehampton and see our seniors,' Octavia said. 'They've all got bobbed hair and they all wear short skirts. It's the fashion.' But talking about them made her aware of how much she was missing them and she sighed.

'Let's get on,' Emmeline said, patting her arm. 'It will be better once the funeral's over. Then you can get back to school.'

'I must go back tomorrow,' Octavia said. 'I can't leave them any longer. There's too much to do.'

'Let her go,' JJ said, when Emmeline asked his advice about it later that afternoon — and in private. 'It will do her good to have something else to concentrate on. It's what she needs. The girls are her family, every bit as much as we are, and you need your family at a time like this, as you know, my dear.'

HE WAS RIGHT. Being back in her familiar chair on her unfamiliar platform with her school assembled before her, smiling and excited, eased Octavia away from the anguish of her loss.

The terrible ache was still there but it was covered by the need to make decisions, to respond and listen, to think and plan. On that first day back there was almost too much to do — undelivered stock to chase, two alterations to the timetable to arrange, lessons to teach, studies to supervise and endless queries to answer, although Morag did her best to shield her from the worst of them. On the second day, at morning break, a deputation of senior girls arrived to see her.

'And what can I do for you?' she asked as they trooped into her study. It wasn't a serious matter as she could see from their happy faces. But it took a little while before their spokesman began to explain.

'It's like this, Miss Smith,' she said. 'You know you said that being in a new school would mean new directions. Well, now that we're here and we've got such a nice lot of room, we were wondering if we could have a place set aside for silent study. Somewhere absolutely quiet where we could just get on.'

'Which you can't do in a study,' Octavia understood.

'Well no, not really,' another girl said. 'Studies are fine if you want to ask for help or you've got something to discuss but they *can* be a bit noisy.'

'And when you're in the fourth year,' a third said with feeling, 'you need a bit of peace from the little'uns. We don't mind helping them now and then, but not all the time.'

'What we really want,' a fourth girl said, 'is somewhere we can depend on to be absolutely quiet.'

It was a sensible request. 'Do you have anywhere in mind?' Octavia asked.

They hadn't. So she promised to bring it up at the staff meeting next Monday and see what the rest of the staff had to say. 'Come and see me again on Tuesday,' she told them, as they left her study, and watched as they walked away through the empty hall. The empty hall! But of course, she thought. It's just the place. Large, vacant and, except for the change-over between lessons and studies, extremely quiet. We could have the tables set up immediately after assembly and use it as a study area for the rest of the day. Just for the senior girls of course, and on the understanding that there will be no staff there to assist them and they must maintain discipline for themselves. It will be an interesting experiment.

The staff agreed with her and thought the hall was the obvious choice. It was almost too easy. Quiet study began on Wednesday morning, at first with the original half dozen who had come to see her. By the end of the day it was being sampled by nearly thirty girls, all of them hard at work and all of them completely quiet. And by the end of the week even the first years had learnt that if they came out of a lesson or a study for any reason, they had to tiptoe through the hall without saying a word.

'I think,' Octavia said at her next staff meeting, 'we can chalk this up as one of our successes.' Then since they were feeling pleased and happy with their decision she went on to warn them that she would have to be absent the next day 'for the funeral'.

They were full of sympathy for her and said so, each in her own practical way. She was not to worry about the school. Everything was well organised. There were no problems. 'We shall be thinking of you, my dear,' Morag said, as the meeting broke up. 'Look after yourself.'

But it was Emmeline who looked after the event, preparing the sandwiches, arranging the cars, even choosing the hymns. And afterwards when the family were gathered in the drawing room, Octavia had to admit that it had been easier and less distressing than she'd feared. 'All thanks to you, Em,' she said. 'I don't know what we'd have done without you.'

'That,' Emmeline said, 'is what families are for.'

CHAPTER 25

Roehampton Secondary School kept Octavia sane that autumn. The new building with all those pristine rooms and all that tempting yet-to-be-used space was an inspiration. Hardly a day went by without someone arriving in her office with an idea or a suggestion for some activity or other.

Jenny Jones wanted to start a school choir. 'They're ever so keen, Miss Smith,' she said, sounding very Welsh in her excitement. 'Now they've heard themselves in a room with good acoustics there's no holding them. And it's such a big room, there's more than enough space for rehearsals.'

Morag and Helen Staples were keen to get curtains for the stage so that they could organise a play for the end of the term. 'There's bound to be something we want to do,' Helen said. The sixth form wanted to put on a pantomime and asked if they could write it and rehearse it 'in secret'. There was some staff discussion about that but in the end they agreed to it, saying they ought to be able to trust the sixth form. Sarah and Phillida offered to make the costumes for whatever play was going and Sarah found an attic storeroom that she said would be an ideal place to store them in. 'You'd never believe the space up there!'

Alice wanted to start an ancient history club. 'With all this interest in Tutankhamen,' she said, 'it's just the thing. There's so much material for display and the girls are really enthusiastic. There's a sort of club already and we could meet in my teaching room. We only need the go-ahead.'

But it was Mabel and Elizabeth who came up with the most far-reaching suggestion and that grew from their concern for the first formers at lunchtime.

'Some of these poor little things are having a really hard time trying to remember where they're supposed to sit,' Mabel said. 'I've been watching them. They get muddled every day. In a place this size, they really need someone to look after them, especially in the first few weeks of a new year. How would it be if we ran a house system?'

It was a novel idea and not one that had occurred to any of the staff until then. In Hammersmith they'd all known exactly where they were and where they were supposed to be because there'd been so little space for them. Here in this big school even the fourth and fifth form had had problems finding their way round.

'Prepare a paper about it for the next staff meeting,' Octavia told her two scientific mathematicians, 'and we'll discuss it.'

It was discussed at considerable length, for although they could all see advantages in such a system, especially in the idea that the girls would sit in houses at lunch time with a senior at the head of every table to look after the first formers, there were differences of opinion as to how it should be organised. 'A house system is bound to be hierarchical,' Morag pointed out. 'It will lead to prefects and games captains — and a head girl, probably. Is this what we want?'

Joan Marshall said she'd love some games captains, for house matches and that sort of thing. But who would choose them?

'If the house were to be organised by the girls, they could choose their own leaders,' Octavia said, thinking aloud. 'They could have regular elections at the end of every school year to choose the leaders for the next year. That would be a democratic way of going about it. We could call them house officers.'

'But if we were to start it now, how would they know who to choose?' Morag said. 'It's a tall order to get to know all the seniors in a new organisation. I can see them being able to do it after a year, as Octavia says, but not now.'

'Point taken,' Elizabeth said. 'They'd need at least a term to recognise the ones they wanted to lead them. But that needn't be a problem. We could start it as soon as we liked — or were ready — and the senior girls in each house could take it in turns to sit at the head of the tables. The first formers would be looked after and leaders would emerge. They always do, if the process is democratic.'

'And how would we sort out who is to be in which house?' Phillida asked. 'If you see what I mean? I wouldn't like to think we were parting friends.'

'We would have to do it very carefully,' Octavia said, 'and take our time over it. If we do it form by form, with each form teacher drawing up a list and everyone considering it, we ought to get it about right. There's no need to rush.'

'How many houses shall we have?' Sarah asked. 'I've got thirty girls in my form. That's seven in each house and two left over if we have four houses. Or five in each house if we have six.'

'When the school is at full strength,' Elizabeth said, 'which will be in another three years, we shall have ninety girls in each year plus the sixth form. That will give us a total of at least 460 girls and probably nearer 470. My vote would be for six houses with about seventy-seven girls in each.'

'As we're into the logistics of the thing,' Octavia said, grinning at them, 'do I gather that the general feeling of this meeting is that a house system would be a good thing?'

It was.

'We could name them after the primary and secondary colours,' Phillida said. 'Red, blue, yellow, green orange and purple.'

'Just think,' Helen Staples said dreamily, 'we could have a house drama festival.'

Her colleagues laughed out loud. 'You and your drama,' they said.

THE HOUSE SYSTEM, carefully thought out and planned, began when they came back after their first half term holiday. By then the school choir was rehearsing every Thursday in the Music room and singing at assembly twice a week, the sixth form had written their pantomime and were busy rehearsing it in the sixth form room, usually to shrieks of laughter, and the Ancient history club had put on its first Egyptian display on the new notice boards all round the hall.

'Everything we touch turns to gold,' Octavia said to Elizabeth as the two of them were walking round the hall with Alice, admiring the exhibits. 'There are days when I feel as if we're living in a fairy story and the good fairies have put a spell on us.'

'Long may it continue,' Elizabeth said. 'I like that picture of Tutankhamen, Alice. What a handsome young man he must have been.'

'I'd like to see the mask itself,' Alice said. 'All that gold and lapis lazuli. It must be absolutely stunning.'

Octavia looked at the picture and thought how magical it was. Myths and fairy stories, she thought, mystery and magic, the stuff of dreams. I ought to read 'Antony and Cleopatra' with the sixth form while this is on the walls. It's just the right time for it. But then she sighed. If only the fairies would cast their spell on poor Pa. He was so very unhappy and she didn't know how to help him. She'd tried special meals but he couldn't eat them, she'd tried suggesting outings, to see Emmeline and the children or to walk on the Heath but he said he didn't want to go out. In fact there were times when she thought he would never want to do anything again.

She'd discussed it with Emmeline, of course, because she was the one person who could really understand the state he was in and Emmeline had been sympathetic but not particularly helpful. 'It takes time,' she said. 'He'll never get over it. You mustn't expect that. You never do get over it. I think of my darlings every single day at some time or another. The best you can hope for is that he'll learn how to cope with it.'

Octavia didn't like the sound of that at all. She wanted him to enjoy his life a little. This incessant dragging unhappiness was dreadful. It sapped him of all his energy and gave him a jaundiced view of everything that was happening. He seemed to be shrinking into himself, doing less and less. Amy's clothes were still hanging in the wardrobes and he wouldn't let her clear them out, her chair was still exactly as she'd left it, crumpled cushions and all and couldn't be touched, her stick still stood in the hall stand. 'No,' he said, when Octavia asked if she should move it. 'Don't change things. Leave it. I want it left.' He read the papers incessantly, but it was all the most depressing and negative news that interested him. He noted that the Germans had had to print an entirely new currency because the old mark had no value at all, that the Labour Prime Minister was being taken to task for corruption, for accepting a car and shares in a biscuit factory from a business man he'd subsequently ennobled, that there was a civil war in China, and riots in India and that they'd passed a new law in South Africa, which would make it illegal for a black man to be given a skilled job. 'Man's inhumanity to man,' he said. 'What a terrible world we live in.'

'How about a trip out into the country?' Octavia tried. 'It's lovely weather.'

'No thank you, my dear.'

'Or perhaps you'd like to go up to town. We could go to the theatre.'

But the answer was always the same. 'No thank you, my dear.'

The difference between her life at home and her life at school was so extreme that she could feel her mind stretching to accommodate it as she travelled from one place to the other. Poor dear Pa. What could she do to help him?

Matters reached a climax at the end of November, when Mrs Wilkins came in to see them after breakfast one morning to say that she and her husband would like to retire at Christmas. 'I wouldn't want to inconvenience you,' she said. 'Not with everything being so difficult, but if you could find someone else, that's what we'd like to do. We've got the chance of a flat by the seaside, you see, down in Devon where my sister lives, and we'd like to take it.'

'And high time too,' Octavia said. 'You've earned your retirement if anyone has. I hope it's a really long and happy one.'

But finding replacements who would do the work they'd been doing and be prepared to live in, was virtually impossible. The best that she could manage was a girl called Dilys who said she was 'from the valleys' and could come in daily for the housework 'if that would suit' but couldn't cook.

I suppose I shall have to do the cooking myself, Octavia thought. She wasn't sure whether she was pleased or worried by the idea. A bit of both probably. It would be pleasant to eat whatever meals she fancied, but would she be up to cooking them? Could she ever make lemonade like Mrs Wilkins or bake a seed cake or cook a Sunday roast? Even the thought of it was daunting. Perhaps, the time had come to buy a house of her own, at last, the way she'd always planned, somewhere near the school, and equipped with all the nice new modern appliances like gas fires and a gas cooker and a geyser for hot water. And lots of electric light, of course, and points for one of those electric cleaners. And a nice comfortable study for Pa. She could move them both in and run the place herself with a char to do the rough work and a girl to help her round the house. A new gas oven would be a particularly good idea. People said they were really easy to use and an old-fashioned stove could be tricky, as she knew very well. They could buy some new furniture that would be a bit more comfortable than the stuff they'd been using all these years. Some of the armchairs were wrecks. And of course they would have to clear out the cupboards and wardrobes if they were moving. Her mind made up, she went to see a couple of local estate agents at the end of the next school day.

They were both of the same opinion. 'Wimbledon Park,' they said. 'That's where you want. There are some beautiful houses up there, Edwardian, good sized rooms, every mod con, very well kept up, and you've got a good road to take you straight to the school. Wimbledon Park. That's the place.'

And so it seemed to be. That weekend she went to see four houses and liked them all although she had to admit they were rather too big for her. They all had at least four bedrooms and three big living rooms, usually a dining room, a drawing room and parlour, and the gardens were twice the size of the one in Hampstead. But the thought of living in one of them, close to the school and with room for family gatherings and parties, was such a temptation that she arranged to return to the two she liked best and bring Pa to see them too.

He wasn't impressed. 'You don't want to move,' he said. 'We're all right as we are.'

It was time to take a stand. 'No,' she said, seriously. 'We're not. When Mrs Wilkins goes I shall have to do the cooking. I can't get another couple to live in and cook and care for us. People don't do that anymore. And I might as well tell you, Pa, I can't cook on that stove. It's far too temperamental. I need something I can depend on.'

He frowned at her. 'What sort of something?'

'One of those nice new gas cookers.'

His eyebrows rose with disbelief. 'You're surely not telling me you want to move house to get a gas cooker,' he said. 'You could have one put in our kitchen here, if that's what you want.'

'No,' she said. 'It's not just the cooker. It's all sorts of things. A geyser to give us hot water for baths and to wash with. Think how nice that would be instead of having to wait hours for the fire to warm the water like we do here. Gas fires so that we can have warm bedrooms first thing in the morning. Think of that. It would be a better life for both of us in one of these houses.'

He was surly with disapproval. 'I can't see the need to go uprooting ourselves for a cooker and a gas fire,' he said. 'No, no, we're all right as we are.'

'You might be,' she told him sternly, 'but I'm not. Oh come on, Pa. I want a home of my own. I've waited long enough for it.'

But he wouldn't be persuaded. 'We're all right as we are,' he insisted.

'WHAT AM I to do with him?' she asked Emmeline later that week. 'I've never known him like this before. It's as if he's a different person. He wouldn't even go and look at them.'

'Give him time,' Emmeline advised. 'He'll come round.'

'Well I hope it's before Christmas, that's all,' Octavia said, 'or I shall be cooking on that awful stove. Thank God for the school!'

THE END of the Christmas term was the most enjoyable she'd ever experienced. The form rooms were hung with paper chains, the cooks produced a Christmas pudding for their final school dinner and the sixth form pantomime was riotous. They told the story of the *Babes in the Wood* but sent the babes to a school which was recognisably Roehampton, for there were all the staff, idiosyncrasies and all, Elizabeth with her pince-nez, saying '*neatness is everything in mathematics*' as she always did, Morag in her long cardigan and her flat shoes, saying '*a little less noise, gels,*' as *she* always did, Phillida in a smock with one paint brush in her hand and another behind her ear, Joan Marshall in a gym slip, carrying a hockey stick, and yelling '*Bully off!*' There were cheers and screams at their every appearance and when the cast took their final bow the applause went on for such a long time that Octavia had to hold up her hand for it to stop so that she could thank '*their talented players*' for the great fun it had been.

She drove home on that last afternoon, happy but exhausted. And there was a letter waiting for her from one of the estate agents. A property had just come onto the market, which seemed to him to be exactly what she was looking for. Perhaps she would care to telephone him about it.

She phoned at once and agreed to go and see it the next afternoon. But I shan't tell Pa, she thought, as she put the receiver back in its cradle. He'll only say no and there's no point in disturbing him until I've seen it. It might not do at all.

It was the best house she'd seen and in quite the most pleasant road, a short, wide, unpaved, cul de sac, avenued with lime trees and bordered by gardens so green and well grown that to walk between them was like walking in a country lane. The house was big like all the others she'd viewed and very handsome to look at. She stood gazing up at it, enjoying the white frontage and the grey slate roof, feeling peculiarly satisfied by the balance of it, the three identical windows on the first floor, exactly balanced by the two on either side of the central front door. It reminded her of something but for a few seconds she couldn't remember what it was. Then her father's voice spoke in her mind '*all designed according to exact mathematical principles, little one,'* and she realised it was the Georgian house she'd lived in as a child, the house in Clerkenwell.

'Yes,' she said. 'It's very handsome.'

'Would you care to see inside ma'am?' the estate agent said, hopefully.

She followed him through the front door rather apprehensively in case the interior was a disappointment. But she needn't have worried. It was such a warm and welcoming place, she liked it as soon as she stepped inside the hall and she soon found that it had everything she could possibly want, a gas cooker in the kitchen, a geyser in the bathroom and gas fires in all the main bedrooms, a parlour and a dining room and a magnificent drawing room running the length of the house, four bedrooms and a dressing room on the first floor and another two rooms in the attic. There was no furniture in it at all — 'An executor's sale, you see ma'am,' the young man explained — but that didn't worry her. The emptiness made it easier for her to imagine how she would arrange things herself.

'Yes,' she said. 'It's an excellent house.'

'I thought you would like it, ma'am,' the young man said. 'Would you care to see the attic rooms?'

'I might as well, now I'm here.'

They were bigger than she expected, with sloping ceilings and dormer windows that let in a surprising amount of light but it was the wallpaper in the room that overlooked the back garden that was the real surprise. It was a William Morris design, and not just any design, what's more, but the one that Pa had always had in his study.

'This,' she told the young man, resting the palm of her hand against the familiar pattern, 'might be the deciding factor.'

He had no idea what she was talking about but he could see that he was within reach of a sale. 'I'm very glad to hear it, ma'am,' he said.

I must plan this very carefully, Octavia thought. I'll wait until after Christmas, until we've said goodbye to the Wilkins, and then I'll cook a few meals on that horrible stove and we'll see how he likes the change of cuisine and if he complains, and I'll bet he does, I'll try to tease him into seeing it. If I handle it lightly I might just be able to do it. I'm not being very kind to him, poor man, but I've got to ease him out of his misery somehow and the longer he sits at home and broods the more difficult it will be. Besides, it's high time I had a home of my own. I've been putting it off a darn sight too long.

She gave a farewell tea to her old servants and invited Emmeline and her children, who turned up in style, Dora looking extremely pretty, wearing red lipstick and a new dress with a very short skirt.

'Although what her father would say if he could see her I dread to think,' Emmeline said. 'We'd never hear the end of it. He thinks lipstick is sinful.'

'All the best things are,' Octavia said, looking at Dora. And was given a conspiratorial smile.

In the New Year, when they'd finished off the cold turkey and eaten all the Christmas puddings, Octavia finally did battle with the stove and produced a roast that was burnt black on the outside and underdone in the centre.

'I'm sorry, my dear,' JJ said laying his knife and fork aside. 'It's inedible.'

'I did warn you.'

'You'll get used to it,' he said. 'Better luck next time, eh?'

Next time she tried to cook a cake and that was even worse. The mixture was only cooked round the edges and the centre of the cake had collapsed into a soggy pool.

'Perhaps we ought to buy one of those cookers,' JJ offered. 'What do you think?'

'I tell you what,' Octavia said, seizing her moment, 'why

don't we go and look at a new house and see what *you* think about *that.*'

'Put like that,' he said, looking at the wreckage of the cake, 'how can I refuse?' And added, with a touch of his old wry wit, 'But you will remember that I've lived in this house for twenty-seven years and I'm in no hurry to leave it.'

They went the very next morning. And although Octavia promised herself that she would be calm and sensible and not rush him and take care to point out all the bad features about the place, so as to show she was taking a balanced view, she forgot her good intentions as soon as she turned into the avenue and saw the estate agent again. She introduced her father but then she couldn't wait to get him into the kitchen and show him all the excellent things that were there, the two walk-in larders and the long Welsh dresser and the shining new gas cooker.

'Yes,' he said, rather dourly. 'I see.'

'It's a very good size,' the young man pointed out hopefully.

'Come and see the drawing room,' Octavia said. 'And tell me if you don't think it would be ideal for family parties.'

'Yes, very nice,' he said, when he'd seen it. But his tone was non-committal.

She showed him all the rooms on the ground floor, took him round the garden, and upstairs to see the bedrooms and finally, having sent a signal to the young man that he was to stay where he was, and with her heart quite beating ridiculously fast, she climbed the last two flights of stairs to the attic.

'There,' she said, throwing open the door to the William Morris room. 'What do you think of that?'

'Good heavens!' he said. 'It's my wallpaper.'

'This could be your study,' she said quickly, 'and you'd hardly know the difference from the one you're in now, except that this is marginally bigger. They both overlook the garden, there's lots of light. Imagine it with all your furniture in it, your desk and your bookcases. It could be a lovely room.' Oh please, Pa, at least think about it.

He walked to the dormer window and looked out at the garden, while Octavia waited. 'You want to move here very much, don't you, Tavy,' he said.

It was time for the truth. 'Yes, Pa, I do.'

'I would prefer to stay in Hampstead even if it means eating burnt meat for the rest of my life,' he said. 'But if you are set on this house, and I can see that you are, I suppose I had better consider it. It has a pleasant balance, almost Georgian.'

'I thought that as soon as I saw it,' she said. 'It reminded me of the house in Clerkenwell.'

He was surprised. 'Fancy you remembering that,' he said.

'You told me how it was designed,' she said, 'according to mathematical principles. I think this is a similar house.'

'Yes,' he said, smiling at her. 'So what with that and the gas cooker and the wallpaper I suppose we must buy it.'

She was instantly wracked with compassion for him. He was so generous and so loving and he missed Mama so much and she'd been putting such pressure on him. 'Dear Pa,' she said, putting her arms round his neck and kissing him, 'you mustn't agree to this just for me. I want you to be happy here. If we buy it, it will be your house every bit as much as mine.'

'I know that, my dear. I have thought about it.'

'I've had the school to keep me going, ever since Mama died,' she said, 'and you've been at home all on your own except for the Wilkins, and it must have been awful for you. And now you're all on your own except for Dilys and I don't suppose she's any help at all, is she? No, I didn't think so. I'd like to give you something to fill your days a bit, something new, something that would make you feel just a little bit better. I hate seeing you so down and serving you awful meals and leaving you alone for so much of the day. If we live here we'll get a girl to come in every day and look out for you, make you tea and that sort of thing —

and put the kettle on when I come back from school. And when I'm home we can explore the common and the village. I've driven round it and it looks pretty. And you can have a wireless in your study so that you can listen to music up there. And there's a theatre just down the hill, we can go there whenever we like, and there are lots of bookshops. I know it won't be a wonderful life, not without Mama to share it. How could it possibly be? But it might be better than the one you're living now.'

He stroked her cheek, lovingly. 'You are a good girl, Tavy,' he said.

So they bought the house and took possession of it six weeks later on a cold February day in the middle of her half term. And although she was trying to be calm and serious about it, so as not to upset her father, Octavia found herself singing as she unpacked.

BY THE END of the summer term they had established a new pattern of life in this new house of theirs. Octavia learnt how to cook on her new gas cooker and spent a lot of time mastering the art of making cakes and pastry; Emmeline came to visit with one or other of her children at least once a week, and they all went for a walk to Wimbledon village or took the air on the common, stopping at Caesar's Well to buy ice creams of course; and in the afternoons, JJ listened to the wireless in his by-now familiar study with his familiar books ranged round him in their familiar order and felt there was some good in his life after all.

The next school year began with an invitation for Octavia from a man who signed his letter AS Neill and said that, like her, he had started an experimental school, in which children were not bullied or coerced into learning but allowed the freedom to learn in their own time and their own way. In his case it was a school for children who were considered 'difficult' or 'failures'; in hers he assumed it was a school for girls who had passed an examination for entry, which presupposed a difference in kind, but he thought that they would find they had much in common and suggested that she might like to come to Suffolk and visit him.

'How would you fancy a trip to the country, Pa?' she asked and passed the letter across the breakfast table for him to read.

It was an interesting experience, for Neill, as everyone called him, was an extraordinary man and his views matched Octavia's almost exactly. One of the things that interested her particularly was the school parliament at which staff and pupils made the rules together. She questioned him deeply about it, asking how often they met (every week) and what they discussed (whatever they want to) and what would happen if they made a rule that didn't work when it was put into practice.

'They'd change it at the next meeting,' he told her. 'Children are practical creatures, if they're allowed to be. And cussed of course. Force them to do something and they'll do anything to avoid it, give them freedom and they use it wisely. As you must have found out.'

As they drove home through the sunset, Octavia mulled over all she'd heard. 'I think a school parliament is a very good idea,' she said.

'So that will be inaugurated first thing on Monday morning I suppose,' her father said.

'No,' she said, grinning at him. 'That will be inaugurated when the need for it arises. I've given up imposing my ideas on people. That's a fool's game. I shall bide my time and wait for the moment to arrive.'

It arrived rather sooner than she'd anticipated and with an uproar over the trees in the school grounds. The original field had already contained several well established trees when they moved in, and as soon as the playing fields and gardens had been planned, several more had been planted. Now, to Phillida's horror the juniors were climbing all over them.

'It's not the old trees so much,' she said, 'they're strong enough to withstand it, but to swing on our little flowering cherry! I mean to say. They'll snap it in two. And then all our beautiful blossom will be gone for ever. We've got to stop them.'

'They have been told,' Elizabeth said. 'The sixth form are always reminding them.'

'It should be a school rule,' Phillida said. 'Freedom is all very well but we're letting them behave like vandals.'

Although that wasn't what she'd intended, she sparked a passionate debate on the value of freedom in education. Some were for allowing the juniors to learn the hard way, '*since that is what freedom entails, surely.*' Others were for protecting the tree, and passing a new school rule. But there were arguments put forward against that. What if it were ignored? Rules were made to be broken. How could it be implemented? As Phillida said, 'We can't be out in the fields all day, even if we took it in turn.' They argued for nearly twenty minutes before pausing for breath and looking at their headmistress to see what she would say.

It was a happy moment. 'Perhaps,' she said, 'we should allow the school to make the rules and then we would be certain of them being kept. What do you think?'

They were interested, wanted to know more, questioned her closely and for another twenty minutes, and at the end of their long debate, decided that a school parliament might well be an excellent innovation. And as a way of testing the idea, they decided to put this particular matter to the school, sending a notice of their concerns to every form and asking for suggestions. 'Then we shall see what happens.'

What happened was that there was overwhelming support for a tree protection scheme. It was suggested by one of the third forms who said they thought the way to deal with the problem was to have '*a tree planting day followed by a week during which all the senior girls would take it in turns to be in the school grounds to remind anyone who needs reminding of the proper way to treat young trees.*' It was a great success, especially as the new tree was planted by the two youngest girls in the school who also happened to be the most agile climbers. By the end of the tree protection week there was already talk of forming a school parliament, by the end of the term two representatives from each form had been elected, the art room had been chosen as the best place for the council chamber, and everything was ready for their opening session, which would be in the first week of the spring term.

THE SCHOOL YEARS PASSED HAPPILY, with a series of academic successes, of problems solved by parliament, and of high days and fun days of every description. By the start of their fifth year, the now renowned Roehampton Secondary Girls had grown out of all recognition and beyond even Octavia's most optimistic expectations. It had nearly five hundred pupils and twenty-four members of staff and even an upper sixth of a select half a dozen who were preparing for the Higher Schools certificate and university entrance. The garden was maturing splendidly, the flowering cherry was superb, all the class libraries were well stocked, the school choir was much admired and had begun to win prizes at competitions, the sixth form play was a regular romp, and the school parliament was such an established institution that nobody could remember a time when it didn't exist.

'Teaching,' Octavia told her father at breakfast, at the start of that fifth year, 'is the most rewarding job in the world.'

JJ dabbed his mouth with his napkin and smiled at her. 'I am glad our opinions concur,' he said. 'I gather things are going well.'

'They are,' Octavia said with great satisfaction. 'Oh they are indeed. There are moments when I feel capable of absolutely anything. As if I could fly through the air if I put my mind to it.'

'I trust you will not put your belief to the test,' her father said. 'I should hate to see you splattered all over the front garden. Think how it would upset the neighbours.'

OCTAVIA'S WAR

BERYL KINGSTON

CHAPTER 1

'Why is it so dark Aunty Tavy?' Barbara said. At five years old she was a sturdy child and curious about everything, so a sudden darkness at six o'clock on a summer evening was something to be wondered at.

'There's a storm coming,' her aunt Octavia explained. 'Look at the sky. Do you see all those grey clouds over there? Well they're storm clouds.'

The child persisted, standing by her aunt's elegant cane chair and squinting up at the sky. The clouds were so very grey as to be almost black and there was something about them that she didn't like at all. 'Why aren't they white?'

'Because they're full of rain,' Octavia said. 'They're like big black ponds up in the sky. Presently they'll make a rumbling noise that we call thunder — I expect you've heard that before, haven't you — and then they'll spill all the water out and we shall have a storm.'

Barbara's baby sister Margaret was standing beside the chair too. Now she edged a little closer to her aunt and held on to the sleeve of her cardigan, just in case. 'Shall us get wet?' she asked.

'We shall if we stay out here in the garden,' Octavia told her.

'But not if we get indoors quickly enough.'

'Shall us run?'

'Like greyhounds,' Octavia said, smiling at the child's earnest face.

'What's a greyhound?' Barbara wanted to know.

'Time for us to go,' their mother said, striding towards them across the lawn. 'I hope you're not being troublesome.'

Octavia smiled at her reassuringly, dear Edith, with that thick auburn hair and those clear blue eyes and that oddly endearing anxiety. 'They're being intelligent and curious,' she said, 'which is exactly as it should be. Ask Pa.'

Her father had been watching the exchange in his quiet way, enjoying the children's curiosity, thinking, as he always did on such occasions, that Octavia was so easy with children and wishing she could have married Tommy and had children of her own. It would have been so good to have had grandchildren. But there, you can't have everything in this life and she was a great lady, one of the leaders in the world of education and much admired.

'They're no trouble,' he said to Edith, 'but Tavy's right. I think we should be getting in. It's all very well for you little ones and your Aunt Tavy with her long legs. You *can* run like greyhounds if it starts to rain but I can't. I'm more of a tortoise.' He picked up his stick like the explanation it was and the movement dislodged the newspaper he'd been reading earlier and had set aside on the garden table. It fell on the grass, where it laid untidily, its pages fluttered by a sudden breeze. He watched as they turned, one after the other, until they gave a final flick and settled at the morning's chilling headline, '*Storm clouds over Europe*'. How apposite, he thought, but even as the words came into his mind, the first thunder rumbled overhead and the rain began to fall, spattering the paper with large damp spots.

Within seconds the garden was full of movement: Emmeline puffing towards them across the lawn, moving as fast as she could, given her weight, and unfurling an umbrella as she ran. 'Quick Uncle,' she called to him. 'Let's get you indoors. I can't have you taking a chill.' Edith grabbed a child in each hand and all three bolting like rabbits, Margaret squealing. 'Us'll get wet Mummy. Us'll get wet'.

Octavia brought up the rear with the paper and the tea tray, skimming across the lawn with the tea cups rattling and thinking it was just as well the milk jug and the tea pot were empty. They tumbled into the drawing room one after the other, dampened, laughing and breathless, and Emmeline took the tray from her cousin's hands and said she'd be back in a jiffy with some towels. By that time it was raining heavily and so dark that Octavia had to switch on the light as though it was already night time.

'That's the trouble with storms,' Emmeline said, busily towelling Margaret's short bob. 'They're on you before you can breathe. You'll have to stay here till the worst of it's over Edie.'

'I can't do that Mum,' Edith said. 'I've got to be back for Arthur's tea and we're late already.' Feeding her man was very important to Edith Ames and tonight's meal was even more important than usual because she had something difficult to tell him and she wanted him to have a good tea inside him before she did it. 'Don't worry. We've got our umbrellas.'

'Umbrellas!' Emmeline snorted, glaring at the window. 'Oh for heaven's sake Edie. They won't be any use. It's coming down like stair rods.' Both little girls turned their heads at once to see if rain really *was* like stair rods and were impressed to find that it was. 'Hold your head still, Maggie, there's a good girl. You don't want to catch cold.'

The instruction was as much a warning to her daughter as her grandchild. But Edith was firm. 'They won't catch cold,' she said. 'They'll run like the wind, won't you girls.'

'You'll all get drowned,' Emmeline warned, turning her attention to Barbara. 'That's what'll happen. Never mind running like the wind. Anyway, aren't you going to stay to see your brother? He'll be home any minute. You'll stay to see *him*, surely to goodness. Ten minutes. I mean what's ten minutes?'

'Enough to make us late,' Edith said. 'It's no good you going on, Mum. I can't be late for Arthur's tea. Not even for our Johnnie. You know that.'

Octavia had cleaned her rain-spattered glasses and was drying her own frizzy hair in her vigorous way, listening to them with her usual concentration, turning her towel-hung head to watch their faces as the argument progressed. She was aware that Emmeline was being overprotective of these much-loved grandchildren of hers, that Edith was being too dogged in her determination and that neither would give way to the other. There's nothing for it, she thought, dabbing at her damp sleeves, I shall have to intervene. As head of the family it was her job to try to keep the peace and to suggest whatever compromises she could, just as she calmed tempers and suggested solutions as head of her school. 'How would it be if you went home in my car?' she said to Edith. 'Then you wouldn't be late and the girls wouldn't get wet.'

Emmeline relaxed at once, saying, 'Very sensible' but her daughter looked worried. 'That's ever so good of you Aunt,' she said, 'but what about your dinner party?'

'I shall be back in plenty of time for that,' Octavia said, speaking with a confidence she certainly didn't feel, for preparations for the meal were well under way, the agency cook and the waitress were busy in the kitchen and in less than an hour her guests would arrive.

'But isn't it Major Meriton?' Edith persisted.

'Major Meriton is a very old friend,' Octavia told her. 'I'm sure he won't mind if I'm a bit late.' But that wasn't true either. Now that he was middle-aged and a senior official at the Foreign Office, Tommy Meriton had become a stickler for punctuality. It was sometimes quite hard to remember what a relaxed young man he'd been when they were both young. Relaxed and handsome and easy to be with. What a long time ago it all seemed!

'I'll keep him amused if you *are* late,' her father said. 'But I'd cut off quickly, if I were you. Time is getting on.'

'There you are, you see,' Octavia said to Edith, handing her damp towel to Emmeline. 'Everything's taken care of. I'll go and get the car out of the garage. Wait in the porch. I'll drive it to the door.'

It was a cheerful journey to Colliers Wood, even though it was so dark that she had to put the headlights on and the rain was torrential, hitting the roof as loud as sticks on a tin drum and sluicing the windscreen with constant streams of water. Propelled by her private urgency, Octavia drove faster than she should have done, persuading herself that there was no danger because there were very few cars about. When they reached the bottom of Wimbledon Hill there were puddles half-way across the road and she drove through them at speed too, so that the impact made a palpable thud and water rose from her wheels in a dramatic white arc. The girls were thrilled with it, calling out 'Wheeee!' at each new impact, and Edith said it was like being in a ship at sea, adding 'Not that I've ever been at sea, but I can imagine it.'

'It was always such fun driving with you,' she said to Octavia as they passed the curved steps of Wimbledon Theatre, dramatic on their corner. 'Off to the theatre to see the pantomime and going home after Christmas at your place in Hampstead all squashed together in the back seat. We had some good times.'

They bumped across the tramlines, heading for the underground at South Wimbledon. The pavements were crowded with rain-drenched women carrying baskets and shopping bags, bent against the wind and struggling with tugging umbrellas. 'Soon be home,' Octavia said. 'And by the look of it, it's just as well. This is getting worse. Have you got your brollies?'

'We shan't need them,' Edith said. 'It's only a step.'

Which was true enough, for Wycliffe Road was short and narrow with the merest scrap of a front garden between the gates and the houses, so she could reach the door of her maisonette in two strides. It only took a few scrambling seconds for all three of them to run into the house.

Now, Octavia thought, waving to them, I can get back. With a bit of luck and some fast driving she could be home and changed before the Meritons arrived.

But her luck didn't hold that afternoon. The Silver Cloud was standing in the drive. On the one evening when she could have done with Tommy's predictable punctuality, he'd decided to come early. Sighing, she garaged her car and let herself into the house. Her guests were in the drawing room being entertained by her father. She could hear Tommy laughing in that throaty way of his and his wife saying something in her soft voice that made him laugh again. And as she hung up her keys on the hall stand, the agency waitress walked out of the kitchen carrying twelve glasses and a dish of peanuts on a tray. The evening had begun. Emmeline must have heard her car and given the signal for the aperitifs to be served. There wasn't time for her to change. Ah well, she thought, removing her cardigan and tucking it into the hall seat, there's nothing for it, this blouse will have to do. She tried to pat her hair into some sort of order, failed, straightened her glasses, and took a deep breath. Then she opened the drawing room door and walked in, prepared to be teased or scolded.

Fortunately, Elizabeth Meriton was the first person to turn towards her, elegant as always in an understated evening dress, in powder blue pleated silk, as Octavia was quick to notice, her short hair immaculately waved, her nails and lips painted the same bright colour, and Elizabeth was every inch the diplomat's wife, smiling warmly and saying exactly the right thing. 'Tavy my dear. JJ tells us you've been on an errand of mercy. Why does that not surprise me? How good to see you.'

The two women kissed cheeks and then Tommy took Octavia's hands in his and kissed her too. There was no teasing or scolding, he was too pleased with himself for that. 'We've had *such* an afternoon,' he said and looked at her eagerly, waiting for her response. 'I can't wait to tell you.'

What's he been up to? Octavia wondered. It had to be something special. She took a Dubonnet from the proffered tray, thanked the waitress, sipped it, and looked a question at him. 'Well tell me then,' she said.

'We've been buying Lizzie's uniform,' he said happily. 'She's all kitted out and ready for school and she looks superb, doesn't she Elizabeth.'

'He's been like a dog with two tails all afternoon,' Elizabeth said, laughing at him. 'You'd think there'd never been another eleven-year-old requiring a school uniform in the entire history of education.'

'Ah but what an eleven-year-old, my dear, and what a school!' Tommy said, beaming at Octavia. 'These were no ordinary purchases.'

Which provoked a murmur of amused agreement, for there wasn't a soul in the room who didn't know it had always been his ambition to send his much loved only daughter to Octavia's school. His sons were settled at Dulwich, which was right and proper, but his daughter had to go to Roehampton Secondary School and be educated by the great Octavia Smith.

Watching his ardent face Octavia was remembering the evening when he'd first told her how important it was to him, here, just outside those French windows. 'There's a war coming,' he'd said, 'and open cities will be bombed.' How terrible those words had seemed to her then but it had been an accurate prophecy and she knew it now after what had been happening in Abyssinia. 'London schools will be evacuated,' he'd said. 'They are already planning it. I want her to be at your school with you. I want you to look after her.' She'd laughed at his eagerness, for Lizzie couldn't have been more than six or seven at the time, and teased him that he'd have to wait till 1936 until she could be enrolled at Roehampton Secondary School. And now it *was* 1936 and she *was* enrolled and what was happening in Europe grew more alarming by the day.

The doorbell was ringing. More guests were arriving. She excused herself from the Meritons and walked across the room to greet them.

IN HER MAISONETTE in Wycliffe Road, Edith had given her daughters their nightly mug of cocoa and put them to bed. Then she'd set the table and cooked Arthur's supper all nicely in time for his return. It was liver and bacon and fried onions, which was one of his favourites, and they'd both enjoyed it. Now he was sitting in his armchair in the kitchen, smoking a cigarette with his legs stretched before him and the lower button of his waistcoat undone to make room for the meal, reading the *Evening Standard*, happy and satisfied, the difficulties of the day behind him.

'Good?' she asked him unnecessarily, as she put the dirty plates in the sink.

'Smashing,' he said, looking up from the paper. 'You done me proud.'

His praise pleased her, as it always did. 'I do me best.'

'You're a giddy marvel how you manage,' he said.

She filled the kettle and set it on the gas stove ready to boil some water for the washing-up, swept the tablecloth, folded it and put it away in the dresser. Then she sat down at the table again.

'Thing is,' she said. 'I got something to tell you.'

'Oh yes,' he said, eyes still on the newspaper.

'Listen to me Arthur.'

'I am,' he said, still reading.

'No really listen. It's important.'

He set the paper aside. 'I'm all ears,' he said, smiling at her.

Now that the moment had come she didn't know how to begin. She looked round at her nice neat kitchen, at her nice dependable gas cooker that she kept so clean and her nice white sink and the pot full of wooden spoons and kitchen knives, at the pretty flowery wallpaper that Arthur had hung for them and the curtains she'd run up on her Singer and the rag rug she'd made for the hearth, at the mantelpiece clock that he'd given her that Christmas because it looked cheerful. And now she was going to lose it all and the clock was ticking reproach at her, in a leaden inevitable way, clunk, clunk, clunk. 'Thing is,' she said again. 'Thing is, I think I'm expecting. Well not think, actually. I know I am.'

He was so shocked he couldn't disguise it. 'Oh blimey, Edie! ' he said. 'That's torn it.' Then he was rescued by disbelief. She couldn't be. He'd always been so careful. I mean, what's the good of being careful if it happens anyway? 'Perhaps you've got it wrong,' he hoped. 'I mean, people do. Women I mean.'

Her distress tipped into anger. 'Women!' she shouted. 'It's got nothing to do with women. This is me. Edie. I don't get things wrong. If I say I'm expecting, I'm expecting and I ought to know.' Then her emotions tipped again, propelled by that awful repetition. She put her head in her hands and burst into tears. 'What are we going to do?' she wept. 'We can't have another baby Arthur. We simply can't. We can only just manage as it is without another mouth to feed. We'll have to leave this house and just when we've got it so lovely. Oh Arthur, I'm at my wit's end. What are we going to do?'

'Come an' sit on my lap old thing,' he said, stretching out to hold her hand. He'd spoken out of turn, by hoping it was a mistake. Now he must make amends. Poor Edie.

She crept into his lap like a miserable child needing comfort, which was most unlike her. Normally she'd have kept him at arm's length for quite a long time after a mistake like that. Now she put her head on his shoulder and wept into his shirt.

He put his arms round her and held her close, stroking her back and thinking hard. There had to be an answer. There were always answers. Come on Arthur Ames. Use your wits. Think. The baby was on the way. There was no doubt about that. So what was to be done? He'd have to earn more money. That's what. He hadn't got the faintest idea how he would do it but it would have to be done.

Edie pulled a handkerchief out of her pocket and blew her nose. She was still awash with anxiety, drowning in it. 'What are we going to do?' she wept. 'What if you get laid off?'

'I'm a skilled mechanic,' he told her, with some pride. 'We don't get laid off. There ain't enough of us to go round.'

She wasn't convinced. 'You very nearly did that time, when the garage closed and everything. If you hadn't been took on by old man Murchison it would ha' been all up with us. We'd ha' been on the dole.'

'But we wasn't,' he said. 'It never come to it.'

'It'll come to it this time,' she said miserably. 'I don't see how we can avoid it.'

And he suddenly saw how. Like a light being switched on. 'I shall join the Territorials,' he said. 'They're advertising for car mechanics. I saw it in the paper only the other day. Good life. Out in the open air. Uniform provided and that'll save on clothes. Good grub and that'll save on food. Good pay or so they said. Can't be worse than what I earn now anyway. Could be a lot more. That's the answer. I shall join the Territorials.'

'But that's the army,' Edie said. 'You'd be a soldier.'

'Only part time. You come home nights. Most nights anyway. You can go on with your trade. That sort a' thing.' He wasn't entirely sure of his facts because he'd only scanned the advertisement but he had to make it sound acceptable. 'Could be just the ticket.'

'But what if there's a war?'

'There won't be.'

'That's not what they say in the *Mirror*. They reckon there's big war coming. They're always on about it.'

All perfectly true but he didn't want to be reminded of it. Not now. He couldn't afford to be faint-hearted now or to think about what might — or might not — happen. He'd made his decision and he would stick with it. 'You don't want to take no notice of the *Mirror*,' he said cheerfully. 'That's all newspaper talk. They don't mean half of it.'

'I don't want you in a war,' Edie said. 'I don't hold with wars.'

'I could do with a cup of tea,' he said, changing the subject. 'What say you put the kettle on?'

AT OCTAVIA'S dinner party the talk had turned to war too. They were twelve to table and four of the guests were old friends of her father's who belonged to the Fabian Society and consequently kept well abreast of the latest news.

'I used to think Winston Churchill was just a warmonger,' Frank Dimond was saying, 'but I'm not so certain now. The situation in Spain is absolutely appalling and as to what is happening to the Jews in Germany...'

'I still think the League of Nations should be taking action,' Octavia said. 'I know Hitler has taken Germany out of the league but that's no reason for the rest of us to ignore what he's doing. That's just playing his game.'

'But what action could we take?' Elizabeth Meriton asked. 'If he ignores the threat of sanctions, as he invariably does, what other weapon do we hold?'

'That,' Tommy said, dabbing his mouth with his table napkin, 'is the nub of the League's problem. Without an army to back up their demands there's nothing much they can do. Any international power needs an international army if it is to stand up to an international bully. It was a major oversight not to set one up right at the beginning.'

The storm had blown itself out and now it was a peaceful summer evening. There was a blackbird singing in the garden and sunlight flowed through the windows in long visible columns, making the glasses shimmer and warming their earnest faces.

'I feel as if we're all drifting,' Emmeline said sadly. 'Nobody in their right mind wants another war and yet we're drifting towards one. That's what will happen isn't it Tommy? If the League can't do anything then we shall have to.'

'I wish I could say no,' Tommy said. 'But I fear you may be right. As far as we can see at the Foreign Office, since Hitler occupied the Rhineland he's had *carte blanche* to do what he likes and so has Mussolini. Gassing defenceless Abyssinians was against every code of warfare that's ever been written and yet he got away with it. It's a very serious situation.'

'What I can't understand is why the government will go on talking about appeasement,' Frank Dimond said. 'They must know it isn't going to work.'

'It's more diplomacy than hope,' Tommy said. 'They know how important it is for people to believe that peace is possible and of course they don't want to spread alarm. It's a different matter behind the scenes. There are no official statements about it, naturally, but they're actually beginning to make preparations, pushing for more men to join the Territorials, manufacturing gas masks, stepping up on the production of arms. That sort of thing. Churchill's pressing for more, as you would expect, but at least it's a start. They've put in orders for the new fighter plane too, the one called the Spitfire. I expect you've heard of it.' Heads were shaken around the table. 'No? It was on show at Southampton. Me and a few chaps went down to see it.

Fastest thing in the air so they say and I can well believe it. Rolls Royce engine. Twelve cylinders. Handsome little plane. Just the sort of thing we shall need if it comes to it.'

'How many have we got?' Octavia asked.

'Six,' he said and when she grimaced, 'but there are more on order.'

Six, she thought, against an entire German Air Force. What good is six? If we're going to fight them we shall need hundreds and the young men to fly them. Then she noticed that Johnnie was listening just a little too ardently and that Emmeline was watching him and looking anxious and she tried to think of another subject to distract them.

JJ was thinking the same thing. Now he leant into the conversation. 'What a topic for a fine summer evening!' he said, smiling at them. 'Have any of you been following the Berlin Olympics, I wonder?'

They had and took his lead at once, grateful to be thinking of something other than death and destruction. The wonderful performances of Jesse Owens in the hundred and two hundred metres were remembered and praised — 'He's the fastest man in the world, imagine that, and he's modest about it' - Hitler's rudeness in snubbing him was deplored — 'But what can you expect? He's a nasty vulgar little man' — the British success in the four hundred metres relay was enjoyed again. The dinner party relaxed and eased. Only Octavia sat a little apart, contributing to the general talk in a vague way but still thinking and worrying. There had to be some way to stop this war. She couldn't just sit there in her comfortable chair in her comfortable room and ignore it. It wasn't in her nature. Once or twice, Frank Dimond looked across the table and gave her a brief smile as if he knew what she was thinking but she kept her thoughts to herself. She would talk to Pa after the guests were gone and see what he thought about it.

But as it happened, it was Frank Dimond who brought up

the topic again and he did it when most of the other guests had left and he and his wife were putting on their coats and saying goodbye to Octavia in the hall.

'A most enjoyable evening,' he said to Octavia. 'And very informative, if I may say so. I had no idea the government had so many preparations under way.'

'Nor had I,' Octavia told him and smiled. 'I think our Tommy was being rather indiscrete and thank God for that. I've never been in favour of official secrets.'

'In that case,' he said smiling at her, 'may I ask you a question?'

'Of course,' she said, wondering what it would be.

'I belong to an organisation that might interest you,' he said. 'Or perhaps I should say a committee, for that's all we are at the moment. But committee or organisation our aims are the same. We are doing what we can to get as many Jews out of Germany as possible. We're afraid Hitler might close the borders, so time is of the essence. Would you be interested in helping us?'

'Of course,' she said again. 'If I can.' It was just the sort of thing she ought to be involved in. 'You must tell me more.'

'I will ask our Mrs Hutchinson to contact you,' Frank said and turned as JJ and Emmeline walked into the hall to say goodbye too. 'A splendid evening JJ.'

'I'm glad you enjoyed it,' JJ said, shaking his hand. 'It was good to have your company.'

'A lovely dinner Emmeline,' Mrs Dimond said. 'Splendid food, lovely wine, good company, what more could anyone want?'

They left smiling and Octavia smiled too although rather absent-mindedly. She was wondering when Mrs Hutchinson would get in touch and what she would say when she did.

Her phone call came two weeks later. And it caused a row.

If you sign up today, you'll get:

1. A free historical fiction novel from Agora Books

2. Exclusive insights into timless fiction, as well as the opportunity to get copies in advance of publication; and,

3. The chance to win exclusive prizes in regular competitions.

Interested?

It takes less than a minute to sign up.

You can get your free book and your first newsletter by visiting

**www.agorabooks.co/
timeless-fiction-newsletter**